VENUS ENVY

RITA MAE BROWN

VENUS ENVY

BANTAM BOOKS

NEW YORK · TORONTO · LONDON · SYDNEY · AUCKLAND

VENUS ENVY

A Bantam Book / May 1993

All rights reserved.

Copyright © 1993 by American Artists, Inc.

Book design by Kathryn Parise.

LIBRARY OF CONGRESS CATALOGING-IN-PUBLICATION DATA

Brown, Rita Mae.
Venus envy / Rita Mae Brown.
p.   cm.
ISBN 0-553-09199-9
I. Title.
PS3552.R698V45   1993
813'.54—dc20   92-39378
CIP

Published simultaneously in the United States and Canada

Bantam Books are published by Bantam Books, a division of Bantam Doubleday Dell Publishing Group, Inc. Its trademark, consisting of the words "Bantam Books" and the portrayal of a rooster, is Registered in U.S. Patent and Trademark Office and in other countries. Marca Registrada. Bantam Books, 1540 Broadway, New York, New York 10036.

PRINTED IN THE UNITED STATES OF AMERICA

RRH   0 9 8 7 6 5 4 3 2 1

Dedicated to
Judy Elaine Hill and Margaret MacInnis
Two very different individuals who when troubles came
behaved with restraint and compassion.
The term for such behavior
used to be "lady."

ACKNOWLEDGMENTS

Medical terminology and procedures were foreign to me so I owe a debt to Dr. Herbert C. Jones for providing me with those facts. As Dr. Jones is one of my most cherished friends he also provided me with laughter.

I wish to thank the American Film Institute in Los Angeles for selecting me for the Directing Workshop for Women, Eighth Cycle, which although focused on film enriched my sense of the novel in unexpected and delightful ways. Much of the delight was learning from the other participants.

Wendy Weil, my literary agent and my friend, was always there when needed.

Beverly Lewis, my editor, as usual made clear and intelligent suggestions and I am grateful.

Robert Lyn Kee Chow, my coach, worked with me for six weeks this summer and drove my body so hard that my mind had time to replenish.

Dr. Frank Kimball buoyed me with his wit, his keen observations on humans and horses and his courage.

I've finally realized that I probably can't live without Gordon Reistrup who is ferociously bright, well-organized and wonderfully funny. We've worked together for four years and I hope he's enjoyed them as much as I have.

Acknowledgments

As Sneaky Pie now writes her own mysteries she helped not a bit on this novel, but the other cats and dogs showed up for work each morning. The offerings of dead mice, moles, shrews, and snakes were greatly appreciated.

VENUS ENVY

CHAPTER

I

"Dying's not so bad. At least I won't have to answer the telephone." Frazier Armstrong breathed deeply, which wasn't easy, since the oxygen tube stuck down her throat had rubbed it raw. "Then again, I will never have to fill out the IRS long form, buy a county sticker for my car, be burdened with insurance payments that stretch into eternity, to say nothing of my business license and the damned money I pay to the county each year on my depreciating business machines. No more mortgage payments and no more vile temptation as the doors of Tiffany's yawn at me like the very gates of Hell." She burrowed ever deeper into the hospital bed. Porthault sheets brought from home made the bed more comfortable but every time she glanced at the saccharine wallpaper, a dusty rose with tiny little bouquets, she thought, "One of us has to go."

1

Nestling should have made her feel better but it didn't. What certainly made her feel better was the morphine solution dripping into her left arm. She laughed to herself: "I pay a business tax, an amusement tax, a head tax, a school tax, a poll tax, a gas tax, a light tax, a cigarette tax. I even pay tax on Tampax. I hate paying and paying and paying. All I do anymore is work and obsess about money, which is how I landed in here. Still"—she wistfully noticed the slanting rays of the afternoon sun through the Venetian blinds—"I wouldn't mind living."

Thirty-five was too young to die, especially for someone with as much energy as Frazier. At first the shortness of breath and tightness in her chest had irritated her but hadn't bothered her. Stress. Well, stress and two packs of Muleskinners a day. Her assistant, Mandy Eisenhart, hounded her to go to the doctor but Frazier had better things to do with her time than plop her butt in Yancey Weems's office. He was a nice enough doctor but too fond of needles.

Over the last year her breathing had deteriorated until she could hear an odd metallic rattle in her bronchial tubes. Billy Cicero, her best friend and rent-a-date, told her she had hairballs. He stopped laughing when she was rushed to the E.R. two nights ago. The pain in her chest hurt so much that each time she breathed, tears came to her eyes.

The admitting physician ordered a battery of tests. She heard the head nurse mumble something in the afternoon about "blood gases were obtained."

Being canny as well as highly intelligent, Frazier paid a young nurse to interpret the lab work currently reflected on her chart. She had bilateral inoperable carcinoma of the lungs which had spread to the chest walls and invaded her spine.

The only remaining test—which seemed a waste of her evaporating time—was a lung X-ray, but the X-ray equipment was under repair, causing a backup mess not only for the hospital patients but for those physicians sending patients to the hospital for the procedure.

Poor Billy, that corrupt choirboy, wept when Frazier told him what she had so recently learned about her condition. She'd known the handsome Billy since their cradle years. It was the only flash of genuine emotion she'd ever seen in him and his response provoked a fierce spasm of love on her part. If only things had been different for them. They weren't exactly star-crossed lovers. Hard to be star-crossed with a man who enjoys snorting cocaine off erect black penises but still, what if things had been different?

No more "what ifs." No more anything. Death, the long dirt sleep, promised peace.

Frazier sat bolt upright in the bed. She emphatically hated the idea of being locked in a casket. Cremation. That seemed more civilized and sanitary. Who wants to be a worm's hamburger? Just yesterday she and her mother, Libby Armstrong, had battled until the tears flowed and the nurses had charged in like a remnant of some old Austrian regiment clothed in sparkling white. Libby just screamed and hollered about a Christian burial and Frazier screamed and hollered right back. "I don't want to get stuck in the ground like hazardous waste!"

Libby's luminous green eyes glowed. "Well, it's certainly preferable to being fried—fried, I tell you, Mary Frazier Armstrong. Just crisp like chitlins. You'll be reduced to ash like the tip of your Muleskinner cigarettes and how many times did I tell you not to smoke? No willpower, Mary Frazier, no willpower and here you are wasting away with lung cancer and I don't know what to do. And your poor brother is just prostate with grief."

"Prostrate, Mother."

"That's what I said. He's on the floor."

"Carter's on the floor because he's dead drunk."

"Don't you talk that way about your brother. He has an affliction. The Irish blood, you know, from your father's mother. Every one of them a victim to strong waters. Now our family—"

"Mother, I don't care anymore. I don't care where Carter's alcoholism came from, he has to stop drinking."

"You didn't stop smoking."

"And I'm about to expire, which I must say will be a relief because I won't have to hear any of this shit anymore!"

"How dare you speak to me that way? I am still your mother."

"Not for long!" Frazier shouted with jubilation. "You know what I think the family is, Momma? The family is the transmission belt of pathology. That's what I think. You always take Carter's part and Daddy always takes mine and who gives a flying fuck? I don't. I'm dying. I'm checking out of Hotel Earth. Sayonara. Adios. Ciao. Toodle-oo, auf Wiedersehen, and bye. Roger, wilco, over and out, Mom."

Libby shrieked, "You are hateful. You've got a mean streak in you, girl."

As the grammar disintegrated, Frazier began to cough violently, her spittle flecked with blood. The nurses rushed in as her mother rushed out, tossing her worn *Common Service Book of the Lutheran Church* onto Frazier's bed. Libby had tried to control Frazier's life. Now she wanted to control her death.

Libby hadn't returned and as Frazier recalled their "little outburst," which was how Libby would describe the scene to her husband, an outburst she would chalk up to the morphine for "pain management," this formerly dutiful daughter hoped she wouldn't see her mother again in this life. And if there was reincarnation she didn't want to see her in any future lives either.

A light knock at the door alerted her that she would endure more human contact before Death snatched her in his cold claws.

"Sistergirl."

"Hey, boy." Frazier smiled as the door swung open and Carter Redington Armstrong entered the room. He was Frazier's mirror image. Blond and good-looking, with a crooked smile that defused any criticism, Carter was what Southern women called a handsome devil. Broad shoulders and a narrow waist proved that, despite his battles with the bottle, he worked out, he tried. According to Big Daddy, Frank Armstrong, he just didn't try hard enough.

"Momma's ass over tit." He scraped a chair next to the bed. "I am her emissary but I'd have come anyway. She wants to make up with you before . . . Well, you know."

"I know." Frazier sighed. "What's the deal? Momma's always got some deal to cut."

"Her Mothership did not entrust me with such details."

"Liar." Frazier smiled, then coughed. "Goddammit, I hate this tube. I just plain hate it. Shit. Fuck. Damn!" Frazier yanked the tube out of her throat and breathed a deep gurgly breath. Blood was smeared over the end of the tube.

"Frazier—"

"Let it be, dammit. If I've got to die, then I am dying without that thing tearing up my throat."

"Yeah, okay." Carter shifted his weight. He noticed the flowers, hard not to notice. Thousands and thousands of dollars' worth of flowers filled Frazier's room, as would be expected given her social status, to say nothing of her business position. His green eyes, like their momma's and Frazier's, fell on an enormous horseshoe. "Billy."

"Billy."

"I hate that sumbitch."

"You used to like him."

"Not after tenth grade, that cocksucker."

"Carter, that was a long time ago. He's found other wonderwands to suck. Anyway, I don't want to talk about Billy. You go home and tell Momma that I am going to be cremated. It's in my will and there's not a thing she can do about it."

He sighed deeply. "Okay."

"She'll bitch and moan, I know, but she won't be bitching and moaning at you."

"The old man been in today?"

"Crack of dawn."

"Dad's not doing so good." For Carter to perceive his father's emotions was a great leap forward, as they used to say in China.

5

"Yeah." Frazier nodded. She reached over and sipped from a glass of water but it burned violently. She quickly put the glass back on the nightstand.

"Bad?"

"I don't care much anymore."

Carter's eyes filled. "Oh, Sis, what am I gonna do without you? I know I've always been a worthless sack of shit but I love you. I always loved you." He dropped his head on the bed and Frazier ran her fingers through his thick curly hair.

"I know, Brudda, I know." She called him by his childhood name. She couldn't say *brother* when she was tiny; she called him Brudda. "It was kind of a setup that we'd be pitted against each other, you know."

"I know, I know." He sobbed. "I could do no right and you could do no wrong."

"In Daddy's eyes. 'Course, if it was Momma it was the reverse."

He lifted his eyes to hers. "But, Frazier, did you have to be so successful?"

"You know, I've had ample melancholy opportunity to think about us. Yes, I did have to be so successful. I just didn't want to be . . . like her. And I guess you didn't want to be like him. Since Big Daddy made himself a ton of money, oh, Carter, I don't know. Maybe you just rebelled and said, 'I ain't doing jack shit.' Well, you hurt him. You surely did hurt him, but you hurt you too. You're as smart as I am."

Carter grabbed a tissue and wiped his eyes, blew his nose. "I don't know about that. I couldn't have started an art gallery. I couldn't abide your customers."

"Maybe not an art gallery, but you could have done something else."

"What?"

"Carter, how many times have we talked about this? You could have gone into the paving business with Dad."

He threw up his hands. "And have him tell me day in and day out that I'm half the man he is? No fuckin' way. Nothing I do is o. was good enough for him!"

"Maybe failure gets to be a habit. Maybe it's comfortable. God knows you've got enough women making excuses for you. Momma, your wife, your mistresses." He didn't flinch at the word *mistresses*, so she continued: "Maybe being adored by women is kind of a curse—know what I mean?"

He nodded. He did know what she meant but he still stalled on the runway. Thirty-seven years is a long time to wait for liftoff. "You think I'm a bum?"

"Sometimes. Mostly I think you're self-indulgent and I think you've wasted a lot of time hating me 'cause I grabbed the brass ring, if you'll forgive an awful expression."

"Dying flushes out the truth, doesn't it?" A rueful smile crossed his chiseled lips. "While we're on the subject of flushing, I don't want Billy Cicero at your funeral. I don't care if he is heir to the largest tobacco fortune in the United States. He's a sleazeball. I mean, Sistergirl, what we don't know about that bastard we can't even imagine."

However, Frazier did know. She didn't need to imagine. "He's got his ways. I don't want to waste what time I have left arguing with you about Billy. I want us to make up. I don't want you to have guilt about me, or harbor resentment. I'm going to be out of this mess. You, Brudda, got another good forty to fifty years of it. Until we resolve conflicts we repeat them."

"Shut up," Carter flared. "Don't rub that therapy bull on me. It's just another form of religion, I tell you, and it's as full of baloney as the old one."

"Then let me put it in plain English. Stop comparing yourself to Dad. Stop comparing yourself to me. Stop drinking. Stop pretending you like selling real estate. If you won't go into Armstrong Paving, then buy a goddam shrimp boat on the Gulf of Mexico and be a captain. It's the only thing you love and you're a damned fine sailor. Screw the country club. Screw the state of Virginia. Screw everyone's expectations of Frank Armstrong's boy. Go be your own man."

"You don't like Virginia?"

"I love Virginia. That's not the point."

He rubbed his chin. A blond stubble accentuated his natural virility. "Well . . . well, if only we could have talked like this years ago. I . . ." Tears spilled onto his muscled chest. "Forgive me, Sistergirl, forgive me."

"For what?"

"For hating you. I should have been proud when you made your first million but I wanted you dead. And now . . ." He broke down again.

"There's nothing to forgive, Brudda, nothing at all. I didn't do anything to make life easier for you. I didn't want you around my customers. I treated you like a dumb redneck and you're not and I sucked up to Dad. Oh, how I sucked up to Dad to get the seed money to start the gallery. I paid him back every penny plus interest but I know that when you wanted to buy that quarry to start your own business he wouldn't give you a dime. I didn't talk to him. I didn't do a damned thing except agree with him when he said you'd get drunk and go bankrupt."

"He's probably right." Carter sobbed even harder.

"It doesn't have to be like that. Believe in yourself. You're the only brother I've got and I didn't. I mean . . ." She was crying too.

The nurse came in to find brother and sister wrapped in each other's arms, crying so hard they were gasping. She gently extricated Carter, then tried to put the tube down Frazier's throat. Carter charmed the well-meaning lady into leaving his sister alone. After she retreated they spoke quietly for a bit and then Carter left. Frazier watched his back as he walked away, wondering if she'd ever see him again, and worrying that he wouldn't change. He could be a happy man, if only . . .

But then, was she happy? She'd made a mess of money and she'd make even more if she could live. She knew her field, she loved it, and she loved profit. Ah, yes, *profit*, the sweetest word in the English language. No, *net profit* was the sweetest, truly the sweetest. Net profit. But had she been happy? She lied to her family. She lied to her friends. She lied double-time to her lover. The only person she told the truth to was Billy Cicero and he was an even bigger liar than she was. Well, no. She told the truth to Mandy. Beautiful, black Mandy, whom she teased and called "Afrodite." She had left the business to Mandy in her will. Mandy wouldn't know that until the will was read. The Stubbs, John Sartorius, the Marshalls, the Herricks, all the fabulous English sporting art, to say nothing of the other merchandise—uh, art, the Thiebaud. The list was glorious and expensive, deliciously expensive. Were she going to live, Frazier would make Mandy her partner on Mandy's birthday. Frazier wished they could have the chance to work together that way. Mandy deserved to be her partner but it gave Frazier some solace to know that Mandy Eisenhart was going to be one of the richest young single black women in Virginia. Maybe there was some justice in this world or the next. Mandy was the only person she would really miss. Funny. They never socialized. The relationship was all business but when she thought about her life, that was her greatest love, that damned art gallery, those incredible paintings.

Maybe she had made some people happy. She'd found them the right painting at the right price. That was something.

Outside her window a robin perched in a tree, the red buds swelling despite a light dusting of snow. Spring would arrive early in Charlottesville this year. Frazier loved spring. She closed her eyes and listened to the determined chirp. There was something obscene and truly offensive about spring coming, about people enjoying themselves and her being dead.

Carter's visit had exhausted her. She closed her eyes for a moment, then opened them again. She didn't want to miss anything. Not one second. And she hoped she'd be spared more emotional farewells. Emotional expression was all very well but she had made a life of emotional repression her very own and she might as well die as she had lived—with distance and reserve.

She dozed off. Her friends, the doctors, and nurses marveled at her ability to withstand pain but she felt very little. No wonder governments declared morphine and cocaine illegal; apart from being highly addictive, those substances made one feel divine. She had heard that for terminal patients a speedball of morphine and cocaine might be mixed, but she was kept to morphine.

When Frazier's eyelids fluttered open, the nasty digital clock read 3:12. The ticking of the pendulum, the little click of hands as they swept the minutes and then the hours, had contented the human race for hundreds of years. The rhythm of the sounds gave signal not so much that life was passing but that all was regulated, harmonious, and in perspective. The great grandfather clock in the hall of her parents' Federal house sang out every fifteen minutes, a longer note on the half hour, and joyous chimes on the hour. The moon phases, as exquisitely painted as the clock face was tooled, announced that time was decorous. But a digital clock announced a paucity of imagination and a break with tradition. No hands. Frazier thought of them as amputees. Well, had anything important ever happened at 3:12 in the afternoon?

Before she could answer her own question Billy Cicero glided through the door. Billy's impeccable wardrobe kept a platoon of tailors busy on Jermyn Street in London. Today he wore a charcoal suit with a pale pin stripe, thin but not quite a chalk stripe. His vest was dove-gray, his bright-white shirt was made of the finest cotton, and his tie was plum with tiny gold snaffle bits embroidered throughout. Billy had attended St. Paul's in America and then Oxford in England. He never wore a school tie because anybody who was anybody knew what college you attended at Oxford. School ties were for people who didn't count, and in Billy's book most people didn't count.

"Precious, you look like shit." Billy smiled and then pecked her on the cheek.

"Really." Frazier agreed with him. "If I'm going to die I might as well be as attractive as possible while I'm doing it."

Billy reached over and picked up the telephone receiver. His strong fingers punched in the numbers. "Terese? Billy. We need you over here at the hospital, east wing, room six twenty-five." He paused. "Hair, brows, makeup, and"—he grabbed Frazier's hand—"manicure too. On my tab, darling. Thank you so much." He hung up the phone. "The miracle worker, Terese Collier, will arrive in this holding pen in two hours. Think you'll live that long?"

"Guess I have to." Frazier squeezed Billy's sun-browned hand.

Billy Cicero possessed a catastrophic beauty. No one was immune to it, least of all Billy himself. He towered over most people at 6′5″. His shoulders were as broad as the continental shelf; his body muscular and well proportioned. His face was as if Michelangelo's "David" had sprung to life with dazzling teeth, deep-brown eyes, and thick black hair.

People oohed and aahed whenever Billy and Frazier made an appearance. "The perfect couple," bystanders whispered. Frazier stood 5′11″ in her stocking feet and when she put on heels she topped 6′2″. She was as golden and tawny as Billy was dark, and with her green eyes, catlike in color and shape, she cast a spell over people, as did he, but Billy was aware of his physical presence and used it ruthlessly. Frazier never did believe she was beautiful, no matter how many times she was told. What she did believe, however, was that she was a natural athlete and she drew more confidence from that than from her exterior.

"You're not really going to die, are you?" Billy kissed her again.

"I tell you it's almost worth it to get away from all these long faces. Mother pitched a hissy yesterday and Carter broke down today. It's more than I can stand. Tell me anything that doesn't have something to do with me. Tell me about work or the stock market or . . . anything."

"Stock market's in the toilet. Atlantic Tobacco is going strong, I'm happy to report. Thank God all those Europeans and Africans love their cancer sticks. Uh—sorry, darling."

"I don't care." She reached into his inside suit pocket and pulled out a soft package of Muleskinners, the cigarette that put Atlantic Tobacco on the map during World War I. It was now enjoying a resurgence as a butch brand, in its original package design. Smoking Muleskinners meant to hell with the health fascists, and plenty of young men were lighting up. While Frazier preferred brown Shermans, out of New York, she smoked Muleskinners in public for Billy's sake.

"Gimme a light."

He plucked the cigarette out of her lips. "No."

She plucked it right back and ran her hands over his body, searching for a lighter. She found the gold Dunhill in his left pocket. "You know, Billy, if I'm going to go I might as well go on my own terms. What's the point of prolonging life if you've forgotten how to live? I could just as easily have gotten cancer of the lungs without smoking. Remember what happened to Sandy Faulconer? Never smoked a day in her life."

"I don't think I'll be as brave as you are." He clicked open the top of the lighter and rubbed his thumb over the barreled dial. A medium-sized flame shot upward and Frazier inhaled with reverence.

"God bless the American Indian." She closed her eyes in ecstasy. "Billy, I'm not brave. I'm accepting the inevitable. Oh, this burns my throat but it burns good. I took that damned tube out which was rubbing me raw and I made the nurse turn off the oxygen machine."

"I'm glad to hear it. Otherwise we'd have been blown to bits." He joined her in a cigarette. "Deep down I guess I don't believe you're leaving me. If God should grant us a miracle, you and I are going to get married. I mean it."

Frazier coolly appraised him. "Then aren't you glad miracles are in short supply?"

"Baby darling, we should have done it years ago. You go your way and I'll go mine and who's the wiser? I suppose I could even sire

and our respective parents would froth with joy.
long, you go along."

I like you." She decided to allow Billy his grand
I make a good team. We always have. I don't guess
n somersaults of happiness."

Kenny played Nothing in *Much Ado About Nothing*.
boredom can I stand? I'm a martyr to Kenny's
meaning. Life doesn't mean anything. Just do
p yourself off the streets, to keep your two brain
lectricity."

Kenny's all right."

et married and Kenny and Annie should get mar-
perfect together." Billy laughed. "Poor Ann, with
ment because we don't take her to parties in New
on the west side of Richmond for that matter.
long drag—"I'm being uncharitable. She does love
e she's good in bed."

hat Kenny is not hung like a hamster." Frazier put
ehind her. "Nor are you, my sweet."

ere are people out there, millions of them I suppose,
x, who don't think we should do it, or that anyone
I guess they don't do it at all. Can you imagine that?
g dead. I mean, honey, a man could at least lash it to
a toothbrush or something. You've got to try."

"Not everyone can be as accomplished an explorer of libido as
yourself," Frazier purred. "You know, I always thought we should
organize a sexual Olympics. A gold medal for best all-round love-
making, best rear entry, best blow job, longest distance for ejaculation, most perfect breasts. What's the discus compared to that?"
This overheated thought was making Frazier feel woozy.

Billy murmured, "Are we judges or participants?"

"Ummm, how about both?"

"Frazier, you've got to live. Where will I find anyone like you:

your general depravity, your sharp eye for a brushstroke, your appreciation for the refinements of the male member? Besides which, no one can dance like you, or play golf like you, and I ask you, who will be in charge of the Dogwood Festival and the Fourth of July fireworks this year at the club? You're going to live and we're going to get married." He leaned over and kissed her on the lips, a long deep Muleskinner kiss, which, although pleasant, kicked over neither of their engines. "You look tired. Why don't you go to sleep, and when you awaken, Terese will be here to fuss over you. I'll try to stop by tomorrow."

After Billy left, Frazier tried to sleep but his left-handed marriage proposal rolled around in her mind like a loose ball from a pinball machine. She'd never have to worry about money for as long as she lived. Billy wouldn't dream of interfering with the gallery. And the thought of being Mrs. Cicero wasn't horrible. What caught her, a tiny golden fishhook to the heart, was that if she married him it would feel as if she'd given in. Ever since she could remember, her mother had pounded at her about the advantages of a "suitable match," the whole country shivered in a spasm of heterosexuality. After a certain age an unmarried person became an object of scorn or pity. Funny, because to Frazier they looked free and she wanted to be free. She never saw the romance part of marriage. To her it was legalized fucking: the correct penis is inserted in the correct vagina and the issue from this moment of hydraulics is declared legal. The issue for those illegal couplings were bastards, a term not used in polite society but a condition perceived and felt.

Movie stars could have children out of wedlock and welfare mothers could have children out of wedlock but other women better damn well watch their step. Actually, it wasn't a step they could watch.

Mrs. William Bennington Cicero. This bothered her also. She'd spent her life as Mary Frazier Armstrong. She had no intention of losing her identity. Armstrong-Cicero might not be so bad but she liked her name and intended to keep it.

Billy was bullshitting. She tried to squelch the turmoil with that triumphant realization. Then she wished she hadn't, because her mind turned to her forthcoming demise.

"How imaginative is Death, how versatile his methods," she thought. "He can snatch you from a sound sleep, or a bullet can shatter your skull. You can drown in water or in your own blood. Then again, you can fall off a bar stool. Really, people fall off bar stools, kaput, every year. AIDS shows Death at his best, teasing, tormenting, and killing by degrees. Momma's family leans toward the furious and fatal heart attack. But oh, the ways to go. You can slip on a banana peel, you can choke on a green pea, you can lose control of your car or die of alcohol poisoning or the nifty and speedier coke slide into oblivion. One has so many choices, or does Death choose? What about multiple sclerosis or an inoperable brain tumor or, then again, that old standby syphilis, a real killer. Death will not fail. If we cure one disease he'll invent another. And he'll hunt you down using surprise and cunning."

The Redingtons, her mother's family, kept a book of pedigree reaching back to 1640 and Frazier loved to read about her ancestors. As a child she'd pore over each page, but one incident always seized her imagination. Rachel Redington, aged twenty-three in 1843, was shelling peas in a large tin bowl one blistering August day when a thunderstorm rolled over the Blue Ridge Mountains. Either the storm appeared with blinding speed, and those summer storms can, or Rachel, sitting on the porch, assumed it would blow over as quickly as it came. A bolt of lightning struck the metal bowl of peas, killing Rachel instantly. This story so impressed Frazier that she would never set foot on a porch during a thunderstorm.

"Like a stalking tiger, Death will pounce," she thought.

"Maybe I'm lucky to have these few days to consider my life. Maybe Death is like a punctuation mark, a period at the end of a sentence. It means the sentence is over and you've been correct. Who wants a run-on sentence?" A tear ran into the corner of Frazier's mouth. "I do," she cried. "I do. I don't want to go. I don't want to be brave, goddammit. I don't want to miss the spring, I don't want to miss the golf season, I don't want to miss anything." She buried her head in her pillow.

When Terese Collier tiptoed in, Frazier was sleeping so soundly that she didn't wake up until Terese had applied the second coat of Raging Raspberry to her nails.

CHAPTER
2

Terese Collier should have taken photographs of Frazier to prove her handiwork. Frazier's shoulder-length hair curved casually forward, smooth and shining. Her eyebrows, plucked to perfection, served as accent marks to her extraordinary eyes, and her nail polish gleamed. Because she felt sorry for Frazier, Terese threw in a pedicure as well. Raging Raspberry startled Frazier each time she popped her toes out from under the covers.

The long twilight surrendered to night. The hospital corridor quieted down and Frazier was grateful that no other family members visited. She didn't miss Ann either, which might have provoked self-questioning in a person more focused on her emotions. Since she didn't miss Ann, she didn't give her absence a second thought.

Tempted to turn on the television, she decided against it. The vacuousness of the shows offended her far less than the relentless juggernaut of commercials. The tinty music of those commercials filtered into the halls, as other patients lacked her standards.

"Boss." Mandy walked in.

"Hey."

"You look good, girl." Mandy's smile was incandescent.

Odd. Frazier thought to herself that she and Mandy had worked cheek by jowl for three years, yet only now did she notice the high cast to her coffee-colored cheekbones.

"Did Mrs. Thornburg come to a decision about the Isidore Bonheur?"

"She's a whirlwind of indecision. However, the small hound picture sold today."

"Good."

Before Frazier could ask, Mandy added, "Darryl Orthwein from New York. I expect he'll roll it over in a year or two but that's okay."

"Shrewd collector, that one."

"I brought you something." Mandy reached into her voluminous bag and pulled out a box of fine French paper. "Here, write letters to Tomorrow."

Frazier opened the box and ran her forefinger over the smooth cotton finish. The pale-blue paper sported a tiny darker-blue freckling. "This is gorgeous. Mandy, where do you find these treasures?"

"Picked up the phone and called Paris. Fortunately, they believe in Federal Express. I love paper and I remembered the time when your father sent you reams of rice paper from Japan. The stuff was so beautiful it took you six months to work up to writing on it." Mandy laughed.

"Had to learn to use a brush." Frazier held the paper on her lap. "This is very kind of you."

"I figure if you write a letter each evening for the next day, there will always be a next day." Mandy fought back the tears.

"Oh, Mandy . . ." Frazier choked up, then gained mastery of herself. "None of this makes any sense. I feel okay, sort of."

"What about the coughing?"

Frazier shrugged. "What bothers me is that every now and then I can't breathe, but I'm not in pain. That's what I hate about the morphine. I click this button here and presto, more drips into my veins. It feels great but how do I know how I really feel?" She turned her face to the window for a moment. "Well, maybe I never knew how I felt, period."

"I have this theory"—Mandy leaned forward, beginning her sentence with a favorite phrase—"that feelings are the essence of being human but it takes probably fifty years to trust them. Most of us are living from the neck up."

"Not Billy Cicero."

"His sex stuff is just another escape," Mandy stated flatly. "Anyway, I'm not sitting here in judgment of anyone in particular. I'm guilty too."

"You know, I was thinking when you walked in the door about how I spend more time with you than anyone but I don't know much about you, other than that you graduated from Smith, top of your class, did your graduate work at Yale, and worked in Rochester after that."

"You met my mother. To meet a woman's mother is to know what you need to know."

"Thanks, Mandy. Mine was in here yesterday sobbing because she wants me buried. My God, I can't even have control of my body when I'm dead. It's my body and I'll do with it what I want."

"Tell that to the anti-abortionists."

"You know what I mean." Frazier placed the stationery on the nightstand. "Is there any subject before the American public today more overworked than abortion?"

"Well, I don't know, but you scooted off the feelings discussion right fast."

"All right then, smartass, what are you feeling right this instant?" A flash animated Frazier's scratchy voice.

Mandy paused a long time, then spoke in a soft voice: "I don't want to lose you. And you look ravishing."

Frazier's chin wobbled. "I thought you tolerated me because I'm your boss. I mean, I'm white. Don't you hate me somewhere in your heart?"

"I'm not that petty, Frazier."

Tears splashed onto Frazier's ample bosom. "How am I to know? It's awkward. Maybe that's why I concentrated on work. I didn't grow up with black people as social equals. Or African-Americans or whatever the hell I'm supposed to call you all. You know what I mean."

"So we both lose." Mandy dropped her head and then lifted it again. "Sometimes I think we'll never stop paying. Not your people. Not my people. It will go on and on like some painful wave that never reaches shore. Since we're telling the truth, I'll tell you why I was reticent. . . ."

"But fun, you were always fun." Frazier wiped her eyes.

"Thank you." Mandy pulled out Kleenex for herself and Frazier. "You might get angry."

"I don't care."

"Okay. I think you're gay. I think you've hidden from me and everyone. You go out nonstop, mostly with Billy, some other guys, too, but you know, I never feel any . . . heat."

Frazier's shoulders tensed. "Maybe they're not the right guys. Or maybe I'm cold-blooded."

Mandy shook her head. "It's not the end of the world, boss."

"And when's the last time you saw anyone rewarded for being gay and telling the truth about it? It might not be the end of the world but it sure as hell isn't the road to success."

"I didn't take you for a coward." Mandy's voice dropped lower, then rose with renewed energy. "Then again, I understand no one has a right to know another person's business. But from my point of view, I'm left out. You never trusted me enough to include me in your life. Do you think I care for one minute about whether you're gay or straight? Don't you know me better than that?"

Frazier's chest tightened. She fought for every breath. No one had ever spoken to her like this before and she'd never told her secrets before, except to Billy, but that wasn't telling—that was sharing. "I trust you, Mandy, as much as I trust anyone." She inhaled and heard that nasty rattle. Mandy stood up and began lightly patting her on the back. That didn't work. Frazier pointed to the oxygen tank. Mandy quickly put the tube into Frazier's mouth and turned on the valve. Frazier took a few deep hits of pure O_2 and then removed the tube. "Sorry."

"I'm the one who's sorry. I should have kept my mouth shut."

Frazier breathed again from the tube. The little iridescent dots that had been dancing before her eyes disappeared. "I guess, I guess I thought no one would want to know the real me and now I'm leaving and no one will ever know me."

"I'd like to know you." Mandy smiled. "You're a genius at what you do. You're a good boss and I think you're a good person basically."

Frazier shook her head. She didn't know what to say.

Mandy spoke again. "Don't die a stranger. Tell the people you love who you are, or write them. Maybe they need you and you don't know it. Maybe you need them."

"I don't want to need anyone." Frazier's hands shook as she placed the oxygen tube back on the tank.

"'No man is an island,'" Mandy recited from the poem.

"This woman has tried to be." She steadied herself and then told Mandy what she had never spoken to another person, other than Billy. "I am gay. Or maybe I'm not. Let's just say I'm operating sexually on all pistons, but emotionally I am much more attracted to women. I've tried to avoid it, you know. What this could cost me . . . My family, such as they are. Not my clients, thank God, but my social position. My reserve turned into a full-scale emotional retreat. So I avoid the issue by not falling in love, by keeping my distance, by . . . by working and working and working. It's just . . . too painful." Frazier fell back on her pillows. "People are cruel. *You* know that."

"I do, but I also know that plenty of them are wonderful and if you don't put yourself out there you'll never know. And you just put yourself out there and I . . ." Mandy swallowed her words, a hard knot of grief like a baseball in her throat.

"Mandy, I don't even know if I'll be here tomorrow. I have a surprise for you after I'm gone. It's the only way I can tell you how I feel. I'm not much good at this. Feelings exhaust me."

Mandy had much more to say but she could see the fatigue and she felt guilty for bringing it on. She kissed Frazier goodbye and left, wondering if she had been selfish in pushing her boss or if she had actually given Frazier a kind of gift.

～～～

Two hours later Frazier's phone rang. It was Mandy apologizing profusely. Frazier, just back from the X-ray lab, was happy to talk to anyone not involved in the medical profession.

"Stop worrying about it," Frazier commanded. "Just live for two when I'm gone—or name your firstborn after me."

"I'm not handling this very well." Mandy sobbed.

"You were the one who wanted to know!"

"No, not that. I'm not doing very well about your being sick. I'm sorry. I should be comforting you, not the reverse."

"Mandy, don't worry about it. Comfort my brother. On second thought, don't comfort my brother. He already has one mistress that I know of."

"Still?"

"Oh, yeah, the one with the cowboy boots and tits big as Texas. In fact, I think she is from Texas. Those girls down there are serious about hair, too. I never saw so much hair on a woman's head. Of course, I've only seen her from a distance."

"What does Laura say about Miss Texas?"

"She thinks he's given her up."

"So how do you know he hasn't?" Mandy's natural curiosity was taking over.

22

"Because when he cried all over me—and I confess I cried back—he stank of Giorgio perfume. The stuff oozed right out of his pores. Laura wears Hermès, as you might suspect. Giorgio is much too loud for Laura. The Garden Club would turn up its collective nose, literally. Even the daffodils would shudder."

"Um, um," Mandy hummed.

"You got it, girl. My brother may be a failure in many respects but when it comes to women he's irresistible. It's hard for a sister to see a brother as sexy but ever since I can remember Carter has been a triumph of androgen, or whatever it is that attracts the girls like flies."

"My mother says women *are* like flies. They'll settle on shit or on sugar."

"Your mother doesn't like women much, does she?"

"Well, this statement was provoked by my sister's falling for a man Mother considered too dark for an Eisenhart. Mom's a horrible snob that way."

"Yeah, so's mine—about suitable matches. Before Charles married Diana I swear Libby would lie awake at night and plot how I might meet the Prince. 'If only he could see you, sweetie,' she'd say. 'They want you when they see you.'"

"True enough." Mandy paused a moment while her dog barked. "Enough, Duncan."

The Scottie barked harder.

"Duncan's true to form," Frazier remarked.

"Am I forgiven?"

"I said you were. Don't repeat yourself. You know how I hate to be bored."

"I know. Well, don't forget to write a letter to Tomorrow. Promise?"

"I will. Bye-bye."

"Bye, boss."

Frazier hung up the phone. Like the claws of physical desire, loneliness and longing seized her stomach. There was so much to live for. How could she have so squandered her time? She thought of the lips unkissed, the thighs uncaressed, the paintings she'd just missed purchasing. She thought of the music she adored and how she wished she had kicked off her shoes and danced in the dew on spring grass. Simple pleasures, animal delights, all were shoved aside in her ascent and in her fear that if she cavorted, frolicked, and played, she might betray herself. Spontaneity evaporated inside her.

Control. Control yourself. Control your destiny. Control your emotions. Well, she controlled all right. She controlled herself right out of any action that did not lead directly to her bank account.

She lay there and wondered why so many people who considered themselves aristocrats violently opposed displays of emotion, honest exchange. Not that the middle classes were much better. They preferred to talk about emotion rather than show it. The joke was that talking about emotion often vitiated the emotion. They wound up bloodless. Frazier's friends, the U.C.'s—the Upper Classes— preferred neither. A single poppy in a round crystal bowl sitting on a perfect terrace could elicit as much rapture from Billy Cicero's mother as an orgasm. Probably more. Small wonder that Billy, like the moon, never showed his mother his dark side.

Frazier kept returning to the lips unkissed. If only she had pressed her mouth between DeeDee Cheatam's shoulder blades in their Tri-Delta days. And Frances Peterson. She was so hot, with her long, long body and her ice-blue eyes. Who knew what might have happened if Frazier had just reached out once or twice or, well, more than that. Then she had spurned Victor Nederlander, which nearly killed her mother. What she remembered about Victor, her beau in her middle twenties, was the downy hair on his chest. She made him crawl over hot coals for sex and then she hurt him by not enjoying it. What would have happened if she'd let go? Every now and then she'd escape to Charlotte, North Carolina, to the Guest Quarters with someone, male or female, only to forget them after the weekend. As Frazier had good taste, they were nice people, people worth remembering.

Keep your distance. Don't get involved. Don't reveal too much.

Keep it light. But people couldn't keep it light. They had emotions, even if Frazier didn't.

She was having them now. All the pain and even the pleasure she'd sidestepped in her thirty-five years had boomeranged into an anguish more profound than any physical pain. Again, Frazier gasped for breath. Her head pounded. She fumbled for the oxygen tube and managed to turn on the tank. The smooth, pure air clarified her mind as well as her lungs.

She had never truly loved anyone. Of course, she had never truly hated anyone either, but this lack of passion seemed a further incrimination of her refusal to become engaged, to connect. She sucked in another breath and with it her mind bent under the weight of her sorrows.

She grabbed for the *Common Service Book*, the gold letters *I.H.S.* beckoning in the lower right-hand corner. A frayed red silk page marker bore testimony to Libby's constant use. Frazier gulped in more air, then replaced the tube and turned off the oxygen. She composed herself as she opened the book to page 430, where her mother had placed the marker. It was the "Order for the Burial of the Dead" and Libby had underlined burial.

Furious, Frazier nearly tossed the book against the wall. The only thing restraining her from this small fit was the realization that the thud would disturb whoever was in the adjoining room, suffering with God knows what. She hoped they suffered merely the pains of their disease and not the pains inflicted by family.

She dropped the book back into her lap and the pages fluttered to 441. Her eyes fell on "Responsories."

V. *In pace in id ipsum dormiam:* I will lay me down in peace and sleep. None of us liveth to himself, and no man dieth to himself.

Verse: Whether we live therefore or die, we are the Lord's. None of us liveth to himself, and no man dieth to himself.

The shroud of mortality drew closer around Frazier's strong shoulders. A blue chill shot down her spine. She closed the book and fumbled in the nightstand for her solid gold Montblanc pen. Billy gave it to her on her last birthday, September 17. He laughed when she turned thirty-five and said that that was the age at which Dante wrote the *Inferno*, for thirty-five was believed to be the beginning of middle age in the Middle Ages. On her birthday card he wrote, "Welcome to the Middle Ages." The next day she called Fahrney's, a pen and stationery store in Washington, D.C., and discovered that the pen cost $8,500.

A phone book would serve as a desk. She yanked the Yellow Pages out of the drawer. When she took out one sheet of Mandy's paper the tube from the morphine drip swung in the way of her writing. Frazier tore it out of her vein.

"Goddammit, if I'm going to die I might as well feel it. I might as well feel something before I go!"

Then she began writing, writing, writing. Mandy suggested one letter per day to Tomorrow but Frazier wrote volumes. She wrote to Billy, to her mother and father, to Carter, to her Auntie Ruru, whom she adored, to Ann, to Kenny Singer, and lastly to Mandy. She was so tired by the time she got to Mandy that she wrote only, "Thank you."

By now, midnight beyond thought, she was withdrawing from the morphine. She felt sick to her bones. She put stamps on the envelopes and placed them on the nightstand by her bed.

She was going to die. She'd never felt so wretched. She shook. Nausea consumed her. She considered jamming the morphine needle back into her vein but she was determined to feel something, anything, this pain in her last moments. At least she would die knowing she had told the truth to the people she could have been close to—perhaps. Maybe her death or her truth could be a spur to them. Maybe they could change and find a few shards of happiness amidst the rubble of their psyches.

Frazier, trembling uncontrollably, clicked off the light. She remembered that it was Ash Wednesday. Why she would remember that she didn't know, but it stuck in her brain like a piece of cotton on the boll. She wondered if she should ring the nurse or call up her pastor for the Last Rites. No, she'd lived this life fundamentally alone. She might as well die alone. Frazier Armstrong fell into a boiling sleep from which she never expected to return.

The descent into Hell had begun.

CHAPTER
3

The official beginning of spring was three weeks in the future but already the predawn light cast a softer gray glow on the horizon. The peepers sang down at the lake, indicating they cared little for official dates. The horses, cats, and dogs were shedding their coats, and bluebirds would soon awaken to dart along fence lines and bushes searching for a suitable nest site. A great heron poised at the edge of the lake appeared ghostly in the pale light.

Jogging along the dirt road through his property, Dr. Yancey Weems breathed in the cool air laden with moisture. Running in forty-degree weather suited him and he had learned to rise before dawn during his days as an intern. Like most early risers he prided himself upon this trait and felt superior to those slugabeds who awakened at 7:30 or 8:00 A.M.

His beeper disturbed his reverie and rhythm. Cursing, he turned and ran back toward his work shed, where there was a telephone.

Yancey picked up his message to call Thornton Rogers, head of oncology at Albemarle General Hospital in Charlottesville. He knew it wouldn't be a happy call. Which of his patients had surrendered at last?

"Thornton, Yancey here."

"Get your ass down here faster than a crow flies, Yancey," Thornton commanded. Thornton commanded everyone, except for his wife. "We've got a problem."

"Who?"

"Mary Frazier Armstrong. Just get here."

CHAPTER
4

Winking over the horizon, the flaming halo of the sun announced hope and happiness and a new day. Apollo had again replaced his sister in the sky, the sun kissed the moon goodbye, and day enjoyed victory.

Yancey Weems, sent on this mission by Thornton Rogers, bent over Frazier's inert form. The nurse quietly rolled away the morphine drip and the other machines.

"Mary Frazier." Yancey sounded shaky. "Mary Frazier, wake up."

Frazier rolled over, the remnants of Terese Collier's makeup more on the pillow than on her face.

"Here." Yancey handed her a cup of real coffee. "Slug up first."

The hot liquid popped her internal clutch into first gear. "I'm here now. I mean, my brain is warming up."

"Uh, Mary Frazier, honey, we've known one another for a long time. I've known your family ever since I moved here for my residency, and well . . ." Beads of sweat dotted Yancey's upper lip, though it wasn't remotely hot. "And well, I have wonderful news but please don't sue me. I'll take care of everything. I swear I will."

"Will you cut to the chase? I may be dying but I'm not dumb."

"That's just it. You're not dying. You're as healthy as a horse except for a severe case of bronchitis and stress—you're under a lot of stress. Work, I reckon."

Frazier didn't move a muscle. Then she felt her face. She touched her wrist to feel her pulse. She pinched her arm, then shouted, "Thank you, Jesus!" She remembered the other patients. "Sorry, Yancey."

"Oh, it's quite understandable. I would dance a jig myself. This whole thing is due to a computer error—I want you to understand that. We enter data according to social security number and a lab-work order number, and somehow your numbers became scrambled with another individual's who, as luck would have it, was having symptoms somewhat similar to yours. I think a lab technician punched up a wrong digit. The X-rays from last night show that your lungs are clear—remarkably so, given that you're a smoker. 'Course, your bronchial tubes are infected but"—he paused to catch his own breath—"Thornton Rogers and I would have caught this right away if we could have gotten the X-rays when we wanted them."

"I don't give a rat's ass how it happened. I'm just glad I'm going to live and oh, God, how I am going to live! I'm flushing my two packs a day as of this moment. Never again. It's too frightening now, the possibility of cancer. I've been spared once."

"I hope, for your sake, you stick to those words," Yancey kindly admonished. "Now I want you to understand we'll give you some pills to help ease you off the morphine. And please let me explain about the morphine. It often acts as a respiratory depressant but, given what we thought was the advanced spread of the cancer, Thornton and I considered pain relief the humane course of action."

"I ripped the goddam thing out of my arm last night. I don't want any more chemicals or drips or doctors." She smiled slyly.

"Still, the stuff is very powerful. Remember, we thought you were in excruciating pain. Our hospital is correct in all procedures for the terminally ill. Anyway, you'll not have too much trouble handling the morphine withdrawal and I'll prescribe antibiotics for your bronchitis. You'll be as good as new in no time."

Frazier's eyes glazed over. She turned from a babbling Yancey and looked at the nightstand. The letters were gone. She jumped out of bed and knelt on the floor, peering under the bed.

"The letters—my letters."

"I beg your pardon?" Yancey squinted behind his horn-rimmed glasses. Why any man thought horn-rimmed glasses were attractive was beyond Frazier. They didn't make men look smart; they made them look like wimps.

"Yancey, I put eight stamped letters here on this nightstand and they're gone."

"The nurse probably put them out at the front desk."

Frazier bolted out of the room like an Olympic sprinter off the blocks. Yancey, astonished for a moment, hurried after her. Frazier skidded into the huge, round reception desk in the middle of the floor.

An older nurse stood up, alarmed. "Miss Armstrong, you've got to conserve your strength. Let me help you—"

"The letters. Where are my letters?" Frazier's pupils were as big as a cat's on the prowl.

Yancey came up behind her and spoke in his doctor voice to the nurse: "The patient has had a shock—a happy shock, I'm glad to say—but she put some letters on her nightstand and she seems quite concerned about them. If you know—"

"Brenda picked them up at seven, just like she always does." The nurse looked at the clock. "Those went out on the mail truck at seven-thirty." Then she smiled. "We're very efficient around here. Don't you worry about a thing. Your letters will be safely delivered,

Miss Armstrong. Your loved ones will be receiving them tomorrow if they're local, and in two or three days if they're not. You just go on back to bed and don't give it a second thought."

The blood drained from Frazier's face. Yancey attributed this to morphine withdrawal. Caused mood swings too.

"I've got to get to the main post office. I've got to get those letters back."

"Can't do that." Yancey put his arm around her to lead her back to her room. "It's a federal offense to tamper with the mail. Once it's in the chute or the bag it's history. Even the President of the United States couldn't get a letter back once it's in the postman's hands."

"The President of the United States couldn't find his ass with both hands." Frazier's color flushed back into her face. "Don't tell me what I can't do."

"Mary Frazier, what's so damned important here? You're going to live. Sit down and call your family and tell them the news. You're experiencing mood swings and possibly a mild obsession. That's quite natural under the circumstances."

"Will you kindly shut up!" Frazier's eyes flashed. "I am not experiencing mood swings. I do not need to be managed. I am in a shitload of trouble because of those *letters*."

Yancey dropped his arm around her shoulders. He was more puzzled than insulted. Anyway, Virginia women were devastatingly direct. He'd come to Virginia from New York University Medical School and discovered that the myth of the Southern Belle was just that. These women were polished, achingly polite, and heroically poised, but damn, they were tough as nails and they were straight shooters.

Frazier inhaled deeply through her nostrils, then coughed. That damned rattle again, the bronchitis. "I wrote everyone and told them the truth—the truth about myself and the truth about them."

He patted her back again. "Is that all? Your family and friends will know you thought you were dying, and besides, it can't be that bad.

You're overwrought. This is a joyful experience but a jarring one. After all, you thought you were dying and that changes everything. Don't worry about it."

Frazier stopped and turned to face him squarely. "Yancey Weems, what do you think would happen if you wrote to the people in your life and told them what you really thought of them?"

He paused for a skinny minute and then spoke in a genuine voice: "I get your point."

CHAPTER
5

Frazier drove herself home. She called everyone: Billy, Kenny, Mandy, Auntie Ru, and Ann, of course. Hosannas filled the skies. What she didn't tell them was that within a day her verbal grenades would be lobbed into their mailboxes. She figured she'd hear about it soon enough and she might as well get twenty-four hours of quiet. She'd given up on peace as soon as she knew she couldn't retrieve those letters.

The other phone call she made was to Harvey McIntire, president of the country club, to inform him that she would be available for fireworks duty on the Fourth of July. Harvey was thrilled on two counts. One, she was alive and two, he wouldn't have to train anyone else to handle the light explosives.

CHAPTER
6

Forcing jonquils tried Libby Armstrong's patience. She was planning a dinner party in honor of Frazier for the following week and she wanted the house filled with blooms, a precursor to Easter and spring.

The odd flap of a loosening fan belt alerted her to the mailman's arrival in the front drive. If she didn't hear the Jeep, the dogs usually did. Libby wrapped a shawl around her shoulders and ran out to the box just in time to wave to the mailman on his way to the next gruesomely expensive house on the country club grounds. In the distance a golfing foursome, bundled against the cutting wind, teed off.

Libby hurried inside to the kitchen. She carefully deposited the mail on the table and made herself a sandwich. Then she sat down to sort the mail into piles. The bill pile grew and grew. That was depressing. A few magazines, including Frank's beloved *Field and Stream,* relieved the bill gloom. Finally there were three letters: one from the church and two on beautiful blue-speckled paper addressed in Frazier's strong vertical handwriting.

Libby slit open the envelope with her name on it, laying down the silver Tiffany letter opener parallel to the magazine pile.

She opened the letter and soon her jaw was hanging open too.

Dear Mother,

By the time you read this I shall most likely be dead. It wasn't a bad life but it wasn't a really good life either. I realize this was mostly my own fault but you had a hand in it.

Not being a mother I can only sympathize with the tedium of the task. Carter and I gave you fits, I know we did, but then children are self-centered little monsters requiring close to two decades of discipline to break them to the minimum of civility. This was a task you chose. Neither Carter nor I chose it, obviously.

We were and remain your hostages to the future. We were trotted out at parties, dressed in whatever was the latest fashion. We were given every lesson conceivable to develop the proper friendships and form: tennis, swimming, golf, music, cotillion—I know my coming out cost a sweet mint. You watched lacrosse and field hockey, which you loathed. You liked Carter's football better, but then you liked everything Carter did better than what I did.

You taught me right from wrong. You performed the endless chores of motherhood. You instilled in me wonderful work habits and a cast-iron sense of responsibility but, Mother, you never loved me. Perhaps I'm just not lovable—to you anyway—or maybe I was a convenient weapon in the low-level war between you and Dad. Whatever, I have no memories of you kissing me or hugging me, if not for show in front of your friends. What I do remember is incessant criticism. I was never good enough.

You're rancid with unhappiness, Mother, and I really don't know why. Did life not turn out as you expected? Does it for anyone? Was it my fault? Oh, I know, it was Dad's. Why don't you let the poor man off the hook? So excitement isn't his middle name. He was a good father, a good provider.

If there were anything I could do to get you to look at yourself, to change, to just let go of all that heavy baggage you cart around with you, I'd do it, but I can't. Your unhappiness has become part of your identity. I don't think you want to part with it.

I could write reams about how you've pitted brother against sister but I won't. Stay out of Brudda's life, Mom. Let him go.

One other little thing. You never really knew me. You never really wanted to. I lived in your house for eighteen years and, after college and New York, not twenty miles from you, but you don't know a thing about me. I used to want you to know who I was, what I thought and felt, but by sixth grade I gave up. I want you to know I'm a lesbian. Actually, I'm bisexual, I suppose, but I have always felt that someday I might fall in love and that it would be with a woman. I wish that fact were not important but in our narrow-minded little world it looms as large as Mt. Rushmore. What I regret is that I hid, that I slithered away from this. I lived as a coward but at least I'm not dying as a coward. You no doubt will be glad I'm dead after reading this. I'll spare you social embarrassment. What would the Garden Club think?

Well, Mother, you'll cry tears at my funeral but you won't really miss me. You've lost more than you can imagine, but then so have I. I never had a mother. I had a drill sergeant.

Mary Frazier

Libby's enormous diamond cast rainbows of light around the room; her hand was shaking so badly that the colors splashed the walls. She ground her teeth in anger, then snatched up Frank's letter. In her distracted state she ran to the bathroom. She couldn't find a place to stash it. She opened the bedroom closet next and flipped through her clothes. Then she spied a hatbox on the upper shelf, stretched on her tiptoes and wiggled it off the ledge. She opened it and placed the letter inside. Then she threw the box up on the shelf but it kept falling down. Cursing, crying, shaking, Libby pulled over the floral-patterned wing chair, stood on it, and finally secured the hatbox on the shelf.

It didn't occur to her to read Frank's letter. Whatever Libby's faults, invading another human being's privacy wasn't one of them.

CHAPTER
7

Mary Russell Spitler, Frank Armstrong's older sister, tore open the end of her blue envelope. Ruru, as she was known, lacked the patience to open anything neatly. She shook out the letter, put on her spectacles, and read.

Dear Auntie Ruru,

By the time you read this I shall most likely be dead. I didn't want to exit without telling you I have loved you always, and I loved being your namesake even though it killed Mother to call me Mary. Well, she never did call me Mary, did she? I guess Frazier suited me better.

I love you because you never tried to be anyone but yourself. You're straight from the shoulder, no airs, just down to earth. I used to wish you were my mother. I still do. I love your sense of humor and I love that you never compared Carter to me and vice versa. You loved us both and accepted us for who we were and who we became.

On the surface of it, I've lived a decent life but, Ruru, I had no generosity of spirit such as you have. I never gave anybody anything without calculating the consequences to myself. Quid pro quo, that's me. I covered it up splendidly, I think, but then after all the money Mom and Dad spent on cotillion and private school I surely acquired manners and a good education too.

I wish I had spent more time with you. I wish I were more like you.

I want to tell you something about me. Why, I'm not sure. It won't matter but I feel guilty keeping me from you, and I did. Don't feel bad—I kept me from everyone. I'm thirty-five years old and I've never fallen in love with anyone. Not once. Oh, I've jumped in bed with people, not that many, but enough to make me think I was doing something. But love? Not me. I'd have to get too close, I guess, or maybe I was afraid I'd wind up like Mom and Dad. The other reason I declined this invitation to vulnerability is that I'm gay, whatever that means. If I let myself go I'd lose everything I've worked for—that's what I thought and I'm not convinced that wouldn't have been my fate.

I'll never feel what you felt for Uncle Paul, God bless his soul, and if I see him I'll give him a huge hug and kiss from you. You knew love and you were wise enough to pick a good man.

I filled my life with things. I was successful. Everyone seemed to like me. I was popular, as we used to say at St. Luke's, but Auntie Ruru, I was as hollow as a gourd.

I'm sorry I cheated me. I hope I didn't cheat you. I did love you so very much.

Frazier

Ruru wiped the tears from her eyes. "Poor baby," she said out loud to herself. Then she thought long and hard about what to do.

CHAPTER
8

The main post office, large, old, and ugly, filled half a downtown block. Carter Armstrong sauntered across the black-and-coral marble floor. He waved to the men and women behind the counter, nodded to acquaintances, tipped his Redskins baseball cap to the ladies, and then reached into his pocket for his box key. Finding it, he swung open the brass door with the little rectangular window. He pulled out a handful of irritants—every mail-order catalogue on the continent found its way into his mailbox. He didn't mind getting them at home, but stuffed into the P.O. box, they seemed sacrilegious somehow.

He accepted his business mail at this box as well as the occasional letter from a lady friend. Everything else was addressed to his home.

Having flunked out of the University of South Carolina, which was hard to do, Carter had slunk home and studied to get his real estate license. Fortunately, when he took it the test was easier than it was now, but then Carter wasn't stupid, merely lazy. He passed the test and worked as a realtor at the offices of Blue Sky Realty for three years. He studied some more and passed his broker's test, then opened his own real estate office, Horse and Hound. Since this was the center of hunt country he decided to specialize in farms and estates. Given his easy manner and his feel for the land, Carter sold real estate and even collected a few energetic agents along the way. With more motivation and less liquor he could have made good money.

Frazier's letter caught his eye. He'd recognize his sister's handwriting anywhere. Her bold wide letters written in real ink stood up like soldiers. His handwriting leaned far to the right and was full of fat loops in the l's, in any letter above or below the line.

He leaned against the big oak table in the middle of the P.O. box area and flicked his fingernail under the envelope flap. He took out the letter and read.

Dear Brudda,

By the time you read this I shall most likely be dead. I meant everything I said to you when you visited me earlier today. I wish you'd cut the traces and go.

What I didn't say is that I know you're still carrying on with Sarah Saxe. I call her Sahara Sex because she must be hotter than those desert sands the way she gets you fired up. I know you promised Laura to give her up. Obviously, you can't.

If you think I'm going to pitch a hissy fit on the page and tell you how rotten you are, I'm not. Whatever this woman has, you need. You've had affairs ever since your voice cracked but this one is different. I don't know if you know that or if you think you're just hanging around because the sex is terrific. I do know she's not "suitable," as Mother would say, and you wouldn't want to bring her to the country club. You've been rebellious about everything else—why are you such a conformist about this? What I'm saying, dear brother, is that I think you're in love with this one.

Love hasn't been high on my agenda. In fact, it isn't on my agenda at all. I've been a major fool, and how funny, because when someone falls in love, usually people say that person's the fool, but I swear to you with my last breath, the fools are the ones who don't try.

Telling you to leave Laura will probably come as a shock to you coming from me, if you'll forgive me for using "come" too often. Your favorite word, animal! As wives go I think Laura is okay but I'm not married to her. She's conventional, she's suitable, she pleases Mother. Give her the house, the car, and enough money to live on until she can get some job skills. It wouldn't hurt Laura to give up her weekly hair appointments, manicures, therapy sessions, aerobics classes, gardening club with our mother, tennis lessons, bridge club, and whatever else she does. Guess I shouldn't forget the Heart Fund. No proper lady forgets her volunteer work. At least it's a worthy cause but aren't they all? A dose of the real world and the value of a dollar would do Laura a world of good.

Today I die. Tomorrow it could be you. Love is worth fighting for, Carter. Do it.

I never did. I'm gay. I don't know if you knew. We never talked about it and I don't think I've ever given any indications that I might favor what is now called an alternative lifestyle. Bullshit. I'm nobody's alternative. Truthfully, I'm a failure as a lesbian but if I had had the guts I think I would have fallen for a woman. Don't confuse this with just sex. Men always do that. Well, it doesn't matter now. I blew it.

You'd rather be wrong by yourself than right with somebody else's help. You're a flaming asshole and a bullhead, buddy, but heed these words from the grave. And as for being a flaming asshole, hey, maybe it's a family trait. Remember Uncle Ray and the time he got shitfaced at the lake and he drove his Volkswagen off the dock into the water? He swam out only to have Mother screaming what a worthless drunk he was. He bowed to her, got into her Volvo station wagon, and drove it off the dock! When I see Uncle Ray in the hereafter, if there is a hereafter, I'm going to tell him it's been dull around here since he's been gone. He's

the only one who'd stand up to Momma. I never stood up to her. I
retreated and did whatever I wanted to do. Better than caving in to her
but still—

If I could live, Carter, I'd give Momma a piece of my mind. No lie.

Okay. That's it. Think about love. Oh, yeah, I did love you, even when
I didn't. Know what I mean?

Sistergirl

Carter reread the letter to make sure he'd understood it. He
thought a minute and then threw back his head and yelled, "Ye-
haw!"

CHAPTER
9

Ann Haviland opened the door to her pretty downtown home. Built in 1892, with high ceilings and ornate fireplaces, the house was Ann's pride and joy. Since housing in downtown Charlottesville was cheaper than out in Albemarle County, she could afford the place. The mail, shot through the slot, was scattered all over the floor. Ann kicked off her shoes by the door and bent down to pick it up. Hurt because Frazier sought solitude after her brush with death, she grabbed Frazier's letter and walked into the living room.

Assuming the letter would be tender and romantic—well, as romantic as Frazier could muster, which wasn't much—Ann built a fire in the fireplace. A cold wind whipped outside, reminding her that winter still had power despite the signs of spring.

She plopped into her favorite wing chair and opened the letter.

Dear Ann,
  By the time you read this I shall most likely be dead.

Ann's eyes moistened in expectation. She read on.

  I haven't given you much in life. Perhaps I can give you something in death. The truth.
  You always said you wanted me to love you. I could never figure out if you wanted love or if you wanted unconditional surrender. Obviously, I'm no good at either. Maybe it's me, maybe it's you, maybe it's the way most women are raised. You wanted to hear about my feelings. You wanted to process our relationship constantly.
  Ann, I didn't want a relationship that felt like another job. You seem to have more feelings than I do. I like to play golf, read a good book, or go to a movie when I'm not working, even though that's seldom. You got offended when I didn't send you sweet cards or tell you how lovely you looked or how much I needed you, or whatever it is that I didn't do. Mostly, I didn't spend enough time with you.
  And the time we spent together we hid. God forbid anyone should know we slept together. We went out in public with escorts. Of course, they're as gay as we are but the facade must be served. I was worse about this than you, I know.
  You said you'd lose your job at the bank. Maybe you would have and maybe not. Better to lose your job than your integrity. Easy for me to say, I know. I'm dead—almost. What I'm realizing is that I was dead while I breathed, dead to passion, dead to honesty, dead to sharing myself, dead to the pain that life brings us all, but it brings it in such a special, vile little package if one is gay.
  Look, I'm probably not making much sense. I tore that morphine tube out of my arm. I feel awful, like I'm spiraling downward into some abandoned canyon of anguish. You like people to be articulate and I'm losing it.
  I'll spare you more of my muddle but let me try to be concise with what I have left in me. You'll destroy every relationship you have if you aren't willing to claim that person as worth your time, your body, your soul, etc.

I was the wrong person for you but I did like you. I do hope you can be happy sometime. Fight for yourself. If you don't think you can be yourself here, then go to a bigger city. You've got a good résumé, you're good-looking, and you're good at what you do. Lots of goods. Go to New York or Los Angeles or Houston. I love New Orleans. Go there. Is there anyone who doesn't love New Orleans? Just go.

And remember, you are as sick as you are secret—so get going!

Love,

Frazier

The sound of Ann's hard breathing filled the room. Finally she gasped, "I will break every bone in her beautiful body!"

CHAPTER
10

The rich glow from the mahogany paneling embraced visi-
tors to Billy Cicero's office. His silver tennis trophy from
the previous year's country club finals had a place of pride
on the mantel. Since he spent more time at work than he did at home,
he kept the trophy there.

Atlantic Tobacco supplied Henrico County and the city of Richmond with thousands of jobs either in the plant itself or in related
industries. Zephaniah Cicero, Billy's great-grandfather, used to say
that Atlantic Tobacco's history was the history of Richmond.

Each day Billy eased into his jet-black Aston-Martin Volante and
drove the forty-five minutes east from his estate in the Green Springs
district of Louisa County to Richmond. Some days when his radar
detector, illegal in Virginia, told him the coast was clear, he could fly
door to door in thirty minutes. He never tired of seeing the Virginia

countryside, nor did he ever tire of the tobacco industry. From the first green shoots triumphantly bursting through the earth to the long fragrant leaves curing in the sheds, he loved the cycle of the weed, as he and his family referred to it. He made trips to Connecticut to inspect cigar-wrapper tobacco and trips to Kentucky for cigarette guts. If there was one tobacco plant in a state, Billy paid it a visit. He knew which leaves to brighten and which to let be. He could take a leaf between his forefinger and thumb, gently rubbing it, and tell you its qualities.

A cigar man, himself, although Atlantic Tobacco specialized in cigarettes, Billy longed to see the great cigar makers of Cuba. If only Cuba would wake up. But he had cast his eyes over the undulating crop of cigar leaf in Jamaica and the Cayman Islands, and sweating like a laborer, he'd bent over those old masters who had escaped Cuba in 1959 and set up shop in Tampa. Old men with nimble fingers could roll a cigar in seconds. Machines were for phonies.

Tobacco, glory of the New World, along with chocolate, the banana, maize, and chicle. Tobacco, that soother of raw nerves, that congenial drug to puff merrily amidst friends. Doctors, health fanatics—oh, sure, they could add a few years to your life, maybe, if you listened to them and gave up smoking. If you didn't live longer, it would seem longer.

Billy believed devoutly in self-determination. No one had the right to tell anyone else how to live his or her life. Smoking, drinking, drugging, and fornication were individual decisions, as well as what career one pursued, where one lived, and so forth. Who the hell were these people swooping down on Congress, that assemblage of carrion, these crows of retro-Puritanism? Except that now Puritanism had to do with your health and not just sex. He sighed and lit up a contraband Montecristo.

His secretary, a curvaceous bombshell, tottered in on her Ferragamo high heels and put his mail on his desk. She also kissed him on the cheek. Georgina adored Billy, but then most women did. He winked and she exited. He observed the sway to her rounded back-side. He didn't get it. How could that turn men on?

He read a letter from the Jockey Club, another from Atlantic's lobbyist on the Hill, and then he picked up Frazier's letter. As he was accustomed to Frazier's personal stationery, he didn't recognize the blue-speckled paper as hers, although the handwriting looked famil-iar. A call interrupted him. He dispensed with that in short order and opened the paper, folded over once.

Dear Billy,

By the time you read this I shall most likely be dead. I shall, however, be a dazzling corpse because Terese worked overtime. Thank you for that gift.

I have many things to thank you for, not the least of which is the gold Montblanc pen, which I cherish and adore. And what about the sensational Jean-Léon Gérôme painting we found in Poland and smuggled out? Or the time we went to Venice to pick up the Tintoretto you just had to have, along with those well-hung gondoliers? I think my favorite memory of you is the summer that you met Kenny Singer and we hopped in the car and drove to Harper's Ferry on a whim. . . . Those little brick buildings with high-water marks on them and the dates that the river flooded. I don't know, there was something special about that trip. And the raid—John Brown wasn't playing with a full deck. Then we climbed up to the rock where Jefferson supposedly said there wasn't a better view in all of Europe and we ate sandwiches and talked about everything and nothing.

We've trotted out to every damned ball in the United States. We've swirled at the Waldorf-Astoria for the Disease of the Week, all those dreary Palm Beach fund-raisers—for new face lifts no doubt—the Polo Ball—that's more fun—and we've never yet missed any ball that Carolyn Devane has organized, whether it's been in Houston, New Orleans, or Timbuktu. We've opened libraries and held vigils at condemned theaters on 44th Street. Town & Country *ought to put us on staff.*

We've even saved the whales but can we save ourselves? Well, yourself. I'm out of this joint. My first thirty-five years were a near-life experience. If I had a second thirty-five they would be very different.

Maybe you're not willing to read on but if I can sit here and write this feeling like death eating a cracker, oops, I guess I am, well, you can read it.

In the slot machine of life you hit the dark side of the jackpot, Billy. You're gorgeous, incredibly intelligent, and driven. You'll double Atlantic Tobacco's profits before you're fifty. If anyone can do it, even in these contracting times, you can and you will. But you've also been abandoned by your parents, oh, abandoned to the best schools, culminating in St. Paul's and then onward and upward to Oxford. Your childhood was a succession of nannies, governesses, trainers, and tutors. Mumsy and Popsy rode camels under the Sphinx's chopped-off schnoz, skied in Aspen during our winter and Bari Loche during our summer. Who ever loved you for you? Love wasn't the operative word but expectation certainly was. You delivered except for one glitch in the program: you're gay. Why tell Mumsy and Popsy? They don't deserve the truth, they don't care, and it would besmirch the postcard family they carry in their minds and display to their friends. So, on the surface everything is okay. On the surface.

You treat people as though they are props in a play, starring you. You even treated me as an extra. Even me, Billy, even me. If I had lacked wit, if I had lacked beauty, I would have been forgotten or passed over. I was convenient. Marriage to me would have been convenient, too, if you meant it and I don't think that you did.

Let me approach this another way because I'm starting to sound like my mother—a fate worse than death and coming from me at this moment you know I mean that. An obsession with style dulls you to suffering. Sometimes it's your own suffering. Underneath your perfect exterior there is a painful and imperfect interior. Stop and look inside. No, I'm not saying this is The Picture of Dorian Gray *but you have so distanced yourself from everybody and everything that isn't shimmering and shining and profitable, you're more lonesome than you know.*

Maybe all the men are a symptom of that or the cocaine. Don't get me wrong—if anyone can handle the stuff, you can. I don't think people become addicted unless it's in the blood, like alcoholism. But you're grabbing at handsome men, white powder, exquisite paintings, all these things, material things, all outside yourself. Don't get hard, Billy. Don't shut people out, or real feelings. Don't repeat my mistake on your grander level.

And stop lying about who and what you are. You're so goddam rich nobody can touch you. What do you care what they think? We both lied and we were so good at it. It frightens me to think about it. If you lie about being gay, doesn't it stand to reason that you'll lie about other things? Lying gets to be a habit. Finally, you lie to yourself. I did.

I know you aren't going to like this letter but I'm praying something will connect, something will get through to you. I never fell in love with anyone. Had you been a woman I probably would have fallen in love with you. I don't know, maybe if you'd been honest and I had too, we would have fallen in love in a nonromantic way. I don't even know what love is anymore except there are more kinds of it than I can fathom. But for what it's worth, I loved you as best I knew how and I want you to come home to yourself.

I left my business to Mandy. When the will is read she will also receive a set of instructions. I forget how long that kind of legal silliness takes but I have willed you the John Frederick Herring, Jr., that you so admire. Mandy is great-looking, great company, and she has poise. Take her out, make sure that she meets the right people. It's good for business and she'll know what to do. Look out for her until she gets her feet under her, okay?

As for me, I'll put in a good word for you with the Almighty. I expect you'll need it.

> *Ta-ta,*
> *Frazier*

"I'll be damned." Billy whistled under his breath.

CHAPTER

II

Kenny Singer, dog-tired and ready to bite, came home late from work. He threw his mail on the bed and took a shower. Then he got under the covers, fought the temptation to "win a million dollars" if he'd subscribe to a magazine, and finally opened Frazier's letter.

Dear Kenny,

By the time you read this I shall most likely be dead.

What good times we had together on our double dates. Billy, ever the center of attention, distracted me from you but upon reflection I realize you have become very dear to me.

I was a fool in this life. If there's such a thing as reincarnation, I'm not going to be a fool in the next one. The trouble is I can't imagine coming back as anyone but myself. I want to be open and loving and warm. How do you do that? You do it all the time. You give of yourself.

Forgive me for not knowing how special you are.

I'm wearing down. I'd best be brief. If you're in love with Billy, well, love is irrational. I can't say much about it but I can say that straight or gay is irrelevant. What matters is that you be in a relationship with someone who respects and honors you. And I hope that happens for you. If Billy can achieve that, great.

No matter what happens with Billy, please think about having children sometime. You were meant to be a father and I believe you will find some kind of fulfillment with that kind of love.

If all the world's a stage and I am merely a player, I am leaving the theater for a brief intermission. Wonder if there's popcorn in the celestial lobby?

May I see you in the next life and may I know, early on, how special you are.

Love,
Frazier

Kenny stared at the letter, then held it to his heart.

CHAPTER
12

"Sir Teddy," a haunting oil painting by Ben Marshall, captured Frazier's attention. Painted in 1808, the subject was a lean and long Thoroughbred, which, on the 27th of August, 1808, beat the mail coach from London to Exeter, doing the 176 miles in 23 hours. Small, yet large in impact, the painting was so unusual not because of the horse but because of the two dogs in Sir Teddy's stall, one of which, a white cur, peered out at the viewer from behind the stall siding. Frazier couldn't take her eyes off the white dog. She felt the dog was Ben Marshall studying the viewer.

The gallery, in the old part of downtown, drew knowledgeable collectors and dealers from the Americas and Europe. When she left Sotheby's, Frazier considered opening a gallery in New York City but the overhead plus the punishing local and state taxes wrecked that idea. She remembered the line "Build a better mousetrap and the world will beat a path to your door." In Frazier's case this was the absolute truth. For one thing, she could offer extraordinary sporting art and the occasional Matisse at far more competitive prices than her big city competition.

In that respect Frazier was a true capitalist. The big city broker sought to make one big hit. Frazier built a loyal clientele and had repeat business. Selling a George Stubbs for $10,000 under market value seemed insane to her competitors but she made ten times that when the gratified customer became a friend and continued buying from her over the years. Her competitors couldn't seem to figure out that being located in central Virginia, in the small but sophisticated town of Charlottesville, was a huge advantage.

Her other two advantages were Amanda Eisenhart and her own sharp eye for the young artist. Not only did Frazier possess an unerring sense of quality, brushstroke, line, and composition—lots of people had that—she also had an uncanny knack of knowing what painters would go the distance. Darcy Weeden, her Delta Delta Delta sister, sang her praises throughout Buckhead, just outside of Atlanta. Frazier sold Darcy a large equine painting by an English artist who was in her thirties. The cost five years ago was $17,000 and Frazier promised the hesitant Darcy she would never regret this purchase. The value of that same work had skyrocketed to $185,000 at last appraisal.

Mandy read her letter from Frazier. It said "Thank you. Love, Fraiz." She folded the letter and walked out of her office into the main room of the three-roomed gallery. She drew alongside Frazier and studied "Sir Teddy."

"You're not going to sell that painting."

"Ben Marshalls are easy to sell even in a depressed market. You know that. Like Herring, Stubbs, Munnings, Bonheur. There are some artists who are golden."

"I know all that, thank you very much." Mandy half-smiled. "You aren't selling that painting, because you're in love with it."

"Well . . . I guess I am."

"Are you sure you want to work today? You're still coughing. I don't mind running the show."

"Thanks, but I'd rather be here than at home. My bronchitis medicine is helping. I threw that damned other crap in the trash can. I'll tell you this: don't you ever mess around with heroin or opium or morphine. They're the same, I think. I mean, they're different but aren't they all derived from the poppy?" Mandy shrugged and Frazier continued, "I was so low, black as the insides of a goat."

"Still?"

"No, but I rock and roll a little bit."

"I just read your letter."

"Shorn of all literary flourish." Frazier put her arm around Mandy's shoulders. "But I meant it."

"Will you ever tell me what the surprise was in your will?"

"If I live through the next few months I'll tell you everything."

Mandy's eyes widened in fear. "Are you still sick? Is there something you're not telling me?"

"Oh, no, I'm sorry. I shouldn't have said it quite that way. Come on over here—let's sit in my office. I'd better tell you exactly what I've done, because there's going to be hell to pay. Big time."

Frazier's office was painted a soft yellow, the yellow that the Metropolitan Museum of Art often uses on its walls. The two sat on the 1930's overstuffed sofa. The office, simple but sensuous, with lots of curving lines, betrayed a secret side to Frazier. Most people would have expected her office to be an homage to Hepplewhite, Sheridan, or Chippendale, a bow in the direction of the eighteenth century.

"Shoot," Mandy said nervously. "No, wait. You've experienced a catharsis. You're selling everything and moving to Hawaii. Actually, for you it would be the south of France, Lake Como, or New Zealand. Am I right?"

"About everything except New Zealand. Beautiful but so far away. Argentina."

Mandy fell back on the sofa. "I knew it. I knew you'd leave."

"No, I just meant if I were to go it wouldn't be to New Zealand. I'm not going anywhere, although I might be run out of town."

"Frazier, what did you do? I mean, what can someone do who is full of tubes and flat on her back in the hospital?"

"You told me to write letters to Tomorrow."

"I got one. Thank you back at you."

"Uh, I did write letters to Tomorrow. I wrote everyone and told them the truth about myself and what I believe to be the truth about them. I begged my brother and Billy to change their ways. I told my mother exactly what I think of her—I emphasize *exactly*. I bequeathed the same favor, different flavor, on Ann Haviland. I wrote my father an exhaustive letter about him, Mom, Carter, and myself. Who else? Auntie Ruru, whom I adore, and Kenny Singer. I opened the whole can of worms."

"Jesus H. Christ on a raft." Mandy was speechless after that. Frazier pulled herself up and opened the little refrigerator. She handed Mandy a Coke and took one for herself, grabbed the crystal old-fashioned glasses, filled them with ice cubes, and rejoined her on the sofa.

"Imagine what would happen to you if *you* told everyone around you the truth," she said.

"I'm doing that very thing." Mandy rattled the cubes in her glass and then poured the Coke. "I've been more open than you are but I guess I've got a couple of skeletons in my own closet and I've got my own stuff right now, you know?"

"I don't know."

A little involuntary twitch, which blossomed into a smile, indicated that Mandy registered this but wasn't sure what to do next. "Right. Boyfriend trouble. We can talk about me some other time. My first question is, do you remember what you wrote?"

Frazier's eyes glassed over. "Kind of."

"What do you mean, 'kind of'?"

"I ripped the morphine tube out of my arm. It swung in my way every time I moved my arm and I couldn't write and anyway, as the night wore on I sank deeper and deeper into the slough of despond or anger or wherever I was. I did tell the truth. I just think had I been in a better emotional state I might have chosen my words more wisely. I don't think I was ugly. Well, I was to Mother." Frazier breathed in sharply. "But she deserved it and I should've laid my mother out to whaleshit years ago. Am I being unfair? Doesn't everyone blame her mother for everything?"

"Uh, I don't. I love my mom. Most times, anyway. Don't start beating up on yourself. I've seen *tua mater* many times. She's no prize."

"Whew." Frazier crossed her legs under her and turned to face Mandy, who did likewise. "Thanks for that. You know, when I was writing Mother from the hospital I kept thinking about how she would read Carter and me stories at bedtime when we were tiny. When I got a little older I wanted to read them myself. So I opened *Babar the Elephant* and *Bambi* and found sentences, even paragraphs, blacked out. When I asked her, she lied and said the book was printed that way. So one day at the library—oh, I must have been in third grade by then—I found *Bambi.* Do you know what she had done?"

"I can't imagine," Mandy replied.

"She'd crossed out every reference to the mother being killed."

"No!" Mandy exclaimed.

"Every syllable. So I marched home and asked her why she'd done that and she said because those passages would have upset Carter and me. She wanted to protect us from Death. Only made it worse, of course. I never really trusted her after that. Of course, I'm not sure I trusted her before that either. *Bambi* and *Babar* made me realize what I had always known, I guess—that Mother wants everything controlled, placid, no involvement. You feel things as a child but you don't know what you're feeling. After that I knew what I was feeling, about her anyway. I sure knew not to tell her my feelings too."

"Who knows what your mother will do now? She can't black out the sentences in your letter."

"I reckon I'll find out."

Mandy sat straighter. "Did you tell them all that you're—"

Frazier interrupted: "Gay? Yes, ma'am."

A long silence followed. "In the long run you'll be glad you did. In the short run . . ."

"In the short run I am going to be sliced and diced, I am going to be barbecued, I am going to be deep-fried southern style, I am going to be trussed and trounced and beat so hard about the ass that my nose will bleed. Honey, I am in deep shit, like all the way to China deep and you goddam well know it."

"Now I feel responsible. I gave you the stationery."

"Nah. This was my doing. I'm taking full credit and if I'd had any ovaries I would've read everyone the riot act years ago. I'm not eager to suffer the consequences though, and suffering is such an important part of Christianity that Mother feels it's her duty to spread it around. Oh, sweet Jesus, I need a friend."

"You got one."

"In a pig's blister."

"Me."

"Ah, Mandy, there's nothing you can do to protect me or save me."

"No, but I can stand by you. And so will Auntie Ruru."

Frazier turned her glass around in her hand a few revolutions. "Billy, maybe."

"Billy?"

"Considering I told Billy he's going to hell in a handbasket, in so many words, I don't know which way he'll cut. I think it's me that will get cut, actually."

"He's gay, too, of course."

"I don't feel it's my duty to blow the whistle on anyone else."

"Bullshit. I'm not an idiot. Anyway, past the age of thirty, roommates look suspicious." Mandy's flash of anger gave her a sultry, sexy look.

"He doesn't have a roommate."

"Oh, Kenny Singer is just attached to his hip, is that it? I mean, if

I'm going to be here in the center of the hurricane, you can't be Little Miss Daisy in a field of cow flaps. You'd better tell me everything I need to know." She put her glass on the coffee table and folded her arms across her chest. "What about Carter?"

Frazier shook her head. "He's going to be the biggest surprise of all, I think. Hell, Mandy, I don't know. Right now I don't know shit from Shinola."

Mandy leaned over and patted her hand. "The great thing about the truth is you're not obliged to remember it. You can claim amnesia. Not that you would. You know what my mother says . . ."

"No, but I have a feeling I'm going to."

"If you're going to be hung for sheep you might as well be hung for a wolf." Mandy finished off her Coca-Cola.

"*Hung* is the operative word, a word I don't wish to hear unless it applies to the male of the species."

"Amen, sister." Mandy uncrossed her legs, swinging them over the sofa. "Know how to tell if a man's well hung?"

"I've got my method. Let's hear yours."

"If there's three inches between the rope and his collar."

"Oow." Frazier squinted. "Mean."

"A small diverting moment from the crisis at hand. All right, let's catalogue the worst. You'll be drummed out of the Junior League."

"My heart is breaking."

"You'll have a devil of a time getting a golf foursome at the country club. Your women friends won't want to be in the bathroom when you're there. Uh, children. Yes, they'll hide their children when you drive by."

Frazier suddenly froze. "Mandy. It's not funny. Some people *are* that ignorant. I'll no longer be Mary Frazier Armstrong. I'll be Mary Frazier Armstrong, comma, Lesbian. My identity will be skewered on a word derived from the name of an island off the coast of Greece, or is it closer to Turkey? I'm about to lose my individuality, my social position, parts of my family, if not all of it, and God knows what else."

"That's why I have the advantage over you."

"What?"

"You can lie about who you are. I can't. My face tells the tale."

"Your face is uncommonly beautiful."

"Thank you, but it bears the stamp of Africa. That's hardly a plus in the land of the Blond Beast. At any rate, I can't be anything or anyone other than who I am. It's better that way."

"I don't know," Frazier honestly stated. "Funny what runs through your mind. I keep hearing a phrase Carter used one time when we got campused by Mother for throwing a party when she and Dad were out of town. It happened to be prom night too. He said, 'It doesn't matter if the rock hits the jug or the jug hits the rock. The jug still gets it.' I'm the jug."

"I hope not, Frazier."

"Me too."

"How much damage did the party do to the house?"

Frazier's voice lifted into the mezzo range. "Oh, nothing. The house was untouched but Carter and I took photographs of various St. Luke's sports heroes engaged in indelicate acts with cooperative ladies. The taking of them wasn't the issue. Circulating them at school for profit landed us in hot water." Frazier burst out laughing. "But it was worth it. The sight of the prom queen giving Ernie Watkins a blow job, tiara and all. Yahoo!"

"Frazier, there's a whole side of you I don't know." Mandy stared at her in wonder and admiration.

"Carter and I could cut a shine—until I had to earn a living. That's when I pulled in my horns, or became mature—take your pick. Yeah, and that's when I began to hate myself too. Have you ever seen rainbow trout? They're shimmering, living rainbows in their element. Take them out of their element and their colors fade. I guess I was like that, or I am like that."

"Sounds to me like you're coming back to life."

That sentence ran through Frazier's head as she walked into the second gallery room. An enormous canvas, ten by fifteen feet, dominated one wall. Painted in the seventeenth century by an unknown artist, it depicted the gods and goddesses on Mount Olympus. Their perfect bodies, except for that of crippled Hephaestus/Vulcan, inspired worship. Zeus/Jupiter, a man at the peak of his powers, forty or fifty perhaps, his body thick with physical might, light shining from his head, gazed over his brood. Their happiness was both earthy and heavenly. Guilt, suffering—well, long-term suffering—and pain had been banished.

His wife, brothers, children, and his wife's children were positioned around the Thunderbolt God in a mix of personalization and parentage that would send a therapist into transports of analysis. Modern man needs to explain everything in order to feel safe—a dangerous illusion, for there is no safety. The ancients didn't need to explain; they needed to experience, and this anonymous artist, no doubt a hearty Venetian, must have reveled in his work as he mixed his oils from mounds of dried powder. He, too, must have craved experience, and his sensual nature was reflected in the Olympians.

Zeus/Jupiter sat on his throne in the middle of a semicircle arranged around him. Hera, or Juno, his wife, stood by, statuesque, at his right hand, her hazel eyes trained on her philandering husband. Clearly she didn't trust him even when he was sitting down.

To her right glowered Poseidon/Neptune. Perhaps he left his mighty ocean kingdom for this family portrait, poised between squabbles for a moment of calm. He strongly resembled his brother, although his beard was golden whereas Zeus's was gray. Poseidon leaned on his trident, casting his eyes not at his overlord brother but at Artemis/Diana, who was standing next to him, her silver quiver on her back, her silver bow in her hand.

Fat chance. Not even the god of the sea could turn her chaste head. The only man the youthful, perfect huntress loved, and not physically, was her twin, Apollo. He sat on a rock slightly in front of Artemis. He wore his golden quiver and his golden bow lay at his feet. The two were mirror images of each other, gorgeous, yet somehow rather cold.

Ruddy Ares/Mars made up for their lack of heat. His red hair was shorn, as one would expect of a soldier. His armor further enhanced his virility. His sword, sheathed, hung by his side. He held his helmet in the cradle of his arm; the flaming-red horsehair seemed to sway in the breeze. His gaze smoldered at Aphrodite/Venus, who sat directly opposite him in the semicircle.

She returned his gaze with equal heat. Here the artist broke with convention. No washed-out blond Venus. Rich, dark curly hair fell to her shoulders. Her eyes glowed a dark blue. Everything about her suggested passion, erotic possibilities allied to tender mercy. This Venus was far more than a sex goddess.

Moving back toward Zeus, Hermes/Mercury, laughing, stood next to Venus—perhaps the only woman, apart from his mother, whom he completely trusted. His long-muscled, slender body gleamed. No beard appeared on his sharp jaw. If paintings could move he would have been twirling his caduceus, and the intertwining snakes on the magical rod would have been dancing with laughter.

In sharp contrast to Mercury stood Athena/Minerva. Her impressive helmet covered the blond hair, which was tucked underneath, a few tendrils escaping. Her gray eyes evidenced no passion but she didn't seem cold, just preoccupied. Her shield rested on a tree stump behind her. She looked at her father, Zeus, and he returned the gaze. She was his favorite child.

Standing between them but a step back was Hades/Pluto. So enthralled was he by his underworld kingdom that he, too, rarely ventured out of it, much less to Mount Olympus.

Hades/Pluto was as dark as Neptune was light and tremendously handsome. All three brothers were powerfully built men with beautiful mouths and white teeth. The finest cloth covered his body. Unlike Neptune he showed little interest in plotting against their brother. Pluto, although distant and judgmental, was a loyal, honest soul.

In the near distance the artist had placed immensely muscular Hephaestus/Vulcan, still sweating from his work at the forge. Zeus/Jupiter couldn't stand him, so Hera/Juno tried to make up for this by taking his part at each opportunity. His crippled leg stuck out at an odd angle from his good one.

Another god at a distance from the others was Dionysus/Bacchus. He lounged in the lower right-hand corner of the canvas. In his late twenties or early thirties, the prime of life, he should have cut a splendid figure. He was slovenly attired, however, which detracted from his beauty. A golden goblet was raised in his right hand, raised not to Zeus but to the painter or the viewer, for Dionysus peered out of the painting, away from the circle of gods. A slight smile played on his ruby lips—a jeer or genuine pleasure?

This florid artwork had supposedly hung in the grandest whorehouse in Venice. The sneaking sensuality of it, the subtle assault on Judeo-Christian priggishness, the sheer grandeur would attract someone, a buyer moved by impulse, an impulse probably not understood.

Frazier especially liked the brushwork, so smooth, so silky, so unobtrusive. The flesh seemed real. She could reach out and caress Mercury's eternally youthful figure or tweak Jupiter's majestic beard. The painter believed in art that conceals art, an attitude in keeping with Frazier's philosophy. She detested artists who wailed about how difficult their work was and then further tried the patience of all the giving saints by telling you how they accomplished their masterpiece.

The front door opened. Frazier's shoulders stiffened. Was it Mother? Dad? Carter? Was the axe raised ready to grind? The Fed Ex man dropped off a package, offered his congratulations upon her good health, and left with a wink. Frazier was relieved and strangely disappointed.

CHAPTER
13

The metallic-coffee Explorer purred down the tree-lined drive. Frazier pulled up at her parents' white brick Federal home. She sat a moment remembering the first time she had driven the Explorer down the brown pebble driveway. Libby had walked out of the house, disappointment etched all over her face.

"You sold the Range Rover?"

"Yes, Mother."

"But why? A Range Rover has some élan."

"Because the dealer is eighty miles away."

"I loved your Range Rover!"

"Then you should have bought it."

Frazier blinked, tried to focus on today, got out of the car, and slowly walked to the back door. She opened the door, hinges squeaking.

Libby, potting plants in her sink, barely uttered a hello.

"Need any help?"

"No, thank you" came Libby's clipped reply. "I want these narcissus ready for your dinner party."

"What dinner party?"

"The dinner party to thank God for the miracle of your recovery," Libby pronounced.

"This is the first I've heard of it."

"I was planning to call you tonight."

"Momma, did you pick up your mail yesterday or today?"

Libby's lips stretched tighter across her face. "I did."

Frazier was losing patience. She hated this trick of Libby's. Don't volunteer any information; don't facilitate a discussion. Force the other party to bring up any unpleasant or volatile subject and declare yourself an unwilling victim of such upset. Upset equaled bad manners. "My letter, Mother? I know you must have gotten my letter."

"I did."

"Well?" Frazier's tone hardened.

"I am putting that right out of my mind because I think you must have been out of yours."

"I knew you'd say that." Frazier crossed her arms over her chest. "If it's not what you want to hear, then there's something wrong with the person telling you. Right, Mother?"

"I see no reason to continue this discussion. You'll come to your senses. In the meantime I advise you to be prudent."

"Prudent? As in shut up?"

"You said it; I didn't."

"I wrote other letters."

"You did?" Alarm invaded every crevice of Libby's body.

"Carter, Daddy—which you know, since you pick up the mail—Kenny, Ruru. I think I forgot a few."

Libby gripped the sink. "And did you tell them . . ." Frazier remained silent, forcing Libby to go on. Nothing like giving your mother a dose of her own medicine. "Did you tell them what you told me?"

"That I was dying? Of course."

"You know what I mean."

"I want to hear you say it. That's probably why I stopped by. I figured you wouldn't phone me or come to my house."

"Say what?" But Libby was losing at her own game.

"Not a goddam thing, Mother."

"Don't you swear in front of me. That you're unnatural," Libby shouted.

Frazier walked away from her and gripped the doorknob. "Nothing is unnatural—just untried."

"Don't you get smart with me. Why'd you come over here? To make me more miserable than I already am?"

"You did that all by yourself. I came over here to warn you. I don't know how the other recipients will take their letters. For all I know it's all over town that I'm gay. I know it's all over town that I'm alive. I thought you might like to pull yourself together, to organize your public response."

Icy fear clawed Libby's entrails. Her friends. The whispers behind the hand. The seemingly innocent inquiries, the too-firm handshake from the pastor after service. She could see it all. The social embarrassment—that would be loathsome—but the true agony would be the pity, the sickeningly sweet smiles and the solicitous tone of voice. Oh, God. "I don't understand you. I never understood you and I don't understand this. Go to a psychiatrist. You don't have to be this way. I don't want you to be this way."

"What do you think I did one day, Momma? Do you think I woke up and said, 'I'm going to be queer today. I'm going to upset my mother, baffle my father, jeopardize my place in the community, and lose a few friends in the bargain? I'm going to join the most despised group of people in America. Hooray for homosexuals. I can't wait to embrace these sorrows.' Do you think I did that? Do you think anyone does that? I regret your hurt, Mother. I regret even more being shoved into a category, being *untermenschen*, as the Nazis used to say, less than human. But you know what? I am what I am. I can't see that it's the end of the world or that I've suddenly turned into a monster."

"Two thousand years of church teaching can't be wrong," Libby railed.

"Until the last century, that same church justified slavery, Mother, because it was in the Bible. I am not going to a psychiatrist. I am not going to suddenly marry and produce the grandchildren you blab about day in and day out. Like I said, Momma, I am what I am. And like it or not, I am your daughter."

"Then I wish you had died!" Libby tossed the pot at Frazier's head.

Quick reflexes intact, Frazier ducked. The pot smashed against the door. That fast Frazier was out of the house, leaving Libby to bellow, "Look at this mess you made. You come back here and clean it up. Frazier! Mary Frazier Armstrong, look what you made me do!"

CHAPTER
14

Frank Armstrong, silver-haired and fit at sixty-three, fiddled with the back door hinges. A screwdriver and a can of 3-In-One oil were his weapons. Cold night air whooshed into the room along with Libby, who entered from the opposite direction.

"Will you close that door before we catch our death?"

"You've been grexing and groaning about the door, so I thought I'd surprise you." He jiggled the tongue of the lock, inserted a few drops of oil, then swung the door back and forth and drenched the hinges.

"Frank, that oil is running down the door."

"I'll clean it up. Why don't you fix me my regular? Better make a double for yourself."

"Why?"

"Because you're edgy."

"I am not." Libby marched out. By the time she returned with their drinks—a scotch on the rocks for Frank—Usquaebach, his favorite brand—and a double of Absolut with orange juice for her—the back door was fixed. Frank wiped the edge of the door and then put away his tools.

They retreated to the den, a walnut-paneled library filled with books Frank would never read. Libby favored romances, gardening books, and biographies. A few large home-decorating books also squatted on the shelves.

Libby clicked on the television for the evening news but she couldn't sit still. She rose to get her needlepoint. She sat down. Then she wanted her reading glasses, which were in the kitchen. The news showed a body being fished out of the river, then dumped in a body bag. The camera distance was far enough away so as not to ruin supper for the viewers. Nothing like a blue bloated carcass with the face eaten up to put you off salmon forever. Still, the sight of something abnormally large and squishy being dumped in the bag, to say nothing of the policeman bent over a bush, plucked at Libby's nerves.

"Why do they have to show something like that? I ask you, Frank, why? I mean, what if that person's family is watching and they haven't been notified yet? Can you imagine? Can you imagine how horrible to be told that . . . that awful mess is your flesh and blood?" She shivered. "People have no respect today. The media."

"Ants at a picnic."

"What?" Libby's darkened eyebrows—she was naturally blond—curved upward toward her very blond hair, a neat trick at fifty-nine.

"Reporters are like ants at a picnic. You step on those that you can and ignore the rest."

"What business is it of anyone's? Why show some poor soul's mortal remains like that? I could see that he hardly had a shirt on. When I go, put me in the ground as fast as you can."

"I have heard enough talk about death in this household to last me until mine. I don't want to hear any more about this. Put your mind off the subject."

"Look, now they're showing us a car wreck. Three drunken kids in Buckingham County." Libby's voice rose. "And a close-up of a blood-spattered windshield!"

"Honey, you usually go for the gory details."

"I do not. I most certainly do not."

"Libby, what in the hell is the matter with you tonight? Did you and Ruru get into it again? You having troubles at the Garden Club?" Frank had fielded a day of decisions, complaints, negotiations, and equipment problems at work but if Libby needed to spew her problems he might as well listen. It was easier than getting his butt chewed off.

"None of those things. I have not heard from your bohemian"— she leaned heavily on the word *bohemian*—"sister since we discussed the good news about Frazier."

"Good news? A blessing from great God Almighty." Frank smiled.

Libby wanted to say that maybe it wasn't such a blessing but she held her tongue, a real victory for her.

In the long silence that ensued they watched commercials. One was for controlling body odor; another dwelt on the subject of constipation; four car ads livened up the fare; a wine cooler promised eternal youth, which would quickly sour if you didn't use the toilet-bowl cleaner that followed the thirty-second wine spot. After this bracing experience the news team filled the small screen with chat about the anchor's new dress and oh, what fun the basketball tournament will be. Meanwhile, half a world away, Eastern Europe struggled to govern itself after nearly half a century of disabling communism. Poor Russia had had the absurd philosophy since 1917. That wasn't newsworthy. Underarm deodorant was. After the contrived byplay between the anchor and the co-anchor, sporting the worst hairdo since Howdy Doody, the sportscaster faking a butch voice, and the weatherman's patter, a brief flash of events squirted across the screen. Fortunately, the content included no body count.

Libby relaxed enough to fish in her needlepoint bag for some lime-green yarn. Lime green was a big hit with Libby. "I think I'll cancel Frazier's party."

"Huh?"

"She needs time to adjust. We can celebrate when she's more herself."

"She's great. She's better than I've ever seen her."

"When did you see her?" Libby held the lime-green yarn tightly in her hand.

"Dropped by the gallery at lunchtime."

"And?"

"And what? She was busy and I had a few minutes. We'll get together for lunch Friday." He noticed Libby's jaw clamp shut. "She's happier than I remember. Almost like she was when she was a little girl. You know, when she was a child she'd walk right up to you and say whatever was on her mind. I don't know." He rubbed his chin. "Something different about Frazier."

"I'll say." Libby jabbed the needle into the belt pattern.

CHAPTER
15

The Southwest Range, a spur of mountains running north-east and parallel to the moody and sensuous Blue Ridge Mountains, offered protection to the lush little towns of Keswick and Cismont. Route 231 snaked alongside these gentle green mountains, culminating in a traffic circle at Gordonsville, where every spring the high school students jammed the 360 degrees with their cars, driving the local police and citizens crazy. If the high-spirited youths shot straight up Route 15 off the circle they would bump into the beautiful town of Orange. If they whipped off about 200 yards to the west on Route 33, then turned north again on 231, they would pass some of the most beautiful land in America. Frazier's house, a Virginia frame farmhouse, circa 1834, lay just off this road, south of the crossroads of Somerset.

She could drive to Richmond in an hour. She could zoom into

Orange in minutes and hop the train to New York City. The airport was only forty minutes away. Washington, D.C., if she headed up through back roads, took two hours by car. On the main drag, without hitting rush hour, she could make it in an hour and a half, and if she boarded the commuter plane it was less than half an hour to D.C.

Apart from the location, Frazier dearly loved the yellow house with the dark-green shutters. Rain on the tin roof always made her think of "Singin' in the Rain." The house, added onto over the decades, bore testimony to good times and hard times. The heart-pine floors, a soft wood, were worn as thin as a bee's wing near the doorjambs. The windowpanes, hand-blown, reflected an imperfect but lovely view of rolling hills lapping up to one of the Southwest Mountains. Hightop Mountain may have been too grand a term but no one dared call them fat hills.

The other good thing about the house, Roughneck Farm, was that it was just enough out of the way that Frazier endured few drop-ins. She was enduring one tonight.

Ann Haviland paced across the old blue Chinese rug in the living room. A blaze in the huge fireplace wasn't the only thing crackling.

Frazier, reeling from her mother and now Ann, was collapsed in a faded wing chair. A tidal wave of exhaustion washed over her. She thought to herself how she regretted her promise to give up smoking. She would have given almost anything for one puff of a divine Sherman cigarette.

"The time I wasted on you!" Ann punctuated her sentence by stopping before Frazier. "To say nothing of the money."

"What money?"

"The earrings from Harlan and McGuire, the tickets to Lake Louise in Canada—"

"Hey, I paid for the hotel room." A flicker of anger lifted Frazier's heavy eyelids.

"Well, what was I to you? I don't want to talk about money—that will get us nowhere."

"You brought it up."

"Don't evade." Ann's pretty features clouded over in anger and anxiety. "What am I to you? What would you make of this letter if you were the one to receive it?" She shook the letter under Frazier's nose.

"Uh." Frazier reached up for the letter. "Could I read this?"

"You don't remember what you wrote?" Ann was incredulous.

"I sort of do and I sort of don't."

"I'm your lover and you don't remember?"

Frazier snatched the letter from her hand. The warm flow of hostility awakened her. "I am tired of explaining to you how I felt, the physical state I was in, the hour of the night. Just let me read the goddam letter."

Ann flounced into the opposing wing chair, crossed her arms over her chest, and stared at Frazier as those beautiful green eyes danced over the blue-speckled pages. Ann's left foot tapped on the rug. The cat, Basil, glared at Ann as Ann glared at Frazier.

Frazier finished the letter and placed it on the coffee table.

"Well?" Ann grabbed it back.

Frazier folded her hands together. "I regret that the fear of dying made me blunt but I don't regret what I wrote. You aren't happy with me. You haven't been happy with me for the last year."

"I hardly ever see you." Ann worried about what was going to happen next, even though she had pushed Frazier.

"We both work hard."

"You're obsessed with your work."

"I love my work and you don't. Maybe if you loved what you were doing in this world, you wouldn't be so jealous of what I'm doing." The merciless truth filled Frazier's voice.

"Thank you for Psychology 101, but while you're at it tell me how I'm going to pay my bills."

"Other people have had to figure that out, Ann. Why should you get carried along? If you want to change your life, you will. If you want to be happy, you will be. Don't use money as an excuse. Right now you'd rather complain than change."

"Death sure has done wonders for you," Ann ruefully noted. "Before, I could barely get you to talk about anything other than work or sports."

"You wanted to know how I felt. I told you. You don't like it. Now you attack me for it. I'm not saying I have any answers for you. And I'm not saying you're a bad person or that you're wrong. But what I put in that letter is the truth as I see it. We aren't going anywhere. Why prolong the agony?"

"It's agony to be with me? I thought we had some pretty good times." The reality of this conversation was seeping into Ann's brain.

"We did. It's always good in the beginning. We just don't see eye to eye."

"If we were together more maybe I'd really know what you think and how you feel. Apart from this." She picked up the letter, then dropped it again on the coffee table.

"Ann, we aren't the right team. Especially since I came out in every letter I've written."

Ann gripped the armrests. "How many did you write?"

"Mother, Dad, Carter, Billy, Auntie Ruru, Kenny, and . . . uh, Mandy. Seven besides yours."

"Did you mention me? I mean it's one thing if you blow the whistle on yourself. Did you blow it on me?" Ann's throat muscles tightened.

"No, but Carter will put two and two together."

"He hardly ever saw us." Ann's hands shook. "And Billy will keep his mouth shut. After all, he has a lot to lose. Mandy? Why would you write Mandy on the night you thought you were dying? I mean, Mandy's an employee."

"Mandy may be the only person in my life who likes me for me."

"Carter's a buffoon. Jesus H. Christ on a raft, Frazier. Why? Why tell Carter anything?"

"He's my brother and I love him."

"*Finally.* Carter is *finally* more successful than you. Oh, is he going to *love* this." Ann clapped her hands together.

"Maybe not."

"If Carter or Ruru or anybody else asks about me you'd better lie through your teeth. You might be going down the tubes in this town but I'm not!"

"You didn't get it." Frazier looked at the letter.

"To come out. Easy to come out when you're dying. You're going to be dogmeat!"

"I intend to find out."

"Am I supposed to admire your bravery?" Sarcasm dripped from Ann's lips. "We'll see how brave you are as time goes by. As you lose friends and, what's closer to your heart, your business."

"For Christ's sake. Why should my being gay affect anyone's wanting to buy art or not?"

"Because you've been perceived one way. You're glamorous. You're on the 'A' list, Frazier. You won't be on it anymore and the social flow was where you drummed up a lot of business."

"Half the art dealers I know are gay."

"They're men." Ann's knuckles were white as she continued to grip the armrest. "There's a double standard for queers too."

"I hope you're wrong, but even if you're not"—Frazier hauled herself out of the chair and walked over to the fire—"I can't go back into the closet."

"Sure you can. You can write everyone or get in the car and visit them. Tell them you were hallucinating. They'll believe you because they'll want to believe you."

"You know, Ann, I've lied all my adult life. I've lied by keeping silent. Somehow that seems worse to me than if I'd actively lied. Maybe someday something will happen to you that will make you look at yourself and the world in a new way. What's that saying? 'The scales fell from my eyes.'" Frazier shook her head because she couldn't remember. "Whatever. I realized some things about myself and about the world I live in, part of which I am responsible for, you know."

"Why? You didn't make it," Ann shot back.

"No, but I keep it going and if I don't do anything, if I just continue to hide, then I'm accepting things as they are."

"Oh, my God, now you're going to change the world. You and Mother Teresa!" Ann couldn't believe her ears.

"No, I'm not. But I'm going to change myself."

Astounded, Ann bounded out of the chair and stood before Frazier, nose to nose. "Millions of people, millions in America, all over the world, manage to live without anyone knowing who and what they are. Not every gay person has to carry a banner. People can speculate all they want. If you don't tell, they don't know. And it's nobody's business. They're happy; their families are happy. Ignorance is bliss. Why, all of a sudden, do you have to be different? You're going to sacrifice everyone else to your own so-called integrity. What gives you the right to make other people suffer?"

"I'm only responsible for myself."

"Oh, yeah. Is that what our great-grandfathers said when the Indians got wiped out by the U.S. government? 'I'm only responsible for myself. Their misery is their problem.'"

"I hardly think the circumstances are the same." Frazier listened. Her anger drained away. She struggled with these new assaults.

"You know what I mean. You don't have the right to make me unhappy, or shame your parents, or expose Billy."

"I'm not exposing anyone. I'm just telling the truth about myself and . . . and if that makes other people miserable, then"—she thought for a moment—"then maybe they need to learn how desperately unfair their attitudes are, how unfair," she groped, "the system is. If you don't know a problem exists or that your behavior harms other people, you can't change it. Maybe my mother and my dad need to think about some things."

"And maybe you do too." A hot ember sizzled out of the fire. Ann moved her foot. "I'm going to avoid you like the plague. Don't call me. Don't write me. When word gets around town that you're gay I'm going to be shocked—oh, how shocked—and then relieved, of course, that I was spared this knowledge before. I mean, what if you had made a pass at me?"

"You've got a diagnosis," Frazier said disgustedly, relying on a phrase from her Tri-Delta days that meant someone was deranged.

"Oh, sure," Ann snarled. "You know, you don't want to be close to anyone. You've admitted that. I didn't want to believe it. Well, you've got your wish now. No gay woman is going to go near you, because if she does, then everyone will suspect her. And in America how many open lesbians are there? Three? Ha." Ann laughed. "In Virginia the word *lesbian* doesn't even exist in a polite person's vocabulary. You did it this time, Frazier. You are going to be alone, but what are you going to do with that revved-up sex drive of yours? One of these cold nights you're going to miss me. Too bad there aren't whorehouses for women like you. That would be perfect for you. You could enjoy yourself and then walk away. No responsibilities so long as you can pay the bill. That's what they'll carve on your tombstone: 'She paid the bills!'"

"Ann, just go."

After Ann left, Frazier crawled into bed. The cat and the dog burrowed in next to her. The night temperature dropped into the twenties. She'd started a fire in the bedroom fireplace to cut the chill, because the old heating system struggled as the temperatures plunged. Well, that disadvantage was offset by the fact that the house breathed, so she suffered few sneezes and allergies.

Frazier pulled the down comforter up around her, as well as a shawl to wrap over her shoulders. She tried to read *Remembrance of Things Past*. The words swam in front of her eyes. People must have had more time to read when Proust wrote his masterpiece. She closed her eyes, then opened them to stare into the flames. She might be alone for the rest of her life. At least she'd be alone knowing who she was. The reward for conformity was that everyone liked you except yourself. If no one else liked her, she'd at least like herself and that was more than she could have said before.

But Ann's words bit into her nerves like voracious drops of acid. How could being yourself make other people so angry, so hateful? Maybe Ann's words stung because there was some truth in her accusations. Maybe she didn't have the right to hurt other people, but no matter which way she turned she hurt somebody. Lying was a slow hurt. This was quicker and cleaner.

Done was done. She'd have to find a way to live with it.

CHAPTER
16

Huge geometric flakes of snow twirled down from the heavy night skies. The cars in the parking lot of Buddy's Restaurant were completely blanketed but the patrons inside the popular bar and grill either didn't notice or were too drunk to care.

Carter Armstrong, in his clear tenor, sang along with the Irish band named for the famous hunt, The Galway Blazers. Deep in Bushmill's whisky, he felt a cloak of invincibility warm his soul. Whisky always made him feel powerful, intelligent, and above all happy. He also loved the taste, the slow warmth as the liquid filled his mouth, the tongue of fire as the amber nectar slid down his throat, finally bursting into his stomach with a blast of pure energy. Bless those brewers and distillers in Scotland and Ireland bending over their copper pots, the smell of sweet grain and fermentation filling their nostrils. Carter raised his glass to men he would never see.

Buddy, a former college football star and the bar's owner, clapped Carter on the back. "Last one, Adonis. It's snowing to beat the band outside and you've got some mean roads before you get home."

"Snowing?"

"Yeah, time to fish out your cross-country skis." Buddy planned to glide over the hills tomorrow.

"Never learned to ski."

"It's easy." Buddy smiled. "Especially the falling down. I don't think I got out of a snowplow for the first two months, but hey, you meet a lot of good-looking women out there. Must be something about a man with snow up his nose and encrusted all over his face that's irresistible to them." He clapped Carter on the back again. "Speaking of good-looking women, that's great news about your sister. We're all gonna grow old together and she'll still be the best-looking thing I ever saw."

Carter beamed. "I'm happy. But the best part, Buddybud, is that my perfect sister, the successful and driven Miss Mary Frazier Armstrong, is a dyke." He tipped back his head and howled. "She wrote me a letter 'cause she thought she was dying and apart from telling me how to live my life, which every goddam woman seems intent upon doing, she confessed to being gay. I love it. I love it. I love it! I don't look so bad now and I bet Daddy is writhing—his Miss Perfect isn't so perfect."

Buddy always listened to news—men called it news, never gossip—as much as the next guy but Carter's crowing revealed more about Carter than it did about Frazier. "Live and let live." He shrugged.

"You know what I think about this town?" Carter knocked back the last of his Bushmill's. "They live and let live but they don't make life easier."

Buddy motioned for the waitress to bring coffee over to the table. He sat opposite Carter. "Other guys go home?"

Carter nodded. "I'm holding the fort until last call." The coffee was placed before him. Since Carter had been tended to in one form or another all his life, this kindness was routine. "Thank you," he said to the waitress. Just because he expected people to take care of him didn't mean he'd forgotten his manners.

"Hey." Buddy leaned over. "Don't be talking about Frazier. If she wrote you a letter, that's between you and her."

Carter glared over his coffee as he sipped it. "I've had to eat Frazier's shit since college. She can eat a little of mine. If she's gay, she can pay. God knows I have."

"It's not the same." The thought of beautiful Frazier being a lesbian pained Buddy. Not that he cared one way or the other about who did what to whom, but to suddenly find such a beautiful woman off-limits was demoralizing.

"Why not?"

"Come on, take another sip and don't get belligerent on me. How many years have we known each other? Since kindergarten. Forever. I'm just saying go light on her. She's had a terrible time. Don't make it worse."

"What do you mean it's not the same?"

"Carter, wildman, you don't do jack shit"—Big Buddy opened his palms as if in supplication—"except where the ladies are concerned."

"Ah, I don't know anything about women." Carter relaxed. "But I've got one."

"Or two or three." Buddy burst out laughing. "I don't know how you do it. My old lady would skin me raw, and on my favorite part too."

"If you don't use it you lose it."

Buddy waved for a refill. "This ought to get you home."

"I'm okay."

"Just in case." Buddy waved to his customers and friends as they filed out. People would ooh and aah when they saw the snow outside, now six inches deep and still piling up.

"Thought we'd have an early spring," Carter said. "The robins are here."

"Winter backlash. He'll loosen his grip soon enough. March raises your hopes and smashes them on the floor every two days. Hey, here's one for you. What do you call a guy who masturbates?" Carter shook his head that he didn't know. "A tearjerker."

"That's bad, Buddy. I mean, that's so bad it's pathetic. Listen to this. A guy goes to the doctor with his wife. She's been feeling bad for a while so they run a battery of tests on her and she's maybe forty, you know, not too old. Two weeks later the doctor calls the guy in his office and says, 'We've reviewed the results of all these tests, Mack, but we can't quite pinpoint your wife's disease. I know this sounds crazy but she's either got Alzheimer's or AIDS.' Alzheimer's or AIDS? The guy can't believe it. 'What do I do?' he says. The doctor says, 'Take her for a nice long walk in the forest and then leave her there. If she finds her way home, don't fuck her.'" Carter giggled. The giggles grew into laughter and then finally he shook.

Buddy laughed, too, but mostly he worried about Carter getting home. As for worrying about Carter doing something useful with his life, he'd given up on him years ago.

CHAPTER
17

The sunrise arrived like the tiptoeing of an angel. Frazier awoke early, Curry and Basil curled up beside her, and watched the soft pink haze spill over the snow. The crystals refracted the light, covering the ground with tiny rainbows. The icicles glowed, changing color with each shift of light until the world was washed in gold.

She tossed out seed for the birds, providing amusement for her and the cat and the dog. The birds' tracks in the snow reminded her of the marks bakers put on pies. Soon the squirrels horned in on the food. She opened the back door and threw out Indian corn for them. They quickly scampered away and fussed over the corn cobs, much to the robins' delight. Blue jays swooped down, squawking. The backyard resembled a feathered convention.

Since most Virginians can't drive in six inches of snow, much less a foot and a half, schools were canceled, along with concerts and sports events. The announcer on the radio listed the cancellations for each county. Frazier figured there was little point in going to work. The town would be vacant.

Frazier waited until 7:30 A.M. to call Mandy, as she knew she'd be awake by then.

"Good morning, Glory," Frazier sang out when Mandy picked up the phone.

"It is a good morning. I'm looking over the rooftops on Second and First streets. Reminds me of that Pissarro, 'Pontoise, The Road to Gisors in Winter.'"

Frazier told her, "Stay home and play. No one's going to work today. I'll check in for messages. You build a snowman. Or snowwoman. Or how about a snow Versailles?"

"With my vast sculpting talent I can hardly wait," Mandy replied. "Hey, don't forget, you were supposed to have lunch with your father today."

"Thanks. I did forget. I'll call him as soon as I hang up. You know what else I forgot?"

"What?"

"To order more Xerox paper. Remind me to do that Monday morning. I programmed it on my Wizard but I forgot to look at the damned thing. I'm better off sticking notes everywhere."

"Like the end of your nose."

"Are you implying that I misplace my notes?"

"Only that you're nearsighted. So what are you going to do today?"

"Are you ready?" Frazier let the suspense build.

"You're not going to write more letters?"

"Very funny. No. I am going to organize my library. Finally."

"Good for you. I hope you'll show me the results. I was supposed to go out with Sean tonight but he won't be able to drive in so I think I'll organize, too—my bathroom. You'll never see the results."

"Have a great day sorting through your lipsticks." Frazier pressed the disconnect button and then dialed her father at home.

Libby answered, "Hello."

"Mother, is Dad there?"

"Yes." Libby's tone was as frosty as the outdoors.

"Let me talk to him."

"Why?"

"Mother, I have a lunch appointment with Dad and I want to reschedule. Put him on the phone."

"You'll upset him."

"I'm not going to upset him."

"Well, don't you talk to him about . . . you know."

"He knows." Frazier was exasperated. "I told him in my letter."

"I didn't give him your letter."

"Mother!"

"Just hold your horses, young lady. He's overworked and overwrought. You know how this recession has affected your father's business. Everybody thinks Frank is so rich that something like this can't hurt him but the paving business has been hit hard. He doesn't need any trouble from you."

"Put Dad on the phone."

"Not until you promise me you won't talk about disturbing subjects."

"You have no right—"

"I have every right to protect my husband."

"Do you really think this news won't get around town? Daddy will hear about it."

"Oh, no he won't. No friend would bring that up to your father."

"Maybe it won't be a friend."

"He is not going to know." Libby held firm. "I'll give him your message." She slammed down the phone.

"Mother. Mother? Goddammit." The clear dial tone filled Frazier's ear. She placed the receiver in the cradle.

Libby puzzled Frazier despite the fact that she had known her all her life. Her mother's rigidity was no surprise but Libby's believing she could keep information from her husband was disturbing. Either her mother marshaled more resources than Frazier could imagine or she had lifted lying to an art form. Then again, maybe Frank wanted to be managed. Libby kept his social calendar, wrote his thank-yous, bought his gifts for family, employees, and friends on their birthdays, anniversaries, and Christmas. Libby decided what charities would receive contributions, where they would vacation each year, and when to buy new cars. All Frank had to do was go to work and come home. Maybe he didn't really want to know anything about anybody. When she was young Frazier had longed for her father to stand up to her mother. By the time she reached her teens she prayed for it but Frank continued on his placid way. If Libby scolded, he chalked it up to that time of the month. If she proved as irritable as a hornet, he declared that she was high-strung. If she lashed out on a two-week rampage, he generally gave her enough money to redecorate the house.

Frazier held her hand up to the light. Her veins shone through a purple-blue. Hard to believe that she was related to Libby, or even Frank, by blood. Hard to believe, too, that had she died the pulsation in her veins would have stopped, the blood stagnating in place. Of course, if she had died sitting up, she guessed the blood would have eventually run to her feet. Wouldn't gravity pull it down? She pondered this for a few moments and then let out a war whoop. She hadn't died. Okay, her mother was a whistling bitch and her father was a weakling where his wife was concerned, but she was alive, triumphantly alive.

She pulled on heavy socks, a silk undershirt, a long-sleeved thermal undershirt, a flannel shirt, her jeans, and workboots. She grabbed an ancient down jacket, whistled for Curry and Basil, and ran outside.

A strong creek with a small waterfall provided the northern boundary for her land. Frazier, the cat, and the dog plowed through the fresh snow to the creek. Although the banks were encrusted with ice, the waterfall cascaded over the rocks. The temperature hadn't plunged deep enough or long enough to freeze the waterfall.

The low rumble of a diesel truck sent Curry bounding through the snow. A smart dog, he followed in Frazier's footsteps as she headed for the driveway. Basil rode on Frazier's shoulder.

"Ruru. What are you doing out on a day like this?"

"Bertha gets through anything." Ruru climbed out of her 1977 four-wheel-drive Ford. "And so do I. I figured that our phone conversation when you came home from the hospital wasn't good enough, and I figured on a day like this we ought to take a walk."

"Sure. Let me put these two back in the house."

Grumbling, the cat and dog were shut up in the house. Ruru and Frazier headed down the road, because a car had gotten stuck by the side.

"No point in using Bertha. We can push this lady out ourselves."

The driver, cold and frustrated, steered the car as Frazier and Ruru pushed from behind. They finally shoved her on her way with a wave and a shout.

"Let's walk down to the old schoolhouse."

"About two miles. Then another two back, Ru."

"You think I'm too old? Boy, you can be a smartass kid." With that the older woman set off at a brisk pace and Frazier hurried to catch up with her. Every now and then she'd have to spit out some of the phlegm that would break out of her bronchial tubes. "Hurts, doesn't it?"

"Uh-huh." Frazier nodded.

"Hopefully you'll be out of the woods soon. Hey, maybe we shouldn't be outside."

"No, this is good for me. In fact, I'm going to start jogging."

"You?"

"Me. I hate it like poison. I mean it's so boring, but"—Frazier inhaled the crisp air—"it really helps the lungs. I don't know where I picked this thing up."

"Runs in the family."

"Yeah?"

"Your Great Uncle Fred suffered from bronchitis all his life. Used to have a funny, metallic whistle when he'd breathe."

"Yeah, I've got that part." Frazier smiled at her energetic aunt. "Gee, I'm glad to see you. Mom's being radioactive. Big surprise. She didn't show Dad the letter I sent him and she's getting hysterical about me talking to him about . . . The Subject."

"I can well imagine what the gracious and socially correct Elizabeth Redington is doing. Your mother and I took one look at each other forty years ago, and what can I say? Hate at first sight. Except hate's too strong a word. Antipathy. I wouldn't pay her no more mind than a goat barking."

"It's so quiet. Have you noticed? All I hear is our breathing and the crunch, crunch underfoot." Frazier looked around as if to remember every detail of this day, of this walk. "Ru, what am I going to do?"

"I don't know."

"Are you upset with me?" Frazier's heart fluttered.

"Me? I should hope to holler. No." She scooped up a big handful of snow and packed it into a ball. Up ahead loomed a stone wall and Ruru threw and hit it. "I just want you to be happy. I don't much care how or with whom, and I suppose I can become accustomed to a woman in your life if it's the right woman. I can't see that it's such a big deal."

"Don't hold your breath. There isn't going to be any right woman."

"Don't get tragic." Ruru punched Frazier. "Love has a funny way of sneaking up on you when you least expect it. Anyway, that's not the issue right now. The issue is what's Libby up to and if you can endure the social fallout without sending someone to the dentist. You've been hanging around with the wrong crowd anyway. This is a perfect chance to ditch them."

"You never said anything before."

"Why? It was none of my business. I hope they bought paintings from you."

"Some did. Most were tight as ticks unless they were buying cocaine."

"Fast crowd. Hope you—"

"I'm not the type."

"No, guess not."

The red schoolhouse came into view. With its long windows reflecting the light, the table and chairs outside were transformed into shapes out of dreams.

"I think I would have been happier going to a school like this than St. Luke's," Frazier commented as they climbed the huge stone steps. They peeked in the windows. The old-fashioned desks with wrought iron on the sides sat neatly in rows. A gigantic black potbellied stove commanded the middle of the room, and the blackboards—real blackboards, not green—covered the east wall. Drawings were displayed above the blackboards.

"Your Uncle Paul used to say that the curse of being rich was that you had to live with rich people."

"Do you think Daddy feels that way?"

"Honey, your daddy surrendered so many decades ago he forgot who he is and what he came from."

"At least he's not a snob."

"Just a fish out of water." Ruru put her hand over her eyes. "Look." She pointed west. "More snow."

"You're right. Let's head back."

The first flakes of the new storm fluttered down as Frazier and Ruru stepped into the mud room, stamping their feet.

Ruru made fried-egg sandwiches with pickles, lettuce, and mayonnaise as Frazier bent over a saucepan of mulled wine. They chatted and enjoyed their visit with each other.

After lunch, sitting before the fireplace, Curry in Ruru's lap and Basil in Frazier's, they laughed about Yancey Weems's fear of being sued.

"Did a brush with death sweeten life?" Ruru asked. The firelight softened the wrinkles in her face, making her appear years younger than she was.

"Uh—yes. But you know, the strangest things rivet you. I kept thinking how beautiful the paper was that I was using, and how balanced the pen. Every object appeared larger to me somehow. Mostly I couldn't believe it was happening to me. There's so much I want to do and see. And I want to play. Really play."

"You've kept your nose to the grindstone, that's a fact. I suspect those balls and social extravaganzas didn't qualify as play."

"Harder work than running the gallery. You know, though"— Frazier leaned toward Ru—"I wish I didn't know I could die. I wish none of us knew that. What it really does is make you a victim, a mark for any phony promising an afterlife. If we didn't know we could die I think we'd enjoy the moment we were in a hell of a lot more. Believe in Me and thou shalt have everlasting life. Of course, people want to believe that. The fear of dying is a whip, a goad, a lash, and oh, how the preachers and pastors and priests and holy toads have used it. I want to live, Auntie Ruru, like I never wanted to live before and I sure as shit don't want to die. I don't even want to think about it but I do anyway."

Ruru stroked the dog, then spoke. "I never thought of it that way. I was grateful for my faith when Paul died. Not that I imagine him cavorting in clouds, wings on his back and a harp in his hands. Paul with a harp! He was tone deaf." She laughed. "But faith—not the church, mind you, but faith. I drew sustenance."

"What if it's not true? What if there isn't a God or heaven? What if Jesus wasn't a savior but a Jewish rabbi?"

"It doesn't matter."

"Huh?"

"What matters is that we live with some decency and respect for one another. You don't have to believe a thing but you can't get in the way of my believing."

"Right."

"Then don't trouble yourself. The Lord moves in mysterious ways his wonders to perform."

"And what's that supposed to mean? I hate it when you get cryptic."

"It only means that one must suffer, lose faith, bump into walls, whatever. Your faith will come. It's not rational. It comes from the heart, and dogma is irrelevant. What church you attend doesn't mean diddleysquat. It's what you feel, and if you feel it, you have everything."

"This is too mystical for me. And I'm not making fun." Frazier meant that.

"I know."

Frazier, a devilish twinkle in her eye, said, "What makes you so smart?"

"These wrinkles. No other way, kid, no other way."

"Well, any other philosophic gem you'd like to bestow upon me as I begin my journey?"

"Yes. Seriousness is the refuge of the shallow."

With that they both laughed and returned to delicious gossip.

CHAPTER
18

B y Monday the main and secondary roads were plowed, and
the weather, so typical for March, blossomed into a gorgeous
fifty-degree day. The sound of running water gurgled
through downspouts, culverts, and street grates.

Outside the large plate-glass window at Terese Collier's beauty
salon, A Cut Above, unopened daffodils brazenly swayed in the
melting snow. If Terese lived in New York or L.A. she could have
rolled in the money. She was a wizard with a pair of scissors.

Frazier stopped in early to thank Terese again and get a light trim.
The manicurist, Jennifer, a vision in pink, and Malibu, Terese's
young assistant, all cheered at Frazier's recovery. Jennifer and
Malibu were, however, a trifle weird. Malibu looked at Frazier with
a searching eye. The manicurist ritually soaked Frazier's hands in

paraffin but the usual snap to the patter was gone. They fell back on that conversational soporific, the weather.

After her fingernails gleamed to perfection, Frazier relaxed in the barber's chair. She made a mental note to find one and put it in her library. Auction season would begin in six weeks and if one was patient, bargains could be found. Even if a person paid the full price for pie safes, cobbler's benches, old harnesses and tools, it was worth it to be part of the auction excitement.

The snip of the scissors lulled Frazier. A thought popped into her head. "Terese, has Ann come in?"

"She came in to cancel on Saturday."

Frazier knew they knew. That reply scratched Ann off the list of suspects. "When was Mother in?" Not that Libby would have breathed a word.

"Mizz Armstrong had the works, uh, Wednesday, I believe. Looked good, too. Then Thursday morning before the storm kicked up bad, Malibu gave Laura a facial. She had mud on her face, oowee." Terese shook her head. "Ready to kill Carter."

"So what else is new?" Frazier was getting the picture.

"Out most of the night before. He said he was at Buddy's and the snow started and he couldn't get home. Except that it wasn't that bad and he drives that four-wheel-drive truck. She's hopping. You know how she gets."

"Do I ever. If she's miserable she's going to make sure the rest of us are miserable too." Well, Laura had certainly found the way to stick it to Frazier.

"Don't see why she don't divorce that man, even if he is your brother."

"I wouldn't want to be married to him."

Malibu smirked. "Laura says you wouldn't want to be married to anybody."

Terese tapped her comb on the counter. "You can shut your mouth, Missy."

"Well, that's what she said."

"Laura can be"—Terese paused—"stressed out."

"Laura is turning into my mother is what you want to say. Nothing's ever done on time, nothing's good enough or thoughtful enough. She didn't used to be that way. You know, it's not just Carter who has his flaws. If I were married to Laura, I'd stay away from home too. She hangs out with Mother all the time. They do Garden Club and Bridge Club and Tyson's Corner for those shopping fits. They're like twins. Mother tells me day in and day out how lucky Carter is and how Laura is like her own daughter—which means, of course, that her own daughter is a disappointment."

"Least she doesn't drink." Terese measured Frazier's ends against a ruler, ever the perfectionist. "Mine gets mean as snakeshit when she drinks. Sent Daddy to E.R. once. Brained him with a number seven iron skillet and we thought he was gone."

"You're right there. Libby prefers the death of a thousand cuts."

"How's that?" Terese asked as Malibu edged closer.

"In China a criminal would be laid out so all the villagers and peasants could walk by and cut his body, a slice here and a slice there. A person could live in agony for days until he finally died."

"Frazier, do you think your momma is that mean?" Malibu adored dirt.

"Not every day. She has to be truly inspired for the death of a thousand cuts." Frazier kept her head still while Terese clicked the scissors.

"That stay in the hospital must have done something to you," Malibu observed. "I don't remember you ever being so . . . uh, forthright."

"Exactly." Frazier proved Malibu's point. "Now what do you want to say to me about getting married, Malibu? I'd hate for you to get your knickers in a twist because you don't know something or because you think you do."

"Uh, well." Malibu faltered.

"It's none of your business, Missy, and why you listen to what Laura Armstrong tells you, or half the sniping, unhappy broads that

come in here, is beyond me." Terese let fly. "Go on in the back and
mix up some shampoo. Frazier needs peace and quiet after what she's
been through."

Malibu, stung, flounced out.

"Now she'll take it out on you."

"And she can find herself a new job if she does. Every day I get men
and women knocking on my door, begging for work."

Frazier's face clouded over. "So do I, Terese. I hate to turn them
away."

"Sleeping down on the Mall now and in the winter, too, and
Frazier, it's not just the drunks anymore. I thought big cities had
these problems, not us."

"And Congress will raise taxes again and further drive down the
productive people. I hate every lying scumbag by the Potomac."
Frazier paused. "I'm not a very political person but it's gotten so bad
these last couple of years that even I notice and I'm . . . mad.
Really mad."

"Amen, sister. Do you know—of course you do—I spend three
days each month trying to keep up with the paperwork, the worker's
comp, the withholding, the payroll taxes, and I can't hire a book-
keeper to do it? I simply can't afford that and truthfully, I can't afford
the time. Change is gonna come. Uh-huh."

"Will it be in time, though?"

"Yes." Terese's voice was firm. "You can jerk around the American people for years, decades maybe, but sooner or later people do
wake up and when they do, watch out, baby, 'cause heads're gonna
roll."

Frazier whispered, "Terese, speaking of heads rolling, Laura shot
off her mouth and said I was gay, didn't she?"

Terese's hand paused over Frazier's golden head. "Why would I
listen to anything that comes out of that bitch's mouth?"

"Better fasten my seat belt."

"Nobody's going to believe her. Don't give it a second thought."

"Except that it's true." Frazier broke into a cold sweat and she hated herself for being afraid.

"No lie?" Terese was curious, not judgmental.

"No lie. I haven't done much about it. I mean, I'm not running the girls."

"You know my Uncle Jake was that way. Sweet man. Honey, I don't care."

"So far you and my Auntie Ruru are the only ones who don't and if Laura's out flapping her gums it will be to Richmond and back before the weekend. Actually, Mandy doesn't give a fig, either."

"You're gonna find out who your friends are," Terese flatly stated.

"I appreciate you having this conversation with me."

"Know what I think?" Terese closed her eyes for a moment, then opened them. "I think the guilty dog barks first. Laura knows better. First off, if it gets back to Libby that she's telling tales, there goes that beautiful friendship."

Frazier interrupted. "Laura will pin the blame on someone else, or other people. Mother will believe her. Mother believes everything that comes out of Laura's Elizabeth Arden hot-pink mouth."

"Maybe, maybe not. But you put this in your pipe and smoke it: what does Laura have to gain? Wouldn't it be wiser to be quiet?"

"She's jealous. Always has been."

"I know, I know, but still, the guilty dog barks first."

"Terese, what do you know that I don't?"

"Nothing, but I know people."

By the time Frazier reached work she was ready to kill Laura, but that would have been too easy. The first thing she did was pick up the phone and order an expensive pool table from Richmond. Mandy couldn't believe Frazier was doing that but she thought it was pretty funny. Frazier had said she always wanted a pool table but would never get one because she thought that's what dykes did—hang around bars and shoot pool. So what. She wanted one. Then she told

Mandy what Terese had said, that Malibu was a turd, and how furious she was.

"Don't confront her," Mandy advised.

"Why not?"

"Because Laura's devious. She'll wriggle out of it and find a way to make you look paranoid in the process."

Frazier appreciated Mandy's viewpoint. "Damn, I hate to let her get away with this."

"You're rich. Hire a private detective for a month."

"What?" Frazier couldn't believe her ears.

"The worst that will happen is that you'll waste a couple of thousand dollars. Remember those crocodile loafers you bought at Gucci's in New York? They were a thousand and fifty."

"Now don't throw them up in my face."

"I'm not. I am merely suggesting that you have tossed around thousands of dollars when you felt like it, so you can afford a detective to follow Laura. If she's Miss Squeaky Clean, well, fine. If not, I say nail her ass to the floorboards."

"You continually amaze me, Mandy."

"Prairie justice."

"Well, you never have taken a shine to her."

"Oh, it's not just that or how she gets all sincere about where she was when Martin Luther King was shot, what she thinks about the Anita Hill/Clarence Thomas hearings, the latest Eddie Murphy movie. Does she think I'm incapable of discourse on any subject that does not involve an African-American?" Mandy sighed. "I think of Laura not as a honky but as a toot."

"A toot?"

"Yeah, she's not big enough to be a honky."

"I think I've got a lot to learn from you, Mandy." Frazier dug out the phone book and flipped through the Yellow Pages for private investigators. She stopped for a minute and winked at Mandy. "There's a lot to be said for being nouveau riche, and Laura means to say it all."

CHAPTER
19

"Riding to the Last," by Lionel Edwards, executed in 1938, brimmed with dash and speed. Frazier loved many of the twentieth-century artists, and one wing of her gallery gleamed with their work. She had Peter Curling's racing paintings and Constance Holford's magical work that seemed to lift off the canvas. Susan Crawford's racehorse studies sold quite well, as did the work of Heather St. Clair Davis, whose hunting scenes were ravishing. Peter Biegel's work now drew good prices and the Lionel Edwards paintings sold literally like hotcakes. Frazier especially liked Cecil Aldin and G. Denholm Armour for their sense of humor.

Surrounded by these paintings, she held the world outside at bay. Fox-hunting attire in Sir Alfred Munnings' paintings and Lionel Edwards's sublime work had changed not a jot. Tradition lulled one into believing life would be similarly consistent. Life had other ideas.

As Frazier left the modern wing of the gallery she passed the huge Olympus painting. She could have sworn great Jupiter winked at her.

The phone jingled. Mandy grabbed it, then silently mouthed, "Ann." Frazier winced but took the call in her office.

"Your idiot brother, one hundred and eighty pounds of condemned beef, is running around town celebrating your lesbianism. Can't you shut him up?"

It took a moment for Frazier to understand, although Ann was clear enough. "I'll talk to him."

"Good." Ann hung up.

Mandy wandered in. "We should introduce Ann to Sean." Sean was Mandy's boyfriend.

"Why?" Frazier asked bleakly.

"They're both violently concerned with their public images."

"God knows Ann is. She's ass over tit because Carter, according to her, is running all over town with the good news about little me."

"Oh, boy." Mandy wrinkled her nose. "Maybe this will make you feel better." She handed her boss a letter postmarked Charleston, South Carolina. "I'll make myself scarce."

"You don't have to. Sit down. Might as well share whatever Jinx has to say." Frazier neatly opened the letter from her college sorority roommate with a heavy silver letter knife. She hummed. "Okay. She's glad I'm alive. She was surprised by my phone call, she thinks it's weird that I'm gay, but everyone is weird in her own way."

"So far, so good."

"She doesn't know why I'd want to be a lesbian, but then she doesn't know why anyone wants to be heterosexual either. People are different." Frazier laughed. "Then she says not to forget Trebonious Volvo." She explained, "We suffered through Livy together in college and we invented a scribe called Trebonious Volvo. He wrote scurrilous comments in the margins of Livy's text, in Latin, of course. Then Trebonious graduated from being a scribe and blossomed into a writer on his own. He used to pen searing and occasionally vulgar letters to the editor of the campus newspaper. Once he printed broadsides for the 'Mr. Pig Contest,' which the sororities seized upon and carried out."

"Mr. Pig. Is this like Miss Ugly?"

"Yeah, exactly. Jinx and I got pissed off, I mean major pissed off, at AAT because they hosted the Miss Ugly contest, a hallowed tradition. Every brother would invite the worst-looking female he could find to the house for a big dinner."

"I thought Sigma Nu was the rowdiest fraternity."

"They would have been, but AAT thought of this decades ago. Anyway, the girls had no idea what was going on and as you can imagine, they probably weren't asked out much by anyone. So to be invited to AAT—and the brothers were good-looking—was really a thrill. Then one of them would be crowned, except she wouldn't know why. The brothers would leave the ladies after dessert, for cigars, they said, but really to vote by secret ballot as to which girl was the ugliest. The winning brother received a keg of beer all for his very own.

"In our junior year the greatest tradition sank to a new low. In the middle of a fried-chicken dinner some bozo cut the lights and a food fight erupted. A chicken bone put out the eye of one of the contestants, if you'll forgive the use of the word. That frosted it for us. Well, it did for AAT National, too, and for the president of the university, who yanked their charter in a hurry. We couldn't let it alone though, and both Jinx and I aren't hard to look at but we thought, how stupid that women are judged by external things. If women judged men's looks as harshly as men judge women's, I can guarantee you that seventy percent of the male species would never get laid, and I mean never. So we instituted the Mr. Pig contest and the best part was—oh, what wimps—the best part was that the fraternities, as well as some other men, rose up in righteous wrath saying that 'Two wrongs don't make a right.' Ever notice how when the tables are turned the boys just can't take it?"

"Yep. A good man is hard to find."

"A hard man is good to find." Frazier smirked.

"Come on, that one's got gray hairs. So what happened with 'Mr. Pig'? Still going on? Still making the boys furious?"

"Yeah." Frazier nodded. "Know what else we tried to institute, and we really ate it on this one—a slave auction. We wanted to auction off Tri-Deltas and Delta Tau Deltas, our brother fraternity, to anyone who needed work done. We figured we'd get some good money out of the Chapel Hill townies who wanted to finally tackle those odd jobs that pile up. My God, our sorority president, Melody—I kid you not, her name was Melody Myers—shit a brick. Not only were we branded as sexists by the wimps, now our own sorority sisters feared we were racists. I still think it would have raised *beaucoup* funds. Am I a racist?"

"Not any more than most Caucasians."

"Isn't it peculiar that we've avoided certain topics over the years? Well, actually, if you know my family it's not peculiar, although Carter's sure making up for it."

"That's a generous way to describe the Mouth from the South." Mandy returned to the previous subject. "Are you burning to give me your views on race? Do you want to be absolved for the sins of your great-grandfathers all the way back to 1640? Isn't that when your people stumbled onto the Tidewater?"

"Uh-huh. I am an old, old Virginian. Whoop-de-do. No, I don't want to be absolved for anything because I didn't do it. I leave guilt to those white people who want to prove they have refined emotions but still don't want to do anything about the problem, which, if you have noticed, and I'm sure you have, is termed *the race problem* or *the black problem.* It's not a black problem; it's a white problem. Pure and simple."

"Whoever has the gold makes the rules. That's the real golden rule, and since that's white folks, they can't see past their blinkers. When I was a teenager I used to fly off the handle about it. Mom and Dad would ignore me, which only made me worse. Now I realize that a small percent of the population will never impose its worldview on the majority. The nature of being a minority is to explain, *ad nauseum*, how you see the world, assuming the majority can take time away from their own self-indulgence to listen."

Frazier stared at Mandy's light eyes, her delicate nose and chiseled lips. The secrets of the blood screamed out for each of us: Irish, Italian, Slavic, German, English, you name it. When, last century, two centuries ago? . . . who knew but what some fine-boned European contributed genetic material to what was now Amanda Eisenhart. Frazier couldn't help but wonder who fed into her own veins, as well. It was a silly Southerner who believed he or she was racially pure whatever side of the fence one fell on. "I think that's absolutely true."

"I have this theory that if a person belongs to a so-called 'oppressed' group they can be defined by that. They can incorporate the master's view of themselves into their minds and never go beyond it. Then there are the people who protest endlessly. They make a career out of expressing the anger of that minority. I don't want to be a professional African-American. I want to be Mandy Eisenhart."

"If people will let you."

"You have to fight for it, fight for yourself."

Frazier folded the letter and replaced it in the envelope. "You have to find your enemies to fight them. See, that's where I get confused. I feel like I've fallen into a vat of Jell-O. Take Billy Cicero, for example. Not a peep."

"Hurts, doesn't it?"

Frazier nodded. "Maybe the longer you put off the day of reckoning, the more painful it is when it arrives. You know what I think about? I think about Jacob Marley in *A Christmas Carol.* Remember when he visits Scrooge, clanking and shuffling fathoms of chain, and he warns Scrooge that the chains he has forged in this life are already far heavier and longer than what Marley's dragging around? Chillingly accurate. That last night in the hospital I counted my fathoms of chain."

"I've only forged ankle bracelets." Mandy giggled.

"You're a real prize." Frazier laughed. "And what's engraved on your ankle bracelet? 'Heavens Above'?"

The remainder of the day passed happily. A dealer out of London cabled to buy John Ferneley, Sr.'s portrait of bull terriers. The detective called to say he would start shadowing Laura Armstrong beginning Monday. Frazier still had her doubts about that but she was angry enough to go ahead with it. The pool table merchant from Richmond promised to deliver the table Saturday before noon. Mandy worked late on billing and Frazier stayed at the gallery with her to make calls to the Coast. Los Angeles was ever a fruitful source of quick cash.

CHAPTER
20

Quick cash dominated the round table where Frank Armstrong joined his paving colleagues. Once a month this small, clubby group of the better contractors in the state gathered in Richmond to discuss business, swap or buy equipment from one another, and compare notes on new methods of paving. The soil varied dramatically from one end of Virginia to the other and this called for different approaches to building roadbeds. Frank generally found himself building roads in the unyielding and badly draining red clay. The fellows in the Tidewater contended with sand. Some of the boys in the southwestern counties coped with shaley rock, a bitch to work with and often dangerous when cutting through a hill or mountain.

Paving contractors, like realtors, were under oath not to discuss their commission percentages or bids, lest there be charges of price fixing. Of course, the realtor discussed the commission with the seller and the buyer but until that commission was written in the listing agreement, the realtor couldn't speak of it. For the contractors the struggle centered on bids. Most of these men would be bidding against each other for the lucrative state jobs the highway department doled out and sometimes they even bid on pieces of federal highway. A good estimator was worth his weight in gold, a lesson Frank had learned the hard way when, as a young contractor, he underbid a job to secure it and then faced losses which he made up out of his own pocket.

Pickens Oliguy, a florid-faced, jocular man, sat next to Frank. "You hanging in there, Frankie?"

"I am, but I had to trim my employees by twenty percent and I can tell you, Pickens, I felt like a worthless sack of shit the day I handed out those pink slips."

"Join the club, Frank," George Demerius called from the other side of the table. "This downturn isn't heading back up. I wonder if we're gonna get the nose of this bird out of the dive." George had been a fighter pilot in World War II and Korea. Aviation remained his metaphor.

Frank shook his head. "Those men have families to feed. I don't know. . . ." His voice trailed off.

"Nothing we can do." George boomed. "If business comes back up we'll all rehire those people, of course."

"It's not just the economy." George spit out his words. "It's the goddam taxes. The red tape! They're telling us to fly and then yanking off a propeller."

"Hear! Hear!" the other men at the table chimed in.

"I will vote for anyone who cuts back taxes. I don't care if he's a Klan member or a faggot or if he's a she." Pickens banged his fist on the table. "I don't even care if it's some dressed-up nigger."

Frank blinked hard. He hated that word but he knew he wasn't going to change sixty years of one man's prejudice. "As I see it," he said, "we have to lobby harder here in Richmond and in Washington, but maybe what we need to do right now is begin to pool equipment. Temporarily. Maintenance costs will eat us alive. And I know I'm not the only person here carrying heavy interest at the bank for some of the stuff. Maybe we need to canvass one another's inventory by region and divest ourselves of what we can part with. They'll buy it out west—Arizona, New Mexico. At least, I think they will."

The other men, surprised at this radical suggestion, spoke among themselves all at once.

Pickens lowered his voice: "Frank, you think we're in for a true Depression?"

"Yeah, I do." Frank's face looked gray.

Pickens nodded. He, too, had come to this assessment.

"Well, how are we going to work out who gets what when? I mean, we could tear each other up." Larry Taylor, a younger man, raised his voice.

Randy Milliken, one of the older men, gruffly said, "This round table was built on trust."

"Hear! Hear!" the others shouted again.

George stood up and tapped his spoon against his beer glass. "Gentlemen, gentlemen, Frank has given us a, well, a most unusual idea and one that is worthy of serious consideration in these times. Obviously, we can't figure this out tonight but we can sure think about it. I guess most of you have heard that Moe Schindler had to bail out—and hey, no golden parachute. So I think Frank's idea is, as I said, worth our consideration. As you know, tonight we have a guest speaker, John Kalergis from Purdue. He's here to talk about drainage materials and stress load, after which Pickens will deliver a short address on the use of the helicopter to . . ."

Randy cupped his hand to his mouth: "Pickens never gave a short address in his life. Break out the sleeping bags, boys."

The small congregation hooted and clapped. Disturbing subjects, pushed into the background for now, would reappear later, usually around three o'clock in the morning.

CHAPTER
21

The Garden Club performed many hours of community
service that beautified the county. They planted and
tended flower beds in front of the Albemarle County Court
House, Lee Park, Jackson Park, and a host of other, smaller parks.
Laura Armstrong, a rising star in this bastion of female power,
developed a plan to transform the Downtown Mall into a riot of
horticulture. She battled for three years to win the approval of the
more conservative members of the club. Once she had it, nothing
could stop her. She organized fund-raisers, she bedeviled the big
nursery over in Waynesboro to lower its already low prices, and she
rounded up her troops for their first assault on the mall as soon as the
last frost was over.

Frazier had declined to join the Garden Club, although she was
asked. This sent her mother into such a tiz that Yancey Weems

temporarily prescribed Valium. Frazier wickedly handed her a bottle of gin to assist in swallowing those nasty pills. By the time Libby returned to consciousness Frazier's rebellion had receded into memory like the taillight of a speeding car.

Not that Frazier wasn't sensitive to gardening. She was. She knew her Gertrude Jekyll as well as the next woman. Mostly she declined to join because she didn't have the time, and if Frazier made a commitment to an organization she wanted to give her best. The other reason was that the group's idea of gardening was too formal and rigid for Frazier. The real radicals were hot-waxed over Japanese gardens. She shied off that. How many koi could you see and why did they always look like goldfish anyway? But her sense of gardening was that gardens should progress from the house to the wild and the stages should be subtle: more formal around the house and more relaxed farther away. She'd spent a small fortune at the farm dotting the woods with rhododendron, red maple, countless species of violets, varieties of oak, sweet gum, black gum, and the inevitable walnuts and chestnuts. And those were just the plants she cleverly placed to look wild. Around the house she allowed the English boxwoods to flourish, planted there long before she came into this world. Her iris beds were the envy of Orange County and she casually littered her lawn with broken columns, pedestals, and even a huge bell, pieces often hidden behind lilac trees or strangled by wisteria or peeking through the wavy leaves of towering magnolias.

This blatant creativity, first practiced in the New World by Thomas Jefferson, irritated Laura Armstrong. Visiting Frazier was like rubbing sand in Laura's eyes. She couldn't accept her sister-in-law's imagination and she loathed her playfulness. Gardening, like clothing, was a way to express status. Naturally, Frazier's backyard exploded with hydrangeas and peonies, which Frazier quite correctly called cabbage roses. The tea roses, yellow and pink, that clambered over her chestnut rail fence drew exasperated protests from Laura because she declared they attracted winged irritants to the house. The only irritant Frazier could see was Laura.

Perhaps it was inevitable that these two women should have strained relations at best. After all, Laura was a Kappa Kappa Gamma and Frazier a Delta Delta Delta. Laura embraced housewifery with post-feminist belligerence. Frazier agreed with Seneca: "Why get married? It's easier to hang myself."

Then again, maybe some people were doomed to combat because of chemistry, because of something fundamentally irrational. They not only didn't click, they clanged in opposition.

Knowing this, Frazier approached her golf lesson with trepidation. Laura usually played tennis at the same time and the two would collide, with large public smiles, at the 19th Hole. The soggy earth, the biting wind, only spurred Frazier to her task. Golf, a game for ancient men in lemon-colored sweaters, had hooked her at age twelve. It wasn't a game for old men, as she had thought; it was a game of intense concentration, physical beauty, and explosive release. She'd become proficient enough to be a scratch golfer.

Today, working with Toby Wentzle, the pro, she marveled at how the game continually unfolded. No one man or woman would ever know all there was to know about golf. Toby, a former touring pro, loved working with Frazier because she was a natural, but even more so because she had the mind for the game.

After one hour absorbing the intricacies of the seven-iron, Frazier tipped Toby and repaired to the 19th Hole for her usual chef's salad. Angie, the attractive manager, greeted her with a cup of hot tea and the Richmond newspaper.

"Aren't you raw from the wind?"

"Yeah, but that's half the fun of it. I'll remember this day in mid-July and think I really did something, you know?"

"You golfers are looney-tunes."

"I don't need golf for that." Frazier slapped at her with the newspaper and Angie, laughing, returned to the kitchen just as Laura flounced through the glass door. The pompons on the backs of her socks were larger than her racket head. She observed her sister-in-law and froze.

"Afternoon, sister." Frazier was overpoweringly polite. "You're looking very well."

"And so are you," Laura cooed, then sat at the table next to Frazier's, turning her back, yet still talking over her shoulder. "Your strength has certainly returned. When we put in those flower beds at the mall your strong back would come in handy. Not that you'll do that, of course." And then she hissed under her breath, "And not that any woman in the Garden Club will want to be seen with you. You'll never ever be asked in again." She glanced up. "Oh, hello, Angie. Thank you for the menu but I have it memorized. I'd like the cottage cheese salad in the cantaloupe and do set out the raspberries on the side and then I'd like some sparkling water, lime on the side—"

"Put the rat poison on the side, too." Frazier beamed over at Angie.

"Isn't she a card?" Laura trilled to Angie. "Always cutting up."

"Well, you're always cutting down," Frazier trilled back as Angie left them.

Laura, returning to a whisper, assumed an air of urgency. "What is the matter with you? Isn't it bad enough you've plunged your mother, that sweet soul, into the depths of despair and heartbreak? You've attacked my husband. I mean, can't you behave?"

"Oh, and what has Carter told you?"

"Just that you raked his entire life over the coals, as if you have room to criticize," she growled.

"I did not rake Carter over the coals. I told him to stand up for himself and to stop drinking."

"He's a social drinker. You make entirely too much of it because you hardly ever drink at all. You people see someone else enjoying their libations and you assume they belong in Alcoholics Anonymous."

"He does."

Angie returned with both their orders, and sure enough, a small tin of rat poison was on a separate plate. She whirled on her heel and winked at Frazier as she left.

"Is this funny? Ha. Ha. Did you pay her off? Sophomoric. You are so sophomoric and don't think I haven't forgotten that you were the one who filled all the footballs with water. Just about ruined Homecoming. You'll never grow up, Frazier. That's really why you aren't married. You can't make a mature commitment to another human being. Then, too, your kind of relationships never last."

"Aha, now you're an expert on lesbian relationships."

Laura shifted in her seat so she didn't have to speak over her own shoulder. "Will you lower your voice? I am hoping—no, let me amend that. I am praying that the family can keep this under wraps until you get some help. I can only pray that those other people to whom you wrote your little bombshells have the sense to shut up about your ill-mannered confessions." Laura lied through her teeth.

"Sugar, you didn't read the letter I wrote Carter? No, I guess not."

"He said it would put me right over the edge. Said you must have been half out of your head." She reduced her whisper some more. "I really don't want to discuss this in a public place."

"The only other person here is Kyle Everly and he's been deaf since 1952, so they tell me. The mob has come and gone, so, honey, it's just us chickens."

Laura shifted back to her original position. "I have nothing more to say on the subject or to you. You're being entirely too flippant and I am going to chalk it up to your recent fright. When you are quite yourself again we can work this out."

Frazier jabbed, lightly, Laura's shoulder with her fork. "I am more myself than I have ever been."

"Stop that. You're not normal." Laura surprised herself with her volume.

"Normal is the average of deviance." Frazier stood up, reached over and dropped the rat poison in Laura's cottage cheese. She trotted out the door before Laura could scream bloody murder.

CHAPTER
22

A slender sailboat, large enough for two people, sat in the driveway like an emaciated banana. Ruru's pride and joy, christened *Zaca* after her hero Errol Flynn's yacht, did not add to the luster of the neighborhood. She trimmed her yard and mowed her lawn but a few of the neighbors winced every time they drove by the *Zaca*. Libby didn't drive by at all. She swore the reason was not that Ruru lived in a modest section of town but rather that Ru fell down on the housekeeping tasks. A maid five days a week contributed to the dazzling appearance of Libby's country club mansion, and when this was brought to her august attention she proclaimed that when she and Frank were married she had been the maid.

It was true that Ruru and her vacuum cleaner rarely saw each other and yes, there were crumbs on the kitchen counter, but what really drove Libby around the bend was the dogs. Two Jack Russells and two Dalmatians, one liver-spotted, controlled the house. They slept on the sofa, the chairs, the bed. One had chewed the carpet when it was a puppy but not at the ends. Instead, small holes dotted the surface of the carpet as though a huge moth had feasted on the threads. The cats, four of them, posed no difficulty other than tearing the arms off one chair. They cleaned themselves, were fastidious in the use of their dirt box, and they terrorized the dogs.

Libby would swoon and decry the commotion. To Ruru the sounds of her brood pleased her as much as Bach pleased Pablo Casals.

Frazier motored over after her strained lunch and found Ruru on her knees beside the bathtub, washing her Dalmatians. The tub water was the color of red brick.

"What did they get into?"

Ruru grimaced as a dog-shake spritzed water over her face. "The usual."

"Mud's still better than skunks. Remember last year when Toby and Lulu got tangled up with one?" Toby and Lulu were the Jack Russells.

"How many gallons of tomato juice did I go through? Goddammit, Chief, sit down!" The liver-spotted dog obeyed for an instant and then stood right back up.

"About two, and those are little dogs. I ought to help you, Ru, but no reason for both of us to get filthy." Frazier reached over for a towel. "But I'll dry Chief while you work on Marco. That way I only get half-dirty."

"A bleeding saint, you are. Sit down, Marco!"

Marco, being more obedient than his sister, sat down and stayed down but he rolled his eyes heavenward and implored the god of dogs to release him from this suffering. Odd, because if there was a puddle he'd sit in it; a river, he'd leap in it. Why was a bath such torture? Probably because it wasn't his idea.

Auntie Ruru rinsed Marco. His black spots glistened. "Here's another one."

"How come Toby and Lulu aren't mudballs?"

Toby and Lulu stayed in the living room as though distance would save them from the fate worse than death, a bath.

"They were in the cab of the truck. These two were in the bed. There now, that ought to do it except that I need a shower."

"You've been dirtier."

"That's a compliment." Ru bent over and patted Marco's head. He totally ignored her.

The two humans sat down in the living room. The Dalmatians ran back to the kitchen.

"I've got to give them a bone. Be right back." Ruru rewarded Chief and Marco with large Milk Bones. She passed out little ones to the Jack Russells, who, although unbathed, couldn't bear to see another dog get a bone. Ruru thought of the unearned treat as a bribe toward future good behavior.

She brought in a bowl of potato chips.

"Not me, thanks."

"Good. More for me." Ru's weatherbeaten hand darted into the yellow pile.

"I ate a big salad at the club. Actually, I didn't finish it because Laura flounced in, plopped at the next table, alone, mind you, and talked with her back to me. Bitch. I put rat poison in her cottage cheese."

"You what?"

"No, no, it wasn't that bad. Angie brought out a tin as a joke and I'd finally had it with her so I dropped the tin in Laura's lunch. She deserved it." Frazier sighed. "And it felt so good."

"I've no doubt of that," Ruru mumbled with her mouth full. "You're not holding back, girl, are you?"

"Uh—no. If I keep this up no one will ever talk to me again but I feel so *good*."

"Laura still hot on the tendril school of coiffure?" Ruru darted into the kitchen and grabbed herself a Coke. The salt from the chips was making her thirsty. She came back and plopped down with her feet hanging over the arm of the chair.

"If she were Jewish I'd swear she was Hasidic."

"If she were Jewish she'd be more intelligent." Ruru reached in for a gargantuan handful. She slipped some chips to the J.R.'s. Chief and Marco began to look interested in joining the party as the little dogs merrily crunched. "'Course, I suppose even a smart girl could fall in love with Carter. He's damnably attractive."

"You know, Mandy told me to put a tail on her and I did."

"Huh?"

"A detective."

"That kind of tail." Ruru knitted her eyebrows together. "Whatever for? Laura would never have an affair. She'd lose her whip hand over your brother. I mean, she has to be a martyr, a sinned-against woman. La-dee-dah and crapola. But hey, you get points for that in this town. Maybe Laura should be Catholic."

"You're awful."

"I'm awful? I didn't salt my sister-in-law's lunch with rat poison. Mary Frazier, do you think you're going through a phase? You grew out of this stuff at puberty. Of course, I liked you better before." Her eyes twinkled.

Frazier played with the signet ring on her left hand. "I'm going through something."

"Now, let's get back to this detective business."

By now Chief and Marco had crept into the living room and lay next to Ruru's chair.

"Mandy suggested I take a closer look. Well, I can't recall exactly how she put it but it was one of her brainstorms, or hunches. She said the guilty dog barks first. Actually, Terese said that the other day when I got a haircut. Well, no matter."

Ru swung her legs over the chair arm and sat upright. "Wouldn't it be wonderful if the detective discovered Laura has a secret life? If

Terese was right? Let's see what would be a deep, dark secret to Laura—abortion counseling."

"Auntie Ru!" Frazier laughed.

"To change the subject, how is Mandy?"

"Breaking up with her boyfriend, Sean. She's been breaking up with him for the last year. Not that I know the whole story. Snippets. Must be tough for a highly intelligent, beautiful black woman to find the right guy."

"The difficulty is in the intelligence. The rest of the package is fine. 'Course, it's hard for a bright white girl too. Men seem to prefer dumb women. Maybe you have to be dumb to work for free, which is what most women do. Ironing for love. Think, if I wrote a book about it could I get on the talk shows?"

"Sure—but you don't iron. You never did."

"Don't be literal, Frazier. It doesn't become you. My husband survived." She sank back into the chair. "Not a day goes by I don't think about my Paul and not a day goes by without my wishing he was here with me but I bow to the will of the Lord. Maybe heaven needed plumbers. Shit, that's what I hate about getting old. You fight the losing-of-your-looks part until somewhere in your fifties and then you give in. That's not so bad. What I hate is the dying part. Everybody dies. The memories they take with them."

"But you hold the memories."

"Only the ones I know. What did Paul know that I didn't? Did he remember when automobile makers created the semiautomatic?—a memory that would mean something to him—or maybe he was alone sailing one day and the light played across the water just so. Who knows what's in another human head and then it's lost. Forever lost." She put the chips on the holey rug for the dogs. Ru was careful to divide the snacks first or an unpleasant fight would have erupted. "How did I get on this subject? Squawk, bleech, reep." She sounded like changing radio stations. "And now back to Mary Frazier Armstrong and her life crisis."

Frazier giggled, her green eyes brightening. "You're nuts."

"I hope so, because what passes for sane scares the bejesus out of me. But really, kiddo, what's cooking?"

Frazier, palms up, gestured that she didn't know. "I feel good."

"You've established that. Feeling a bit impulsive, are we?"

"Yeah." Her grin revealed those perfect teeth.

"That's fine but remember that people aren't accustomed to your behaving that way. They're accustomed to me being spontaneous but not you. Add your recent revelation to the picture and you can understand that, well, things are dicey right now. I haven't heard a peep, so it's not around town just yet."

"No one will ever see me as the same person, will they?"

"Probably not. If you continue to place rat poison in other people's food, I would have to say their view of you will change forever." Ru spoke kindly. "And, darlin', some people will never get past it once the word's out that you're gay. You will be reduced to an object. It's not fair but that's the way it is. If you wear a purple skirt people will say it's because you're a lesbian. You own an art gallery. They'll say that gay people are always artistic. You have a dog and a cat and live alone. Lesbians always have cats, don't they? You'll be shorn of your individuality. But to those people who are full people themselves you'll be what you are and what you choose to share."

"I think"—Frazier groped for words—"I know that. But I don't feel it yet."

"You've spent most of your adult life repressing your feelings. Give them time to catch up to you. You're not used to you."

"Auntie Ru, what would I do without you?"

"Stumble around in the dark and feel wretched," Ru kidded.

CHAPTER
23

March 17, that lucky day, turned icy as a witch's tit. The wind had teeth; the daffodils and croci˙ bent to the ground. Saint Patrick's Day provided climatic memories. One year the holiday would be deep in pure snow and the following year it might be sixty degrees with bright sunshine. Neither snow, nor sleet, nor driving rain could keep the Irish from their exuberant frolic.

The ballroom of the country club, a cavernous but well-proportioned space, was festooned with green and white. White silk parachutes hung from the ceiling, creating a cozy atmosphere, a triumph considering the architecture. Beautiful ceramic pots overflowing with shamrocks in bloom provided centerpieces on each table. Monumental green sashes topped with golden and green ribbons covered the walls, and the bandstand had been transformed into a corner of the Emerald Isle. The bandleader, trumpet in hand, stood on sod. Leprechauns served drinks.

The gentlemen were in white tie and many wore shamrocks as boutonnieres. The ladies, resplendent in jewels and gowns, glided across the dance floor like colorful moving sculptures.

Laura, a paradise of chinchilla, entered on Carter's arm. Libby and Frank had arrived before them and were seated at a table some distance from the dance floor because Libby always complained that the band was too loud and she couldn't hear herself think.

As Carter and Laura pushed through the crowd they waved at friends. Arriving a few minutes after her brother and sister-in-law came a solitary Frazier. Her low-cut dress, dramatically white, snapped heads around. She wore her emerald and diamond choker with matching earrings. The green was her nod to the Irish.

She'd debated whether to come or not. Billy Cicero was to have been her date but he never called, not even to cancel. She was determined not to call him. Coralling a date, an acceptable male, at such late notice was like the search for the Holy Grail. She could have stayed home and avoided the stares of those who knew, but the more she thought about it, the more determined she was to attend. If you hid away, then it looked as though you were ashamed of what you were. She was going to the ball and if people wanted to talk, let them. What had they done for the world lately?

She sat between her father and brother, wisely avoiding Scylla and Charybdis—Libby and Laura—who already glared at her like clashing rocks. Frazier smiled at the two women and talked to Frank.

"Where's your date, honey?"

"I don't know."

Carter butted in. "I'm delighted not to have to sit with Billy Cicero."

"Riding to cocktails, I see." Frazier spoke acidly to Carter. He'd already had a few. "No, you don't have to sit with Billy. Kenny called and left a message on my machine but the machine cut it off. So . . . who knows?"

"Guy could screw up a wet dream." Carter failed to clarify which man he meant.

Frazier wrinkled her nose. The distinct scent of Sarah Saxe curled into her nostrils. She patted Carter's broad shoulder. "Let's dance, creep."

Carter stood up and held his sister's chair.

Laura pouted. "You're supposed to dance with your wife first and last, Carter, darling."

"Not this time . . . darling." Carter smiled the smile of a man utterly disgusted and bored with his wife.

Out on the dance floor brother and sister synchronized their bodies. They had grown up practicing various dance steps with each other.

"Brudda, what are you doing running around town telling people I'm gay?"

He pressed the palm of his hand into the small of her back. "I got drunk at Buddy's. Anyway, if you are, you *are*. Why should I hide it? Don't tell people news if you want it kept a secret."

"The circumstances were bizarre."

Carter thought about that a few moments. "That's the truth." Then he added, "But once you're out of the closet you can't go back in again."

"I can rattle off a few famous names who have tried."

"Candyasses."

Frazier considered Carter's summary judgment, as well as his sentiments concerning her. "Look, you're right. I am what I am but don't use it against me as a weapon. My letter to you wasn't ugly. I meant it. Cut the traces and run."

Carter peered over his sister's creamy shoulder and beheld his wife busy in conversation with Isabelle Harper, another Garden Club member. "I wish I could—but I'd lose every penny. She's vindictive. She'd take me to the cleaners—and I don't have much to take."

"What if you had just cause?"

"That would simplify the process but Laura is perfect, you know—and as cold as a wedge."

"Who knows? Something might turn up." At that moment Frazier prayed the detective would dig up some dirt.

"Damn," Carter exclaimed, then twirled Frazier around so she could see Billy Cicero lightly jump down the steps into the ballroom, then turn and hold his hand out to Ann Haviland. He was followed by Kenny Singer, escorting Courtney Wood.

"Billy and Ann—the Immaculate Deception," Frazier blurted out.

"Fuck 'em," Carter said.

"No, un-fuck him. Fucking's too good for him." She put her head on Carter's shoulder. "I smell Sahara's perfume on your neck."

"You do?" His eyes widened; then he laughed. "There are many parking spaces in my heart."

"That's not where I'd put them."

Carter and Frazier returned to the table, where Carter ordered and downed two scotches in quick succession while Laura grilled Frazier about why Billy was squiring Ann and not her.

Libby inserted her two cents: "He's flighty. Guess he wants to play the field."

"Oh, Mother, he's a flaming faggot." Carter draped his arm around his mother's chair.

"Don't use those kinds of words around me." Libby ruffled her feathers.

"Son, it's not proper to be talking out of school about a friend of Frazier's."

"Hell, she knows, Daddy." Carter let the cat out of the bag. "She's as queer as he is."

"Carter, Carter, you take that back this instant. I demand that you apologize to your father." Libby's jaw clenched shut and her voice rasped.

Frazier felt this was like watching a train wreck, and she was a passenger.

"Sistergirl, I didn't mean it exactly the way it sounded." Carter, ignoring his father, apologized to his sister.

"What's going on?" Frank couldn't stay out of this one.

"Billy Cicero's a jerk, that's what's going on. He was supposed to bring Frazier to the dance but when she thought she was dying she wrote him one of her notorious letters and he's avoiding her. That's as near as I can figure it." Carter sounded almost sober.

"He's drunk." Libby grabbed Frank's hand to pull him up for a dance.

Frank remained in his chair like a carved granite statue of Buddha, too heavy to budge.

"I'm always drunk." Carter grinned at his mother.

"Now this is silly." Laura's voice dripped in honey and falseness. "Carter, darlin', let's dance."

"No." Carter flatly refused.

"Then dance with me." Libby swayed in her seat like a cobra.

"I want to get to the bottom of this." Frank could be stubborn on occasion. This was the occasion.

"Big Daddy," Laura hummed, "this is just a little misunderstanding. We can clear it up after the dance."

"Did you write letters?" Frank directed his hazel eyes to Frazier.

"Yes, I did, Pop."

"Frank, I want to dance." Libby ran her finger up the back of his neck. He ignored her.

Carter, sensing what he'd done, joined in Laura's appeal for a postponement. "Dad, we really can sort this out later. I opened my mouth before thinking."

"A not uncommon occurrence." Frank shot him a withering look. "Frazier, you thought you were dying, you wrote letters, and you didn't have anything to say to me?"

"Frank, forget this." Libby was desperate.

"Daddy, I wrote you a long letter and I can't remember all of it. It was a painful and miserable night but I don't think I put down anything I didn't believe to be true and I wrote that I loved you."

"Where's my letter?"

Libby rose to find a dance partner. Frazier pulled her back down.

"You'll hurt her wrist," Laura cautioned.

"Stay out of this, Laura," Carter warned.

"Did you mail my letter? Could it have gotten lost? Carter got his."

"Yes, and Mother got hers." Frazier couldn't resist as Libby's face turned puce.

"Where's my letter?"

"It's not rocket science, Dad. Figure it out." Carter reached on the table behind him and drank every one of the drinks belonging to the people out on the dance floor.

"I don't appreciate your tone, son."

"Never do. Never do." Carter replaced the last glass on the neighboring table.

"I feel sick. Frank, let's go home." A silence followed this suggestion as everyone at the Armstrong table looked at an extremely healthy Libby. "I didn't do anything. I must have dropped the letter coming back from the mailbox, or maybe the mailman put it in the wrong box, or maybe—"

"Or maybe you should tell the truth." Frazier folded her hands together.

"There's been quite enough truth told, girl." Libby spat venom at her daughter. She could have passed for a mamba snake at that moment.

"You took my letter." Frank finally got it.

Libby pointed her finger at Carter. "I'll never forgive you."

"Momma, you never forgive anybody," Carter said.

Libby, in a rhapsody of irrationality, turned Frank's anger into an opportunity to inflict guilt and avoid the issue. "And that's the thanks I get from both of you! Laura, take me home. I am not going to sit here and be insulted by my own children and given the cold shoulder by my husband."

Laura obediently rose to guide a trembling Libby out of the room. Frank, Frazier, and Carter mutely observed.

Finally Frazier broke the silence. "Dad, we better talk."

CHAPTER
24

The spillover of light from Frazier's office faintly illuminated the paintings in the main part of the gallery, casting an ethereal glow over the artistic labor of centuries. Inside the office Frazier and her dad sat on the sofa. Both had deemed it unwise to talk at the ball or anywhere in the country club, where the walls have ears.

Carter, happy to be excused from any duties involving emotional responsibility, merrily stayed on and danced with every woman in sight. Before ten o'clock he was three sheets to the wind and each time he'd lift a glass to his lips he'd declaim, "Couldn't hurt a baby rabbit."

It was just as well that Frazier and Frank missed the remainder of the ball, because Carter progressed from three sheets to the wind to bombed to finally shitfaced. When he left with Kenny's date—not that outrageous in their part of the world, where people did seem to be oversexed—he grandly opened the door for Courtney. She didn't mind getting into his souped-up iris-colored Ford flare-side pickup. The purple truck glittered with excitement amidst the dull Mercedeses, Cadillacs, Buicks, Range Rovers, and sundry station wagons. So far so good, but when Carter slid behind the wheel he noticed that Yancey Weems's 560 Mercedes was in front of him and Billy Cicero's Volante behind him had squeezed him in so tight he couldn't get out. He just backed up and crashed into the Aston-Martin, then popped the clutch into first gear and smashed into the Mercedes. The lady of the evening screamed in amazement and quickly opened the door, launching herself onto the sidewalk in a heap of satin and tulle. She must have decided that anyone crazy enough to do that was too crazy to sleep with. Carter, laughing, continued on his collision course until he could wriggle out. He waved to the damsel as he sped into the night. When Yancey Weems beheld his Mercedes, its trunk resembling an expensive accordion, a friend had to administer smelling salts. He'd fainted dead away. Billy Cicero, made of tougher stuff and having learned from paying hefty insurance fees, quickly lined up witnesses, although Courtney, the best witness, had fled. He then strode back into the ballroom and hauled out his local lawyer to witness the hard evidence.

Maybe the booze couldn't hurt a baby rabbit but it sure desecrated the Mercedes and the Aston Martin.

Both father and daughter struggled with their own problems. Tomorrow, when news of Carter's folly would hit them, they'd handle that too.

Frazier remembered the opening line of her letter, since it was the same for each recipient. "By the time you read this I shall most likely be dead." She pieced together what she could. Frank, a man wedded to rationality, listened intently.

"You always worry about money, Daddy. I guess if I had a wife who spent as much as Mother, I'd worry too. Anyway, I hit you pretty hard for that in the letter and I begged you to enjoy what you have and most especially to put Mom in her place. She says 'Jump' and you say 'How high?'"

"That's the problem. You take her seriously. I let her blather on, I agree with her, and then I go and do what I want to do. As long as you don't offer your mother any resistance you'll usually get your way. You butt heads with her."

"I think your way is devious."

"Might be devious but it works. Libby needs to think she's in command. So do you."

Frazier bristled. "I do not. I happen to be more efficient than most people, so they might as well do it my way."

"Okay." Frank smiled. She had proved his point.

"Great, now you're going along with me. Dad, don't you ever get tired of women telling you what to do, when to do it, and whom to do it with? If it isn't Mom, then it's Mildred at the office."

"Best executive secretary in the state. Honey, I need help. You don't. Anyway, I tune out your mother when she starts listing my shortcomings. That's her way."

"Well, I don't want to be in a relationship where I have to tune out my partner." Frazier spoke sharply. "Sorry, Dad, I didn't mean to sound that harsh. But it hurts me when I see you cave in to Mom, and it hurt me when I was a kid and you'd let her jerk Carter and me every which way she wanted. You never stood up for us."

Frank ran his fingers through his thick silver hair. "I regret that, baby. But you know, when I was young things were different. The wife ruled the house and the kids. I built a good business and paid the bills. Division of labor. In retrospect I think maybe we should have been more flexible. I wish I had spent more time with you kids. I guess being Libby's child is harder than being her husband. I'm going to retire soon, honey, and when I do I'm going to spend more time with the family and on the golf course too. The clock's ticking, you know."

"Yeah, I do know, Dad. That's why I wrote those letters." She gulped in air and worked up her nerve. "What Mom's fussing about is that I'm gay. I wrote everybody that. She says it will kill you. Damn, I don't even want to repeat the stuff she said. I guess that's why she destroyed your letter."

"I'm not keeling over dead." He ruefully smiled. "You're a beautiful woman. I thought those girls were, uh, masculine. I don't know how something like this happens and I think life would be a lot easier if you weren't." He paused. "But if that's what you want out of life I'm not going to stand in your way. You're still my daughter." He reached out and brought her hand to his lips.

Frazier fought back the tears. She tried to speak but she couldn't. Finally she whispered, "Thanks, Daddy. Why is everything so easy with you and so hard with Mom?"

Frank patted her hand and continued to hold it in his big paw. "The oldest story in the books. Fathers and daughters are close; mothers and sons. I get along with Carter about the way Libby gets along with you and yet I love him. He's my son." Frank's voice rose in bewilderment, for he was not a man accustomed to discussing his own emotions, although he was ever prepared to absorb other people's. "I love him but I can't talk to him. I can't reach him and he's throwing his life away. Yet I can sit here and talk to you and it's like seeing myself again, young. We don't have barriers. I look around at my buddies. Same story mostly. Tension with the sons and ease with the daughters."

Frazier shrugged. "Different expectations, I guess. I think fathers are hard on sons."

"I was. But I thought I was providing discipline, and I was hard on you too. You could take it. You were tougher. Funny what makes you know. I remember watching your lacrosse game, St. Luke's versus St. Catherine's, senior year. You were down two goals."

"That wasn't lacrosse—that was war."

"Well, I saw you with new eyes. That monster back for St. Catherine's slashed at you with her stick when the ref, or whatever you call her, had her head turned. She broke two of your fingers. I could see your little finger dangling. You kept your mouth shut. You scored a goal. You scored a goal! Now most kids would have run for the sidelines to bleat and wail and point the finger—forgive the pun. A smaller percentage of kids would have vowed to get even with the back and their focus would have been revenge. Your focus stayed on the game. You scored another goal in the last period. By the time the game was over your hand was so swollen it hurt to see it. I don't know when I've ever been so proud of you. That's when I knew you were something special. Carter would have taken his stick and brained the guy. He can't control his emotions. You can."

"Best game I ever played," Frazier recalled. "I learned that from you, Dad. You used to tell me the secret of success is to watch the doughnut, not the hole."

"Honey, we'll get through this somehow. And if you have a friend, you can bring her around. Mother will have to get used to it."

"I don't have a girlfriend. Right now I'm not sure how many friends I do have of any nature, but I've got you and I'm sorry your Saint Patrick's Day dance went pfft."

"I'm not."

They talked a bit longer and then Frank left with a heavy tread, for he would have to face an hysterical Libby. Frazier elected to stay in the office and clear away paperwork. She was too keyed up to sleep. She finally turned out the light at 1:30 A.M. As she walked through the darkened gallery a sliver of light, like a silver arrow, shone from the street lamp into the deeper recess of the gallery and played over the Mount Olympus canvas. Frazier stopped to admire the effect. She blinked, involuntarily stepping back. She could have sworn the wings on Mercury's sandals fluttered. She hurried to the wall switch for the room and flipped on the light. She stared at the painting. The wings remained perfectly still, although Mercury appeared to have a smug expression on his face. She laughed at the tricks light can play on you and locked up for the night.

CHAPTER
25

Blasted out of bed at 7:00 A.M. by the telephone, Frazier rolled over onto Curry's leg, provoking a muffled yelp. The dog raised her head as Basil leaped onto the dresser for a better view.

Frazier would have consigned this unwelcome call to her answering machine but whoever was calling would ring three times and hang up to avoid the machine's pickup on the fourth ring. After a series of these incessant jangles Frazier succumbed.

"Hello."

"Don't try and be nice to me," Libby shrieked. "What a hellacious mess and it's all your fault."

Frazier sat up. The cold gave her goose bumps. "What in the hell are you talking about?"

"Don't you swear at me, young lady. I brought you up better than

133

that. If you hadn't kept your poor father up until all hours of the night, you'd know."

"Mother, I haven't had much sleep. I haven't even had my first cup of coffee. What's wrong?"

Libby sputtered but her desire to slap guilt onto Frazier with a trowel overcame the desire to take deep offense at her daughter's tone. "Your brother, beside himself from the scene at the club, overindulged and wrecked his truck getting out of a parking space. That beautiful truck!"

"He wrecked the Ford in a parking space?" This made no sense to Frazier.

"He also wrecked Yancey Weems's brand-new Mercedes and Billy's expensive whatever-it's-called."

Frazier developed a sense of the accident. "He wrecked their cars too?" Frazier stifled a laugh.

"Yes. This is terrible. But you haven't heard the worst part. Courtney Wood says he pushed her out of the truck. They found her wandering down by the swimming pool. Her dress was torn. She was scratched and bruised. Broke both heels on her shoes too."

"Mother, how did she get into the truck?" Frazier positively enjoyed this.

"She left with Carter. Billy made an indecent proposal when Kenny was out of the room. Carter offered to carry her home."

"Did Carter tell you this or is this your theory?" Frazier heard Mandy's echo: "I have a theory."

"Carter told me nothing. He's hungover and sick as a dog, which I suppose he deserves. Laura called, frantic, just frantic, because Bobsy Krent at McGuire, Woods, Battle and Boothe phoned to discuss damages. Can you imagine the shock? 'Damages for what?' Laura asked. The sordid details immediately followed, I can assure you. Bobsy represents Billy. And, well, they say Yancey Weems is in a coma of grief, yes, a coma of grief. Laura couldn't get Carter to the phone. He used the 'f' word, she said."

"We'd better wait for Carter's version." Frazier, like a skilled acupuncturist, inserted the needle. "Now, Mother, you don't think Courtney had something else on her mind—taking advantage of Carter in his weakened state?"

"She's no better than she should be," Libby sagely noted. "And since Kenny Singer fires blanks, you might say, she wanted a real man. If her bodice were cut any lower it would have been at her navel. And Carter, with diminished judgment. . . . What southern gentleman would refuse a lady a ride home?"

"You're right, Mother."

Libby, lulled by her daughter's agreement, dropped her tone to "confidential." "Ann Haviland found Courtney by the pool, freezing her assets I should think, and the story there is that Billy, when told of Courtney's condition, said Courtney was a silly cow and only wanted Carter for his . . . part. Can you imagine such talk? And then Kenny socked Billy in the jaw."

"That is news."

"It got worse. Billy called Kenny a catamite! Kenny hit him again and then left with Courtney Wood, where Laura believes him to be even as we speak. They say Ann almost passed out at such an exchange."

"As it's now seven-thirty, I'd hazard a guess that wherever Kenny is he isn't awake." Frazier shuddered at Kenny's public humiliation. It was a sure bet he didn't call Billy any names.

"That means he's seven come eleven." Libby again sounded conspiratorial.

"Mother?"

"Eucie-ducie?"

"Oh, AC/DC," Frazier corrected her. "Who knows?"

"I thought you people knew one another. And you have secret signs like Masons."

Frazier shook her head in case cobwebs still lingered. "I don't know anything about secret signs."

"Oh." Libby was disappointed. "What did you and Dad talk about?"

"Everything."

"Be specific," Libby demanded.

"Mother, Dad was great. This isn't a big deal for him. What did you talk about when he got home?"

"He said he was tired and he went to bed. All this has worn him out. He doesn't show you how he feels but I *know*."

"Does he know about Carter's escapade?"

"He's not awake yet. He needs to sleep."

"But I don't?"

"You're younger. I can't talk to Laura anymore. At least for another hour. She's fixated on Courtney Wood. If I were Laura I'd be much more concerned with where Carter will get the money to pay for damages. Those five-sixties cost more than a hundred thousand dollars! Stupid to pay that much for a car. The cost of Billy's car, they say, is astronomical. A king's ransom. Carter's totaled so many cars and trucks, Laura says she doesn't think the insurance company will pay."

"Hanckel-Citizens is the best, Mother."

"He's not there anymore. He had a fight with his agent and he shifted over to Central Insurance."

"Well, he's about to find out how good his insurance company is." Frazier longed for eggs and sausage. "I'm glad I won't be there when Carter wakes up. Whooee."

Niceness permeated Libby's voice. "I was thinking, perhaps you could help your brother."

"He needs Alcoholics Anonymous, not me."

"He does not. He most certainly does not. We do not have drunks in our family. High spirits, perhaps, but there has never been a drunk in the Redington line. Now in Frank's . . ."

"Uncle Ray."

"He's been dead for years."

"Doesn't change the fact that he guzzled beer."

"Sometimes I think Ru drinks, the way she acts."

"Not really."

"Go ahead. Stick up for her. You two are thicker than thieves."

"If you want me to pay for Carter's demolition derby you ought to keep buttering me up, Mother. It's more effective." Frazier twisted the imaginary acupuncture needle.

"Butter you up? It's your duty. He's in this mess because of you."

"Sure, I held the bottle to his lips. I didn't do a goddam thing."

"Don't swear. This *is* your fault. He was terribly upset at the dance. This whole gay"—she nearly gagged on the word—"business has shaken him to his core. I can tell. I know my boy. Think of his standing in the community."

"Carter's recent unpleasantries have nothing to do with me. He suffers from testosterone poisoning."

"I can see I'm getting nowhere with you. You won't be content until you ruin this family. Why? So you can be queer?" Libby was ripshit.

"The only people who are queer are the people who don't love anybody. That means you, Momma. You are incapable of love!" Frazier slammed down the phone so hard she scared the cat.

CHAPTER
26

"Maybe we need a better light on the canvas." Mandy stood in front of the Olympus painting. "One that gives us a wash with the tiniest hint of rose."

"That means a trip to Eck Supply," Frazier grumbled, in no mood to run errands or to have Mandy do them either. An avalanche of paperwork awaited them, as tax time lurked six miserable weeks in the future, immediately before Easter, an ugly way to screw up the holiday.

"I'll call them. I bet they've got what we need in stock and I can pick it up on my way to work tomorrow. If they haven't got it I'll order one. No big deal."

Both heads turned as they heard the front door open. Courtney Wood, dressed for success, stepped inside. As the second showroom could be seen from the front door through the large archway, Frazier and Mandy appeared almost a part of the huge canvas, an optical illusion.

"Good morning, Courtney," Frazier greeted her as Mandy waved and walked to her office to call about the lights.

"Well, hi, Frazier. I was on my way to work and I thought I'd pop in and see what's new and if you still had that James Seymour painting—1744 or something like that."

"Good memory." Frazier smiled. "Good scarf too."

Courtney glanced down at her silk Hermès scarf, tied around her neck so a point would hang over her left shoulder. "Thank you. I don't see the Seymour."

"That sold just about two months ago to a couple living outside of Nashville."

"Was it awfully expensive?"

"I can't divulge the cost of a painting unless my clients instruct me to do so, and they did not, but it went for six figures. Wish I could tell you more. That's the advantage of auctions—you know what price each painting brought. It's a good way to track the market. Would you like coffee or tea? I have cold drinks too."

"Oh, no, thank you." Courtney held up her hand to her eyeballs to indicate she'd imbibed enough liquids this morning. Frazier wondered when she'd get to the point of her visit.

"Would you like me to leave you alone to study in silence?"

"Oh, no, you see, uh, well, Frazier, I wanted to talk to you about the Saint Patrick's Day Ball and the mess with Carter. Billy's lawyer called me this morning and how he found out that I left with Carter I don't know. . . ." Courtney wanted to believe hardly anyone knew about her exit with Carter. This was one of those pathetic flights from reality so prevalent in small towns.

"Billy told them."

"How do you know?"

"I don't, but I know Billy. Carter's handsome—raffish, I guess you'd call it. He was alone. You may not have been having the best time with Billy and Kenny, and Carter smiled that big ole crooked smile."

Courtney, bewildered, fiddled with her purse. "Close enough. Billy can be so beastly, even if he is divine-looking. I don't know. He's got ice in his heart, and what he said to Kenny, who is such a sweet guy. . . . How could you stand dating him for so many years?"

"Mutual interests," Frazier truthfully replied, but she didn't list the interests and Courtney was too preoccupied to ask.

"Well, I don't want to testify against Carter if it gets that far. He had one too many, that's all."

"Did you tell him?"

"Laura, the Dragon Lady, won't put me through."

Frazier laughed at Courtney's description of her social-climbing sister-in-law. "Call him at work."

"He's not there yet but I'll keep trying. I do hope he'll talk to me and that's where I was hoping you could help me."

"What can I do?" Frazier made no move one way or the other.

"In case he's mad at me and won't talk, will you tell him I am not testifying against him and I hope he can clear this business up."

"Yes."

"And I'm here to bring you a message from Kenny. He'd love to see you toward the end of the week."

Frazier brightened. "Thanks, Courtney."

"Kenny is a teddy bear. Not like Billy. I don't know how they can be friends, they're so different from one another. Guess you and Billy had a fight, huh?"

"A one-sided fight. He's angrier at me than I am at him but if things continue I guess I could work up a case of the mean reds."

"Men." Courtney's tone implied one could do nothing about their apparent irrationality.

"Some men." Frazier smiled.

Courtney checked her watch. "Well, I'd better run. Thanks for giving Carter the message."

As she left Frazier sighed with relief. The bombshell fragments hadn't fallen out yet in Courtney's social set. How refreshing to have a normal conversation, free of hidden agendas. Courtney's agenda was clear enough.

Frazier called Carter at his office. He picked up the phone himself, since his secretary was lying in bed with the flu.

"Horse and Hound Real Estate. Good morning."

"Wildman . . ."

"Don't get on my case about the little incident at the club. There are too many people ahead of you. You'll have to go to the end of the line."

"I don't give a rat's ass, Carter. But Courtney Wood's been calling you at home to tell you she won't testify against you should it get that far and Laura, lovely Laura, wouldn't put her calls through. Courtney stopped by the gallery to ask me to call you in case she couldn't reach you from work. Guess she felt people there might overhear."

"Oh." Carter's anger drained off. Then he laughed. "You should have seen me, Sistergirl. Richard Petty, move over."

"I hope you enjoyed yourself. The bills—"

"Shit, I don't care. I don't have any money anyway. I think the insurance company will ditch me after this."

"Assuming they pay."

He sighed. "There is that, isn't there? If they don't I'll dig it up somewhere. Still, it was worth it."

"Exactly what was worth it? I want to know. Really."

"Every day I walk around and I do what I'm told. I don't just mean Laura and Momma. I pick up the groceries when I'm told, and I pay that gas tax at the pump like I'm told. And if a client wants to look at a house in Orange County, I drive them there like I'm told. I feel like my life is proscribed or prescribed or circumscribed or something. The only adventure I have left is women. My life frittered down to one long set of rules, none of which I made. Rules and bills. Damn, Frazier, I feel trapped and I feel old—sometimes."

"I know. I know." And she did.

"When we were kids, even up through college, we could pick up and go. Oh, yeah, Dad bitched at me about being responsible but he'd reverse himself and say go on and see the world while you're young. Why do we have to stop? I look around and I see my buddies with potbellies, balding, and you know, they get laid every Wednesday night. They go to the Tap Room on Thursdays for the club specials. It's like everyone is moving through this routine but nothing happens, very slowly." He stopped a moment and then added, "You thought you were dying in the hospital. Sistergirl, I feel like I'm dying now by inches."

"You can change. If I can change, you can change."

"So you told people you were gay."

"You don't think that's a change? I was unhappy and too dumb to know it. Shit, Brudda, I love my work and I love my house and the kitty and doggie, of course, but I was rolling in my own rut. I'm trying to get out."

"You wanna stay here?"

"For right now, I do, but if it gets really awful, I don't know—I reckon I could leave. But it would be hard. I do love it here and I'm not sure people would be any more forgiving or generous anywhere else."

"If you went to New York or a big city you could be with your own kind." Carter thought he was being helpful.

"What's my own kind? Lesbians? Why should I want to socialize with people because of their sexual habits? You're my flesh and blood. Aren't you my own kind? Maybe Delta Delta Delta alumnae are my own kind. It gets confusing, doesn't it?"

"Seems to me," Carter said, lighting a cigarette, "it would be more comfortable being with people who felt what you feel and who aren't going to judge you harshly for it."

"Maybe so but how do I know they won't judge me harshly for something else? For me maybe it's a case of better the devil I know than the devil I don't. But for you, you never did get out. I had those years in New York City, so when I returned here I was sure about it, plus I'd been seasoned up there. I became somebody other than Libby and Frank's daughter. You got to hit the road, Carter."

"I reckon I'd just take my problems to a new location," Carter mused.

"I didn't say that. Go reread my letter and this time don't get pissed at me."

"Sis—I'm really fucking up. I know it."

"Maybe I am too. Maybe we're at this big old crossroads of our lives and one turn means more of the same and the other turn means all kinds of new stuff, but it's scary as shit because you don't know how it's going to turn out. If we pick more of the same, we get to be safe, bored, but adored too. All the other safe people—which is to say probably ninety percent of the people we know—will hail us as prudent, responsible, and mature people. We'll even know where we'll be buried. Right, the plots will be chosen. Isn't that what you do when you sit and rot? I guess it's a secure feeling to know where you'll be even when you're dead. We've got to go with the ten percent, Carter. I don't know how I'm doing it but I made a beginning when I wrote those letters and I'm not backtracking. Maybe every human being has only one question to answer—"

Carter, listening intently, interrupted: "What's that?"

"Do you want to live or do you want to die?"

CHAPTER
27

The flannel sheets warmed Frazier as she climbed into bed, exhausted. The day that began with Courtney ended with Ann charging into the shop in full cry about a variety of sins. All Frazier's sins. When Frazier mentioned that Ann had vehemently expressed no desire to see her again, lest she be tainted with the deadly lavender "L" for lesbian, she hollered some more and left as abruptly as she came. Mandy, who had been in the storeroom, finally crept back into the gallery after Ann's flaming exit. In a funny way both Frazier and Mandy felt sorry for Ann. She wouldn't be making Frazier out to be such an awful person if she weren't in love with her.

Piled next to the bed, a mountain of books teetered precariously. Frazier intended to read each one but time scooted away from her. Most nights she was so tired she couldn't keep her eyes open.

Tonight she reached over and plucked up the little Bible she had read in the hospital. Libby urged her to reacquaint herself with the Good Book and she reread her favorites, especially the Book of Psalms.

She liked to shut her eyes, then open the pages, plunk her finger down, and read. This game had saved her during Catechism or she would have perished from fear and boredom. Their pastor, fierce in his biblical lore, expected his charges to know everything backwards and forwards. Frazier, not religiously inclined, struggled with the forwards, and even at that age, twelve and thirteen, she realized that religion, at least her religion, was predicated on fear. How could God love you if He was trying to scare the shit out of you?

She closed her eyes, felt the thin pages between her fingertips, and stuck her right forefinger on the bottom right of the page.

She read II Timothy, Chapter 4, Verse 7. "I have fought a good fight, I have finished *my* course, I have kept the faith."

Closing the book, for she had no desire to read on, given that although she loved that verse she could barely abide Saint Paul, she thought about the concept of reward. External reward surely pleases because everyone sees your victory or the fact that the Lord has shone his love light upon you. The concept of internal reward was more demanding. No wonder those jackleg preachers stressed money. Christianity, a demanding religion, spawned a host of false prophets to make it easier for people.

Frazier didn't much think of herself as a Christian but when she read bits and pieces from the Bible she knew something remained in her brain. She also knew the Good Book would be used as a weapon against her.

Funny how so many people leapt up to judge homosexuals. It was as though every bad feature of heterosexuality was projected onto those men and women who found themselves in love with a member of their own sex. They were scapegoats for the culture. The common run-of-the-mill adulterer created more damage than a lesbian could dream of doing. The adulterer betrayed his wife, wounded his children, and used the woman with whom he slept for pleasure. But he was not so bad, not so hateful, even though he took down at least two women and however many children he had sired.

Frazier held the small old Bible in her hands and wondered how people could read so selectively, but then maybe she was reading selectively. She did get one message clear though: "Judge not lest ye be judged."

CHAPTER
28

The wind stung, tiny needles impregnated with moisture. These sharp gusts alternated with dead calm, the sun shining—another March day. The temperature edged into the high fifties, giving Frazier the excuse to play her first round of golf for the season. Mandy and Ruru accompanied her.

Although it was a weekday Frazier hung a sign on the door of the gallery: OUT. The Puritanical dedication to work meant a few passers-by would scowl and shake their heads. These were the "Keep thy shop and thy shop will keep theè" people. Not that their world-view lacked truth, merely that it was their truth. Frazier's hospital scrape encouraged her to play more, period. Mandy volunteered to hold the fort but Frazier beguiled her outside too.

A long fairway harboring hidden sand traps greeted Auntie Ruru as she sank her yellow tee into the soft earth. She studied the situation.

Frazier motioned toward the right. "Green's over there, Ru. If you hit straight you'll be in good position for the next shot."

"Five hundred and forty yards," Mandy read aloud from the small diagram placed at the ladies' tee.

"For you." Frazier always teed off from the men's tee, since she hit the ball about as far as any woman in the club and most of the men. Frazier's driving powers impressed everyone. Putting, though, gave her fits. She'd run hot or cold. There would be days when she could do no wrong. Unfortunately these days would be followed by weeks when she could do no right. Cigarettes had helped during those "no right" times. Her golf bag was stuffed with last year's cigarette packs, and as this was the first time she had played this season, she hadn't cleaned them out.

Around the slow, graceful curve of the fairway reposed Libby Armstrong's house. This would become visible on one's second or third shot, depending on how strong one's second shot turned out.

Ru performed the obligatory wiggle, her number one wood poised dangerously over her right shoulder. She uncorked her drive, the splintered tee flying into the air. The ball, also bright yellow, sailed low but straight.

"Good shot!" Frazier appreciated the feat.

Mandy grimaced because now she would have to tee off, and as a beginning golfer, she was hard on herself. She felt she slowed down everyone's game. She did, but what she couldn't believe was that they didn't care. Mandy had taken up golf at Frazier's urging. Since the game made her boss happier than anything, Mandy figured there must be something to it. There was: blood, sweat, tears, and an expansion of her vocabulary of abuse. Worse, golf's cruelty lay in the fact that every now and then she'd hit the ball sweet and true. It felt so wonderful—to her bones wonderful—that she'd brim over with enthusiasm, sure she could master this game. Of course, the next shot would take care of that glory. For all Mandy's suffering she was

hooked and while not a natural like Frazier—then again, who was?—
she learned quickly and she was developing into a nice player.
Another year and she'd be an asset to any twosome or foursome.

Ru and Frazier respectfully fell silent as Mandy pushed her orange
tee into the ground, topped with an orange ball. She slipped her
driver out of the bag. The woods proved more difficult to handle
than the irons for Mandy, so she'd psych herself out, worrying
instead of simply hitting the ball.

Frazier read her mind: "Think of it as a fat iron."

Fat iron, hell. The woods felt unwieldy. Mandy wished she made
enough money to buy graphite clubs. She kept trying out the set in
the pro shop and they felt fabulous in her hands. The price was
equally fabulous. Now *those* woods—yes, with those woods she could
accomplish miracles.

Mandy took a few practice swings. Then she stepped up to the ball.
She tried to relax. Slowly she brought the club up over her shoulder,
she paused for a moment, and then tried to do what Frazier told her
over and over again: "Let the club head do the work, the club head
and gravity." Gravity was off today. The ball sailed way high like a
balloon escaping, only to hook off the fairway.

"Damn, damn, double damn." Mandy voiced her disappointment.

"Honey, if I could have hit a shot like that after playing two years
of golf I'd have bought beer for everyone," Ruru encouraged her.

"You're in the rough, not the trees, so you're in good shape,"
Frazier called out from the higher tee.

Mandy and Ruru stepped off the ladies' tee, out of the way of
Frazier's ball, and turned around to observe her swing. She made it
look so effortless. She'd limber up, then stand still, lifting the club as
though it were a feather, only to swing it down in an arc of grace and
power.

The ball soared, climbing like a homesick angel, screeching in the
distance even as it gained altitude. After what seemed a long time the
white dot dropped into the middle of the fairway.

Mandy and Ru looked at each other and then at Frazier. They

shook their heads in admiration and climbed into the green golf cart. Frazier joined them.

Now the second shot called for an interesting decision. Depending on where the ball rested, depending on whether one could really handle a wood without the help of a tee, there was an opportunity to use a four wood. It was tricky.

Mandy wisely chose her four iron. Even though she would be sacrificing distance, she was worried about getting back out onto the fairway. Ruru, in good position, grabbed her four wood, as did Frazier.

Frazier and Mandy studied Mandy's predicament.

"Okay. See that hillock? You aim for that and you'll be in good shape."

Mandy, relieved that the grass wasn't as high as she had feared, punched the ball out and hit stronger than either she or Frazier had anticipated. The orange globe disappeared over the manicured hillock.

"What a shot!" Frazier placed her hand over her eyes to shade the glare.

From down on the fairway Ruru cheered.

"I didn't think I'd hit it so far." Mandy blinked.

"You're in Mom and Dad's backyard," Frazier said.

After Ruru hit her second shot, a straight clean strike but a bit short, she joined Frazier and Mandy as they clambered over the hillock. Frazier's ball lay farther still up the fairway. The three women gazed down at the white brick Armstrong house. Perched like a brilliant oriole by the back door sat Mandy's golf ball.

"Uh-oh." Mandy despaired.

"There's a creative way out of this." Frazier rubbed her palms together.

"Well, if she takes her five iron she can pitch up and over Libby's boxwoods. It will cost her a shot, plus another one to get on the fairway, but it could be a lot worse." Ruru slung her wood over her shoulder.

"Ru, it will cost me more than a shot. I don't know if I can get the ball up and over like that and think of the divot I'll make in Mrs. Armstrong's lawn. She'll have a coronary."

"We won't be that lucky," Frazier replied. "Follow me. I know how to do this. It will cost two strokes but it's going to work."

Frazier and Mandy strode into the backyard, followed by Auntie Ruru driving the golf cart.

"Seven iron," Ru puzzled.

"Nope." Frazier opened the back door. As this was a Federal-style house with a large central hallway, a clean expanse dotted with grotesquely expensive chairs along the wall beckoned the threesome. "Ruru, hold open the front door."

"With extreme pleasure." Ruru giggled, her gray curls dancing.

"Your mother will kill us."

"She's at Garden Club, so she'll never know. Now you do what I tell you to do. Take your pitching wedge, because you have to get the ball over the lip of the back step. But it's not much, see. So a soft, soft swing, using your wrist, or you'll put a hole in the ceiling. Not that I care. In fact, I'd pay to see Mother's face when she discovered it and I'd love to hear the explanation she'd concoct to explain the sudden depression in the ceiling."

"Frazier, I don't think I can do this."

"Yes, you can. Remember, soft." Frazier handed Mandy her pitching wedge, then held open the door, standing well to one side of it.

Mandy gulped and flicked her wrist. The ball popped up over the stairs and landed in the middle of the hall, where the heart-pine floorboards glowed with decades of waxing.

"Roll, you sucker, roll!" Ruru yelled from the other end.

The orange ball died by a Queen Anne chair but not under it, thank God.

Frazier grabbed Mandy's putter. "Come on."

Mandy dutifully followed. "I was too soft."

"Hey, this is an original golfing situation. Don't worry about it."
She handed Mandy her putter. "Aim for Ru."

"Thanks." Ru ducked her head.

"Don't hold back."

Mandy followed Frazier's instructions and knocked the ball way out into the front yard. Ru shut the door and scurried around the back for the golf cart.

Cheering, Frazier and Mandy dashed out to see if Mandy had any kind of shot. She did. All she needed was a strong smack and she'd be under the green. She had to clear some hedges about twenty yards off but Frazier told her that was a piece of cake and after Ruru arrived with the clubs she discovered it was.

Laughing like grade schoolers, the three finished out the day rejuvenated by the situation, by the sport, and by one another.

That evening Libby called Frazier. When Frazier picked up the phone she groaned because she assumed she'd hear yet another chapter in "A Day in the Life of Carter Redington Armstrong and His Mother."

Instead Libby fairly shrieked, "You'll never guess what happened to me!"

"What?" Her mother's tone worried her: sickness, money losses, more Carter troubles, someone at the club picking on her because of Frazier's sexual orientation—such an interesting way to put it.

"My hallway floor has pockmarks! You can't believe it—you just can't believe it. That was the first thing I noticed when I came home from the club late because Florence Grissom had to tell me everything I never wanted to know about her vacation on St. John Island. Pictures too." Libby's voice shivered with distaste. "How many wild donkeys can you look at, I ask you? She must have shot five rolls of wild donkeys and the ocean. I know what the ocean looks like. It's big, it's blue, and it's boring. Well, so I came home, my arms falling off from carrying the groceries—they were having a sale on steak at Giant so I thought it prudent to load up the freezer. Well, anyway, I barely had my toe in the doorway when I noticed these tiny marks, like teeth marks. I put the groceries down and I looked. Then I got down on my hands and knees. My hallway, from front to back, is pockmarked. Pockmarked!"

"Smallpox."

"What?" Libby's voice hit the soprano register.

"You said the floor is covered with pockmarks so I figured it was smallpox."

"If that isn't comfort to your mother," Libby growled. "I'll tell you what happened. Some of those terrible golfers walked through my house! My house! And in their golf shoes. I know that's what happened. I am never leaving my house unlocked again. You can't trust people anymore. I am sick, sick, sick, and believe you me, the country club is going to hear about this."

"Mom, I am sorry," Frazier lied through her teeth.

CHAPTER
29

"Love inspires me to nausea." Billy Cicero leaned against his backup car, a metallic-silver Range Rover. Since he worked in Richmond, servicing the vehicle was easy and he really loved the car.

Frazier watched the numbers on the gas pump flip over. Gas prices were like slot machines—from week to week prices popped up or slid down. She'd run over to the station by Zion's Crossroads early this morning because she needed to check on Carter's truck, which was being repaired. The body shop was nearby. She'd noticed she needed gas, and as luck would have it, she pulled in as Billy was filling up his Range Rover.

Both parties were surprised at each other's presence but Frazier figured Fate was throwing them together for one last roll of the dice, or a new game altogether. She asked Billy if he loved Kenny. Nausea was the reply.

"That's too bad. He's a good man."

"Fray, I've never been interested in long-term deals. Why would I change now? Kenny became an exercise in monotony."

"Ann too." Frazier couldn't resist a dig at her ex. "The Princess of Lingerie spends more money at Victoria's Secret than most families spend on food."

"I won't be taking her out much." He smiled. "I had to escort her to the Saint Patrick's dance. She's so petty, and it provided her with a lurid glory if only for a moment—then, too, I enjoyed the look on your face."

"Billy, why are you so mean to me?"

"Because"—his lustrous eyes flashed—"you spoiled everything. I would have married you. It would have been perfect. Then you wrote those bleeding-heart letters. God, Frazier, I would never have thought you'd cave in to cheap emotion. Who cares if you tell the truth? People want to be lied to, cajoled, jollied along. Don't disturb them with the facts. You made an ass of yourself and I'm going to make certain you don't make an ass out of me."

"Having a lesbian friend doesn't mean you're gay. Come on." The pump rang behind her. She withdrew the nozzle.

"Why take the chance? Life pleases me right now. I had no choice but to dump you and Kenny."

"Why is it so hard for you to tell the truth?" She gripped the nozzle until her knuckles were white.

He put his hand on her gas pump, leaning on it. "Frazier, people don't deserve the truth. Look around you. Do you want to tell the truth to that bozo behind the counter in the store? His I.Q. hovers at his body temperature. Do you think the so-called average American thinks about anything else except his stomach and his dick? As for the American woman, she doesn't think at all. If she did, there would have been riots during the Hill-Thomas hearings. You girls are conditioned to be fucked over. It's normal for you. Why, tell me why, you would want to share precious information about yourself, about your business, about the world with these disasters on legs?"

Frazier's jaw clenched and unclenched. "Maybe I don't think the average American is so stupid. Maybe I think Jefferson, Madison, Franklin, and Washington were right."

"They were hardly average and every one of them was rich. Democracy, like most beguiling ideas, is impossible to practice. If you read the Bill of Rights to ten people, picked at random, off the streets of Richmond or San Francisco or Lincoln, Nebraska, for starters they'd tell you it was too radical. Secondly, the assholes wouldn't even know it was the Bill of Rights. Shit, give them a Bill of Wrongs and Bill of Goods and keep the common man away from the voting booth. Tell them nothing. You had to go and shoot off your mouth or your pen. Damn, Fray, we could have enjoyed a fabulous life."

"Lying?" She waved to the man in the store, indicating she'd be in soon.

"No, protecting our interests. Let me tell you how life works in America, honey. Michael Milken sits in prison. Bad. Right? Wrong? It's not a high-security place so he doesn't have to rub shoulders with the men who stink. He doesn't have to worry if he bends over to pick up his soap in the shower. He has only to sit and wait because when he is released he will still have about a hundred and twenty-five million dollars and that's after he settles the lawsuits. The savings-and-loan debacle is the theme song of the Republican Party and no one is batting an eye, Michael Milken least of all. Drexel Burnham Lambert, his former employers, will pay out about one-point-three billion on the lawsuits and the poor dopes in the streets will pick up the tab on the S and L con. And you want to tell the truth? Michael Milken has shown the way, along with a host of others. While they're cleaning out the till the administration is making august pronouncements about economic recovery. The truth will not set you free. The truth will not win you any admirers. The truth just gets in the way."

"Guess I agree with you about the National Administration of Federal Neglect"—she sighed—"but not about the truth."

"It's not even Federal Neglect unless you're black or poor or female or all of the above. This is about greed and they haven't bothered to legalize it, which at least the Internal Revenue Service has done about its thievery. This is outright bold robbery with barely any punishment, and as long as that wonderful average American you seem to trust doesn't fight back, those folks will keep stealing. Wake up, Frazier. Only fools tell the truth."

"Billy, I can't live and be that cynical."

"Okay, forget the larger issue. Think about being gay. Half the women you meet will be nervous. The other half will also be nervous but secretly furious that you haven't made a pass at them. You will be accused of doing things, all sexual, of course, that you never did. If you date a younger woman you will be accused of being an older, manipulating, seductive lesbian who preys on the young and innocent. If you date an older woman they'll say you're looking for a mother. If you date a woman your own age they'll say it's like being sisters and won't last. You can't win. The Born Agains, those wonderful people with fish on everything, will assault you at every possible convenience and guess what, other lesbians will accuse you of not being gay enough. No respect. No support. No nothing. I don't want that kind of life."

"I don't either but I'm not sorry I wrote those letters."

"I am." He glanced at the man in the store. "Look at that guy. He's so ugly he's a Dairy Queen." That meant he fucked cows.

Frazier laughed. Billy was heartless yet funny in his cruelty. The fellow behind the counter would surely have difficulty attracting a female companion. "Billy, will you ever grow up?"

"The secret of youth is arrested development." He grinned. "I know, you think I'm hard. I'm not. I see the world exactly as it is. Americans want an uncrucified Christ. In the meantime, they crucify anyone who shows the least bit of brilliance, the least bit of individuality. And, baby, that's you. Even more than me, that's you. How dare you be an independent woman? How dare you be rich? You'd better suffer." He put his hand on her shoulder. "It would have been so perfect."

"No, it wouldn't." She covered his hand with hers. "Because you didn't love me. I don't think I would have minded so much that you weren't in love with me. Like you, Billy, I have always been suspicious of romantic love. It looks too much like a narcissism shared by two, but I would have liked to have been loved by you, loved for myself. So let's part neutral. Don't be angry at me, if you can help it. I'll try to remember the good times and we had plenty of those." She started for the cashier inside the store.

He reached out and pulled her back. "The higher emotions aren't necessarily in my realm but I'll try. I won't be seeing much of you, for obvious reasons, so let me fill up your gas tank. One last present, okay?" Billy's face, when he smiled, radiated such handsomeness.

"Okay." A tear ran down Frazier's cheek.

Billy pulled out a gas card. "I envy Christ. He was born before the credit card." He walked to the store and waved with his back to her.

Frazier slid behind the wheel and drove away. She gave up fighting the tears. What the hell, no one could see her. She would miss him, miss his linguistic brilliance allied to total disenchantment, miss his take-charge attitude and I-can-do-anything outlook. She would miss the kisses even if they were Judas kisses. And she had to think about what he had said to her, because she lived in a country where her love was a felony.

How savage to be persecuted for what was best within you. Maybe Billy was by far the wiser person.

CHAPTER
30

The first thing Frazier noticed when she unlocked the front door of the gallery was the smashed windowpane. When she found the rock, which she picked up with a piece of paper in case of fingerprints, she recoiled in disgust. Painted on the rock in red letters was the word QUEER. Well, that was one way for word to get out.

She placed the rock back where it had landed and then double-checked her inventory. Nothing was touched. However, Dionysus' wine cup sat on the floor in front of the Olympian painting. Frazier rushed over to the painting. Again she declined to touch the cup. But there it was, a handsome golden goblet filled with wine. In the painting Dionysus now held sumptuous grapes in his hand.

Frazier shook her head, opening and closing her eyes as if to clear them. The cup shone; the wine beckoned, emitting an unearthly radiance.

She ran to the phone and called the police, and the next call she made was to security. She needed a better system. How could someone get into the gallery and put an extremely valuable gold cup on the floor without tripping the alarm?

This made no sense at all.

When Mandy arrived, Frazier, nearly the color of the gallery walls, grabbed her by the hand and pulled her into the interior room.

"Look!"

"At what?" Mandy glanced around. "That light won't be in for a while. I ordered a dozen."

"Goddam, son of a bitch, I can't stand this!"

"Oh, Frazier, some people are real ass-wipes. It was probably a kid that threw the rock."

"Not that. There was a gold goblet right here filled with wine."

"You mean like the one in Dionysus' hand?"

"Yes!"

Mandy pointed to the painting. The cup was poised in the right hand of the strangely handsome and disturbing god. "I don't remember him smiling that broadly."

Frazier trembled. She was losing her mind, or maybe someone wanted her to lose her mind.

"Boss, come on. You need to sit down. You're more upset than you realize."

"Mandy, it was right there and he had grapes in his hand instead of the cup, and the cup was filled with wine. I mean it and I don't make things up."

"I know you don't." Mandy soothed her and it was true. Frazier was straight as an arrow that way. "But let's sit down, okay? And the police will never believe you, so we'd better concentrate on the rock. You know what I mean?"

Frazier knew exactly what she meant. They'd write her off as an hysterical woman, an overimaginative artist or queer and aren't all queers artists? Oh, shit, she didn't know what to think. She whispered, "Mandy, I swear to you on the blood of Leonardo, the goblet was sitting in front of the painting, and the wine, well, it sparkled."

"I believe you—thousands wouldn't."

Mandy's ready humor and genuine support pulled a smile out of Frazier and she allowed herself to be led into her office.

"It was there." Frazier clasped Mandy's shoulder.

"Maybe you should consider leaving your subconscious to science." Mandy slipped her arm around Frazier's waist. "Something's going on in there." She tapped her finger to Frazier's forehead.

"Don't say that." Frazier was frightened.

"You're assuming it's something bad. What if it's something wonderful?"

"Well, what in the hell would you have done if you'd seen the damned thing?"

"Drained it dry."

CHAPTER
31

"Honey, relax." Sarah Saxe's lip gloss glowed in the dim light of a flickering candle. Her blouse, unbuttoned but still tucked into her jeans, revealed two good points about Sarah.

Carter leaned against the brass headboard of the bed, his cowboy boots dangling over the side of the down comforter. Whatever Carter's other faults, dirtying the furniture wasn't one of them. "I am relaxing."

"Then why are you clenching your jaw?" She caressed his jawline, five o'clock shadow adding to his rugged appeal.

"Ah, nothing." He ran his finger between her breasts, the skin, soft and sugary, distracting him.

"I can tell something's nibbling at you. It helps me if I can talk about stuff. Go on. It will do you good, and me too. I hate to see you worried."

Carter admired Sarah's profile. "That goddam Aston-Martin Volante will cost forty-five thousand dollars to fix. Billy wants it shipped to New York City in a goddam boxcar and the entire machine repainted, not just the front where I messed it up. He says the black metallic paint is impossible to match so the whole car has to be repainted. Son of a bitch. Yancey Weems's damages are less expensive but he's worse than Billy. That silly sack of shit told me I was acting out and needed to understand my hostilities. Said I needed therapy. Flaming carpetbagger." Carter struck the pillow with his fist.

"Maybe therapy isn't such a bad idea."

"Not you too!" Carter started to shout but she put a finger over his mouth and then licked his lips and her finger.

"Sex therapy."

He rolled his eyes in relief. "Yeehaw! I feel better already." Then he tightened up again.

"Let me rub your shoulders." Sarah had anticipated her evening with Carter the entire day and she wanted to enjoy his company. She never minded doing little things for Carter. The act of loving made her happy. Whether the object of her devotion was worthy or not wasn't as important as the devotion itself.

"You know what else?" Carter sat up and swung his legs off the bed. "Some asshole threw a rock into my sister's store. Painted 'Queer' on it." He angrily pulled off one boot. "If I catch the creep I'll tear his balls off—if he has any." He nuzzled Sarah's hand as she rubbed the top of his shoulders, kneading into the deltoids. "That feels good, baby."

"I thought you were upset about Frazier's being a dyke."

"*Upset* is the wrong word. *Rejoicing* is the word. Finally I wasn't the loser, you know? I mean, I can make fun of her and give her a hard time but no one else can."

"Why don't you take off your other boot?"

"Oh, yeah." Carter pulled off the worn boot. It hit the floor with a thud.

Sarah reached around and massaged his pecs. She gently pulled him back onto the bed, propping him up on the pillows. Using her fingernails, she ran her hands between his pecs, finally resting her left hand over his crotch.

Carter considered this an excellent idea and he slid Sarah's blouse from her shoulders. Deftly he flicked the right sleeve off her upper arm.

"What kind of girl do you think I am?" She unbuttoned his 501's.

"The kind of girl I like."

"I can see that." Sarah unbuttoned the last little button, reached in and wrapped her fingers around an ever-swelling cock.

"Thank you, Jesus." Carter closed his eyes while holding two perfect breasts in his hands.

Sarah, still in her jeans, vaulted onto Carter, rubbing him between her tight thighs.

They drove each other crazy until finally he couldn't stand it anymore. He lifted her up, placed her on the bed, and yanked her jeans right off her smooth body.

That was act one. Carter and Sarah plunged into every available orifice. If their nostrils had been big enough they would have tried that too.

She loved to tease him, to keep him hard but not let him come. Carter possessed stamina. He needed it tonight.

After forty-five minutes of unfulfilled ecstasy, Sarah disappeared into the bathroom. When she reappeared all Carter could do was murmur, "Oh, my God."

She wore black pigskin chaps with fringe, black cowboy boots, and a long black quirt hung around her neck like an unclasped necklace. Rawhide thongs dangled from her left hand. The chaps framed her pocket of pleasure, a visual instruction that drove Carter nuts.

She stalked over to him. His eyes were big as eight balls. "Baby, trust me. You're going to love every minute of this."

"Does it hurt?" He couldn't take his eyes off the quirt.

"Not the way I do it."

She didn't lie. She tickled him with the lash of the quirt all over his body and then took twenty minutes to tie him to the bed with the thongs, taking time every now and then to stroke his cock. This alien, immobile sensation, unlike anything he had ever felt in his pursuits of pleasure, unhinged his body. His cock thundered. Surely he had the biggest erection in human history. Yet he was being nudged, slowly, ever slowly, into some deep recess of his soul. He felt like a man and a woman simultaneously. He had to trust Sarah because he was helpless. She wrapped the lash of the quirt around his cock, tightening it and then loosening it, mounting him at her pleasure. Convulsions wracked every cell of his muscular body. It lasted so long that his mouth became parched and he rasped and gasped for air.

Sarah slowly moved on him, sometimes gliding upward, then descending again. They had waited so long that their orgasms detonated like the atom bomb. Her chaps were pliant with sweat and she dropped, exhausted, onto his chest.

Later, when Carter kissed Sarah good night and shut the door to her small apartment behind him, he could barely pick up one foot and put it in front of the other. It was as though he were on a down escalator trying to run up. He wanted to spend the night with her. He wanted to sleep wrapped around her, his nose buried in her red hair.

By the time he opened the back door to his own home he missed Sarah so much he hurt.

The grandfather clock in the hallway chimed ten times. The television flickered in the living room. Laura sat on the sofa, her feet propped up on the coffee table. Her gardening drawings dotted the floor.

"Hi." His voice wavered.

"You got the good news, I see."

"What?" He tensed, instantly wary.

"Your insurance company says, 'Fuck you.' I knew they would."
Oh, how Laura loved to be right.

"Oh—that." Carter pretended he had known.

"Well, what are you going to do about it?" She continued to
repose on the sofa, although her back was rigid.

"I'll think of something." Carter swayed on his feet. He wanted to
go to bed and pull the covers over his head.

"Ask Frazier. She's rich."

"I'm not asking Frazier."

"Oh." A drop of poison coated Laura's vocal cords. "Are you
going to run to Momma?"

"No." Carter blinked.

"Good. She's been through enough already. I worship and adore
your mother because she worships and adores you." Laura showed
her fangs.

Was this the mongoose and the cobra? Carter wondered. "Mother
likes the idea of a son. She doesn't like the idea of me. At least Frazier
knew that about Mom. It took me until now to figure it out."

"Well, aren't we insightful." Laura crossed her legs and swung
them off the coffee table. "What brand of bourbon produced that
realization?"

"None. I haven't touched a drop since Saint Patrick's Day."

Laura clapped her hands together, the action accentuating her
mockery. "Turning over a new leaf?"

Carter walked toward the bedroom. "Yes." He closed the door
behind him. The poison hung in the air, a mist of marriage misery.
He gulped for clean air. He didn't know what to do or how to do it
but finally, finally, he was ready to try.

CHAPTER
32

The rain on the tin roof tapped out a code, a rat tat, rat tat tat. Frazier strained to hear the message, a code from Zeus/ Jupiter, for he was the real rain god. Perhaps all natural phenomena—rain, snow, sunshine, an early blossom of pussy willow, a lost swallowtail butterfly, the green eyes of a kitten, a sweet wind from the south—perhaps all these carried messages and we had lost the ability to read them.

Frazier could read the newspaper though, and her eyes rested on a searing headline: DON'T BE AFRAID TO TRY CHEESE SOUFFLÉS. This encouragement boldly jumped off the page in sans-serif twelve-point type.

She mouthed the headline out loud: "Don't be afraid to try cheese soufflés. Why, yes, what if the soufflé falls? I mean, does one's sense of self fall with it, kerplat?"

The cat rolled over on "kerplat" and purred.

Frazier directed this discussion at Basil: "Are cats afraid to try cheese soufflés? I mean, if you could cook, Basil, would fear of failure paralyze you? Paralysis through analysis. There you'd be, frozen in front of the oven, door ajar, gaping at you. What else can we fear? The heartbreak of psoriasis. Offending thy neighbor with body odor. Hell, it's not so bad if you covet your neighbor's wife but don't have B.O. South Africa's ready to blow. Eastern Europe is shaky. Abortion protestors litter the pavement with their bodies but a flat cheese soufflé is a terrifying prospect."

She threw the paper on the floor. The rustle caused the Jack Russell to bark.

"Shut up, Curry."

If Curry could, he no doubt would have replied, "Shut up yourself, crab."

Frazier glanced over the bed and noticed that she had been reading the food section. Reportage of South Africa rarely appears in the food section.

The patter increased; the clatter filled her bedroom. A sizzle provided counterpoint to the music as an errant raindrop slithered down the open flue and fell into the fire. Curry and Basil curled up together at the end of the bed. The temperature in the low forties, raw, crawled into the bones, whether human, feline, or canine.

Burrowed into the down comforter and flannel sheets, Frazier opened Bulfinch's *Mythology*, which she had bought on her way home from the gallery. Her hands would chill. She'd hold the paperback with one hand, keeping the other under the covers. When the holding hand tingled with cold she'd switch hands.

Dionysus' goblet unnerved her. She decided to reacquaint herself with the Greek myths, but on a night like tonight concentration proved difficult.

For one thing the downpour reminded her that the last time she'd made love was four months ago, with Ann during a storm. How did Carter do it? She limped along with one woman and her brother used to knock them off like ninepins. She considered asking Carter how he convinced these damsels to go to bed with him and then, more impressive, how he slid away from them. Not that Ann clamped down for a lifetime commitment. Poor Ann, so far in the closet that she was in danger of turning into a garment bag, trembling at the prospect of being unmasked. Commitment by its very nature unmasks us. Time does the rest.

Frazier wondered if she'd ever make love to a woman again, or a man for that matter. She wasn't that picky. She preferred to think of her attitude as a whimsical disregard for gender. But she knew that her deepest affections, if she could locate them, were reserved for women. Right now, hands cold, fire crackling, deepest affections paled before animal sex.

Well, it was a sure bet no one in town would go to bed with her. Now that the news was out, thanks in part to Carter's drunken night at Buddy's and Laura's sly hints and judicious indiscretions, no one remotely homosexual would go near her. That was the great Charlottesville way: straight in Charlottesville, gay when you left it.

A life of aloneness. Not so bad, really. A life with no sex. The absolute, rotten worst.

She switched hands. Thoughts of sex drew her back to the painting of Mount Olympus. With the exception of Artemis and Athena, the gods frolicked without guilt. But then guilt was a later invention creeping out of the deserts of the Middle East. Jews invented guilt. Christians refined it.

Why was everything so complicated? After all, a simple matter of human plumbing should be of no concern except to the individuals exchanging fluids.

Frazier gave up, closed the book and snapped off the light. The firelight danced over the walls, creating shadows. As she dozed off she awoke for a moment and one big shadow looked like Vulcan at the forge.

The goblet. She rolled over and moaned. She must have been hallucinating, and wasn't Mandy great about it. Still, it was so real.

The rain drummed in waves of energy. Frazier listened and thought that Zeus/Jupiter was as good a god to believe in as any other: we need to explain what we can't understand. Thunder and lightning must have terrified primitive peoples, as it still terrified young children. Why not invent a majestic god of flowing beard who hurled perfectly fashioned lightning bolts onto the earth? And as for the goblet brimming with wine as deep as thought, her mind was playing tricks on her. Or maybe it was the god of bad lighting.

For a moment between consciousness and sleep she wished there was a Venus. Perhaps the goddess would take pity on her and bring her love—or a perfect cheese soufflé.

CHAPTER 33

"I'll kill the bitch," Laura muttered under her breath.
This rage erupted, overflowing her carefully put-together face, contorting her features. Once she regained control of herself Laura carefully replaced Frazier's letter in Carter's manila envelope with *miscellaneous* scribbled on the tab. Knowing her husband's traits, Laura had instigated her search feeling certain that he would have filed Frazier's letter somewhere. In his way Carter was a meticulous man.

She expected an agonizing confession from Frazier over being gay. Just like that confident—no, arrogant—sister of his to make no apologies at all. By God, she should suffer for what she wrote. Telling Carter to leave her. To make her work for a living, as though living with that goddamn brother of Frazier's wasn't work enough. How dare she?

The blow—Sarah Saxe—wasn't entirely unsuspected. Laura's nose had picked up the scent on Carter's clothing. She believed his lies because she wanted to believe them. Why rock the boat? He trimmed back his wild running after women, but then real estate sales were down, so he no longer made much money to squander on them. Laura steeled herself for the inevitable concurrent rise in Carter's libido with the economy, but Frazier had written that he was in love with Sarah. A little wandering any wife could stand. So what if Carter strayed off the reservation? He returned at night. Besides, her patience and outwardly "good wife" demeanor won her high, high points from the other women in the Garden Club. Obviously, male unfaithfulness bound more women together than they cared to admit, so how a woman handled the problem indicated her status among the Old Guard—the old and guarded.

Had she been a passionate woman Laura would have wrapped her fingers around the cool handle of a .38 and blown off Carter's balls. Ah, but that would be showing some emotion. God forbid. Far better to drain him drop by drop, to humble him with forgiveness, a technique she had not yet mastered. But then, if Laura understood forgiveness she would have understood a few potshots with a .38. Laura opted for the tiny cruelties: the cold looks, the acid comments away from other female ears. In public she placed her hand on her husband's forearm and smiled brightly. One would almost have thought she was a political wife, but then perhaps all wives were political.

She threw on her luscious neon-green tights, her matching aerobic sneakers, her green athletic bra, which could be worn alone, and over that she tossed an electrifying pink T-shirt. Time for classes over at the Boar's Head Sports Club.

And who should be in her aerobics class, the toughest of the day, but Ann Haviland. Laura, now fully in command of herself, fluffed up her hair in the mirror, reapplied her lipstick, and hummed to herself.

No fool, she hazarded a guess that Frazier and Ann probably were an item. Why would any woman hang around Frazier if it weren't for sex? Flawed though this thinking was, Laura did ferret out the buried bond between Ann and Frazier.

The physical act of sex between two women didn't offend Laura. After all, she'd seen porno movies, and the sight of a perfectly turned-out woman diving into the shaved and pomaded crotch of another, while not visually stimulating—after all, what can you see?—wasn't horrendous. Other than that, what could they do, poor things? That didn't bother her. She could even stretch herself to see that Frazier's beauty, smoldering despite her blond exterior, could unbalance another woman. Weren't Frazier and Carter so alike in that way, two shockingly good-looking people? No, that didn't offend her. What offended her to her very core was that the facade was marred, rather like a new car with a scratch on it. Frazier should have married according to her station, borne children, raised them, and if she indulged in a little muff-diving here and there, who was the wiser? At least no children could spring from such a union. Laura vibrated with outrage because now she had to face an uncomfortable issue publicly. People would hint. They already had. There weren't many points to be won for enduring a lesbian sister-in-law, either. Worse, she'd better be careful about how she was perceived with Frazier.

Darcy Schleswieg so much as stated at bridge the other day that she had heard lesbians were very seductive. They especially targeted vulnerable women, the assumption being that no strong woman would hop in the hay with another strong woman. Darcy, that fountain of cosmopolitan knowledge, had opined over a bid of four hearts that the public was wrong, wrong, wrong about lesbians. They weren't those butch creatures trudging to the softball diamond. No indeed, they were really terribly gorgeous and that's how they gained access to your person. You never suspected. Read in: Darcy never suspected Frazier. Laura smirked. She might also read in that Darcy was put out that Frazier never made a pass at her.

Darcy's entire life revolved around her ability to attract men sexually. It was the expression of her power. Not such a jump to figure that this might extend to Frazier, whom Darcy would then publicly spurn as having come on to her, thereby gaining a double victory. Laura knew how these women thought. She should. She was one of them.

Laura slung her brightly colored gym bag over her shoulder and headed for the obligatory BMW. She really wasn't prejudiced against Frazier and she believed this of herself. But she was bullshit mad, rapaciously angry at Frazier's heartrending letter to Carter. She was going to make them both pay, brother and sister, the twins like Apollo and Artemis. And Ann Haviland would be her cat's paw.

CHAPTER

34

"We cuddled." Kenny half-hid his impish smile. "The whole night was thoroughly enjoyable, although I've got to get used to bosoms again."

"You're telling me you're going to date Courtney Wood?" Frazier laughed as she and Kenny Singer walked along the road to her house.

"Yes. What do you think of that?"

"I think you should both get blood tests."

"I have. Negative."

"Thank the gods, Kenny." Frazier's relief was genuine. "I worry because of Billy. . . ."

Kenny smiled but it was a smile of pain. "He'd fuck a dog if it shook its ass right, but he uses condoms and he uses spermicidal jelly."

"With you. But when he gets ripped on coke, who knows what he does."

"Things you could never imagine." Kenny sighed, not in resignation but with marvelous memories.

"Kenny, I feel responsible for Billy's dumping you. He wanted to cut me off and you didn't."

"It was time for that relationship to be over. Billy will use anyone or anything as an excuse—but that's never the truth. Don't worry about it."

She sighed. "I'm so glad you decided to be my friend—now."

"I need a shot of imagination. I need to live vicariously."

"Well, if you're going to play with the girls you'll have to make trips to New York or Denver or some town full of great-looking ladies. I pick Denver myself. More outdoorsy kind of women. Gee, Kenny, why don't you take over my life?" Frazier laughed.

Curry dashed on ahead amidst furious barking while Basil, with regal dignity appropriate to her name, stayed at Frazier's heels. The buds had swollen to a dark maroon but the only shrubs with opened leaves were the forsythia bushes, and the yellow peeked out from partially opened buds. Spring behaved like Carter in his truck, knocking back and forth before finally wiggling free.

Kenny ran his fingers through his close-cropped seal-brown hair. At thirty-two, with few job skills but a pleasing personality, Kenny recognized he'd better get serious about something. "I'm going back to school."

"U.V.A.?"

"No, Virginia Commonwealth in Richmond. The graphic arts department is pretty good and they work a lot with computers. I'm going to be the oldest student in the class, I guess, but I've drifted too long."

"You used to be Snow White but you drifted." Frazier laughed at Tallulah Bankhead's famous line.

"Time got away from me."

Frazier kicked at a mud ball. Curry raced back and picked it up in his mouth, only to have it crumble, making Frazier and Kenny laugh at him. Basil grandly swept by as if to say, "Stupid dog."

"V.C.U. sounds great." Frazier paused. "Are you still in love with Billy?"

"I think I will be forever. I know that sounds dramatic but I can't get Billy out of my system, although he's out of my life. He's a perfect shit but he's never ever dull."

"That's the truth. What about Courtney?"

"I genuinely like her. I told her I was bisexual and I hadn't exercised the *bi* since high school. You know she's not the brightest person in the world or the most mature—but then neither am I—but she's kind. She said that was okay with her. She said something I'd never thought about. She said, 'Men only like me for my tits. Maybe you'll just like me for me.' I found that touching."

"I know exactly what she means." And Frazier did.

"I'd like to have a friend that became a lover. I'd like to sidestep all that obsessive crap we go through in the beginning and call love." Kenny exhaled. "Christ, Frazier, it's exhausting and it takes about a year to find out who that other person really is. This way I can get to know Courtney and she can get to know me. We can date. Sounds corny."

"Sounds wonderful."

"Want a piece of unsolicited advice?"

"From you, yes."

"Find a way to"—he paused and groped for the right approach—"to be with Mandy Eisenhart."

"What?"

"She's the right person for you."

Frazier, discombobulated, sputtered, "She's straight. She works for me and furthermore, I don't know if she'd, uh, take to a white person that way, much less me. I mean, she's seen me at the bottom of my life just dragging my butt."

"Exactly."

"Exactly what?" Frazier's eyebrows knitted together.

"She *knows* you. Knows *you.*"

"Kenny, you're as cracked as the Liberty Bell."

Kenny laughed and slipped his strong arm around Frazier's waist, pulling her next to him. "Sometimes another person can see what's right under your nose. Mandy loves the arts. She is a magical-looking creature. She must be all of five foot two but what a package—those light-hazel eyes and that exquisite mouth. The two of you in bed would drive any man berserk. I mean, even the impotent would get hard-ons thinking about that combination."

"You flatter me."

"I know, I know, sounds crazy but over time, when the dust settles after your coming out—did you come out?"

"I backed out." Frazier laughed at herself. "And bumped into a few trees in the process."

"Women drivers." Kenny shook his head. "Anyway, sooner or later this will calm down, if for no other reason than that this burg generates a juicy scandal about once every three or four months. They'll be on to someone else, shaking their heads, clucking their tongues and judging—oh, how our friends and neighbors and the people we hardly know, how they love to sit in judgment of us. Must be wonderful to be so right all the time."

"Yeah."

"Anyway, when this calms down you'll see that you do have a life. There will be a person just for you and maybe you can live with some integrity as a couple. Not that it will be easy. Shit, look at how I turned myself into a pretzel for Billy. If I'd had any balls I would have told him to shove it. Easier said than done. I guess watching you and reading the letter made me ask some questions about myself and I thought since you'd done me a favor without actually knowing that you had, I'd do you one. Mandy."

"I'll have to think about it." Frazier evaded.

Kenny nodded in agreement. He could have said many things to

Frazier but he chose to keep them to himself. One thing at a time with Frazier. He guided her over to a field of huge daffodils, a bright cloud of spring, just shouting yellow.

"A nimbus of hope," he said.

CHAPTER

35

The remains of their impromptu lunch were scattered on the table like the detritus of earlier conversations: a slipped verb here, a tired adjective there, a discarded noun. Laura spun her web with skill. She waited to capture her prey until the arrival of the crème brulée, which they both felt they had earned, since they ate only a salad for lunch.

"I hear that Frazier isn't going back on the board of the Cancer Ball." Laura stirred her espresso.

"Oh, I haven't heard anything about that." Ann's long fingernails clicked against the countertop as she put down her spoon.

"Darcy told me the other day at bridge that Frazier's been dropped from the committee and they'll ask Billy Cicero to replace her. Too busy, Darcy said, but we all know why. Personally, I think people should be direct and get these things out in the open. I hate the behind-the-back stuff," said she who was an expert at it.

Ann's hands nervously fluttered over the delicious dessert. "Frazier calls those committees 'The Disease of the Week' but she does raise money. She's good at that."

"You two were very close, weren't you?" Laura's blue eyes softened with understanding.

"No, I wouldn't say that." Ann's upper lip twitched slightly. "I love art. Frazier and art are synonymous."

"Did you know—about her proclivities, I mean?"

"Uh—I never thought about it. She was usually with Billy Cicero. . . ."

"And you were usually with Kenny Singer," Laura interjected. "Now if I'm thinking along those lines, you can imagine what the rest of the town is thinking, which is why I wanted us to go to lunch. Just thought you'd like to know so you can be, well, ready."

Ann blanched but kept her voice steady. "Ready for what?"

"Ann, don't be dense. What if you aren't asked back to serve on your various committees, and I know that Allied Assets Bank is a fine firm but people expect a kind of reliability, should we say, from their bankers."

"Laura, don't be absurd. I'm not a lesbian. I like men as much as you do."

Considering the fact that Laura hated men, Ann's statement was loaded, but of course Laura was married. It didn't seem to occur to people that being heterosexual didn't absolve anyone from hatred of the opposite sex. Sleeping with people didn't mean you liked them; it meant you'd borrowed their bodies. In Carter's case Laura merely borrowed his penis, since the rest of him held no interest for her. Lately, she didn't even borrow that.

"I'm glad to hear that," Laura cooed. "Now if you'll heed my advice you'll steer clear of Frazier for a while."

"That won't be hard," Ann truthfully noted.

"The Armstrongs are a peculiar breed. . . ." Before Laura finished her thought Sarah Saxe emerged from the back of the restaurant where she had been sitting in a booth with Carter. She spied Laura and whirled around to warn Carter to duck. Carter followed Sarah's eyes and noticed his wife. Instead of ducking he slid out of the booth and stood beside Sarah.

"Carter, get out of here," she whispered.

"Not on your life." He guided Sarah by her elbow toward the front door.

"There's got to be a back door." Her heart was pounding.

"Alarm system on it. Head up, girl."

They drew alongside Laura and Ann. Carter stopped. Sarah stopped, too, although cold sweat trickled down the small of her back.

"Hello, Ann, nice to see you. Hello, Laura." Carter smiled. "Ann, I don't know if you've ever met my friend Sarah Saxe."

"No, we've never met." Ann nodded a greeting.

"Nice to meet you." Sarah smiled in reply although the smile felt plastered on her face.

Laura, nonchalant despite her fury, spoke to Carter: "Darling, you'll carry a pitchfork into paradise."

"Uh, well, it was good to see you all." Sarah started off.

Carter bored into Laura but his voice was soft. "You know, honey, you nourish grudges. They're the children you never had."

"And whose fault is that?" she hissed.

Sarah, hurting for Carter and for herself, watched as Carter leaned over and said in a low voice to Laura: "Well, darlin', you just suffer an amorous martyrdom, don't you?"

As she watched her husband's back move toward the door, Laura smiled and drank her espresso. Ann, paralyzed by the intense moment, gobbled her crème brulée.

"You know, Ann, maybe you'd be better off gay."

"I'm not gay."

"Then maybe I'd be better off. That man is impossible." Laura feigned insouciance.

"Runs in the family." Ann blushed, realizing that perhaps she had betrayed both a love and a wound.

CHAPTER

36

"'So who died and made you God?' I said. Oh, you should have seen his face. Not a pretty sight." Mandy pushed away the catalogue from England she had been studying. "I let this whole thing go on too long. It's my fault."

"You know what Auntie Ruru says." Frazier quoted her aunt: "'It's easy to get them in and oh so hard to get them out.'"

"Ru has a saying for everything but I have this theory—"

Frazier laughed, "Yeah, yeah . . ."

"No, really, I have this theory that we grow through one another. It's not just books and solitary experiences. I mean, I think there's this subconscious river flowing, this subterranean water . . ."

"Mandy, I can't bear water images for emotional states. Really."

"Frazier, don't be a bitch."

"Well, don't be conventional."

"As I was saying"—Mandy's clear eyes widened—"I think we pick people as lessons. We grow through one another or are retarded through one another."

"So, what was the lesson with Sean?" Frazier folded her arms across her chest.

Mandy imitated her, "What was the lesson with Ann?"

"*Touché.*"

"Oh, I can get tougher than that but being a good sort, I will answer the question. Sean is handsome. Obviously, I can't see myself with an ugly man. My ego depends on his looks. He was bright. He was also so centered on his career that he barely perceived me except when he needed me. And when you get right down to it, how many attractive, well-educated black men are there?"

"Plenty."

"In central Virginia?"

"Maybe you need to—"

"Go on a vacation. No. I need a break but not that kind. Same kind of break you need, I suppose."

"God, I hope not. I'm not getting a break. I'm getting flogged. I mean, this morning I stopped to get scrambled eggs and a bagel and standing next to me in line was Olivia Marshall, with whom I have served on every committee except the King James Version, and she moved away from me, didn't even say hello. Like I carried the plague. If we hadn't been standing in the middle of Bodo's I would have called her on it but that's the point, isn't it? They derive their gray little pleasures from cutting you down when you can't fight back, or when if you do fight back you look like the irrational one. Not that what's happened to me is as bad as breaking up with Sean. I thought he was kind of cute."

"What do you think of my theory?"

Mandy never strayed off the point for long, which was one of the qualities Frazier loved about her, because from time to time Frazier could fly off on a tangent. "Your theory has merit."

"Then why did you pick Ann? What was there to learn?"

"Wait a minute. You didn't tell me what you learned from Sean."

"That men are selfish pigs."

"Come on. That's not true."

"Easy for you to say. You're not going to live with one."

"You never know." Frazier's green eyes brightened.

"What did I learn?" Mandy paced. "Okay, I learned that the package, no matter how great it looks to you and others, isn't as important as what's inside, and I know that's a platitude. I know but I still had to learn it inside. Knowing something intellectually doesn't mean very much if it isn't connected here." She thumped her solar plexus.

"My turn?" Mandy nodded and Frazier spoke: "I have never believed that I would marry anybody. The rest of the world seeks to rush in twos but this coupling holds no fascination for me. I figured that my life would be a series of discreet affairs. Every now and then I would find someone marginally captivating, sleep with her or him but most likely her, and when she pushed for a commitment with a capital *C*, I'd terminate the relationship with as much civility as possible. Ann reads, which is a big plus these days. She can carry on a healthy conversation, although she's far too fond of psychoanalyzing herself and everyone else, but if you can get her off that self-indulgence she has a lively mind. She likes golf. She likes museums and she's always happy to attend the theater. Seemed like a good deal to me." Frazier held her palms upward.

"Did you love her?"

"Of course not. She's not very lovable but then again, neither am I."

"Sean, too, and he would say I wasn't lovable. How can I address that? What's lovable . . . his definition not mine."

"Hopefully, they'll be lovable to other people. I mean, I'm not implying that Ann is permanently unlovable. She was just unlovable to me or for me or—I'm losing the preposition here. God, I hate grammar."

"The kids who were good at grammar were like the kids who were whizzes at spelling bees. Real wienies," Mandy agreed. "Anyway, here we are. What's interesting is, whatever we've learned they will deny. They'll have their version of the relationship which will cast us in as dim a light as possible."

"Ann can't very well do that, since her ovaries would shrivel if anyone knew. She can stew by herself."

"Never underestimate the human capacity for revenge, as well as self-service. Everyone has pure motives. Everyone is the pure little daisy in a field of bullshit. There's such honor in being a victim, especially the love"—she drew out the word *love* until it had three syllables—"victim. Women wallow in it and men, bearing their hurt with wounded virility, rise above it. Ah, how we rise to the heights of post-amorous recrimination." Mandy's hands spiraled upward. "Your phrase when people break up."

"Like the four Bernini bronze columns swirling upward toward Michelangelo's dome in Saint Peter's."

"What in the world are you talking about?"

"Your hand motion"—Frazier repeated it—"made me think of the columns but also how these angers, these rejections, become the foundation of people's domes, if you will. Their very identity depends on their victimization. Take away their litany of woes, their novenas of being done-to, and the dome collapses inward. Crash. Boom. Bam. They'd have to build from a new base. They'd have to be human instead of these befouled secular saints."

"Girl, you're on a roll—and I thought I was the one."

"Mandy, I never was a conventional person. I was the kid in Catechism class who wanted proof of transubstantiation, how wine and bread can become blood and flesh, and if it does, then communion is a cannibalistic festival, primitive beyond belief. I now realize that this is my sin, this is my cross to bear, if you'll allow me to continue in this vein. It's not that I'm gay—that's the stigmata. Everyone can see that and recoil from the wounds. No, the problem is that I don't think like them, I don't want what they want and they can't stand it. They think that my life somehow detracts from theirs.

I am a living reproach to their mediocrity, and maybe they aren't even mediocre—just mainstream. How dare someone go on a separate journey? And my answer is, how can I not go on a separate journey? Someone has to push on."

"The artistic impulse."

"I'm not an artist but I'm fortunate enough to live amidst the work of others who are. It's an impulse toward independence. Women aren't supposed to be independent and if the truth be known, men aren't either. We offer them up, fodder to the corporations where they are ground to a red pulp, pulverized by tedious meetings, diced by internal politics, frightened for their children and how to support them, and all too often burdened by the wife who was supposed to be the helpmate. She turns on him with a vengeance somewhere in her forties and accuses him of stealing her best years. How we hear about women's sacrifices. What about men's? Don't you see, the whole system is geared to make sheep out of us? We have children. We don't live with an extended family, so each little unit needs a refrigerator and a stove and two cars and a house, and you see how it escalates. So we march lock-step to the bank and we borrow money for these necessities which further enslave us to the corporation or whatever it is we do to earn our keep. People drag home and open the microwave. There's a generation out there that thinks hamburger tastes like cardboard! Independent? I feel like we're squirrels in a cage—sure, some of us are in a gilded cage—but we're still running, spinning and only going in circles. No wonder our emblem is the cowboy. He's the furthest creature from our true reality. No home. No skills other than roping cattle. No family life. No therapist. No face-lift. No low cholesterol. Just a life of unrelenting labor—yet freedom." Exhausted, Frazier grabbed a Coke and drained it in one gulp.

Worn down from the implications of this outburst, Mandy took one too. "Is there a way out?"

"I found it—for me."

"You own a house and a car. Christ, you're rich."

"These things came to me because I followed my heart. The only time I did. But, Mandy, even if they were taken away from me, if I lost everything, I have me. Me! That's what the hospital did for me. I'm not playing by the rules anymore."

"You never did."

"The hell I didn't. I trotted everywhere with my rent-a-date. I rarely spoke from my heart but because I always spoke my mind people thought I was forthright. No, I wasn't. I swallowed my own voice just to get along, to fit in with people I wouldn't ask to my house for dinner, to please my mother too. Bad enough that I secretly despised them for being so, so average. Worse, I hated myself for pandering to their prejudices. I laughed at gay jokes. I turned my head when someone made a racist statement. I covered my eyes when the drunks fell down on the mall. Little sins but they add up like those links in Marley's chain." She reached in for another Coke—a revolutionary act, as she only allowed herself two a day. "I hoped somehow you wouldn't do as I had done."

Mandy held the cold can to her forehead. She was burning. "I don't know. Life gets away from you sometimes. I find myself flinching when another black person says 'wif' instead of 'with.' I don't know."

"Are we two peas in a pod or ducks out of water?" Frazier laughed.

"Both, maybe." Mandy kicked off her shoes. "Life isn't like I thought it would be. When I was little I thought that being ten would be Nirvana. So on my tenth birthday I discovered that that wasn't enough. I wasn't perfect. Then I thought being really popular in high school would do it. Didn't. Okay. The best college, the best boy-friend, and then the best job. It's harder than I thought but somehow maybe better. I just thought there would be this day when everything would fall into place, I'd be really smart, on top of the world, and the gods would smile upon me."

"They have."

From the next room thunder shook the walls. Mandy walked over to the window. "Not a cloud in the sky. That's strange."

"Came from the painting."

"Frazier, you're not knitting with both needles when it comes to that painting." Despite her protest Mandy walked into the room, followed by Frazier.

The Mount Olympus painting seemed even larger than before, as majestic as Bernini's columns in Saint Peter's, as massive as a Rodin sculpture, yet light, filled with light and laughter. Zeus seemed especially expansive in this light. He defined jovial. Frazier couldn't help smiling as she gazed on his joyful countenance.

Mandy whispered to herself, "May the Lord bless thee and keep thee, may the Lord shine his face upon thee and give thee . . . laughter." Then she laughed, genuine deep laughter. "Frazier, where did you say you found this painting?"

"I told you—in a whorehouse in Venice. The man from whom I purchased it, uh, it was his house but he was two years older than God and he said when he was a boy, before the Great War—tells you how old he was—that it was a house of pleasure. His mother, apparently, owned it. Rather hard up, the poor fellow. I fell in love with it."

"But who told you about it?"

"A gondolier as we passed the house. Coincidence."

"Fate." Mandy kept smiling at Jupiter. "It's magic, you know. I hope you never sell it."

"First, you don't want me to sell the Ben Marshall—"

Mandy interrupted, "You can't bear to part with that painting of Sir Teddy. It's too wonderful."

"I'm in the business to make money. If I keep every painting I buy or take on commission I'll be in the poorhouse."

Mandy shrugged. "Maybe 'Mount Olympus' is one of those paintings that changes the life of whoever owns it."

"And you thought I wasn't playing with a full deck. Now you're going to get mystical on me. Has breaking up with Sean lifted the scales from your eyes?"

"Very funny." Mandy placed her finger on Jupiter's lips. They felt warm. Must be the light on the canvas. "You know, I bet he knew the Wife of Bath."

"Today she'd be the Wife of Shower."

Mandy punched Frazier in the arm for that, then laughed again, harder and louder. Jupiter's radiance curled around her nostrils, feathered down into her lungs. "Oh, what the hell," Mandy thought. "We're going to live until we die and we'll be dead a long time, so better get on with it, just get on with it and let the drudges of the world worry about being silly. We're not here for a long time but we're here for a good time."

CHAPTER

37

L ent dragged on, as Lent always does, and Frazier found herself giving up far more than she intended. She bought Carter's Ford F150 four-by-four flare-side pickup. He needed the money and once she satisfied herself that the frame had withstood the carnage, she forked over $16,000, which was really more than it was worth, considering.

Carter laughed and told her that now she would be a mothertrucker, a true dyke in her pickup. She fired back that it was Miss Dyke to him. No matter how feckless or destructive he was, Frazier couldn't help but love her brother.

She then paid an impromptu visit to Dr. Yancey Weems, who, still fearing she would come to her wits and sue his ass into next week, leaped up to greet her with open arms. He sat down fast enough when she bargained for Carter. If Yancey would forget this episode and accept the repairs being picked up by Carter, then Frazier wouldn't dream of suing him for malpractice. He accepted this bargain, which wasn't so damned hard. If he sued Carter what would he get? Blood out of a turnip? Carter's house? It wasn't even in Carter's name. Frank, knowing his son was a spectacular fuck-up, had kept the property in his name when he gave it to his son, so to speak, for a wedding present. That preyed upon Laura's devious mind. What if Carter walked? What if he filed for a divorce? She certainly couldn't file, no matter what that bastard did. She'd lose her house. Sooner or later Frank, a decent man but a businessman nonetheless, would sell the house.

Meanwhile Ann, riven with fear, whispered about town that Frazier had once made a pass at Laura, but Laura, blessed art thou amongst women, never so much as breathed a word because poor Libby and Frank would die and Carter would kill his sister. This smear campaign showed a certain vulpine skill in Ann. Had she told the tale on herself it would make a few of the smarter residents of the burg scrutinize her. This way Ann, perceived as a handmaiden to the beleaguered Laura, would gain points as a dear friend, and Laura would emerge with even more luster around her name. No doubt about it, Laura was on her way to becoming president of the Garden Club, to being raised up by the hagiolatry of suffering women, a splendor all the more shining because she herself never complained.

This dreck finally reached Ruru as she was buying flats of pansies at Elzroth's Nursery. Wilfreda Gimble, the tiny stalwart of the hunt club, intoned the gossip as though sharing a sacred sacrament, the bond of female victimization. And what a joy, Laura Armstrong was victimized by both brother and sister, and utter ecstasy, it was sexual. This was scandal too good to be true. Wilfreda gained her status by being the first in the community with news, bad news. She specialized in it; she reveled in it. She made Dan Rather, Sam Donaldson, and the other tarted-up boys and girls on television look like pikers. The theater of her ambition, to be the first with the worst, gave rise to a performance of high caliber. She lowered her voice as she sidled over to Ru. Wreaths of concern wrapped around her tiny brow.

"Oh, Mary Russell, getting an early start for spring?"

"And you, too, Wilfreda? How are your horses?"

"Fine. Now if I could just get you on a horse, Mary Russell. You're only as old as the horse you're riding, so it's a way for us girls to stay young." Hearty laughter. "Say, I am sorry about this terrible triangle with Carter, Laura, and Frazier."

Ru set down the flats of purple pansies. "Triangle, as in Bermuda?"

A flutter of hand to heart completed the stylized gesture. "Oh, dear, you haven't heard?"

"Apparently not. You're dying to tell me. So go on. I'd rather hear it from you than someone else." Ruru was telling the truth because she marveled at Wilfreda's inauthentic emotion. She studied her much the way an entomologist might examine a cockroach.

"Frazier made advances at Laura, poor dear."

Ruru tilted back her head and howled. This disconcerted Wilfreda, who was depending upon a response of shock and deep concern, depending upon it so she could trumpet Ru's reaction to everyone she saw for the next week. Something was wrong with the script. "Laura flatters herself."

"I beg your pardon?" A chill came over Wilfreda's voice. She might have to back-pedal quickly and act as though something was wrong with Ru or else that Ru had misunderstood.

"My niece has better taste, Wilfreda. I doubt she'd make a pass at Laura if she were the last woman on earth. I still can't figure out why my nephew married that calculating bitch."

Ruru whistled the whole way home, which drove Chief, Marco, Toby, and Lulu into harmonious howls. She couldn't wait for the phrase *calculating bitch* or some variant thereof to reach Laura's ears.

Carter, like many men, had married a woman much like his

mother. Since Ruru never liked Libby, Laura didn't stand much of a chance either. Perhaps both Libby and Laura chose to live through a man, whereas Ruru thought you lived as a separate being. Your man was your partner but not your reason for living. No person can bear the weight of being so central to another person's existence. Sooner or later the woman becomes disenchanted; the man suffocates.

It seemed so obvious to her that such relationships would culminate in varying degrees of estrangement. Yet millions of people fell for the old romantic bullshit: You are my everything. I can't live without you. I was nothing until I met you. Et cetera, et cetera.

She pulled a U-ie on Avon Extended and headed toward the country club. Why wait? Why not tell Frank what the hell was going on and Libby, too, if that blowfly was hanging around.

And Libby was. She was terrorizing her maid about polishing the silver, the usual Georgian stuff, which Libby had bought at a London auction and passed off as a family heirloom. She passed it off, as Frank passed out when he received the bill. That was the last time he ever let his wife hop on the Concorde by herself. Crossing the Atlantic was a joint venture after that or Libby would have looted Europe. Field Marshal Göring must have been her secret role model.

". . . and that's the story." Ruru folded her arms across her chest.

"I can't believe it! I can't believe it," Libby shrieked.

Frank shook his head. The pettiness of people disturbed him. Maybe that was one of the many reasons he kept his emotions to himself. That and the fact that he realized decades ago that no one really wanted to know what he felt anyway. Maybe Ru and Frazier wanted to know, but not sharing had become a habit, and habits, as any smoker could tell you, were the devil to break.

"A rumor has a life of its own but we have to stand together on this one. If anyone even hints at this, let them have it."

"Why doesn't Frazier leave town?" Libby suggested. "It's all so embarrassing."

"Libby, you don't believe this tripe?" Ru shouted.

"I don't know what to believe. I don't know what these lesbians do, thank God."

"They do what you and I do, or did, with our husbands. They simply do it with women." Ru wanted to strangle Libby.

"Well, if she's got to do it, then she could shut up about it!" Libby snapped. "See how worn-out poor Frank is . . . because of this."

"I am not worn-out," said Frank, who was but not because of Frazier.

"Darling, you don't see yourself. You drag in from work at night, gray in the face. It breaks my heart to see you." Libby trawled from her depths.

Ru didn't believe this performance any more than she had believed Wilfreda's. If Libby was so concerned about Frank, she could spend less of his money. "Frazier shoulders more than her share of the blame, Libby. Carter hasn't been walking on water recently."

"The poor boy. The real estate market is down, way down"— Libby's voice dropped—"and well, it had to be a shock to learn about Frazier. After all, they were devoted to each other when they were children."

"A devotion you tore apart every chance you got." The cords stood out on Ruru's neck.

"Girls, we're getting off the track." Frank agreed with his sister but if he said that, he'd have two months of bleeding hell with Libby. "Ruru, people are like vultures. They feed on other people to make up for their emptiness."

Both women stopped to stare at Frank. He so rarely spoke in such a fashion that the effect was powerful.

"Oh, Frankie . . ." Tears snuck into the corners of Ru's eyes.

"They'll chew on this until another scandal comes along and then they'll chew on that. If anyone says anything to me about my girl, so help me God I will smash his face in!" He slammed his paper on the armchair and stood up.

"Now, honey, don't be upset," Libby cooed.

"Upset! I was born and raised here. I work hard. My daughter works hard and has made something out of her life. And this is my reward? To watch Frazier be picked apart by vultures, none of whom are her equal in any respect? Do I know what this lesbian stuff is about? My God, I can barely remember my own sexuality, much less understand hers!"

Libby blushed. "Now, honey, don't tax yourself."

He brushed past his wife, a wife he had realized within the first two years of marriage was an empty gourd, but Frank had made a vow before God and man and he intended to keep it. And by the time he realized he was truly alone in this world he had a son to support. His generation didn't think about divorce. Frank discovered golf, and then when Frazier came there was another woman to steal his heart.

"Frank, I do understand it." Ru surprised Libby and Frank.

"What do you mean?" Libby's eyes narrowed to slits.

"Frazier needs nurturing. I don't mean mothering. I mean nurturing, and women do that better than men. Refute me if you think I'm wrong, Frank."

"No, I don't think you're wrong." He sat on the edge of the armchair. Libby noticed but shut up.

"I guess hormones are hormones," Ru kept on, "and no doubt there is lust. We don't feel it but it can't be any different than what we did feel. It's what's underneath. It's the caring part. She needs more help than we knew. Frazier was the perfect kid, straight A's, the best athlete, president of her class, but we didn't stop to look inside her. Carter commanded most of our emotional attention. His need was, and remains, obvious. She needs nurturing. It's as simple as that."

Libby felt this was a sly attack on her maternal job description. However, Ruru so cleverly phrased it that she wasn't sure how to fight back.

Frank's voice wavered. "If only I could have back the years." Ru walked over to her brother and put her arm around his shoulders. Libby seethed. "If only I had paid more attention to my children."

"Poppycock. You were a good father." Libby's defense was really an offense.

"You know, in our time, in my time"—he half-smiled—"we didn't think of that. I thought if I made money, that was it, you know, and if I took the kids fishing sometimes. Now, now I know what a mistake I made. I lost my children."

"You did not." Libby's upper lip curled.

"Maybe I didn't want the emotional responsibility. Maybe it was easier to push it off on my wife."

"Frank, you're being too hard on yourself. A mother naturally has a stronger bond to the children. That's Nature's way," Libby said, ignoring the fact that her bond to Frazier was one of unremitting hostility, and perhaps a part of that hostility lay in Frazier's youth and beauty. The daughter had surpassed the mother.

"It's never too late, Frank." Ru hugged Frank and noticed how thin he was between the shoulder blades. "And you did the best you could with what you had. That's all any of us can ask of ourselves."

"Sounds like something you heard on *Oprah*," Libby sniffed. "You could go on the show as the Phantom of the Oprah." Since Libby rarely evidenced a sense of humor she must have been thinking extra hard to get one up on the quick-witted Ru.

"I like her and I like her show." Ru released Frank. She nearly said, "And I don't like you," but then that was obvious.

Frank sighed. "What this town needs is an enema."

CHAPTER
38

Despite the sunburst of forsythia and the swelling of the redbuds, spring stalled. Gray clouds slid down the Blue Ridge Mountains to spread their gloom over central Virginia. The robins puffed up their red breasts to keep warm and humans grumbled in their winter sweaters.

Frazier escaped the elements by walking through the covered shopping mall, a place she usually avoided but she'd run out of her favorite Lancôme body lotion, and the only store that carried the expensive stuff was in the mall. As it was six-thirty in the evening, the place reverberated with the click of human heels, the slow scrape of teenaged boys in high-top sneakers, and the occasional pop of walkers as the aged participated in the orgy of commercial display.

Frazier passed two athletic-shoe stores selling sneakers at exorbitant prices, especially those endorsed by a basketball player. Basketball, a game played by chromosomes, captured the marketeers of Reebok, Nike, Puma, and other assorted brands. Hard by the sneaker stores were clothing franchises brimming with men and women rummaging through the spring sales. The smell of chocolate cookies, yogurt, and McDonald's assailed her nostrils. Bad as that was, turning into the cosmetics department of Stone and Thomas, a decent store for a mall, was worse. Surely this was what a cheap whorehouse in Paris smelled like, a signature scent laden with lusty promise.

A fine-looking redhead, in her early thirties at most and serious about her hair as only Texan women can be serious about their hair, bent over the counter as she lined up bottles of Red, Poison, Opium, and Cinnabar. Although she had never met the woman, Frazier knew this was Sarah Saxe. The prospect of conversation lured her, probably as sailors were lured by Circe.

Frazier reached out for Ysatis. Sarah, a friendly sort, cheerfully said, "I've never tried that but I am tired, truly tired of Giorgio."

"Too overpowering." Frazier smiled, and when she did her resemblance to her brother was uncanny.

"Haven't we met?" Sarah uttered the oldest pickup line in the world.

"No, but I believe you know my brother."

"Oh." Sarah, unwary, beamed.

Frazier marveled at how open the woman was, how utterly different from Laura. "I'm Mary Frazier Armstrong." Frazier held out her hand. "But everyone calls me Frazier, except for Carter, who calls me Sistergirl."

Sarah clasped her hand. "You look like twins. No wonder I thought I knew you." She quickly withdrew her hand, fearing that Frazier might be judging her for having an affair with her brother, but Frazier thought it was because Sarah had heard that she was a lesbian.

"Yes, everyone says that."

"I, well, I'm glad to meet you."

"I'm glad to meet you too, and, Sarah, if you think I don't approve of your time spent with my brother, you're wrong. His wife is a whistling bitch. At least you make him happy."

Sarah glanced around. "Would you like to have a cup of coffee? I mean, there are never enough salesclerks in here."

"We could go into menopause waiting to buy the perfume."

Sarah laughed. "We've got time."

"Time. We've probably got another twenty-five years and I would like to know what a lesbian needs with a period."

Sarah doubled over. She hadn't expected Frazier to be light-hearted. Then again, Frazier usually wasn't and she had not referred to herself in this manner in public before, but perhaps the two women, bound by love outside the bounds, found they could be free with each other.

"You're not at all what I expected," Sarah confessed as they sat down at a table.

"You are." Frazier opened her napkin.

"Oh . . ."

"And I'm glad. I'm thrilled, actually, that he's not fooling around with another proper Virginia woman, a woman who knows her pedigree, your pedigree, and who wears pastels in springtime."

"Uh-huh."

"You look like Texas to me, sugar."

"And you look like something off the cover of *Vogue*. Carter never told me that you were beautiful."

"No sister is beautiful to her brother, I guess."

"You all are getting close again?"

"Oh, Brudda and I are best friends except when we're enemies."

"He's sure glad you bought his truck." She ordered coffee while Frazier settled for Perrier. "Too late for coffee?"

"I'll be up all night."

"Doesn't affect me much one way or the other." She lifted her eyes to Frazier's. "When Carter first told me about . . . things, I made a couple of cracks, you know, dyke stuff, but I don't believe it."

"You don't have to tell me this."

"I know that I don't, except that I feel like I know you. It's weird. Anyway, I've had my share of threesomes so maybe I know a little more about the subject than Carter—but he doesn't know that yet."

"Is this a sexual confession? Because if it is, I want to hear everything." Frazier leaned forward. She understood instinctively why Carter loved this woman. God knows, the girl was hot.

"Uh, well, yes, in a way. I mean, when I met Carter, I figured, wow, what an animal. I just wanted to jump his bones, which was easy enough."

"Isn't it always?"

"Yes." Sarah laughed. "But one thing led to another and I discovered I liked this guy and he was so miserable—I mean, as miserable as a puppy with a stomachache."

"Have you ever seen his wife?"

"Once. But she can't be the only source of his misery." Sarah hit the nail on the head. "He doesn't believe in himself."

"Yeah, I know."

"Well, after like comes love and I love your brother and I don't know what's going to happen. I don't want to get hurt, I don't want him to get hurt, and I'd like to say I don't want his wife to get hurt but I really don't give a flying fuck about her, you know? I suppose I should. I wouldn't want a husband running out on me."

"Your husband wouldn't." Frazier listened to the ice cubes tinkle in her glass as the waitress placed the beverage before her.

Sarah half-smiled. "Every woman would like to think that, but time changes people and men get restless."

"How is it you never married?"

"Never wanted to. It felt like a trap to me."

"Would you marry Carter if he asked you? Sorry if I'm being too direct."

"I don't know. I want to say yes, but his drinking worries me—not that he gets ugly or anything when he does. He's actually kind of fun until he passes out but he isn't doing his liver any good."

"You don't drink?"

"Not like that, I don't."

"Well, for what it's worth, he's been unfaithful as long as I've known him but I think he really loves you. That's a change."

"He does?" Sarah's innocent need to know was touching.

"I figure I know him better than anybody. He does." Frazier rested her chin in her hand. "Give him a cornucopia of sexual dramas with himself as the star, and I figure if his brains don't fry or if he doesn't wear out his part, he'll be yours forever."

"Why do you say that?"

"I just this minute figured it out. He has energy but he doesn't really have imagination. Supply the imagination, especially in bed, and he doesn't need to sleep with other women, does he? And as we all know, there is no right or wrong way to make love. So . . ."

Sarah shook her head. "You're not at all what I expected."

"I'm not what I expected."

As they roared with laughter Kimberly Noakes passed by the table.

"Kimberly, how are you?" Frazier called out.

Kimberly blinked. "Oh, fine. I'm so happy you're well."

"This is Sarah Saxe." Frazier introduced the women to each other.

Kimberly eyed Sarah with heightened interest. "Pleased to meet you. Frazier, I'm glad I did run into you because I need to chat with you sometime soon."

"About the Girl Scout board meeting?"

"Well, yes, and I'll call you early tomorrow, okay?"

"Kimberly, you look pale. Why don't I save you the trouble and resign?"

A wave of pure relief washed Kimberly's sallow features. "I surely didn't expect you to be so understanding but you can imagine the position we're in and these are impressionable young girls. It's so unfortunate and—" She inhaled as Frazier cut her off.

"As far as I know, Kimberly, young women are quite safe from older women as sexual predators. I can't think of one example where something like that has happened. Sure happens all the time with men though. A high school teacher seduces the best-looking girl in the class."

"You got that right, girl," Sarah echoed.

"Now, Frazier, I knew this would upset you. I did, and I'm sorry and I don't want you to think for one instant that any of us thought that of you. We know you better than that, but think how it would look."

"I have. That's why I'm resigning, Kimberly, but I ask you to think about something. Out there right now there are girls who are in tremendous turmoil. Sexual identity isn't easy at that age, even when you're straight. Think of the pain the gay kid endures. Who can she talk to? Her family? You, Kimberly? Her pastor? A friend in school? Don't you think there are girls in scouting suffering with the issue right now?"

"Well . . . well, to tell you the truth, I never thought of it."

"No one ever thinks of it. That's my point. Maybe if there were gay leaders in scouting or in the schools or the churches, at least those kids wouldn't have to go through what I went through, and what I'm going through now. They'd have someone to talk to even if it's only me."

Kimberly, shaken but listening, spoke: "I am sorry. I really am."

"So am I. I'm not mad at you though. I'm not mad at anyone and that's what scares me. I think I'd be better off if I were."

As Kimberly left, Sarah and Frazier sat for a moment. "Sarah, I get the feeling people would have preferred that I died. It would be better than having to face things. Or maybe saying that they want me dead is too strong. Maybe they just want me to get a pink slip, you know, so I could be excused from life."

CHAPTER
39

Frank bent over Mildred Saviano as she pointed to the right-hand column in the accounting books. Mildred had worked for the company for thirty years. Loyal, efficient, and fond of numbers because they always produced a right answer, she was an unadventuresome soul. But then, Frank thought, perhaps he was also. He arose each morning at seven. Drank his first cup of coffee while he shaved. Joined Libby at the breakfast table at seven-thirty, where discussion centered on the scheduling of the day. He ate half a grapefruit, two pieces of toast, drank one glass of orange juice and then his second cup of coffee.

He usually ate lunch at noon, and in the warm weather he left work at four, if possible, to play golf. Sometimes he thought that he and Mildred were a matched pair, whereas Libby craved excitement and power. His wife's ceaseless rounds of meetings, charities, bridge, and dress-up luncheons, her travel brochures tossed on his side of the bed, her lists of chores—all this exhausted him. In her cups she would accuse him of being boring and he couldn't refute the charges. But he didn't bore himself. Frank was a man who wished the trains would run on time. Mildred would have been the better choice for a mate, but when one is young one rarely considers compatibility.

Frank had looked at Libby's full bosom, her long sleek legs, her fine features. The rest, as they say, was history.

His eyes followed Mildred's finger as she slowly ran down the column.

"It's these uncollected bills that are killing us." Mildred strongly identified with the company.

"I know."

"Frank, we write, I call, nothing happens. Okay, then I call Richardson, Fuqua and Garrick. *They* write. They write again. We've either got to press on and sue or turn these accounts over to a collection agency and give them a percentage—I think that's how those things work." She stuck her pencil in her hair alongside her ear.

"I hate to do that." He tapped one line. "Pete Barber. Overbuilt. He's got a house sitting in Raintree that lists for seven hundred and twenty-five thousand. In fact, he's got houses sitting all over and he has to service the interest on those loans."

"That was his decision. I don't have sympathy for the developers whose eyes were bigger than their bellies." Mildred pulled the pencil out of her hair and made checks against the names she disliked. "Lionel Jacobs. Went wild putting up office buildings. Why? This isn't New York. And here, here's that private asphalt driveway you put in for Fred Vanarman's house. Well, the driveway is half a mile long. He sat his rear up there in his big chair at Strong and Simon churning everyone's portfolio. The market goes bust and he decides you can wait for your money."

"I know these guys."

"And they know you. Come on, Frank, you just can't let people take advantage of you this way. You let go of six employees last month. If these bills had been paid you could have held back half the men. Let's face it, Pete and Lionel think you won't fight back. Oh, Frank Armstrong, what a nice guy. It's not right. You've got equipment loans, remember?"

He ran his hand through his thick silver hair. "Mildred, you're good for me."

"Then why don't you listen?" came her tart reply.

"I'm listening now. What do you suggest? Our lawyers or a collection agency?"

"Our lawyers. On a per-hour basis they are more expensive but everybody knows everybody. Lionel Jacobs isn't going to want to be golfing at the club when Ned Fuqua rolls by in a golf cart after Ned's sent out the papers. Know what I mean? A collection agency is far away, and despite their success ratio, letters from them and subsequent proceedings lack the hometown punch."

"You should have gone into politics."

"Thanks, I can't sink that low." Mildred swiveled in her chair. A photo of her grandchildren commanded the right-hand corner of her desk.

"Do it your way then." He sighed. "Any call-backs on the grader ad?"

"No."

"Hmm. Let's run it again."

"Haven't heard anything back from your meeting with the other contractors?"

"Uh, no, and I thought I had made a good suggestion."

"You did, but you know what I think about meetings, especially professional meetings. What happens is a big nothing or, worse, a giant pamphlet is issued on the new rules and regulations for blowing your nose."

"All right, Mildred, you're burning to tell me what you think."

She laughed because he knew her well. "Make some calls yourself.

Don't wait to do it as a group. I bet you some of those other guys are calling. Pickens Oliguy."

"He wouldn't do that."

"That young flash would—Larry Taylor. Probably burned up the phone wires between here and New Mexico."

"I'll call the guys and tell them what I'm doing first."

"I knew you'd say that. Just do it. It's easier to apologize than to ask for permission. Why ask? It was your idea!"

"They're my friends."

"So are Pete and Lionel and Fred. Frank, get tough."

"I'll think about it. About the calls to the West, I mean. You might be right." He folded his arms across his chest. "That it?"

"That's it except that the dirt about Frazier is all over town. When it reaches my hairdresser, who is the Ancient of Days, you know the gossip has made a complete cycle. Want me to tear off anyone's face?"

"What's wrong with people?" Frank shook his head.

"Petty envy. Frazier is beautiful, bright—always was the brightest little thing—and successful. Finally, she's proved to be human. They all need to crow a little bit. Makes them feel bigger, or if not bigger, at least not such failures."

Frank had not brought up the subject to Mildred. They were so close that about many things he rarely needed to speak. Mildred just knew. But he felt compelled to say something now: "Mildred, I'm a man. Men look at these things differently. Now if this were Carter I'd be furious—my son, for God's sake. But I don't mind so much with Frazier."

Mildred smiled broadly. "Sure, no other man will have her. You'll always be number one."

"You think that?" Frank was incredulous.

"Got any other woman in your life that makes you feel good?" Mildred hit the bull's-eye.

"You."

"Ha!" Mildred spun around and slapped him in the stomach.

"You do."

"You know what I mean. Who fills your heart? Your daughter. Always did."

This disturbed Frank. Could he be so selfish that he was happy his beloved daughter was a lesbian? "I never thought of it that way."

"You don't think about a lot of things and that's why I'm sitting here pulling the hair out of my head over these damn bills. It's a good thing to keep your nose to the grindstone but every now and then, Frank, take a look around—and a look inside."

"The only thing that bothers me about Frazier's choice"—he emphasized *choice*—"is that she'll never have children."

"Nor legal protection. I read in the papers about these galimony suits. That could happen to her. She won't get a break on her income tax or her insurance. Seems to me she made an expensive choice. And what if she lives with someone who won't work? A lot of women won't work in Frazier's social circle. Frazier's going to pay the bills. I mean she's got the worst of both worlds, if you ask me."

"Well, I did ask you."

"And she's so beautiful she'll be besieged by these gold diggers, you mark my words."

"Isn't that funny. I fear just the opposite."

"What do you mean?" Mildred's eyes widened, for she couldn't imagine a scenario different from her own.

"I'm afraid she's going to spend her life alone. She's a good girl. I want someone to take care of her when I'm not here."

"I don't want to hear that kind of talk." Mildred slammed her hand on the table. "No talk about not being here. Anyway, Frank, she's supported herself since college."

"I know, but I'm her father. I want her to be loved. I want her to be protected. I want to know I can entrust her to someone special. I don't know if another woman can do that."

"Apparently not."

"Why do you say that?"

"They don't make as much money as men. How can they take care of one another? And men have their little groups, their cronies. They pass business around to one another. Women don't. I mean, how can they? So Frazier's going to carry the ball and that gets wearisome, especially if she winds up with some damned bitch who wants to live at Tiffany's!"

"Mildred, I didn't expect you to be so vehement."

"I love her, too, you know."

CHAPTER
40

" I 'm no longer the good gay Girl Scout." Frazier finished relating
her story to Mandy and Kenny Singer.
"Sucks," Kenny responded.
Mandy paused before a perfectly shaped black urn from ancient
Greece. The Virginia Museum in Richmond owned a good basic
collection of art and artifacts, which was continually replenished by
revolving shows.

Frazier paused to study it also. "Roberta Saunders has one of the
most marvelous collections of both Attic black figure and red figure
vases in this country or any other."

Kenny asked, "Is she as sexy as everyone says?"

"Are you asking me as a woman or are you asking me as a man?"
Frazier put her hand on her hip.

"For you, as a lady," Kenny replied.

"Smoky, smoky sex. Drives men wild. All she has to do is walk into a room."

"Works for you too," Mandy complimented Frazier.

"Thanks, but I'm icy-looking. It's a different hit, I think." Frazier moved down the corridor. "Mandy, you're pretty much a hit yourself."

"Right." Kenny picked up the theme. "Broad shoulders, narrow waist, uh, ample bosoms, great features, and white, white teeth."

"All black folks have white teeth." Mandy laughed. She changed the subject. "Now, Frazier, I didn't study as much art history as you did. Why do so many of the men on those vases or urns or amphorae—I never do get it right—have erections?"

"Because they're happy."

Kenny's rich tenor purred, "From the looks of it there must have been a lot of happy men in Athens way back in B.C. Too bad no one has figured out how to do time tours."

"What—Courtney isn't making you happy?"

"We haven't gotten that far yet and I'm out of practice. I'll probably forget myself and tell the poor girl to bend over." Mandy and Frazier howled at that. Kenny continued, "Then again, she won't know until she tries and I'll certainly attempt more conventional methods."

"I'm so glad to hear it. The late, unlamented Sean, my ex—I mean he's not dead, just in my heart—well, he was button-down, tortoise-rimmed glasses, straight through. A real three-speed guy."

"Is this the one you described as resembling a Ken doll with anatomically correct parts?" Kenny wondered.

"No, that was Frazier describing Taylor Anderson."

"That wasn't Taylor Anderson. He may not have been greatly endowed by Nature but he was okay. That was Sam Krueger and that was a long time ago. My, how you remember."

"I love girl talk—girls." Kenny smiled. "Something tells me if there were time travel we would have thoroughly disported ourselves in ancient Athens."

"You would. Women bore the usual sexist burdens, as well as the children."

"How sad." Kenny meant it. Now that he had reconceived of himself as bisexual he was in favor of sex for everyone with everyone in every available combination. It was an endearing philosophy.

"You know, Frazier's fixated on that painting of Mount Olympus, which, while painted much later—like the seventeenth century later—carries the flavor of the vases, you might say. Anyway, she's convinced the painting is alive, sort of, and I say she's under a lot of stress so this is . . . a kind of relief."

"Mandy, dammit, Kenny doesn't care about the Mount Olympus painting. And I never said it was alive. I just think there are some things about it that are peculiar."

"Such as?" Kenny asked, his dark, glossy eyebrows curving upward.

"Oh, nothing really."

"In the middle of a bright day we heard thunder. Jupiter's laughter." Mandy supplied an answer.

"I didn't say that exactly. But there wasn't a cloud. I called the power company to find out if a transformer blew—"

"Got obsessed and then she called the police to find out if a bomb had gone off."

"Mandy, come on, I was curious. It was so unusual. Anyway, I'd rather have the thunder be Jupiter's laughter than a bomb. Everything's so upside down right now, someone better be laughing. I'd hate for this muffled misery to be for nothing."

"Yeah, everyone is overpoweringly polite. What was it that Tennessee Williams said? 'A faggot is a homosexual gentleman who has just left the room.' Applies to women, too, I guess."

"It's like an undertow. I can't always see it but I can feel it." Frazier slowed her pace. "I'd feel better if they came out of the closet, the people who sit in silent judgment."

"I hardly think your mother sits in silent judgment." Mandy snapped her fingers together.

"Mother is in a class by herself. Oh, yeah, I forgot to tell you. I received the first detective's report."

"And?"

"Nothing."

"What report?" Kenny smelled gossip and he was never one to pass up a delicious story.

"Mandy told me to put a detective on Laura."

"Our Lady of Perfection?" Kenny was amazed.

"She's not so perfect." Mandy defended her instincts. "She hates her husband and she hates Frazier too."

"Oooee." Kenny sucked in his breath. "Blunt but true. You think she's rolling in the hay with someone other than Carter, the original forty-balled tomcat?"

"No." Frazier shook her head. "She visits different doctors. Apart from her various activities—aerobics, tennis lessons, bridge, the Garden Club—just the usual."

"Maybe she sleeps with the doctors." Kenny, a Southern gentleman, glided down the stairs before the ladies and walked in front of them, the reasoning being that if a lady should lose her footing the gentleman would be there to catch her. The reverse applied on climbing the stairs.

"I thought of that." Frazier glared at Mandy. "You have just perverted my mind, Eisenhart. Anyway, she wasn't in the offices long enough for that unless these guys are adept at speed-fucking."

"Most doctors are," Kenny drawled.

"Is this spoken from personal experience?" Mandy's hand slid along the highly polished railing.

"It is."

"Doesn't count."

"And why not?" He turned his head to look back at Frazier.

"You guys can dart in and out of one another's, uh, nether regions faster than I can put on panty hose."

"And you're telling me a doctor can't fast-forward into someone's vagina?"

"Of course he can," Mandy said, "but the lady of his momentary lust probably won't get much out of it."

"What if he arrives at the other orifice?" Kenny twirled his hand upward.

"My point stands." Mandy sounded triumphant.

"Oh, dear. Does this mean that when I finally do achieve the desired intimacy with Courtney Wood that she isn't going to enjoy oral sex?"

"How do you even know she'll do it?" Frazier drew alongside Mandy as they stepped down the last step.

"You're kidding?" Kenny was shocked.

"No. Some women won't." Mandy backed up Frazier.

"Not you two." Kenny's eyes twinkled.

"Depends on the man." Mandy volunteered a bit of her sexual history. "If he's not hot, never. If I like him, okay."

"But do you like it?" Kenny adored sex talk.

"It's not my fave" came the dry reply.

Now both sets of eyes fell upon Frazier.

"Hey, I'm the lesbian, remember?"

"Oh, bullshit, Mary," Kenny shot back using the gay term "Mary." "Didn't I just hear you discussing the members of some fortunate gentlemen, fortunate enough to have enjoyed your favors."

"You are courtly, Kenny. Why are you both looking at me? Do I like giving blow jobs? Is that the question?"

"It most certainly is." Kenny nodded.

"Loved it. Loved every minute of it."

Mandy's eyes grew larger. She was surprised at this because since she didn't like it, she couldn't imagine Frazier, who was supposed to be gay, liking it at all. "Now wait a minute. Just wait a minute. I'm straight and I don't like it. You're gay and you do?"

"How straight are you, sugar?" Kenny, had he been a cat, would have curled his tail around himself at that very moment.

Now both sets of eyes were on Mandy. "You two are demented."

"I hope so." Kenny grinned.

"Let me put it this way . . ." Mandy began.

"Brace yourself, Kenny. I think we're in for a bout of diplomacy." Mandy laughed. "Hey, you're my boss, remember."

"I remember only too well. So tell . . . the truth. Even if you think it will offend me."

"I have never been to bed with a member of my own sex, but once when I was seventeen I did kiss Meredith Burns in the boathouse at the University of Pennsylvania."

"You had to go all the way to Philadelphia to kiss a girl?" Frazier couldn't help but prolong Mandy's agony.

"We were visiting colleges together." She stopped. "Why am I telling you this?"

"Because we asked and because it's fascinating and because apart from money, sex is the most wonderful, the most engaging, the most memorable subject on all the earth." Kenny sighed.

"Been a long time, honey?" Frazier slipped her arm through his and Mandy did likewise on his right side.

"I consider two months an eternity. Billy and I usually had sex four or five times a week and not always alone."

"Kinky." Mandy noticed an Isidore Bonheur sculpture and thought of his sister Rosa, a painter of restrained passion, a passion focused more on animals than people.

"Very. I have had all my orifices stuffed simultaneously and been stuffing someone else's, often unknown to me—the person, not the orifice. Billy's lust exceeds even my own, but what I really want is to be close to someone. After a time, sex with him became gymnastics—or traffic control. I just wanted to be held, corny as that may sound."

"Sounds pretty good to me," Frazier admitted. "Oh, Mandy, you didn't tell us if you enjoyed kissing Meredith Whoever."

"If I tell, will Kenny tell about his perversions?"

"Deal."

"Meredith Burns was one good kisser."

"But you didn't go further?" Kenny pressed.

"No. I didn't think about it. Girls can do those sorts of things. Kissing, I mean, and it's not a big deal. But if you're asking if I am capable of making love to a woman—sure. Will I? How the hell do I know? I'm like a trapeze artist. I swing from boyfriend to boyfriend. Maybe if I sat down and thought about what I was doing I'd think about that too."

"Serial monogamy." Frazier's voice sounded grave.

"It's not a disease."

"I know. It's just what I observe. I wasn't making a judgment. If anything, Mandy, I give you credit. You're out there trying. On the other hand, you can sit home and conceive of the perfect relationship. You can reconstitute yourself, too, you know. Attack your own neurosis. Imagine how the next relationship will be. While you're sitting home creating this perfection the world goes on. And when you emerge from the cocoon to actually find someone, they aren't perfect and neither are you. At least, if you're out there having relationships and trying and loving and crying and whatever, you're learning, which is a lot more than I ever did. I would have a furtive relationship here and there with someone usually as repressed as myself. Close personal friends, you bet—the byword for a lesbian couple, only I never even coupled. Fucked, yes; coupled, no. I qualify as a major coward."

"You don't know, sister, you don't know," Mandy said, and Kenny nodded in agreement. "And now, Mr. Singer, a perversion. Like what is the wildest thing you ever did?"

He sat on a bench in the middle of the room. The two women sat on either side of him, and as the room was empty, he spoke in a normal tone of voice. "Last year for my thirtieth birthday Billy flew me to Florida and we embarked on a Caribbean cruise on this stunning big cruiser, long as a city block. Two other couples joined us, all gay men, and the crew were all gay, too, or bisexual. I mean, when you're fucking someone you don't care a bit if he's fucking women too. I never did, anyway. On the actual day of my birth we sat down to a white-tie dinner, and dessert was served in this fashion: the crew member with the biggest cock was carried in on a platter they had made, covered in grapes and fruits. We nibbled the fruits. Then we nibbled him. Then we carefully removed our clothes, as did the crew, except that they were ordered to keep on their white caps and navy blazers with the brass buttons. Oh, the sight of those big pecs, a trickle of sweat lazing between them! Billy stroked those crew members' members who were not white. He delicately poured lines of cocaine on these erect penii which the white members of the party and crew sniffed. Then the black crew members and guests—one couple was mixed—placed us on our stomachs while they formed lines of cocaine on our buttocks which they then sniffed. We applied more of this controlled substance to various anuses and entered at will. In order to sustain our erections we dabbed the powder on the heads of our own cocks, which does delay ejaculation, and we combined and recombined in every number and position imaginable. I couldn't sit down the next day. One of the rules of the birthday party was that you must both pitch and catch. I'm not much of a catcher and believe me, I was glad for the cocaine on my poor little poop chute. Damn, did I hurt the next day. But I will never, ever forget my thirtieth birthday . . . and don't worry, we practiced safe sex. I don't want to die as a result of turning thirty."

"Is this what Courtney Wood has to look forward to—snorting cocaine off your part?" Frazier asked while Mandy pulled up her jaw, which had dropped.

"Doesn't look as good on a white cock."

"She doesn't know that."

"Well, I'd prefer to have sex with Courtney without drink or drugs. I'm tired of all that, and as for the, uh, creative stuff, I don't think women are as wild as men."

"I beg your pardon." Frazier was indignant. "Mandy, are you going to let that go unchallenged?"

"I sure as shit never did anything like that."

"Did you?" Kenny asked Frazier.

"No."

"So what's the wildest thing you've ever done?"

"Kenny, I haven't been very wild but not only because I am a woman, and yes, I agree, sadly, that women are repressed prisoners in their own bodies—"

Mandy jumped in. "When you're the one who carries the unwanted pregnancy it pays to be a little repressed."

"I don't know. I think it's dull. I don't want to be repressed. I want life to be a cocktail of silver, sensual pleasures but I can't do that by myself. If I ever find the right woman I intend to incinerate the sheets."

"Mandy?" Kenny was relentless.

Her voice shrank and she whispered, "The wildest thing I ever did was sit on Sean's face." She blushed.

"God, wouldn't that be absolutely, positively the best. To sit on someone's face!" Kenny shouted just as a tour of elderly people stepped into the room.

CHAPTER
41

Route 64, a four-lane interstate running east to west, filled with cars at rush hour. Like Easter eggs of bright and metallic colors, the vehicles moved along at speeds less than sixty-five miles an hour, but moved nonetheless. Frazier drove toward home.

Kenny invited both Frazier and Mandy to stay over and play in Richmond. Mandy declined because Duncan needed to be fed and let out. Frazier volunteered to pick up the Scottie and take him to her place, since Duncan, Curry, and Basil knew one another and got along fine. Mandy thrilled at the break from routine and then elected to stay, which delighted Kenny, as those two were discovering each other. Finding a friend was as exciting as finding a lover. Frazier thought of friends as family without the bullshit.

A thick mist enshrouded the city. As she passed the Hyatt she couldn't see the buildings at all. She could barely make out the exit sign for Broad Street, West. Traffic slowed even more as the translucent platinum clouds settled down farther toward earth, touching everything with a magical radiance, a sense of mystery and possibility. A sense of fender-benders was heightened also, since people often shot through the fog only to crunch into the car in front. By the time she reached the Parham Road exit the mists had lifted enough for her to see the cars coming in the opposite direction, but it was as though they carried the clouds on their rooftops. A light drizzle dotted her windshield. The dogwoods, white and pink, splashed the woods with color, and heavy-headed tulips, flaming orange, red, yellow, magenta, and white, beckoned with each sway. Life was calling. Calling to whom? Frazier felt more alone and confused than ever in her life. The only good thing she could determine from this was that in their own lopsided fashion she and Carter had drawn closer again.

"Every day I count my blessings and every day I'm a few short," she thought to herself, but then thinking again that that wasn't a hundred percent true. She had her health. She had a closer relationship with Mandy and Kenny, and Ruru had come through, but then Ruru always did. She had formed a separate peace with her father and accepted that he would never fight back against Libby. And that included not fighting back to protect her, but she had needed that from him when she was a child. Now perhaps he needed her, if Frank bothered to examine his emotional needs. So there were blessings. The nonblessings piled up like Pelion on Ossa. The only thing she could think of was something Auntie Ruru once said when Frazier was a teenager upset over losing a golf tournament. "You don't grow up until you learn to thank God for your troubles as well as your blessings."

Try as she might, Frazier hadn't reached the thankfulness stage for her current situation.

The mists shone silver now and in the opposite direction she thought she saw Andrea Bittner in a yellow Saab. Hair in a French twist, well-dressed, the driver could have been Andrea. The Volvo station wagon following the Saab had a curly-haired square-jawed man behind the wheel. Taylor Anderson. He was smoking a pipe. So did Taylor.

Galvanized by the parade of people passing her in the opposite direction, she intently stared at each driver, scrutinizing his or her features. A parade of ex-lovers, bedmates, enemies, friends, ghosts. A parade of souls, some of whom she once held to her body, some of whom she thrust away, and some from whom she ran away. Could it be? Was that the reality of relationships? They pass you in the opposite direction as people move relentlessly toward their individual destinations?

And how many lovers had she had? None, in truth. She'd slept with people, starting with a Wolf's Head man at Yale, a fine fellow, really, but just not for her. The first woman she'd slept with, a creature with shimmering black hair, majored in marine biology at the University of Miami. Furtive fucks. And fucks devoid of any technical skill. They didn't know what they were doing and Frazier certainly didn't know what she was doing except for wiggling around and wondering if any good would come of all that sweat.

Those drivers in the other lane moving into the city as she was moving out, out into the pastures and rich forests of Virginia, the mother of the nation, did they, too, stumble backwards into the future? We can clearly see the past or imagine that we do but who could see the future? And the square-jawed man you clasped to your chest tonight might awaken tomorrow to be an ordinary fellow who had a hard-on but not a heart-on. And sometimes she awakened and she was the ordinary fellow. She shot out of their apartments and homes like a greyhound out of the gate, chasing a fake rabbit.

A sense of loss engulfed her as the mists lowered again and she could no longer clearly distinguish the facial features of the people she had imagined were her lovers. Did the center hold? If people didn't stay together, then what held was the individual. If all relationships were transitory and quid pro quo, you'd better like yourself a lot because you were all you'd got. Frazier thought about this and she did like herself a lot, even though she'd never been in more pain in her three and a half decades on this planet. She may not have known shit from Shinola but she wasn't a liar. That was some kind of moral victory in this time of trickery.

But the lovers, enemies, and friends—where were they going? Did she know when she was with them? And who became her enemies? Laura Armstrong certainly. And Billy—probably. And before that, those people she had refused, or slept with and then with whom she refused to become further involved. Those clients who wanted something for nothing. She'd tangled with a few of those. Weren't enemies people with expectations you couldn't fulfill? It wasn't as if she'd set out to anger Laura or Billy. The simple act of being who she was, truly owning her own soul, disturbed them plenty. She didn't play the part they had written for her in the scenario of their lives. Perhaps they didn't know who she was, nor did they care. She was valuable when costumed and clearly enunciating her lines. As for the friends she let slip away, sometimes people grew in different directions. There were no fights, no spectacular blowups to demarcate a new and necessary barrier, no wrangling over an emotional Alsace.

Had Frazier failed somehow or did everyone feel this way? Those people passing her—did they, too, chalk up their losses, wonder if they had mistreated a friend or harshly criticized a child, or perhaps not criticized enough? How did you know? Two people slept in the same bed but had different dreams. How did you know that what you said, sensible to you, might not be misheard, misunderstood, mis-everything? Did each of us speak a private language with our own multicolored metaphors?

The traffic thinned out and the light, opaque in the silver, faltered. The mists darkened to Prussian blue and the rain slashed against the windshield. Frazier picked up speed and the faster she went, the more the raindrops sounded like bullets. A flash of lightning and a roll of thunder startled her and she understood to her bones why those ancient Greeks made a thunder god the head of the gods. The animal in her told her to run and hide. The twentieth-century woman, on the verge of the twenty-first century, told her to keep driving. She had a schedule to keep, a fax machine to check, a Scottie to pick up, phone messages to answer, and she knew, again in her bones, that it was all make-believe. The thunder was real.

CHAPTER
42

Duncan slept next to her on the passenger seat of the car. An adorable mop of black hair, he loved his Mandy. If he didn't like someone, Duncan elegantly lifted his leg on their feet. Once he was so enthusiastic in his animosity that he fell over and peed straight up in the air. Unfortunately, what goes up must come down, so Mandy rushed him into the bathroom for a good scrub.

The rain drummed a steady beat. Frazier pulled into her driveway. She still hadn't gotten used to the sight of Carter's now-repaired truck in her garage, so it gave her a start. She liked sitting high up while driving, so she was happy that she'd bought the truck after all, even though her left leg ached from shifting gears.

The dog and the cat greeted her rapturously and touched noses with Duncan. Everyone went to the bathroom quickly because they didn't like getting wet. After she'd fed her little charges Frazier went into the bathroom and removed her hoop earrings, her exquisite Cartier Panther watch, her signet ring, the crest of the Armstrong family hand-engraved in the gold, and her three-gold rolling ring, also from Cartier. When she opened her jewelry box she noticed that four pairs of earrings and one necklace were missing. A sick feeling hit the pit of her stomach and she hurried to the drawer where she kept her household cash. Untouched. Then she ran into the closet where she stacked the stereo equipment. Also untouched.

It wasn't until she entered her clothes closet and noticed that a pair of Larry Mahan ostrich boots was also missing that she began to get the picture.

"Ann, what the hell were you doing in my house and why did you take my boots and my earrings?"

A pleased-with-herself voice on the other end of the line said, with great self-righteousness, "I gave you those and I wanted them back."

"Then you can give back the Tiffany bracelet, the lapis box"—her mind raced because she couldn't remember what tokens she had tossed to Ann during their flingette (her term)—"and all the earrings I gave you, goddammit."

"You hurt me! You made me suffer and the whole town knows you're gay. This is my reward for putting up with this crap. If you play, you've got to pay." Ann was winding up for a litany of her wounds, the horrors of a relationship gone bust, when she heard a click on the phone.

Frazier hung up and dialed Brown's, the best locksmith in the area. "Hi, I know it's late but if anyone picks up this message could you meet me at my house tomorrow morning at your convenience? It's Mary Frazier Armstrong in Somerset. Thank you."

She put down the phone. After five minutes of fury she laughed at herself. "You lie down with dogs, you get up with fleas."

CHAPTER
43

The large Alfred Munnings painting graced the center of the cream-colored room. A lady riding sidesaddle on a beautiful chestnut beguiled the viewer from the center of the canvas, which, although not beige or pink, somehow gave that impression.

Frazier listed the painting at $225,000, which was fair market value. A dealer from San Francisco called and she flipped through the transparencies to find one she thought best represented the painting. She loved Munnings's work; his sense of restraint and power appealed to her as much as his tirades against modern art repelled her.

"Hey, Sistergirl," Carter hollered.

"In the center gallery."

He strode in, wearing his oldest jeans, the ones with patches on the patches. "What you doing?"

"Sending out transparencies on the Munnings."

"Where's Mandy? Can't she do that?"

"Mandy's still in Richmond with Kenny. I gave her the day off. She needed it."

"Hope she's not fucking him. Those guys are walking time bombs."

"She's not fucking him and he's had his blood tested. Negative, and it's something you ought to do, the number of people you've crawled into bed with, Brudda."

"Shit."

"I'll go with you and get tested too. Not that I've got anything to worry about."

"I have to think about it." Carter hated needles but didn't want to admit it. "Seen Dad lately?"

"No. Why?"

"Just wondered if he was in a good frame of mind."

"How can anyone be in a good frame of mind when he's married to Mother?" She tidied up the pile of transparencies.

"You've got a point there."

"Carter, spit it out, will you? You look like the cat that swallowed the canary, number one. Number two, you've come into this gallery maybe five times since I opened it."

"I've been here more than that."

"Yeah, yeah—so?"

"I left Laura."

Frazier clapped her hands together. It was involuntary. "Sorry, Carter. I don't mean to, uh, rejoice at what may be painful, but you know I've never liked that woman from the day you dragged her out of the Chi Omega house."

"What can I tell you? She unzipped my pants and my brains fell out. Anyway, I was very young." He coughed. "But I've thought it over. She'd never leave me. That's her glory, you know, so we're chained until death do us part. Someone had to go or I'd perish a drunk."

"Are you going to live with Sarah?"

"No. My lawyer says I have to keep my nose clean for six months or Laura can peel me down layer by layer, except that I've got nothing much to take." He walked over and sat heavily in a Barcelona chair along the gallery wall.

"The house still in Dad's name?"

"Yeah, that's why I want to see him."

Frazier sat next to her brother in a second Barcelona chair, the two of them looking like twins. "When did you legally separate?"

"This minute. I just came from my lawyer's office."

"You're doing the right thing, Brudda, although there are going to be some rough bumps along the way. Laura is vicious, as only a spurned wife can be vicious."

"I don't give a good goddam what she says about me. They can all talk. Hey, the Armstrongs are giving the town a real show."

Frazier snapped the fingernails of her right hand under those of her left. "Remember when we used to do that?"

"Yeah. I remember feet-to-feet the best." He smiled, recalling when they'd bound into each other's beds at night, put their feet together, and see who could push the other one off the bed. The loser usually retaliated with a pillow fight.

"You okay?" She leaned against him, bumping the chairs together. "Don't give up on love."

"I'm not giving up. I'm, uh, I don't know. I'm treading water for a while. In some ways I can't be but so mad at Laura. She thought we'd live forever after like the bride and groom on top of the wedding cake. I didn't turn out to be the most responsible guy in the world. She felt abandoned maybe, or cheated. Her response was to keep the house as clean as a museum and to take more classes. That's the deal, right? I bring home the bacon and the wife cooks it? She kept up her end of the bargain with a vengeance and I didn't do shit. And I didn't give her children. I knew I wasn't ready for fatherhood." He put his arm around Frazier's broad shoulders. "You sorry you won't marry?"

"How do you know I won't marry?"

"Seems unlikely. Probably okay with me. There isn't a man good enough for you."

"Don't brown-nose your own sister."

"True."

"What if I married a woman?"

He waited a moment, considering this new possibility. "Be okay with me but it would put Mom six feet under." He straightened up. "You know, I made fun of you when all this started but I'm not making fun now. If you want to walk down the aisle with someone, okay. Okay. I don't know if it would seem weird to me or not. Guess it doesn't matter as long as it felt right to you. I've been thinking about how wrong Sarah is. You know all the reasons but she feels right. Well, if that can happen to me, maybe what's happening to you isn't that different. Maybe it's right."

Frazier shrugged. "I don't know my ass from my elbow, except in a curious way I feel lighter."

"Think there's someone out there for you? You know what Aunt Ru says: 'There's a lid for every pot.'"

"Who would want me? Most gay people I know are so busy lying about who and what they are to people who aren't gay that they aren't going to want to be near me. I'm tainted with the truth. Tarred and feathered by honesty. Straight people are furious because I've disturbed their false picture of the universe, and gay people fear me because my actions might rub off on them and blow their cover. It's a real sinkhole, Brudda, and I'm going to spend my life alone."

"Got me."

"Is this a case of blood is thicker than water?"

"Long as we don't fight over the same girl."

"Scumbag." Frazier laughed.

He laughed in return. "You know what I forgot to tell you?"

"God, now what? Who am I accused of seducing now?"

"You heard that mess about Laura then?"

"What?"

"Oh." He plopped back against the wall.

"Tell or I'll pull the hair on your arms."

"There's a rumor that you made a pass at Laura. Believe me, I laughed when I heard that."

Frazier shot off her chair. "Jesus H. Christ on a raft. Talk about adding insult to injury. I wouldn't touch your wife, soon to be ex but not soon enough, if she were the last woman on earth."

He roared, "Neither would I."

"So what did you want to tell me?"

Carter, still laughing, choked out, "That weasel Billy Cicero is marrying Camille Kastenmeyer—like in six weeks." Frazier's mouth dropped open. Carter continued: "Heard it over at Court Square. Be in the papers, like all the papers, *The New York Times* on down, Sunday. Indecently fast is the word. I hear she's pregnant and I bet it's not by Billy."

"Who knows? But he'd like us to think he's the father."

"Unbelievable."

"Wonder if Kenny knows."

Carter hadn't thought about that. "Oh, yeah. Hurt his feelings, I bet."

"Or make him bullshit mad. What a sneaking coward Billy is. He avoids me like the bubonic plague, dumps Kenny in a skinny second, and now is ready to waltz this poor creature into a state of matrimony. Unbelievable is right."

"Maybe he'd lose his inheritance if his people knew he was gay."

Frazier snorted. "No, he wouldn't. What he would lose is his image of himself. He likes having secrets. He likes believing he's smarter than other people. If he fools them about being straight or about some business deal it means he's superior. He's twisted that way but maybe that's what lying does to the liar. It isn't that they feel bad about themselves or they'd stop. Right?"

"I guess so."

"It makes them feel smarter than other people."

"Too deep for me. I'm just trying to separate from my wife and survive."

"You will. I'm worried about the money."

A crease deepened alongside his mouth. "My money's tired—it doesn't work for me anymore." He lowered his voice. "I was hoping I could live with you for a little bit."

"Oh, Brudda, I knew you were broke when you walked through the door." She touched his big forearm. "Come on home. We can fight under the same roof again. It'll save on gas."

CHAPTER
44

The slam of the back door awakened Frazier, as it did Curry and Basil. Curry yapped and Basil shot off the bed to investigate. Frazier jumped out of bed and glanced at the lovely Cartier enameled clock on her bedstand. 7:45 A.M. Throwing her red silk robe over her shoulders, she hurried down the stairs, fearing it would be Laura just spoiling for a fight.

Worse, it was her mother.

"Where is he?"

"Asleep in the guest room."

Libby charged off toward the back of the house. "He's in this terrible state because of you. Your confession has rattled him. I just know it. He can't think straight and . . ." She reached the door to the guest bedroom and barged right in.

"Mother, leave him alone." Frazier uttered the battle cry of her childhood.

Carter lifted his head off the pillow. Upon viewing his mother in full cry he flopped it back down again.

"Wake up! Wake up and get out of here. I'll help you pack." Libby flounced to the side of the bed.

Carter groaned, then sat up, his curly blond chest hair matted against his body. "Mom, give me a break."

Libby tugged on him. "Come on. You can go home with me."

Frazier leaned against the door, wondering if her brother would fight back.

"I'm staying here."

"You can't stay here. You don't know what kind of people Frazier will bring home. It's not healthy."

"Mom, you're smoking opium." Frazier rolled her eyes but she was beginning to sizzle.

"You stay out of this. You're a bad influence on Carter. He's having a nervous breakdown. Men always leave their wives when they have nervous breakdowns and he's getting to that age." She underscored *that age*.

Carter threw back the covers and headed for the bathroom. His nakedness bothered neither mother nor sister. He called from the bathroom, "If I'm going to be blasted and beaned, at least let me have my caffeine fix."

Frazier pulled her mother by the arm off the bed.

"Let me go."

"Come into the kitchen."

Once in the kitchen and joined by Carter, Curry, and Basil, Libby escalated her entreaties. The caffeine hit her, too.

"You can't stay here, Carter. You come home or you go back to Laura. She's a good wife and she loves you. You don't know what you're doing."

He cut his gaze toward her. "I know exactly what I'm doing and I should have done this years ago. I just thank Jesus we don't have kids so I don't have to drag anyone else through the slime."

Libby glared at Frazier, radiant in the morning light and free from artifice, not a dab of makeup. "You and your damned letters. He's confused. You've got him confused. You've given him crazy ideas."

"I have not!"

"I've seen the letter." Libby triumphed.

"She doesn't miss a trick, does she?" Carter referred to his wife.

"Carter has always been the emotional one and you've been the intellectual one. You made a rude appeal to his emotions, knowing he was approaching middle age."

"I'm thirty-seven!"

"As I said." Libby relished the moment.

"Carter has never listened to me in the past. Why should he listen now?" Frazier defended herself. "Mom, you can't stand the fact that your perfect family isn't perfect. Never was but even your powers of denial are too weak for this dose of reality."

"Don't you lecture to me, missy." Libby raised her voice. She turned to her son. "She's a bad influence on you. People can't just go out and live their lives as they would wish. One makes commitments. One makes sacrifices. Frazier told you to run away in her letter, or words to that effect. You can't do that. You stay right here and you stick by Laura. She's a good wife, and let me tell you, you won't find any better."

"Then you live with her." Carter, usually able to defuse his mother's anger, became angry himself.

"Yeah, Mom." Frazier enjoyed echoing her brother.

Libby ignored her and reached over the table for Carter's big paw, which he withdrew from her touch. "Laura will take you back. She'll forget all about this woman you have on the side. Men do those things. We women know that. She wants you back and she swears to me she'll never ever mention a word of it."

"Christ, you two are a real duo." Carter pushed away his coffee cup. "Mother, I am not a particularly good specimen. I'm fresh out of money. Fresh out of patience and fresh out of prospects but I feel better than I have felt in years. Years. I will never go back to that rigid bitch. Don't even think it for one second. I hate her friggin' guts and if you don't shut up I'll soon hate yours."

Tears sprang into Libby's eyes. "How can you talk that way to me? It's Frazier's fault. She's fought me since she was little. Now she's taking you away from me. My boy wouldn't talk to me like that."

"Yes, and maybe that's why your boy drank like a fish and fornicated like Don Juan. If I'd had any balls I would have talked to you like this when I was in college. Well, it's balls to the wall now. You stay out of my life. You get off Frazier's case. If you prefer the adored Laura to either of us, fine. Just goddam shut up about it!"

Libby rose, shaking, and headed for the door. "I will not sit here and be insulted by my own son." She moved slowly and with offended dignity, expecting Carter to call her back, to sing out an apology, to ease her advertised pain. Silence greeted her stately exit.

When they heard the door slam, Frazier and Carter exhaled with relief simultaneously. When they heard the motor turn over and the crunch of stones as she backed down the driveway, their shoulders dropped.

Frazier spoke first: "I try to recall moments when she was loving."

"The thunderstorm story," Carter said. "Remember that?"

"Oh, yeah." Frazier smiled. "I was afraid of the thunder and lightning and you laughed at me."

"Actually, at the advanced age of six I think I was probably afraid too. We were out in the backyard and a storm, black as pitch, appeared out of nowhere and the wind started blowing. Mom ran out to get us and I remember lightning striking close to the house. The lightning was lavender."

Frazier did remember. "Then she told us never to be afraid of a thunderstorm because God was putting on a show for the angels. The bigger the thunderstorm, the bigger the show. The lightning was the house lights going up and down and the thunder meant the angels liked it, they were applauding."

"After that I wasn't afraid."

"Me neither. Not of thunderstorms, but I could still be afraid of Mother." Frazier sat up in her seat. "Except years later when she used to tell us about the Redington genealogy, she used to emphasize the Rachel Redington story."

"Shelling peas." Carter nodded his head. "Lightning hit the colander or the paring knife. But I didn't think the story of our ancestor's speedy demise took away from Mom's thunderstorm story. That was more proof that anything can happen—absolutely anything."

"Ah, I took it to mean: now you see her, now you don't. Funny how neither of us ever forgot it."

"Who could?" Carter changed the subject: "You know, all my life there's been some woman telling me what to do and how to do it. Sometimes I hate 'em all and other times I'm scared shitless by myself." He lifted his head and gazed at her. "You're the only person I trust."

"I'm a woman, in case you haven't noticed."

"You're my sister, and"—he blinked—"you're gay. I'm safe because you're not one of them. Sometimes I think there's this conspiracy by the entire female sex, the heterosexual ones, to weaken men and drive us down, to work us to death, to just use the living shit out of us."

"Honey, in the war between the sexes I feel like a referee. I can see both sides clearly."

He reached for a blueberry muffin. "I'm getting to know you all over again. Up until college we were best friends and then, well, you went your way and I went mine and maybe that's just the way it is. I'm kind of glad all this has happened. I haven't paid much attention to you or to anybody."

"Me too."

"Think it's the way we were raised up?" He generously applied unsalted butter to the muffin, the blueberries peeking out of the dough.

Frazier thought a long time. "In some ways it is. Let me put it this way: we were never rewarded for showing genuine emotion. Remember when Uncle Ray died? I was in fourth grade, so I guess you were in sixth, and we started to cry at the funeral and Mother got after us about that? We learned to hide everything, I suppose. Being a man you could act out, as they say, in ways I wasn't supposed to, but I think ultimately we both took our revenge on the emptiness of that. I will never be empty again. I may be on the floor wretched but I won't be empty. Anything is better than that."

"Kinda scares me."

"What?"

"Feeling the pain. That's why I love booze. Deadens the nerve endings. I can slide by." He made a sliding motion with the edge of his hand.

"Least you had lust."

"You lusted after money. Is there much difference?"

"Uh, my lusts lasted longer." She smiled.

"Yeah, but mine were more fun." He got up and started another pot of coffee. "Sis, think you would have changed if you hadn't thought you were dying? I mean, did you lie there and bargain with God—you know: 'Dear God, if you let me live I'll give myself to charity,' or something like that?"

"I've asked myself that a thousand times since. I actually think I would have made some changes but I would have taken my sweet time about them, tried to cover my ass, tried to play safe. If nothing else, I've learned that if you can't take a chance, to hell with you." Her eyes snapped.

He lifted his coffee cup in a toast.

CHAPTER

45

Like a backbeat, the steady thump of emotional turmoil kept Frazier moving fast. Her every action seemed punctuated by underlying tension. When it would surface she'd push it out of her mind and return to work.

Outside, the apple trees blossomed and the dogwoods, buds barely open, still gleamed a pale green tinged with white or pink.

Mandy, sensitive to Frazier's moods, steered clear of her today.

Laura Armstrong didn't. She swept through the front door, ignored Mandy, and charged into Frazier's office.

"How dare you!"

Frazier, bent over more transparencies, research books spread over her desk, didn't at first look up to behold the righteously enraged sister-in-law. "You'd prefer he sleep out on the street?" She waited a moment, then wickedly added as an afterthought, "Or with someone else?"

Mandy hovered at the doorway. Laura spun on her heel. "Get out of here, you snoop."

With a quickness Laura hadn't imagined, Frazier was in her face. "Don't you ever speak that way to her. Ever!"

"Oh, is she your new darling?" Laura's lip curled.

The room resounded with a crack as Frazier slapped Laura so hard a red hand-mark remained on her expertly cosmeticized face.

Mandy, now by Frazier's side, gently backed her employer away from a gasping Laura.

"Why don't you leave, Mrs. Armstrong?"

Laura, with a new target for her curdled unhappiness, spat, "Stick to your own kind."

Frazier brushed past Mandy and threw Laura against the wall. "You're sick!"

Mandy, agile and clear-headed, wedged herself between the two women. She placed her hands on Laura's shoulders and propelled her toward the front door, where she managed to get her out on the street. Two white women on the warpath was not her idea of a good day.

She returned to find Frazier quivering with rage.

"I'll kill her. I will fucking kill her."

"She wouldn't be worth going to jail for. I'd settle for permanent scarring. Or you could shoot out her kneecap."

"What?" Frazier paused in her fury.

"Shoot out her kneecaps. Imagine. No more aerobics. No more tennis lessons. She couldn't dance at country club parties anymore. She'd have to walk with a cane unless you blew out both patellas. Need a wheelchair then. You'd be sued, of course, but you wouldn't go to jail. Temporary sanity would be your plea."

Frazier, relieved by Mandy's humor and assistance, laughed. "Sanity?"

Mandy gravely nodded. "Be doing the town a favor. Actually,

slitting her tongue would be even more thoughtful. Think of the peace and quiet."

"She could write notes."

"Cut off her hands." Mandy chopped at her right hand while imagining the gush of blood, the exposed bone, the thunk as the liberated hand would hit the floor.

"Where did you come from?" Frazier sighed, filled with gratitude for this wonderful spirit in her life.

"Birmingham, Alabama, as you well know."

"Well, God bless Birmingham." Frazier reached over and embraced Mandy, then stiffened and let her go.

"You don't hug people of color?" came the sharp retort.

"Fuck you, Mandy." Frazier put her hand to her temple. She could feel the blood pounding. "No. What if someone walked by. How would it look?"

"Like two people hugging."

"Don't be purposely obtuse. If Laura said . . . what she said"— hearing her sister-in-law's voice in her mind infuriated her again— "then she'll spread it all over town, if it isn't already. That's not fair to you."

Mandy drew herself up to her full five feet two inches. "I'm a big girl. I can take care of myself and there are plenty worse things than being called a dyke."

"Such as?"

"Nigger." That hit the room like a howitzer shell. Mandy added, "Or stupid. If a woman's afraid to be called a lesbian, then she's afraid to be a woman." Mandy saw that Frazier didn't follow. "It's all part of being a woman. A wife. Girlfriend. Sister. Lesbian. A man can't be a lesbian. So what's the big deal? There really are worse things than being called a dyke."

"I think you're smarter than I am." Frazier, suddenly humbled, meant it.

"You made the millions—I didn't. I've never felt compelled to defend my femininity, if you know what I mean."

"Maybe I think too much and feel too little. You're smarter about feelings." A wave of exhaustion swept over Frazier.

"Fray, are you all right?" Mandy noticed her pallor.

"Yeah, yeah. I think I'll sit down for a minute." She slumped into a chair.

"Whatever you avoided in feelings, you're making up for it now."

"Boy, is that the truth." Frazier dropped her head back and stared at the ceiling. "Mandy, it's one damned thing after another. Mother flew in this morning, the proverbial wet hen. Accused me, in so many words, of perverting my brother. You know, he fought back. To her face. I could have kissed him. Guess I should tell him Laura was here."

"Tell him tonight."

Frazier sniffed. "Smell that?"

"Your perfume?"

"No."

"It's someone's perfume, only"—Mandy drew in air deeply—"something else. Something richer. Maybe it's Laura's scent."

"Ha! Laura never cast a scent of intrigue." Frazier stood up. "What are you wearing?"

"Jardin de Montacatini. Number VI." Mandy, with her forefinger, wrote out the Roman numerals. "What are you wearing?"

"Ysatis. The usual."

Mandy walked over and leaned close to Frazier's neck. "Very nice."

A slight shiver darted up and down Frazier's spine. "Thank you—but that's not the fragrance. There's something, uh, joyful. Do you know what I mean?"

Mandy sucked in as much air as her lungs could hold, then exhaled with a laugh. "Yes."

Laughter, a low roll like the lap of an ebb tide, soft and sweet, filled the room.

Frazier tore into the big room. Mandy followed. They both stared at the Mount Olympus painting.

"It's coming from them." Frazier pointed to the assembled gods and goddesses. "I swear it."

Mandy, at a loss to explain the extraordinary fragrance or the laughter, studied the painting. The great chiseled face of Jupiter glowed with radiance. Venus, wrapped in a golden light, smiled, a heartening smile. Juno, majestic, surveyed the other gods and goddesses. Mercury, so gorgeous and young, wings on his heels, had a devilish look on his face. Apollo, the ideal of reasonable art, plucked at his lyre. Vulcan, sweaty and huge, paused in his labors to attend to whatever his mother was saying. Neptune and Pluto, fearsome in their separate power, nonetheless exerted a masculine charisma oddly lacking in Dionysus, who exerted something sexy but not male. Diana, chaste and pure, seemed achingly young, while Athena encompassed a clarity and dignity that underscored her beauty, an unadorned beauty.

Finally Mandy whispered, "It can't be," yet even as she opened her mouth the scent was stronger and she felt an inexplicable happiness.

The telephone, that invention from the bowels of hell, broke the spell. Mandy walked into the next room to answer it. It was Harvey McIntire, president of the country club, for Frazier.

Frazier grabbed the phone. "Harvey. Hello. Are you calling to tell me I've been drummed out of the country club?"

"Uh—what?" Harvey was thrown off balance.

"Are you going to eighty-six me from the club? I mean, everyone else is on my case. And I know I'm not the only homosexual in the country club. I'm just the only person honest enough to admit it."

"Mary Frazier"—Harvey's gravely voice soothed as he spoke—"your private life is your business."

"Thank God," Frazier exclaimed in relief.

"Now, girl, don't let this get you down. I know how people can carry on in this town. Just remember it's the best fruit the birds pick at first. Let me tell you why I'm calling. This year the Dogwood Festival committee has decided to use fireworks to herald in spring, shall we say? We want to celebrate on the lawn, pretty much like the

Fourth of July, and well"—he cleared his throat—"we need the extra revenue. We're going to charge a little more for this party and the ball that follows. Black tie."

"That's a great idea."

"Would you do the honors? I know it's a last-minute call but I didn't want to involve you until I had the approval of the festival board."

"I'd be delighted."

After more chitchat Frazier hung up the phone. "Mandy?"

"Yes."

"Maybe it's not such a bad day after all. Harvey and the club are putting on a special festival with fireworks and I'm in charge, as usual."

"While you were on the phone so was I. It's a very good day. They bought the Munnings."

"Yahoo!" Frazier clapped her hands together and then in unison both Frazier and Mandy sniffed the air.

That made them laugh.

CHAPTER
46

When money leaks out of a rich person's purse he or she hopes no one sees the dribble. The word generally employed in such circumstances is *discreet*, as in "be discreet," which is what Frazier was hearing. Kelso McConchie, owner of a gargantuan estate in Orange County, a stable of show jumpers, and a wife who wasn't an easy keeper, was no longer leaking—he was hemorrhaging.

Frazier walked through the 15,000-square-foot mausoleum appraising works by Sir Edwin Landseer, Henry Alken, Jr., Jacques-Laurent Agasse, John Ferneley, J. N. Sartorius, Jr., John Wootton, Francis Sartorius, George Stubbs, Ben Marshall, Rosa Bonheur, and sculptures by Isidore Bonheur and Herbert Haseltine. As McConchie still couldn't bear to part with his nonsporting art, Frazier tactfully circumvented the issue by suggesting to Kelso that if he ever wanted to sell the Caravaggio, she thought she knew of a buyer.

On the drive home the pastures shone like emeralds, thanks to the spring rains. The dogwood dotted the forests and velvet lawns; splashes of creamy white and beguiling pink lifted the spirits. The country club picked the perfect time for a Dogwood Festival and dance. A few early azaleas were opening, the colors ranging from white to the deepest magenta. Life. Spring is life, and the tears spontaneously ran down Frazier's face as she relished the frolicsome charm of being alive.

This private rapture and humility in the face of Mother Nature's bounty vanished when the car phone rang. Not only could the invention of Alexander Graham Bell jolt you out of bed at three o'clock in the morning, take you away from dinner or an emotional conversation, it could now reach into your automobile, the last bastion of personal privacy in America. Some fools even put fax machines in their cars. Perhaps these modern conveniences made people feel in touch, as they say, able to communicate instantly with whomever they chose, but the communication was never a poem by Shelley or an elegant cartoon. It was "Meet me here" and "Pay this" or "When will the job be finished?" The fax machines and telephones escalated the demands one person made upon another, whether it be business or a wife asking you to remember to pick up the dry cleaning. The violent thrust for efficiency and more productivity came at the expense of the quiet each human being needs in order to replenish. Ultimately, the machines destroyed the people who used them, for in losing playfulness, poetry, and solitude in the mad rush for productivity and profit, people became less efficient. There were moments when Frazier felt strangled by all these electronic nooses, but her clients and other dealers expected it. Not to funnel thousands of dollars into the latest car phone, fax machine, Xerox, VHS, and high-definition television meant you were falling behind. God forbid. And if you were falling behind, maybe you weren't keeping up with trends in your profession. The logic spiraled downward from there until a person looked hangdog and who would want to do business with you?

So, both furious and disappointed at this rude interruption, Frazier picked up her car phone. Then she was really furious. Mother.

"Mary Frazier, your attitude about your brother's marriage appalls me. I do not appreciate your behavior and I especially do not appreciate you and Carter ganging up on me this morning. I am going to tell your father. I don't want to, he's got enough on his mind, but this is the limit. Do you hear me? The limit."

"Yes, Mother."

"Well?"

"Well what?"

"What do you have to say for yourself?" Libby's voice crackled as the car dipped below a small spur of the Southwest Range, a part of the Blue Ridge Mountains that lay across Orange County like a long rat's tail.

By the time Frazier replied, the transmission was clear. "I have nothing to say, other than Carter should have left that bitch years ago."

"What a way to talk about your sister-in-law, who is one of the nicest people—why, everyone in the Garden Club adores Laura."

"Mother, I haven't liked her from the day Carter brought her home. You like her and I don't. You're not going to change my mind—well, actually, the only person who could change my mind is Laura. And I sure know I'm not going to change your mind."

A small pause on the other end gave evidence that Libby was firing up her pistons. "You people don't believe in marriage. That's the root of the problem with Carter. You're swinging him your way."

"My people?"

"Gay people. Just flit from one person to another. I know all about these things."

"How wonderful. I have a mother who's an expert on queers."

"You people have different values. No permanence to the relationships. No marriage papers. That's what's going on."

"Might I remind you, Mother, that every gay person comes from a straight home. If you have a problem with my values, then you'd better examine your own. And I happen to believe in marriage with all my heart and soul, for your information."

"I made you gay? I knew you'd get around to that. Everyone blames the mother. A criminal goes on a killing spree. Who was his mother? Did she drink and beat him? Oh, I knew you'd sink this low. I can't wait to hear how I made you a, a—I can't say that word. I hate that word."

"Lesbian? I'll spell it for you. L-e-s-b-i-a-n." Actually, Frazier didn't much like the word either. A dolorous quality attached itself to it. Perhaps it was the number of syllables or too many consonants. *Gay* pleased her. It had a frivolous, lighthearted quality and it made her laugh, especially when she thought of the opposite of gay—grim. Maybe she'd start calling straight people grims, or how about dire straights? If people wanted to start name-calling, then everyone might as well do it. Turnabout is fair play.

"You think you're above it all," Libby growled.

"I'm not blaming you. I am what I am. To me it's the difference between being right-handed and being left-handed. I'm left-handed in a right-handed world. Simple as that. But you could use your left hand if you had to and I can certainly use my right. Nothing is ever as clear as we think it is."

"You are telling me, your mother, that I could be a, a you-know-what?"

"Only if you're lucky." That was a smart-mouthed thing to say but Frazier was steaming.

"Are you trying to make your brother one too?" Libby's voice was ice-cold.

"No, Mom, only you could do that." Frazier argued against her original point, which she truly believed, but at this moment she felt like hurting her mother.

"You said just the opposite. What's the matter with you?"

"Wanted to get your goat. Because I am sick of this, Mother, absolutely, positively *sick* of this!"

"Everything in this family was fine until you had to go and tell. Why couldn't you keep it to yourself? We don't need to know."

"I thought I was dying. Hell, I thought I was doing you and everyone else a favor by being honest for a change. Honesty is the best policy, and didn't you tell me that over and over as a child?"

"This is different!"

"No, it isn't. You either love me as I am or you don't love me at all. And maybe that's my lesson, too. I'm not going to change anyone unless it's myself. So if you or Carter or Mandy are in my life, then I take you as I find you."

Libby switched tactics and hit the offense button again. "Are you sleeping with Mandy? Have you converted her?"

Frazier saw red. *"No!"*

"She's extremely beautiful for one of those people. And wouldn't it be like you to compound the problem by taking up with a person of another race? Miscegenation may be off the law books, my dear, but it certainly exists as a social concept. You can't go about breaking every rule in the book."

"Mother, you are so vile I can't even reply to that flowering"—she passed a huge dogwood—"of racism."

"If God meant for us to be one color, we would be. To each his place. You haven't answered the question."

"You have no right to my life, but no, I am not sleeping with Mandy. I haven't even thought about it and to tell you the God's honest truth, Mother dear, I think she's too good for me, apart from the fact that she has never given any indication of liking women physically."

"Too good for you?" Libby was baffled.

"Yes. She's true blue, she's kind, and there's no falseness to her. She just puts it right out there, Mother—rather the opposite of you and me."

A long silence followed this revelation. "If you want to ruin your life, so be it. Leave Carter alone."

"I love him."

"Then let me ask you this. Do you love me at all?" Libby demanded. Love sounded like a balance due being called in by a solicitor.

Now it was Frazier's turn to be silent. She noticed that her foot was heavy on the accelerator and she eased off. Was she really committed to the truth? Then she had to tell it. "No. No, Mother, I don't love you and I haven't loved you for many years, but I thank you for all that you have done for me. I don't think any child can ever pay back the work that a parent does for her."

"That's all I wanted to know." Libby hung up the phone.

As Frazier turned left at Somerset store, heading down Route 231, her mind boiled over. She couldn't know what it was to be a mother, although perhaps, if fortunate, she would find out someday. Frazier loved children but would only consider being a mother herself if she was in a long-term relationship and if the father was a dear friend. Billy crossed her mind. He was going to be a father. How curious. She wondered if it would change him.

Frazier couldn't know the trials she'd inflicted upon her mother: the vases broken, the chicken pox, the golf lessons, the broken leg, the orthodontist, the ferrying back and forth to private school, the absurd recitals, the constant call for clothing and new this and new that, and worst of all, the constant interruptions with those childish voices piercing the quiet, "Mommy—" How could she know? She hadn't been awakened in the middle of the night with a kid throwing up all over the bedroom. She hadn't taught a child to skate or endured slumber parties or the steady flow of teenaged boys as they courted her daughter. Nor had she hauled herself out of bed Sunday morning after a Saturday night dance at the club to make certain the family went to church on time. At all these sacrifices Libby excelled. And for these sacrifices Frazier felt gratitude.

Before hearing the shadowing wings of Death's vulture she hadn't given much thought to what her parents had done for her, other than the knee-jerk response in public to thank them. She was reexamining everything, everyone, and, most of all, herself.

Libby did everything just right. She was the perfect mother, except that she never sat and listened to either child. Oh, she was harder on Frazier than on Carter but that was to be expected. Libby wanted external results, children praised by her friends. She didn't want to know her children as people. They were display objects, further proof of her prowess as wife, mother, and lady. For Libby, everything was an extension of herself, and Frazier had picked up on that while she was tiny. She couldn't have understood it but she had felt it. Now she understood it. Libby physically did everything just right but she never loved her children—not real, accepting, nurturing love. She probably didn't have it to give, and what Frazier felt she needed to do was forgive her mother. Libby might be able to be more open, to be giving, but that was Libby's struggle, a struggle she seemed to sidestep or ignore. Or maybe her mother was so far away from her own self she didn't even know how empty she was.

As Frazier pulled into her driveway and saw Curry's and Basil's faces in the window she realized those two furry creatures had given her more love than her mother had ever given her. Maybe her examples of goodness in this life ought to include her cat and her dog. Maybe she should strive to be more like them and less like a human. At any rate, she knew she didn't want to be like her mother and she prayed that she could forgive her mother. It sounded easy enough but it was proving ferociously difficult.

If Libby and Frank proved templates, her primary examples, she feared her own ability to love. Forgiving her mother was going to have to take a distant second to reaching down in there and trying to make a place in her heart and her life for other people. She'd spent three decades steeling herself against people, hiding, and not just because she was gay. She trembled at the thought of being inadequate even more than at the prospect of being hurt. But those infernal letters had taught her who did love her and that was a beginning. Surely, she had done something right in this life and she was going to have to learn to do more.

CHAPTER
47

A thin blue line of smoke hovered in the air over the heads of Frank Armstrong, George Demerius, Pickens Oliguy, Randy Milliken, and Larry Taylor. With the exception of Larry, in his late thirties, all the men smoked, but then Larry also didn't drink, worried about high cholesterol, and wore sneakers. He'd spent too much time out of Virginia, but on the positive side he evidenced a sharp business mind.

The temperature dropped rapidly as yet another cold front whirled in from the west, blustery clouds visible even in the fading light. Frank glanced out the restaurant windows and wished he were closer to home. He'd be driving forty-five minutes in whatever rolled in behind those clouds.

Lately his mind wandered in and out of the moment. He'd find himself vividly alert, interested in his immediate surroundings and the conversation, and then he'd be back decades, standing in front of the sagging chain-link fence where he first set up business. He could smell the oil that he laid down over the dusty bluestone. He could feel the worn gears grind under his feet when he shifted the ancient dump truck. He felt the energy that filled his young body. He worked morning, noon, and night. He'd walk down the driveways of people he didn't know to ask if they wanted a load of stone or if they wanted to move up to asphalt. Yes, it was much more expensive, but depending on the quality you put down, it lasted seven to fifteen years and he would guarantee it. He patched holes for free. He sweated in the sultry Blue Ridge summers and he shivered in the raw frost of countless gray winters. He plowed out neighbors' driveways in the snowstorms for nothing. He lent equipment to struggling friends. He gladly shared his experience with other paving men and he soaked up whatever they could tell him too.

The years sped by until, like Sambo's butter, they ran together in a golden path. He remembered Frazier taking her first baby steps. He remembered Carter's tree house, which he'd helped him build. He especially remembered Frazier's last high school lacrosse game, but when he thought of his children he could recall only isolated incidents. Yet when he thought of his business he could recall the color of the ink on his first set of books. The day Mildred, in a crisp sundress, knocked on the ramshackle building by the Rivanna River, the steam floating up even though the hour was 8:30 A.M. He remembered her perfume on that August morning and although he never made love to the woman—hadn't really thought of it—he came to realize he loved her more than anyone, other than his daughter, on the face of the earth. Why? Because she learned to love the paving business too.

Not content to do just the books, Mildred started to go out on bids. She studied the various surfaces one could use and she studied soils. She learned good grading of roads from so-so. She inspected culverts, drove trucks when a man called in sick, and still got out the bills on time as well as the correspondence.

Armstrong Paving became their baby. Frank was amazed that he didn't realize this until his sixth decade. Was he abominably slow or were men dumb about these things?

The major disappointment in his life also centered around Armstrong Paving, for he had built the business to pass on to his son. Carter seemed bored shitless by it. Frazier adored it but Frank had been too much a product of his era when his daughter was young. He discouraged her. Now, well, why kick himself in the pants? Frazier would have turned Armstrong Paving into a multistate empire. But she shot off on her own path and built her own business. She loved her business as much as Frank loved his. In his heart he knew Frazier forgave him for his conventional thinking. He was beyond that today. Unbeknownst to his wife, he'd willed the business to both his children, with the proviso that Frazier run the company. If she couldn't run Armstrong Paving and her gallery simultaneously, she'd find the right candidate to steer the ship while she set the course.

Libby, well provided for in the terms of his will, wouldn't even notice what became of the goose that laid her golden egg. His wife never once asked him one question about his business. Libby didn't know a dump truck from a bulldozer, or bluestone from crush-or-run.

The excitement of building his business from the ground up so occupied Frank that he didn't realize he was quite alone, emotionally, until two years into the marriage. Then the children came and they held him. Of course he would have stayed no matter what. Frank believed that when you married there was no back door. If you made a bad bargain, then you made the best of it. Perhaps he wasn't so wrong in marrying Libby. She was a beautiful woman. She knew how to work a party. She happily organized social gatherings for his clients and peers. That she could spend $2,000 on floral arrangements alone stunned him but she explained that this was her form of dump truck: one needs the right equipment to get the job done. In her way Libby had been a partner, socializing for the business. Perhaps the only foolish thing in marrying Libby was in believing that she would love him for himself. She didn't. She wouldn't. She couldn't. Frank was loved because he was a provider.

He swept his deep, clear eyes around the table and wondered if these men, most of whom he had known at least thirty years, felt the same way? Did they think of it at all?

And why was he suddenly pulled into his past, swirling backwards in an emotional wind-devil? He had lived a good long life but only now was he beginning to understand his life and himself.

Perhaps men grow reflective in their sixties. A glance at George Demerius's wobbling chin disabused him of that notion. Frazier's revelation fired Frank to examine himself. While she was sick, the terror at the possibility of losing his beloved child sent him to his knees before God Almighty. That was a lesson but her incredible shift was another. The lesbian stuff baffled him but what affected him was her change in attitude. Cool, aloof Frazier was becoming direct, emotional, and spoiling for a fight. She'd sent Libby into the strato-sphere. He wouldn't mind sending Libby there himself. If his daughter could change, he could change.

"Then this sumbitch says to me, 'You sent in the wrong form.' The wrong form? I was building off-ramps before this toad got his first hard-on!" Pickens expostulated.

Frank drifted back into the conversation. "People who work for the government, whether it's federal, state, or local, don't live in the real world, Pickens. They've even got a form for when they can get a hard-on, how many hard-ons they're allowed in one twenty-four-hour period, with whom they can get a hard-on, and to whom they should complain if the hard-on isn't sufficiently satisfactory."

Randy laughed. "Sounds like a bunch of dickheads to me."

"The women are bowheads," Larry Taylor chimed in.

"Bowheads?" George asked.

Larry spread his hands out behind his head. "Yeah. Haven't you ever noticed that the higher up they go in the bureaucracy, the bigger the bow? They start out as toddlers with little pink or yellow bows, plaid for Christmas. Then in grade school they wear sparklers. In junior high they use those little terry-cloth things, and by high school they use black silk, or some kind of silk. The kind of bow a woman puts on her head tells you what she expects from life and whether or not she'll give you a blow job. Bowheads."

"No shit." Pickens scratched his own head.

"What does it mean if a woman doesn't have a bow in her hair?" George wondered.

"Can't be in the government without a bow." Larry smiled. "But if she's a civilian and she doesn't have something stuck up there she's probably a little on the wild side, you know, especially in Virginia."

"Hey, I want to know that girl." Randy clapped his hands.

"What I want to know is what kind of bow means she'll suck my cock?" Pickens returned to the more important subject.

"I'm not telling. Otherwise you'll be bird-dogging my quail, buddy."

This elicited a huge round of appreciative laughter.

Pickens shouted above the laughter, "Hey, you know the difference between a bitch and a whore?" The other men shook their heads, so he continued: "A whore does it with everybody. A bitch does it with everybody but you."

Frank ran his fingers through his hair, a nervous gesture. He couldn't help but laugh. When you got down to brass tacks the tension between men and women called for some kind of relief. Then again, what was offensive? What was offensive to women didn't seem all that bad to men. He reckoned he'd never figure it out.

"Back to the prick—I mean no-prick—who fried your ass about the correct forms for the bid," Randy said. "What did you do?"

"Sent my girl down for the correct form. See, that's what pissed me off. I did have the correct form but the state has changed it slightly in the last year and this is the newer form. The changes are so small you need a magnifying glass to find them."

"Asshole." George clipped the word.

"Yeah, but he's an asshole with job security," Frank added. "Why the hell do you think those people can act the way they do and treat people the way they do? Ever look at the qualifications for those low-level state jobs? Not one of us at this table would hire one of those people to work in our companies." He placed his knife across his plate. "Now the higher-ups, maybe. If nothing else, they've learned how to climb and whose ass to kiss. In this world that amounts to genius."

"You got that right, brother." George nodded.

"What really rips it for me"—Randy shifted his weight in his seat—"is that those guys down at the highway department know repaving an off-ramp in Louisa County is a six-hundred-thousand-dollar job and I don't care who does it."

Larry Taylor quietly got up and walked out of the room. The other men barely noticed as they continued to rag on about the state highway department, the state government in general, and finally, what were the Orioles going to do this year? Clearly that was the premier subject.

An hour passed before George asked, "Where's Larry?"

CHAPTER
48

The dismal answer to "Where's Larry Taylor?" came the
next morning before ten o'clock, when Frank Armstrong
received a phone call from the Virginia State Corporation
Commission concerning price fixing. Mildred's face drained of color
when Frank relayed to her how he had gotten together for dinner
with George Demerius, Pickens Oliguy, Larry Taylor, and Randy
Milliken in the beautiful little town of Orange. Nothing had seemed
unusual except that Randy Milliken spent half the night bitching
about filling out forms for the state highway department. Each of
them had bid on repaving the Louisa off-ramp on I-64 and Randy
mentioned that he thought it was a $600,000 job, whoever did it.
Larry had left the table.

"He obviously left the table to call the appropriate department to report price fixing." Mildred rubbed her temples with her thumbs. "Damn, what's the matter with him?"

Frank perched on the corner of her desk. "I don't know. I've built a good business and a good reputation. Larry knows I wouldn't engage in price fixing and with Randy, well, he was hot, a slip of the tongue. No more than that."

"Sounds like Larry Taylor's a real Boy Scout. Probably carries a copy of the Ten Commandments and the United States Constitution in his back pocket."

"Well, I wouldn't exactly call him a flexible person." Frank rubbed his chin. "Mildred, get me George on the phone. Let's see what he thinks."

"Hold the phone away from your ear."

"Why?"

"Because it'll melt." Mildred began dialing.

Frank walked into his small office and picked up when Mildred hollered, "George."

"I'll kill that cocksucker! He's out of his fucking mind! I'll swoop down on him from twelve o'clock and blow him out of the sky."

"Have you talked to him? I haven't called yet."

"I've been calling that sorry son-of-a-bitch since I took the goddam call from the commission this morning, hell, not an hour and a half ago. I mean, shit, I walk into the office and the phone is ringing. My girl isn't here, so I pick it up. Under investigation for improper conduct of bidding procedures. Or some such bullshit. I demanded to know who would do anything like this, you know, and then I got that clear, like crystal clear, so I call the asshole and he isn't available for comment. Not only is he a walking hemorrhoid, he's a chickenshit too!"

"Once the first domino falls, there isn't anything we can do," Frank said, half to himself.

"You got that right. The commission will investigate. Depositions up the wazoo. Hearings behind closed doors, supposedly to protect us, but it won't stay closed for long. Never does, good buddy, never does."

"Guess I'll call my lawyer." Frank sighed. It wasn't just the money that depressed him; it was the colossal waste of time.

"Milliken's doing the same and Pickens is out on a site. Poor bastard probably don't know what hit him yet. If you hear from them before I do, call me back."

"Sure thing."

"You know what I'm going to do?" George launched in. "I'm getting old, Frankie. I worked hard and I may not be the smartest guy in the world but I did pretty good. I believed this was the land of opportunity, and I emphasize *was*. Now you can't even take a shit but what somebody's going to scream, 'Is it ecologically sound?' Know what I mean?"

"Yeah, I do. It's harder and harder to do business."

"I'm not, anymore. This is the straw that breaks the camel's back. I'm selling out. I know I won't get what my business is worth in these times but I ought to get enough to retire, and Lorraine and I are going to Arizona. I've had it."

"I understand." Frank felt weariness wash over him.

"Frank, get out while the gettin's good."

"I can't do that, George. I want to leave my business to my kids. Frazier is a quick study, you know."

"I have no doubt of that but it's a matter of time before this gets into the papers. Paving cartel, old boys' network, greedy businessmen—you know what I mean? Shit, I fought in Korea. I've paid enough taxes to build an interstate between Richmond, Virginia, and Louisville, Kentucky—you know what I mean? Not only will this suspend business for a while"—he stepped on the word *suspend*—"those press nancyboys will ruin my good name. And you know what? Even if we're cleared there will forever be shit sticking to our names because some pissant thought he heard us discussing bids. Look, I could wring Randy's neck right now but he mentioned a ceiling price. He didn't actually pin down his bid, nor did anyone else pick up the ball—you know what I mean?"

"I do and I hope this will be cleared up during the investigation."

"Cleared up or not, we'll be dragged through the mud and I'm out of here."

"George, I'm sorry to hear that but I understand."

"Hey, buddy, cover your ass."

Frank pressed the disconnect button, then dialed his lawyer. She advised him to say "No comment" when the papers called—and they would. She also told him to meet her for lunch.

When Frank finished with Barbara he walked back into Mildred's office. "I've got to meet Barbara Garrick for lunch."

Mildred rolled her chair back. "She's a killer. She learned at her Daddy's knee."

"Yeah." Frank remembered Weed Garrick, Barbara's father, who had been his lawyer until he died suddenly of a massive coronary. "You know what George said?" He paused a second. "He's selling out. He says he's worked too long and too hard for this shit. He and Lorraine are moving to Arizona."

"Too hot."

"Yeah."

"What are you thinking, Frank?" Mildred peeped over her half-moon glasses at her beloved boss.

"I'm thinking that when it rains it pours."

CHAPTER
49

The black penumbra of asphalt surrounded the shopping-center buildings, threatening to eclipse their brightness. As it was an off time, the dark surface showed more than usual. There weren't many cars to cover it.

Frazier noticed it and, being a paving contractor's daughter, roughly figured in her head what it would cost to pave this parking lot retail. Her father often didn't take a fee for such work but rather a percentage of shop rentals over a period of ten or fifteen years. This kept money flowing in instead of arriving in huge chunks from big jobs that would blow apart his taxes for that year. Frank Armstrong would never cheat on his taxes but he would never pay more than he had to either. This technique he passed on to his daughter.

Frazier rolled out her cart of groceries, a shopping long overdue.

Lingering over the artichokes with the girls wasn't her idea of fun, so Frazier put off the chore until the cupboards were bare.

Out of the corner of her eye she had seen Laura Armstrong and Ann Haviland in their aerobic togs, wearing neon-colored visors with the country club logo slicked on the front. They hadn't seen her yet and if possible she would scoot out of there before they did. Ann's snarls irritated her but Laura's sanctimonious attitude about Carter, marriage, and womanhood gagged her.

Mandy had told her at work today that Ann had pitched many a public fit over Billy's engagement. How convenient. She could mime heterosexual drama with no heterosexual pain, and declaring that Billy had broken her heart spared her dating men for perhaps six months. As it was, Ann had dated Billy three whole times after Frazier's letters. Apparently this was enough for a delicious intimacy in the public's mind, an intimacy drummed up by Ann, the born-again heterosexual.

Frazier wondered what woman she was busily seducing now. It couldn't be Laura. Not even Ann would step on that buried land mine. Besides, who would want to crawl between the sheets with someone that bitter? Also, rolling around like that might break Laura's hair. A major tragedy.

Frazier had lied about her sexuality before the hospital stay. She was now ashamed of her cowardice but she was also learning to forgive herself. Ann, cut from a different cloth, actually relished the drama of being gay. She employed the secret language so as to speak to a member of the tribe right under the noses of the enemy. Ann would whisper to Frazier, "So-and-so is a friend of Bertha's," or "She worships at our church." The excitement in her voice proved her need to participate in the subterfuge. Who knows, who doesn't, who will, who won't. It was all so terribly important. The weekend binges at safe places sequestered from hostile eyes and disapproving attitudes provided the very fuel for Ann's life. Being gay added glamour to an otherwise listless life. Maybe the only thing remarkable about Ann was that she was gay. If homosexuality were accepted, out in the open, the Anns of this world would feel robbed of their furtive thrills, their specialness. The lure of the forbidden attracted Ann even as it repelled Frazier.

Caravaggio excited Frazier. Not who was and who wasn't. She hadn't the time for information breathed sotto voce, for well-manicured women leaning over and saying, *"Contra nous,"* when they meant to say *"Entre nous,"* et cetera, et cetera. She never gave a big rat's ass about who was straight and who was gay. Frazier always figured that if you were happy about yourself, if you had a decent sex life, you didn't have the time to worry overmuch about what anybody else was doing and to whom they were doing it. In that respect she found most people, regardless of persuasion, sorry little creatures, bored with their lives, desperately hoping that someone had hot sex somewhere and then resenting the hell out of them for having it. They were like hungry children with their noses pressed up against the bakery windowpane until in anger they smashed the windows.

Frazier felt no responsibility whatever for any other human being's sexual misery. One might not be able to vault out of the ghetto, one might not be able to climb the corporate ladder, there were countless might-nots, but surely one could improve one's own sex life, one's own emotional life, without having to destroy someone else's happiness.

Frazier clung to a vain hope because as she reached her Explorer, both Laura and Ann bore down upon her, twin avenging Furies.

"You tell my husband that if he doesn't straighten up and fly right I'll take him for every penny he's got," Laura seethed. What happened to the long-suffering wife routine?

"Tell him yourself." Frazier opened the driver's door.

"After all that you've done to your family and your friends"— Ann's voice filled with tinny righteousness—"the least you could do would be to help Laura and to help Carter too. He's at a crisis point. He needs his wife and family."

"I am his family." Frazier slid into the driver's seat and closed the door.

Ann rapped on the window. Frazier ignored her and pulled out. In her rearview mirror she could see the two of them, heads together, their brightly colored visors nearly touching. They looked like two chickens picking over a succulent Japanese beetle.

CHAPTER
50

"I thought this was the Rolls-Royce of wheelbarrows." Mandy wobbled behind the laden piece of equipment.

"It is. It's got two front wheels and it's perfectly balanced," Frazier replied.

Mandy set her burden down. "Well, it weighs a ton."

"Here." Frazier grasped the two wooden handles and easily lifted up the wheelbarrow, rolling it toward her outer flower beds. The rich topsoil exuded a pleasing fragrance to a gardener.

"I forget how strong you are." Mandy bent over and picked up the tools scattered by the back door, the dog and cat racing in circles around her. "I'll be glad when we get more light. This weekend."

"Me too. I can work outside up till nine at night. I love the long soft evening light." She set down the wheelbarrow and took the shovel Mandy handed her. "I'll spread a thin layer on what I've dug up here. See, you've got to work the fertilizer down into the ground. That's why I try to get old man Hitchcock to come over with his plow and disc it for me but the weather has been so bizarre he's behind in everything. Didn't hurt me to turn it up by hand."

"'Cept for the blisters."

"And that was with gloves." She tossed the brown earth over her rectangular beds. These were the fall beds, which by mid-July would be putting forth early mums, the huge mums, and the zinnias that heralded the end of summer.

Lines of marigolds alternated with grass strips between the rows of her vegetable garden. The fall flower beds bordered her backyard at the sides. The rear was a two-foot stone wall with a white gate set in the middle.

"This is about as quiet a weekend as either of us has had in a long time," Mandy said as she raked over the new soil.

"My mother's no longer speaking to me, so that helps. Carter took off with Sarah Saxe for Nags Head. Kenny's in New York and Auntie Ru, to whom I spoke at the crack of dawn, is tending her own garden. Apart from them no one else calls me anymore. I guess I'm both freed and abandoned."

"I'm glad your business doesn't depend on this place."

Frazier heaved a big shovelful. "And not just for the obvious reasons. People here are tight as ticks. Try raising money for charity."

"It is odd."

"Plantation mentality."

"Huh?" Mandy paused a moment.

"In the old days you took care of your people. Why take care of anyone else's? Giving to strangers isn't part of our heritage. That's not the best explanation but it's the only one I have, because I can't say that I've found my people to be ungenerous in other fashions."

"Funny how ways hang on long after the means." Mandy wiped her neck with a kerchief, which she stuck in her back jeans pocket. "Are you getting used to it? Being iced out, I mean?"

"Yeah. I'm learning to live with quiet—and you know something? It's a good thing."

"You're better about it than I would be," Mandy said truthfully.

"Oops." Frazier turned up a bulb and sank to her knees to dig a hole for it. As she smoothed over the bulb with her two hands she felt the cool grains of soil slip between her fingers. This was the source of all wealth, good soil. In this part of the world about the best one could hope for was Davis loam. But Frazier had seen the rich black earth of Iowa, the endless fertile prairies of America. She stood up. "Mandy, if we ever forget what made this country great we deserve to fail, you know. It's the earth, the rivers. We're so rich we could be the breadbasket for the world."

"You and my momma." Mandy broke up a clod. "For the record, I think you're taking this, uh, change remarkably well."

"Maybe I figured out I needed to do this myself. No point in bitching and moaning and pointing the finger at other people. This was my own work and I had gotten so far away from *me* I suppose only a major mess and a half would force me to do something about it. You know, Mandy, my mind was like a suitcase with the clothes haphazardly tossed in, then slammed shut because I was in a rush to some destination—only I didn't really know where I was going. If I hadn't gotten sick, if I hadn't written those letters, I probably wouldn't have thought about the nature of my life, the course of my actions, until I was old. I believe people can change at any age, but how much better to do it now. At least the second half of my life is going to be richer than the first half. When I laugh now it's from my belly and not those polite little gurgles in the throat, you know."

"Uh-huh." Mandy wiped her hands. "Think Carter can change?"

"He's trying but he doesn't have as much to work with. I don't mean that in an ugly way but, well . . ."

"I know. Maybe it's the way men are raised or maybe it's Carter, but my experience with men is they won't do any emotional work unless a woman is there to pull them through it: Mommy, the wife, the lover, whoever. It must be awful to be so dependent on women. Would sure make me hate women."

"Never thought of it like that." Frazier dumped out the last of the soil. "Once this divorce is final I hope he's got the guts to go or get serious about a career."

"Yeah, me too. Think he'll stick with Sarah?"

"She's good for him and she's real. He's gotten pretty far away from his own self, too. How does that happen, Mandy? I look around me and I don't see all that many people who are their true selves."

"*Authentic selves* is what the therapists call it."

Frazier, who didn't know bugfuck about therapy, stopped and considered the term for a moment. "Whatever you call it there's not a hell of a lot of it. I don't think my mother has ever had an authentic emotion in her life. As for Dad, well, he gave in to her so long ago it probably doesn't matter anymore. Maybe in your sixties you forget." She spoke with a sudden vehemence: "God, I hope not. I love my dad even if she has whipped up on him. He's weak that way but he deserves to be happy. Carter too. I want him happy."

"Families. We're so different and so alike. It's the source of every deep sorrow and rage we feel but if there's any kind of strength it comes from that same bunch of people. I love my momma and my daddy. I can tolerate my two sisters occasionally. Oh, I love them, I guess, but I'm damn glad everyone stayed in Birmingham. I couldn't have them around me like you do. Why'd you come back here?"

Frazier smiled and pointed to her feet. "The answer's underneath you. I'm like Antaeus. If my feet can touch this Virginia soil I'm indestructible. If you lift me up, the way Hercules did Antaeus in the wrestling match—'course he had some help; a goddess told him what to do, since he was losing, but when he lifted the Titan over his head Antaeus could no longer receive nourishment from Mother Earth and he weakened and was defeated. I have to have this, Mandy. I have to have this earth and I have to have those paintings. I don't have to own them but I have to find them, research them, know the painter's history, and then find a home for them. Painting, sculpture, music, literature—it's the best that other people have left for us. No matter what I did to myself I clung to that, you know. There was some kind of emotional intelligence at work within me, no matter how frail."

"Maybe it's the same—the earth and art. They both feed us—one the body; the other the mind. And I know right about now you're going to tell me how lucky we are, and I know we are, but my back hurts and I want to sit down."

And so she did. She sat under the baby green buds of a sweet gum tree and watched as Frazier kept working. And Mandy wondered how it must have felt for her ancestors to work land they would never own. The more she thought about it, the more she realized that different as her journey was from Frazier's, here they were in the same place, at the same time, with the sun shining like a beacon of joy on their heads in Somerset, Virginia.

CHAPTER
51

"Will you back me up if I bring Sarah to the Dogwood Festival?" Carter asked.

"Yes, but I'll be running the fireworks. If the shit hits the fan on the club lawn there's not a lot I can do," Frazier warned him.

"Laura and Mother will be joined at the hip." He rubbed the blond stubble on his chin. It was seven in the morning and he hadn't yet shaved.

"So what else is new?"

Carter grunted. The phone rang. "Who in the hell?"

Frazier picked up. "Hello. Aunt Ru, what's the matter?" She listened intently, then paused. "Carter, put on your shoes and run down to the mailbox."

"Why?"

"Just do it!" As he obeyed, Frazier listened to her aunt, in a total fury. "It's fantastic."

"How can they do this to him?" Ru fought back tears.

"Auntie Ru, until I read the article I can't say much except it sounds like lies to me. Have you called Dad?"

"No. He doesn't get up until seven-thirty, but I will call him before that nosebleed sits down to her morning coffee and orange juice, flops open the papers, and has a *grand mal* seizure. Just fry her creativity." Ru displaced some of her hurt and anger onto Libby, a handy target regardless of the circumstances.

"Mother's very creative. I just wish she'd express it in ways other than mental anguish. Uh, here's Carter."

"My God!" Carter handed Frazier the paper, the Central Virginia section. As she also took the *Richmond Times Dispatch*, he leafed through that and found offending material there as well.

Frazier quickly scanned the paper. "Oh, my God."

"Sistergirl, there's some here too." He shoved over the Richmond paper.

"Ru, it's in the Richmond paper too."

"My brother never so much as overcharged a customer in his life. He's the most upright and decent man I have ever known, just like our daddy, and I will wring the neck of the sorry son of a bitch who did this to Frankie. I'll kill!"

Frazier continued reading. "I'll help you."

"Improper procedures—what? They're accusing him of monopoly. They're accusing him of—"

"Price fixing. Poor Daddy. Poor Daddy." Frazier felt helpless, then tried to crank over her brain—hard, since she needed her tea. As if reading her mind Carter poured steaming water onto a teabag, sliding the cup to her. She grabbed his hand and held it for a moment. "Auntie Ru, you'd best tell Pop. When you've spoken to him ring me twice and hang up. Then I'll call. By eight o'clock everyone he wants to talk to and everyone he doesn't will have read this story and the phone lines will melt. Okay?"

"Okay."

"And Auntie Ru, you show up at the country club tomorrow night for the Dogwood Festival. I'll be damned if we'll hide away. It's all hands on deck."

"I'll be there with rings on my fingers and bells on my toes. Bye-bye, honey."

Carter passed a plate of glazed doughnuts to her. She waved them away and sipped her tea in fierce concentration. He was morose. "Guess I'd better not ask Dad for a loan now."

"You should never ask him for a loan anyway."

He shifted uneasily in his seat. "I've never been as smart as you."

"Bullshit. Anyway, Carter, Dad might be needing our money—"

"Your money," he interjected. "I haven't got any."

She sat down opposite him. "This could really hurt his business, and the recession has cut into him pretty deep as it is. Carter, we might have to go to work for Dad for a while."

"You'd be crazy to do that." He sat up straight in his chair. "You make a bloody fortune doing what you do, and good as Mandy is, she doesn't have your contacts or your eye."

"Well, thanks, but we can't let Daddy go under."

"Listen, if it's that bad, Auntie Ru can work with me. Damn, she's not afraid to break a sweat and I can operate that heavy equipment. It's been a while but I'll remember it soon enough."

"So you will help?"

"Yes—if he'll let me." That was the easiest decision Carter ever made in his life, and if someone had asked him about such an event even yesterday he would have been tortured by weighing both sides of the issue, by his thorny relationship with his father, by remaining close, geographically, to that *vagina denta* Laura.

The phone rang twice. Frazier jumped up and dialed Dad. Carter stood up and walked over behind her.

"Mom, may I speak with Dad, please?"

"This is a disaster!" Libby wailed. "No, he's trying to eat his breakfast and you'll only upset him more."

Carter, his ear close to the phone, heard this and yanked the phone out of Frazier's hand. "Mother, get Dad on the phone right now."

As her adored child had only once before spoken to her in such anger, Libby, presumably in a state of shock, handed the portable phone to her husband. Carter handed the phone back to Frazier.

"Daddy—are you all right?"

Frank swallowed a mouthful of food. "This is a tempest in a teapot. It will work out. Don't you worry about me."

"I am worried about you. You're a wonderful businessman, Dad, and this is just . . . ridiculous. I want to help."

"You can help me by taking care of yourself, and then I'll have only one child left to worry about."

Carter heard that. Frazier quickly replied, "Daddy, I don't think you have to worry about Carter. In fact, he's right here and he wants to talk to you." She handed the phone to Carter.

He gulped, squinted hard, then began in an unusually husky voice: "Dad, I haven't been worth a damn. I know that but I'm turning over a new leaf. I haven't had a drink since I smashed up Yancey Weems's Mercedes and Billy's Volante. I'm realizing some things. Uh, I'm not making any excuses for myself, Dad." He breathed deeply again. "What I'm trying to say here is that I'd like to come work for Armstrong Paving and I don't expect much money at all. Just enough to cover groceries as long as Frazier will tolerate me. I can operate the equipment and with a little work I can learn to bid out on the jobs—well, a lot of work really, but I can do it, Dad, and this way you can save one salary. Times are bad and this asinine article might slow things down further. And Frazier said Ru can come on in and work too. We can do it. We can get through this—if you'll just give me a chance."

A long, long pause on the other end of the phone was agony. "That sounds like a good idea, son."

A flush washed over Carter's cheeks. Frazier put her arm around his shoulders. "Just one little thing—will you go to bat with Mildred for me? You know she can't stand me."

Frank laughed. "Carter, don't give it a second thought. I'll see you in, uh, how about an hour?"

"Great."

"Tell Frazier not to worry. You know how she gets."

"Yeah, I'll tell her. Bye."

"Goodbye."

Carter held the phone in his hand. He couldn't hang it up. Frazier pressed down the disconnect button. "He said for you not to worry. You worry too much."

"I'm proud of you, Brudda."

"Yeah?"

"Yeah."

She would have been proud of her father, too, if she could have seen him in Libby's country kitchen. When he told his wife she blew a fuse, said it would ruin what was left of his business—not that Carter wouldn't be of some help but father and son fought like cats and dogs. She then indicated that this would just break Laura's heart.

Frank might not have been the most perceptive man in the world but he figured out that his wife feared he would forge a closer relationship with his son and then she wouldn't be needed as a go-between. Libby lived by "divide and conquer." She ragged on until he finally told her to shut up.

Libby, misreading Frank's determination—an easy enough mistake to make, since she'd led him by the nose for four decades—pressed: "Then you insist he give up that girlfriend of his. She's a person of low degree. It will hurt your image. It will hurt your business. Carter has got to give her up."

Frank bellowed, "Shut the fuck up!" and hurled his cup and saucer against the wall, smashing both and leaving a coffee stain on the wall. He grabbed his car keys and left Libby to reassess her position.

CHAPTER
52

T he warm bricks of the country club, set off by a linen-white entablature, contrasted with the spring green from the surrounding walnuts, chestnuts, red oaks, and maples. Soon enough the three-story magnolias would open their enormous buds as if on cue, the white flowers seeming to float like waterlilies amidst the glossy dark-green leaves.

The roads into the club were clogged with cars, and people walked as far as half a mile for the dance and the fireworks.

Tables with pastel tablecloths dotted the undulating lawn, bouquets with hurricane lamps gracing the center of each table. Liveried waiters and waitresses served the guests. A dance floor, used for outdoor gatherings, squatted over the expansive lawn. Under the lingering twilight the bandleader—wearing a toupee so bad that if he threw it in the middle of the road, drivers would think it was a dead cat—rapped his baton on a music stand. The small orchestra picked up their instruments. Thirties and forties tunes floated over the boxwoods and azaleas.

Everybody who could walk, run, or be carried was in attendance tonight. The spring gowns of the ladies shimmered in pastels, while the men looked like smart penguins. Frank and Libby headed a table on the west side of the dance floor. Libby seethed when Carter arrived with Sarah, overdressed but sexy nonetheless. However, Frank's outburst yesterday kept her lip temporarily buttoned. She allowed herself to be introduced to Sarah but remained frosty. Ru diverted Libby's attention at every opportunity. Frazier sat on the other side of the sultry woman. They engaged in a lively conversation while Mandy, wearing a peach chiffon dress, chatted up Frank. That didn't sit too well with Libby either, having a person of color at her table. She elected to be heroic about it so her gang could feel for her, comment on her grace under pressure. The recent riots in Los Angeles had instilled in Libby a fear that any show of distaste on her part would induce violence on the part of an individual who was not white. Libby's racism, like Libby's other "isms," managed to incorporate current events in such a way as to reinforce her prejudice, not challenge it.

Laura Armstrong, starved to perfection, sat at a table with Pete Barber and his wife. Laura had shipped in a date from New York to prove to the masses that she was capable of attracting a handsome man—but then who wasn't if she paid the bills?

Laura had other bills to pay too. The last detective's report had informed Frazier that her sister-in-law visited doctors in Richmond, Washington, and even Norfolk to keep getting prescriptions for that old stand-by Valium and a host of mood elevators.

Frazier paid off the detective but kept the information to herself. If the divorce got ugly she would give it to Carter's lawyer.

Then, too, it gave her some pleasure to know that Mrs. Perfect wasn't.

Pete Barber paid his bill to Frank the minute he read the newspaper attack. Frank was finding out who his friends really were and he hadn't expected this of Pete. It was as wonderful a surprise as Fred Vanarman, the stockbroker, was a disappointment. Fred's response to the price-fixing allegations was to ask his lawyer to investigate the tab for his quarter-mile driveway. He made a point of snubbing Frank as he walked through the tables, passing and repassing.

Wilfreda Gimble, that worn coin too long in circulation, relished the spectacle of the Armstrongs *in extremis* or what she thought to be *in extremis.*

Billy Cicero, Camille Kastenmeyer on his arm, paraded onto the dance floor. He made a special point of coming in from Richmond to show off his bride-to-be as well as his white tie and tails. Kenny Singer, back in town, sidled over to Frazier and leaned down. "Nothing wrong with Camille except she doesn't have a chin."

"Neither did the Hapsburgs. It didn't hurt them any," Frazier replied.

"True, but they were smart enough to grow beards." Kenny laughed. He paused. "I'm sorry about this thing with your dad."

"Me, too, but it will blow over. Dad's on top of it. There must be something wrong with Mother, though. It's not like her to miss the opportunity to wallow in a major tragedy."

"Speaking of wallow."

Laura Armstrong whirled by in the arms of her wavy-haired date. She smiled lavishly at Libby, who returned the gushing tribute. Laura followed this display of dentistry with an animated conversation in the ear of her date.

Carter didn't even notice. Sarah did.

Courtney walked over to retrieve Kenny. She paid her respects and Kenny promised to come back for a dance as Courtney hauled him out onto the floor. Frank asked his wife to dance and Carter followed suit with Sarah. She belonged to the python school of dance.

The three unescorted ladies, Frazier, Mandy, and Mary Russell, observed the writhings.

"Shall I assume my nephew is a happy man?" A wry smile played over Ru's lipstick, pure red.

"Rapturous." Frazier folded her arms across her chest and watched people watching her. Oh, it was a small town indeed.

"How much do you think Laura spent on that dress? A thousand at least. Carter's money. Poor Carter." Mandy cupped her chin in her hand.

"Carter's plastic. He doesn't have any money," Ru informed her.

Billy Cicero, enlivened by a malignant gaiety, twirled Camille close to Frazier's table and she could just overhear him say to his fiancée, "Lifelike, isn't she?" Camille's laughter twinkled.

"Bad to the bone." Auntie Ru reached for the wine bottle on the table, thought the better of it, and called the waiter over for some coffee. "Billy's the result of too much money too soon. That and being told by every woman in his life, beginning with his mother, that he's charming. It takes a mother twenty years to make a man out of her son and another woman twenty minutes to make a fool out of him. Of course, in Billy's case he never made it to being a man."

"Because he's gay?" Mandy innocently asked.

"Hell, no." Ru dumped cream in her coffee. "Because he won't assume responsibility."

Frazier spoke up. "I'm not his biggest fan right now but he runs Atlantic Tobacco with brio and brilliance."

"I mean emotional responsibility. Watch out, girl," Ru said to Mandy. "Dr. Yancey Weems is bearing down on you like a freight train."

Mandy hadn't time to turn around because Yancey appeared beside her and asked her to dance. She graciously agreed to do so as Ann Haviland, already tanned and in pink, glided onto the dance floor too. She pointedly ignored Frazier and all the Armstrongs but she smiled big for Laura.

Frazier moved to the next chair to be closer to her aunt. "I think Dad's going to be okay, especially if Mom leaves him alone."

"He's a strong man. Still waters run deep. People mistake Frank's quietness and gentle manners for weakness. He's a tank when the bomb drops. He didn't win those medals in Korea for nothing and he never talks about them. Won't talk about the war," Ru said.

"Dad wonders why a man should get a medal for killing other men. Speaking of military heroes, did I tell you that George Demerius is moving to Arizona? Selling everything."

"Frank told me. Told me about Carter too. This may be Carter's turning point and you know, Frank has to rely on him. It's good for both of them. I love Frank but he was hard on Carter. Not that I expected Carter to extend his adolescence to age thirty-seven." She scanned the room. "But then, Wilfreda Gimble has pushed hers into her fifties. I believe she's in her sixties myself." She swallowed more welcome caffeine. "Honey, why don't you get up there and dance? You're a beautiful dancer."

"Now that the whole goddam town knows I'm gay I suppose they think I don't like to dance with men. I don't know. Maybe they think it rubs off—you know, you'll get a little queer juice on your palm or something."

"Or that you haven't gone to bed with the right man. One spectacular roll in the hay and you'll be cured. Ah yes, male vanity marches on, oblivious to reality."

Oblivious applied to Yancey, who sought to impress Mandy with his liberal credentials. She politely listened but wished white people would keep their guilt to themselves.

"Being a physician, I see things you wouldn't believe," he said. "For instance, the best families in Albemarle County, the best white families—I mean we're talking aristocracy here, Mandy—they're suffering from sickle cell anemia. Not that I tell them that. I tell them they have leukemia. They couldn't face the truth about their ancestors, you know."

While Yancey continued, Laura, that ruthless monologist, prattled to her date, and Carter, feeling the music, feeling good and feeling that he had the most beautiful girl at the party in his arms, couldn't resist brushing by his wife. She recoiled for an instant, then relaxed into her date's arms, her eyes growing particularly lustrous. That and the fuck-me dress she was wearing—a side-slit up her thigh—made her feel fetching, even if Carter was, in her opinion, being crude and trying to hurt her. What Laura couldn't grasp was that she wasn't the center of attention in her husband's mind.

"Those two must be joined at the hip," Laura giggled to her date.

"That's not where they're joined," he said.

She threw her head back, making a big show of laughter.

"Academy Award performance." Frazier tapped the table with her fork.

"Carter married in haste and repented in leisure. Wonder how much it will cost to dump her?"

"Ru, whatever it costs, it's worth every penny." She glanced at her watch. "I think I'll go down to the fireworks. I checked out every-thing this afternoon but I'll check once more. Send Mandy down when she's finished her dance."

"Frazier, it's hard for you to sit here, I know, but I'm glad you're doing it. People need to see that you're not ashamed, that you have nothing to hide. Same with Frank. You have as much right to be here as anyone else."

"You're the best, Auntie Ru."

"Well, I don't know about that, but being an old lady I sit home and think a lot. I think a lot in the truck too. And you've got to give people a chance. You can't expect them not to be blown off course a bit. They've known you as one thing and now they have to adjust. You haven't lied but you've not told the truth either. Maybe we can say you were flying under false colors." Ru patted her hand. "But give people a chance. Imagine if the situation were reversed."

"What do you mean?"

"What if homosexuality were the norm and heterosexuals had to hide? Well, who would we see? We'd see pimps and prostitutes. We'd see dysfunctional people because the productive ones would pass, as you passed. Under those circumstances you can't expect that anyone would have a good opinion of heterosexuals, right?"

"I never thought of it that way."

"As I said, I'm an old woman. I have the luxury of time to think. So give people a chance. And if more women and men like you would be truthful, I think our society might grow up a little. People are people."

"Oh, how I'd like to believe that, but as long as women can lose their children, lose their jobs, lose their standing in their communities, I think there's more reward for lying than telling the truth. God, it's all so sick."

"How do you feel inside now?"

Frazier played with her napkin, turned the question over in her mind. "I feel clean. I feel whole but I feel a rage I never knew I carried. I don't know if it's over this gay crap or if it's directed at Mother or the insane pressure to conform but I'm willing to bet what landed me in the hospital in the first place was nerves. I plain couldn't breathe. I can breathe now and I'm breathing fire."

"So far you've been a paragon of poise. The fire isn't showing. I guess all that money Frank dropped for cotillion paid off." Ru laughed.

Frazier rose and headed back toward the fireworks. As she did so, Debbie Noakes, Kimberly's twelve-year-old daughter, in her first grown-up dress, rushed out to greet Frazier. She knew her from Girl Scouts, and Kimberly, in typical indirect, middle-class fashion, told her daughter that the reason Frazier wasn't participating any longer was because she had too much work to do.

"Miss Armstrong, I'm so glad to see you."

"Me, too, and how pretty you look. This is the best party because everyone dresses up."

Kimberly, prodded by her mother, rose from her chair and called with saccharine smiles, "Debbie, honey, come on back to the table. You know how busy Miss Armstrong is."

"Mom is being weird. She's always weird," Debbie moaned but did as she was told.

As Frazier moved by the table she heard Kimberly's own mother, the ancient Tiny Lockett, say, "You shouldn't expose the child to those kinds of people."

Frazier kept walking but she heard Debbie ask, "What kind of people?"

By the time she reached the fireworks Frazier was grateful to be away from the crowd. She wondered how she could give people a chance when most of them preferred to sit in judgment rather than learn about another complicated human being. She crouched behind the scaffolding. A giant dogwood would be the last firework lit. The various types of explosives and the lighting tapers were neatly laid out and numbered, as she liked to set off her fireworks in splashes of color. Every time she performed this task it made her think of Monet, Renoir, Pissarro. She thought of fireworks as celestial impressionism, something seemingly dashed off at the moment but requiring technique and planning.

The image of Vulcan standing at a distance from his father on Mount Olympus crossed her mind. Was Vulcan in charge of fireworks? Perhaps he should be. Even on Olympus there are outcast children, less than perfect offspring, and for an odd moment her heart went out to the sweating, crippled god, yoked to Venus, who at least didn't hate him but didn't love him either.

"Il Penseroso." Mandy plopped down beside her.

"Don't remind me of John Milton, now or ever."

"You looked thoughtful." Mandy smiled.

"Thinking about the fireworks and if they're under the protection of Vulcan."

"The painting again." Mandy smiled again. "Some kind of mojo in that painting."

Jim Burguss joined them. "About time. The band's playing its theme song."

"'Dixie,'" Mandy wryly noted.

"Nah." Jim patted her on the back. "'Red Sails in the Sunset.' It's more their speed."

"Now that Russia's cracked up we could amend that to 'Red Sales in the Sunset.' S-A-L-E-S." Frazier spelled it out.

"You're slipping, Frazier, slipping. Then again, our government is slipping too. If we let Russia get away from us this time, if we don't help, then we've failed twice, you know. First at Archangel in 1917 and now."

"Jim, I forget that you're a student of history."

"If more people studied history we'd save ourselves a lot of trouble." He saw the band stand up. "Okay, there's the signal. I'm going back up to the patio."

"Fine." Frazier reached down and lit her first taper. Mandy stood at the ready. The first rocket up was a screamer with a boom, followed by a sunburst that faded out into spangles and glitter.

The oohs and aahs of the crowd gave Frazier a shiver. She loved pleasing an audience.

"Wow, that blue star is incredible." Mandy shielded her eyes. "Say, did you see Ann?"

"I was spared that."

"She's overdoing the femininity thing." Mandy watched a red burst go up, followed by green, then iris with a screamer ripping through the air. "Wow, those are sensational! Well, anyway, Ann is tottering on stilts, as in high-heeled shoes, and her voice is so high only a dog could hear it."

"Wonder why men like all that phony femininity?" Frazier bent over the next batch. "Doesn't turn me on. Gags me. Hand me that, will you?" She pointed to a fresh taper.

"Hey, maybe it does to them what 'Honey, don't you worry your pretty little head about a thing, I'll take care of it' does for us."

"I hate to admit this but no man in my life ever offered to take care of anything. Guess I don't arouse their protective instincts."

"Could be. Showing more cleavage would help."

"You're on a roll. Hey, how do you like those golden fishtails?"

"My fave." Mandy plugged her ears for the boom to follow. It was delayed and went off just as she took her fingers out of her ears. "Sneaky. Very sneaky."

Lurching out of the crowd, dragging her crewcut date, Bob Alton, behind her, came Ann. She'd been deep in the grape. She neared Frazier and pointed. "Why, if it isn't the little match girl."

"You're drunk, Ann," Frazier warned her.

"Yes. But tomorrow I'll be sober. You'll still be a lesbian." She laughed hysterically.

Bob, more sober, reached for her as Ann was picking up speed, heading toward the fireworks display. "Ann, hey, slow down."

More fireworks illuminated the sky and Ann stumbled into the carefully set-up sequence Frazier had laid out. "I forgot how compulsive and organized you were." Ann knocked over sequence seven.

"Get out of here, Ann." Mandy grabbed her arm as Bob grabbed the other.

"Let go of me," she snarled.

"Go on, Ann, you're making a spectacle of yourself."

Ann wobbled toward Frazier. "I'm making a spectacle of myself? I am? My father's not a crook and I'm not Miss Gay America."

A small wire snapped in Frazier's head and she threw a right cross that connected with Ann's jabbering mouth. Ann sank to her knees, then flopped over on her side, knocking a live taper into fireworks that had also fallen all over. Within seconds fireworks shot up the lawn like tongues of flame.

Mandy, with Bob's help, dragged a kicking and screaming Ann, mouth bloodied, out of the fireworks. The crowd screamed. Hundreds of people hit the dirt and Tiny Lockett shouted, "Save the children!"

Tables were knocked over as people ducked behind them. Billy ran into the main building, leaving the chinless Camille to fend for herself and perhaps wonder what sort of man he was. Carter pushed Sarah behind the table with Ru, Frank, and Libby, then dashed across the lawn to pull a child to the ground.

"Mandy, get the fire extinguisher!" Frazier smothered a taper into the grass but another was lit by the fireworks going off on the ground, and every firework setup now shot into the sky or up the lawn in a crescendo of such light they could probably see it all the way to Nelson County. The dogwood went off, too, sending white sparkler trails onto the ground.

Mandy trained the nozzle on the tapers. Frazier madly stepped on flickering embers.

After the last fallout waltzed to the ground, spectators crawled out on their bellies. In the far distance a siren gave evidence that someone was smart enough to call the fire department. Yancey Weems sputtered, "I'll sue for emotional distress and extreme negligence."

Stunned, Frazier swayed, then sat on the ground.

Mandy stood over her. "I have this theory—"

Frazier hoarsely interrupted, "That love—is a very destructive emotion."

"No shit, Sherlock."

Up at the lawn Debbie Noakes was ecstatic. "Best Dogwood Festival ever!"

CHAPTER
53

The front page of the local newspaper carried a color photo of the fireworks debacle at the country club with the headline EXPLOSION! The newspaper, tossed on the office floor in disgust, bore testimony to the fact that Frazier had repeatedly walked over it. The staff photographer had captured good photos. That didn't bother Frazier. What bothered her was the story. The reporter—a generous appellation—got Frazier's occupation wrong, her age, and misspelled her first name as well. Strung-together quotes from eyewitnesses revealed that the reporter couldn't pull the story together so he thought quotes would do it for him.

How could those people be eyewitnesses? They cowered behind tables. At least no one had interviewed Ann. She would have declared that lesbians are unstable, hostile, hate men, and can't handle fireworks. She then would have thrown Bob on the ground and humped him to prove her heterosexual credentials.

The phone rang. Mandy picked up, as she had done all morning. In fairness to the town, most of the calls had been to inquire if Frazier was all right and to find out what really happened. Frazier was known for her attention to safety—first, last, and always. How could she tell them what really happened? If she did, she'd have to reveal that she and Ann had an affair. Much as she loathed Ann she felt bound by the old code Not To Tell about anyone else. Then again, would she want to claim having slept with such a bonehead? Being known as a lesbian was far less embarrassing than being known for bad taste in women. So Frazier hemmed and hawed about a spectator being inebriated and falling into the fireworks, the tapers catching the fuses, and boom! Everyone accepted that.

Mandy tiptoed in. "Her mothership. Should I tell her you're out?"

"No, she'll keep calling to catch me. I might as well get it over with." She lifted the receiver off the cradle as Mandy left. "Hello, Mother."

"You've read the papers?"

"I have."

"What would the *Central Virginia Tribune* do without the Armstrongs?"

"Pick on someone else, I guess. Look at it this way, Mother. If we're getting it, it means someone else is getting a rest."

Libby's voice dropped. "I don't *care* about someone else. Now I want to know exactly what happened. I was so distraught last night that your father took me directly home and then I woke up in the middle of the night because I thought Frank was having a heart attack." Libby waited for the desired response, which she got.

"What?"

"Oh, yes, all this commotion—starting with you, Miss Mary Frazier—has caught up with him. That hideous article in the papers about his business and then last night. Oh, I don't know how he's managed and it caught up with him. He complained of pains, woke me by getting out of bed—you know any little motion awakens me, I'm such a light sleeper—and he went into the bathroom. Well, he had every medicine out on the counter. I asked him what was wrong, he was sweating so. He put his hands over his chest and I knew it was his heart. I ran for the phone but he stopped me. 'Heartburn,' he said, and I said, 'At your age I don't know. Let's call a doctor.' Your father hates doctors and he said, 'If it is a heart attack I prefer to suffer it alone and die in peace. If Yancey Weems were the last face I saw on this earth I'd be furious.' As it turned out he was right about the heartburn, but he's under so much pressure and you and Carter add to his woes. He was appalled by Sarah."

"He didn't look appalled to me. Her boobs were pushed to high tide and I thought Dad got a kick out of that."

"Your father is a leg man. *You* were probably the one peering into her cleavage!"

Braking for an instant to let her mother's comment pass, Frazier rejoined, "It's hard for me to fathom how unhappy and full of hate you are." She hung up the phone and dialed her dad. "Hi, Mildred. Is Pop there?"

"Listen, honey, what a mess last night. I'm so sorry, and of course you've got to be shaken up too."

"Thank you. I'm just glad no one was hurt."

"I'll punch you through to Big Frank."

"Dad?"

"Yeah."

"You okay? Mom said you were sick last night."

"Oh, that damned crab. The new chef at the club puts all those sauces on everything and I think it was too rich for me. Your mother thought I was having a heart attack." He paused. "Maybe she wants me to have one so she can control everything again."

"Dad?" Frazier couldn't believe her ears.

"Things are changing at home. I should have taken hold a long, long time ago, but better late than never. Frazier? Frazier, are you there?"

"Yes. Just amazed."

"One day at a time. I don't want to be ugly but I can't stand it anymore. What a jellyfish I've been. And, Frazier, I want you to be the first to hear this: if we can't work things out, then I am leaving your mother. I don't know how many years I have left in this life but I want them to be . . . peaceful. I gave up on happiness when I came home from Korea."

"Dad, don't ever give up on that."

"I'll try, and you try to forget the article in the paper. Both articles. It's all shit."

"I know."

"Say, Carter came in to work early this morning and checked out equipment with me. After last night, and his girlfriend—isn't she a hot tomato, whooee!—I figured he wouldn't get to work until late but he was here at seven-thirty."

"He's trying, Dad. He's a good man."

A silence followed. "Frazier, I think I have a lot to learn."

"Daddy, so do I."

"Talk to you later. Goodbye."

"Sure." Frazier hung up and thought that maybe her father *would* talk to her later. Maybe those bottled-up decades would finally be decanted.

The phone rang again and this time it was the lovely and mature Ann Haviland. "I'm suing you for bodily harm."

"That's a nice hello." Frazier blinked.

"I've had photos taken of my bloodied face and I have a chipped tooth and I just wanted you to know that I'm suing you before the papers come in the mail."

"Calling me first means in your mind that you're responsible and a Virginia lady? Ann, if you were a Virginia lady you wouldn't have gotten drunk in the first place, and in the second place you wouldn't have tottered down the lawn to harass me. Get a grip."

Ann retreated into frosty superiority to prove, against all odds, that she was mature, responsible, and in control. Ah yes, the great

American vice, being in control. Her voice sounded as though it issued from the bottom of a well. "We'll let the courts decide."

"You know, I'm sorry." Frazier could hear the eager intake of breath on the other end of the phone while Ann waited for Frazier to grovel. "I'm as sorry as I can be that I didn't tear your face off. My lawyer will call your lawyer and I hope that makes you happy, you dumb bitch, because it means you'll still be connected to me in some way."

"I don't want anything to do with you!"

"Hey, if you're suing me you're going to have a lot to do with me. What's the buzz, Ann? If you can't be the positive center of my attention, you'll be the negative?"

"I was never the center of your attention. You think only of yourself. You never wrote me love letters. You rarely sent me flowers. You never loved me."

"I never said I loved you. You said you loved me. Sounded like a baited trap to me. A woman says, 'I love you,' and if you don't return the compliment you're heartless and if you do and you don't feel it, you're a liar. Which is worse?"

"I don't know. In your case you're both."

"Are you smart enough to tell the difference? What the fuck are you complaining about? We dated for a year or so—"

"A year and a half! Don't make light of it."

"I paid for the trips for the most part, I took care of things. I remembered your birthday and Christmas, and for me that's a big deal. I didn't want to settle down and if you think about it, with both of us lying through our teeth about being gay, how could we have lived together without creating ten times more stress? I didn't love you? What am I supposed to do, pay forever because I didn't? I wasn't mean. I tried to be good company. That was it."

"I feel sorry for you." Ann's voice embraced the superior tone. "Sorry because you'll never let yourself be vulnerable to another human being. You'll be alone—old and alone."

"*Vulnerable* seems to be the catchword these days, doesn't it? You tell me what intelligent animal wants to be vulnerable? Nature gave animals fangs, claws, hooves, speed, whatever, so they wouldn't be vulnerable. I think you people who use words like that are so goddam far away from reality that the only reality you have is the vocabulary you use with one another. I didn't love you. I liked you but I didn't love you. Big fucking deal."

"You hurt me and you're going to pay."

Frazier calmed down and said quietly, "Thank you, Ann. Finally you told the truth." She hung up the phone. "Jesus H. Christ, what's going on? Is Mercury sliding through the slops of the universe or what?"

Mandy called in from the other room, "Retrograde. That's when Mercury travels backwards."

Frazier walked out. "Aha! You and the Reagans. I knew it. I knew you were going mystical on me."

"Nah, I just like astrology. It's the wisdom of the millennia, and the Christians wrecked as much as they could but the remnants are better than nothing. Anyway, you don't want to hear about how I know you feel about things you deem irrational. I want to know what's going on."

"Mother is majoring in child abuse and Ann is suing me for bodily harm."

"You're kidding me?" Mandy's deep eyes widened.

"I wouldn't kid about a thing like that. Better to fall into the hands of the Devil than those of lawyers. But then again it's better to feed one cat than many mice, so I'm calling my lawyer and he can handle it. Be back in a flash."

Mandy pulled the aluminum stepladder out of the closet as Frazier reappeared. "So?"

"So, I'll run up a bill but I think Ann will back off."

"Why? She'll see how much it costs her to get her rocks off via the legal system—you realize I use that term in jest—and depending on how angry she really is, she can keep it going for years."

"I suspect when Link Critzer lets her know that the nature of our relationship will be central to the case, she'll shut up. She'll fume at me, of course—can we deny her the emotional satisfaction of screaming and hollering about what a victim she is and what a powerful, mean, manipulative person I am? Ever notice how both parties in a busted relationship are just dying to be the victim? Women are much better at it than men."

"Maybe they have to be."

"Why the hell would you say that?"

"Because men reward women when they're weak, and being a victim means that you're weak and you need a protector."

Frazier helped Mandy to set up the ladder. "Mandy, one of these days you and I are going away for a day and I want you to talk to me about everything. You see things I don't."

"Your vice is my versa." Mandy smiled. "We're supposed to see things for one another. We're a herd animal, remember? Anyway, the lights finally came in from Eck Supply, so let's try this over Mount Olympus."

"Let me get up there. I don't know if the light is on the fritz or if it's the bulb. Is the switch off?"

"Yes."

Frazier climbed up the ladder and reached down for the pink bulb. "Did you hear that?"

"What?"

"A giggle."

"I think it's on the tape that's playing."

"The 'Divas' tape?"

"Uh-huh."

"I don't remember giggles on that tape. I remember people talking. Don't you hear it? Damn, now I don't hear it either."

"Frazier, watch what you're doing up there."

"Well, hold the ladder."

"I am holding the ladder but if you step off, what good's it going to do you? Goddammit. Listen to me for once."

"I used to change the light gels when I was in junior theater. I know everything about lights." She reached up and unscrewed the defunct bulb. "Life's been so hectic I keep forgetting to tell you that I've made you a partner in the corporation. I sent off the amended corporate report to Richmond, and Link completed the rest of the paperwork."

Mandy dropped her hand a moment. "Are you serious?"

"Absolutely. I should have told you over lunch or some significant moment, but the last of the paperwork went out Friday and I sure didn't want to talk about it at the Dogwood Festival. It's been crazy. Actually, I made up my mind when I thought I was dying. I left you the company, but since I lived you'll have to settle for a partnership."

"I don't know what to say." Mandy gulped. "Do I know enough?"

"If you don't, you will. You're attuned to different periods than I am. I think you'll bring a lot of money into the company and an expanded clientele. I'm happy about this."

"Thank you." Mandy reached back up to hold the ladder as Frazier reached into the light fixture to push back the cup, which had slipped.

A jolt seared through Frazier's right arm. When she looked up she was flat on her back, staring into the face of Mercury. He was laughing at her.

CHAPTER 54

"What are you doing here?"

Frazier peered into Mercury's smooth face. "I think I need a cigarette."

"Thought you gave those up?" The god of communications nudged her with his winged sandal.

"What?" Frazier, befuddled and feeling highly peculiar, felt the hair on the back of her neck stand up.

"When you lay dying, or so you thought, you promised to give up cigarettes."

Dionysus butted in. "Don't turn into a health fascist." He raised his golden goblet to her, the very goblet that she'd seen sitting on the floor of her gallery.

Venus leaned over Frazier, placing a hand on her shoulder. "Come on, honey, let me help you. You've had a shock."

Frazier felt golden light suffuse every pore. She couldn't look the goddess full in the face; she was too beautiful.

"Hardly a shock. More of a buzz." Jupiter studied her, his stupendous visage bemused by the sight of this beautiful but confused human.

Frazier stood up, wobbling, and Mercury slipped his strong arm around her waist. "I think I'm going crazy." She addressed Mercury again: "How do you know me?"

"I've been keeping an eye on you for some time now." His smile, high voltage, hurt her eyes. "Do you know my family?"

"Yes, I do."

"I told you they hadn't forgotten us." Neptune struck the earth with his trident in emphasis.

"Don't do that—please, brother." Jupiter smiled benignly on the powerful sea god, who plotted against him too many times. "Think of the San Andreas fault."

"I've practiced restraint for too long," Neptune growled. "Tokyo? Los Angeles? San Francisco? Or how about New York? That would send them into a tizz. They're too complacent down there."

"But here's one who knows us." Juno's cool voice commanded attention.

Apollo leaned toward her, his golden curls shining like silk. "We've gotten together for this family portrait, Frazier, and we've forgotten our manners. Would you like anything to eat or drink?" He nodded and Ganymede, the cupbearer, appeared with nectar.

"Thank you." Frazier sipped from the magnificently tooled cup as Ganymede winked at her. She felt fabulous after one sip. "What beautiful workmanship."

"My husband." Venus smiled in the direction of Vulcan, god of the forge.

Frazier called to Vulcan and he moved closer. "You truly are a god to create something this beautiful."

"Oh, balls," Diana said. "Watch this." She slipped a silver arrow out of her quiver, put it next to the enormous bow, and aimed at a distant spot on the earth. The arrow hit the Times Square teletype on the side of the Allied building. The lights fizzled and went out. The close-up of this event then faded from the large screen Mercury had instantly supplied. "What do you think of that?"

"You're, uh, divine." Frazier gulped.

"Diana, don't be so selfish. This mortal was praising my son and he gets precious little respect from the rest of you." Juno defended her boy. As Diana and Apollo were not her children but twins sired by Jupiter on another woman, she couldn't stand them. Nor could she stand the fact that her husband detested Vulcan just because she bore him without help from his sperm. She really did it just to get even with her husband, who said he gave birth to Athena from his brow.

"Do you know there's a statue to you on top of Iron Mountain in Birmingham, Alabama?" Frazier innocently asked the muscular blacksmith.

"Oh, so what. Nashville's got a statue of Athena, and Rome is full of statues to all of us. Don't encourage him or he'll—"

Vulcan cut off Diana. "What the hell have you ever done except run around and kill animals?"

"Don't talk that way to my sister!" Apollo leapt up, his lyre clanging to the ground.

"You think you're so goddam beautiful," Vulcan spat back at him. "Well, you've never been lucky in love and human women even pass you up, given the choice."

A huge row broke out, with Pluto, god of the underworld, remaining silent but keenly observing.

Frazier whispered to Mercury, whom she instantly adored: "Are they always like this?"

"What family isn't?" He shrugged.

"Aren't you supposed to be above all this?" Frazier innocently inquired.

Venus drew nearer to her. "Why would you want gods who

couldn't feel as you feel?" Her breath enveloped Frazier in a pleasurable cloud.

Frazier, feeling giddy, replied, "I never thought of it that way. I mean, I was taught that there was only one God and He was perfect. Humans are worms by comparison."

"Yeah, well, don't believe everything you read," Mercury solemnly said. "I ought to know. After all, I am the god of communications and this is my century."

"It's mine," Vulcan shouted, his brow furrowing dangerously.

"The nineteenth was yours, darling. Now you've got to give ground. Everyone gets a turn." Venus smiled.

"The twentieth century is mine." Mars smiled broadly.

Pluto spoke at last, his voice cool, stentorian, and deep: "Every century is yours, Mars. As Vulcan gives them better and better technology, they use it to kill one another. After World War Two, I had to judge fifty-five million of them. I've never worked so hard in my life."

"You could have jobbed it out." Dionysus stood up, then plopped back down on his haunches.

"That would have been irresponsible," Pluto, who considered Dionysus a lightweight, shot back.

"I don't see why we should be responsible when they're not." Neptune pointed his trident at Frazier, and a ragged rip of pure fear scared her so, she nearly jumped out of her skin.

"I wasn't even born during World War Two." Frazier tried to keep her voice from betraying her terror.

Mars stretched, his tight, gorgeous body enticing Venus, who could never rid herself of her deep attachment to him and vice versa. Whatever the war god's faults, he remained in love with Venus and ducked around Vulcan whenever he got the chance, but then so did Mercury. "World War Two was interesting but I liked World War One better. It was far more profound because it changed the human notion of warfare forever."

"Not enough to keep them out of the next one," Jupiter growled. He hated Mars as much as Juno loved her other son.

"May I have another drink, please?" Frazier's throat was parched.

Ganymede handed her the goblet. The gods watched her imbibe the nectar.

"Don't drink too much," Athena counseled. "You aren't used to it."

"Thank you." Frazier handed the cup back to Ganymede. "Have I done something wrong?"

"No. Why do you ask?" Jupiter observed her with veiled interest. Juno, right by his side, rarely missed a trick and he didn't want to betray his keen physical interest in this extraordinary-looking human.

"You're all staring at me."

"We haven't allowed one of your kind up here in quite some time," Apollo answered.

"I have," Dionysus bellowed.

"You don't count." Apollo waved his hand at him. "Your mother was human, so keep out of this."

"You're a real pain in the ass. Go ahead, torture me with logic. Force me to listen to your carefully modulated songs." Dionysus rolled his eyes. "I can't wait to see, one more bloody time, how much better you are than me. Well"—he raised his voice—"I invented sex, drugs, and rock 'n' roll. What the hell have you done recently?"

"Don't answer him." Diana entered the argument. "You'll lower yourself to his level." She observed the light. "I'm going hunting. Want to go with me?" She nudged Apollo.

"Maybe later."

Diana glanced from Apollo to Frazier, rolled her eyes at her brother, then walked off.

Mercury touched Frazier's hand. She nearly melted. "We're staring at you because you're beautiful."

Frazier perceived Juno's eyes narrowing, so she quickly bowed in the direction of the queen of the gods. "No human can possibly compare to the queen." Frazier dimly recalled her mythology but she instinctively knew that if she was going to survive on Mount Olympus she'd better butter up Juno. Of course, Venus was the most beautiful goddess but Frazier, also instinctively, trusted Venus. She knew she could tell her the truth. Juno was a different matter entirely.

A slight smile played over Juno's lips. Jupiter, appreciating Frazier's quickness, slid his hand into his wife's. "I am fortunate our visitor is a woman. A man would find you irresistible, my dear, and naturally I'd have to do something awful to him." Truthfully, Jupiter would have welcomed a human competitor. In the old days he would have killed the fellow or turned him into a wart hog, but century after century of being the center of Juno's hot attentions had worn down even his magnificent constitution. She rarely gave him a minute's peace and if he wasn't complimenting her or fussing over her she'd pout, feel hurt, or worse, take it out on a human. Granted, she'd had just cause with some of the women in his past but her rage could be pure evil.

Unfortunately, Juno was ruthlessly faithful and Jupiter felt more trapped by his wife as the centuries piled up.

Juno affectionately put her arm around her husband's massive shoulders.

Venus turned her head to giggle and Mercury pinched her to stop. He knew as far as Juno was concerned that if Momma ain't happy, nobody's happy, to borrow a phrase.

"Do we have any business left?" Neptune asked.

"No." Jupiter held his hands palms upward. "Unless someone else has something to say."

"What do we do with her?" Apollo eyed Frazier greedily.

"Oh, I'll take care of her." Mercury stepped beside Frazier.

"I bet you will," Apollo muttered.

"Perhaps the lady would like to decide for herself." Jupiter shifted his weight and again felt his wife's arm around his shoulders.

"I'd like to go home," Frazier said.

"Consider this a vacation. You'll go home soon enough." Jupiter smiled.

Frazier realized that if she couldn't go home she'd better watch her step. She'd seen enough jealousy and spite to get her antennae up. "If that's the case, perhaps I should stay somewhere by myself. I just dropped in unexpectedly, sort of, and I don't want to put anyone to trouble."

"You're no trouble." Mercury seduced her with his merry eyes.

"No, but you are." Apollo stepped toward Mercury.

"Gentlemen and ladies, gods, I mean, your divinities . . ." Frazier stumbled. "Perhaps I should go home with a goddess."

"Come home with me." Venus moved toward her.

"Out of the frying pan and into the fire." Apollo, disappointed, turned on his heel and left.

CHAPTER
55

F razier expected a flight to a Greek island or perhaps the
Temple of Aphrodite at Knidos in Turkey. She was quite
surprised when after a short walk she and her hostess came
upon Sans Souci.

"But this is in Potsdam, Germany?" Frazier was ferociously confused.

"No, Frederick the Great got the idea from me. Usually when you
find a residence of surpassing beauty, I was the source of inspiration.
Think of Rastrelli's fountains at the Peterhof just outside St. Peters-
burg. I create beauty in all things"—she paused and slid her forefinger up Frazier's arm—"and you are one of mine, although your
temperament needs work."

"My mother says that too," Frazier replied ruefully.

Venus led her to a graceful, understated room at the rear of the

3 0 3

palace overlooking the rose garden. "You'll be comfortable here. Would you like anything?"

Frazier wanted to say "You," but thought better of it. Could humans proposition goddesses and gods?

"How did I get here?"

Venus's clear eyes softened. She ran her long fingers through Frazier's blond hair. "Accept what you cannot understand."

"Well, can you tell me why you don't visit us anymore?" Frazier's temples burned with desire.

"Boredom. Humans used to live in red and gold, green and silver. Now they indulge in gray little pleasures. They've surrendered joy to reason, and reason is a pathetic little god. Even Apollo loses his reason sometimes—usually over a woman, or occasionally a young man."

"I think I offended him."

The goddess's silver laughter filled the room. "Offended him? You turned him on."

"Me?"

"You."

Frazier was immensely flattered, although Apollo was not her type. "How is it you speak English?"

"We can speak any language. We invented them."

"Oh." Frazier folded her hands together. "I guess the human race has become dull. I know I have."

"I'll take care of that." Her smile was blinding.

A thin blade of sweat ran between Frazier's breasts. She struggled to breathe. "You're not at all what I expected."

"And what was that?" Venus reclined on a Madame Récamier lounge. She patted the plush upholstery, indicating that Frazier should sit next to her.

"I thought you'd vamp around. You know, the tits-and-ass school of femininity."

"Too crude. You know I once had great power. It's not so easy anymore. For one thing you people don't really want to love anyone but yourselves. You make Narcissus look good. Then, too, the Christians took over and tried to cheapen me into some slutbunny. It's sex, sex, sex with them and I take deep offense at that."

"Why don't you get even with them?" Frazier was falling into those inviting deep-blue eyes.

"Then I'd no longer be the goddess of love, would I? Do you remember your mythology? I am the only Olympian who doesn't demand blood sacrifices."

"I don't think they've destroyed your power. You've been driven underground. Can anyone or any institution destroy the power of love?"

"They can cheapen it into the power of sex."

A cold spear pierced Frazier's stomach, or it felt like that. Did this mean Venus wouldn't sleep with her? "Yes, well, they've done that. But, uh, how shall I address you? Your Majesty?"

"You can call me Venus, or Aphrodite if you prefer the Greek. Juno thrives on formality. I don't."

"Ah, what I was going to say is that the female principle can be suppressed but never truly vanquished. Those early Christians couldn't eradicate your power, so they gave your robin's-egg blue and many of your attributes to Mary, the Blessed Virgin. Basic theft, I'd say."

"Yes." Venus propped herself up on her right elbow. "Now let's discuss you. You violated your true self. You thought you were dying and told the truth and now"—she reached out with her left hand and ran her forefinger from Frazier's shoulder to her hand—"now you're paying the price for love—no?"

"There hasn't been much love in my life. I'm really paying the price for an idea."

"Ah, is it my fault—?"

Frazier interrupted, "Oh, no. How could any of this be your fault?"

"I made you almost divinely beautiful but I forgot to give you a partner."

"I think I'd prefer to find my own," Frazier blurted out.

"Willful."

"Uh—yes." Frazier smiled. "That's a polite way to put it. Venus, it's not your fault there hasn't been a deep love in my life. It's my fault. I valued success and money more than people. And I was chicken to admit that I loved women best. I just lied and lied and lied until there wasn't much of me left. No wonder I thought I was dying."

"Perhaps part of you has."

Frazier twisted on the Récamier chair to better face Venus. "Good. Now maybe there will be room for love and friendship. I was so goddam busy—excuse me. I didn't mean to swear." Venus waved it off and Frazier continued: "So by trying to control life, I wasn't living it. And, Venus, the machines we have now. In a way it's awful, because you can never get away from business. Americans, some of us, even have phones in their bathrooms."

"Yes, I know all that. Alexander Graham Bell held no allure for me. My husband was close to him. Do you think you can open yourself up to life?"

"I'm trying. It sure hurts more than I thought it would."

"Do you cry?"

"No." Frazier shook her head. "I'm not a crier. I'm a fighter in my own quiet way."

"There's no shame in tears. The shame is in not feeling. Just as there's no shame in loving women. The shame is in not loving at all."

"I don't remember any stories about you making love to women." Frazier's heart slammed against her ribcage.

"Men fear any pleasure women experience in their absence." Venus laughed. "Do you think they'd tell the truth about me? Much as I liked the Greeks of the fifth century, they were petty little patriarchs. Certainly I make love to women. I believe one should be able to make love to one's partner as a woman to a woman, as a man to a woman, as a man to a man. Why limit yourself? You should be all things to your partner."

"How imaginative." Frazier's mouth was again parched. "Might I have another drink?"

Venus clapped her hands and Eros appeared with a cup. Frazier eyed him suspiciously in case he was hiding his arrows in a quiver. Virile and handsome, he resembled no Cupid she had ever seen. "Madame."

"Thank you. Is this nectar again?"

"Yes," Venus's son answered, "but I've also brought a Coca-Cola, since I know you are from the American South. As I recall, you all swim in Coke."

"Well, it does taste pretty wonderful." Frazier polished off the nectar and then chased it with the best Coca-Cola she had ever drunk in her life.

Venus nodded to Eros and he quietly left.

"He's not what I expected either."

"Who is? You're not what I expected."

"Really?"

"I knew you were beautiful, of course, but I thought you'd be more frightened. Most humans are overwhelmed when they meet one of us, although usually we're in disguise. Especially Jupiter and Mercury. Those two are always transforming themselves. How is it you're not afraid?"

"Well, I'm rather afraid of Pluto, Neptune, and Juno. And I'm not at all sure about Dionysus. He doesn't seem to be wrapped too tight. But I'm not too frightened. I don't think you or the others want to kill me. You might use me for sport though."

"I had other uses in mind." Venus leaned forward, her left breast brushing against Frazier's back.

Electrified, Frazier stiffened. She felt warm, sweet breath on her neck and then a tongue flicked just beneath her ear. Venus then bit her on the neck and languidly fell back on the couch. Frazier turned and met Venus's eyes, sparkling eyes, kind eyes. "Has anyone ever resisted you?"

Venus laughed again, that silvery, feathery sound. "Well, if they did they missed a good thing." She reached up and pulled Frazier down onto her. She closed her lips and kissed Frazier's closed eyes. Then she returned to Frazier's lips and kissed her.

The intensity of the kiss befuddled Frazier. Heaven or earth, alive or dead, sane or insane, she had no idea where she was, why she was there, who this woman was really, but her blood turned to lava. Who needed to know?

Losing her inhibitions, she ran her hands over Venus's strong body. She could spend a decade just moving down those long, lean thighs.

Frazier kissed the sole of Venus's foot, noticing as she did that the goddess's toenails were pearl, catching the light with an opalescent shine. Her skin, smoother and opalescent, glowed with an inner light and Frazier was bathed in a soft peach haze.

As she ran her tongue along the inside of Venus's calf and then her thigh, she wondered if she ought to stop at the soft curling mound beckoning—but that would be too soon. She bit Venus's groin, then slid her tongue up the tight stomach to a breast that swayed like a chime.

Frazier felt a strong hand press down on the small of her back. She rubbed her face against the goddess's left breast, then circled the dusty rose nipple of the goddess's right breast with her tongue.

Frazier hadn't made love in so long that inserting and removing her Tampax qualified as pleasure. The months of her relationship falling apart with Ann, then the severe bronchitis eroded not only her sex life but her desire. Now in her arms writhed the apotheosis of love, not just physical love but waves of tenderness that rolled off Venus's body. A sweetness wafted from the goddess, a sweetness born of truly caring about someone. Frazier had no idea why Venus would care for her, but this was hardly the moment to question.

The hand on her back pressed harder and, as Frazier lifted her head to kiss those full lips she looked into the deep eyes. Venus opened her mouth slightly.

Frazier pressed her lips to Venus's and a surge of blazing heat shot through her body. The more she kissed Venus the lighter she felt until she was floating in the air.

The next thing she knew Venus was on top of her, kissing her, biting her neck, licking the palms of her hands, sucking her fingers, nuzzling her breasts. The light emanating from the goddess forced her to squint.

"What a gift," Venus murmured. Frazier blinked in noncomprehension. "What a gift love is," Venus continued.

"You're the goddess of love." Frazier felt truly stupid.

"Everyone asks me for love. It's a gift when someone gives me love. Your body is a gift. Your flesh is so warm and I can taste the salt on your skin. What a delicious experience."

Venus kissed her on the lips and then put a leg on either side of her torso. Slowly she moved up Frazier's body until her crotch was over Frazier's face.

Venus parted the curls to reveal herself, glistening and deep pink. Then she opened herself and Frazier beheld a pink hazy light coming from inside the goddess. As she moved closer to the source of this fragrant haze, the hot pink vagina pulsating, she saw secret worlds within the goddess. Cities and symphonies echoed in her vagina.

Drawn into the body of Venus, a womb of fire cleansed her. As Frazier swirled around, she felt she was in a platinum washing machine on a hot rinse cycle. How long she burned in this state she didn't know, but suddenly she was thrown back onto the bed, her whole body gleaming with fire. She gasped for breath, her bronchial tubes, still unreliable, scorched and hurt.

A strong hand slipped under her head and cool nectar was poured down her throat. Venus wiped her lips. "I'm sorry. I forgot you're human."

Frazier sucked in as much air as she could. She was shaking and bathed in sweat. She reached for the cup. Venus poured more of the restorative liquid down her throat, as well as Coca-Cola.

Frazier finally caught her breath. "I think I'm supposed to ask 'Was it good for you?'"

Venus laughed so loudly that the chandelier in the next room crashed to the floor. The walls reverberated with her joy. "It was heaven." Then she laughed some more at her joke and so did Frazier. "You must have lost ten pounds with that orgasm. Let me feed you."

CHAPTER
56

Huge flapjacks swimming in thick German honey enticed Frazier nearly as much as did Venus's body. The sight of the goddess flipping pancakes at a stainless-steel six-burner Vulcan stove gladdened her heart. Venus wore nothing but a red-checkered apron and she sang to herself as she cooked.

"Juno says she can make pancakes big enough to cover Nevada. Who cares? Who wants to eat a pancake that big? Even my husband isn't interested in that, and he can eat morning, noon, and night. Don't you like this stove he made for me?"

"Very much. I'd like to have one for myself but they're quite expensive."

"Anything good is, I'm afraid. Here." She tossed a bronzed medallion of dough and it fell on top of Frazier's other pancakes. "As I recall you once wanted me to show you how to make a cheese soufflé." Then Venus filled her own plate and joined her guest. The teakettle whistled.

"I'll get it." Frazier leaped up. "You remember everything. I'd been reading the paper, the food section. It seems so long ago." She grabbed a hotpad. She lifted the kettle off the stove and groaned, "Damn, this is heavy."

"Here." Venus joined her. She easily lifted the pot, spilling the steaming contents into a beautifully enameled teapot.

Frazier sat back down with her hostess. "I haven't seen you at full strength, have I?" Venus shook her head. "Well, in human terms, how strong are you?"

Venus got up, walked to the Vulcan stove and with one hand lifted it off the ground, then put it back down. "It's hot or I'd have lifted it over my head."

Frazier's eyes were as big as saucers. "You could have killed me in bed."

Venus waved her hand, airily dismissing the statement. "Any woman worth half her salt can fuck a man to death. Women are a little tougher in that regard, but given enough time and energy you could probably do one in too. Multiple orgasms."

"I've often thought that's why men want to control us—because we are stronger sexually." Frazier merrily ate her pancakes while the tea steeped.

Venus sighed. "It wasn't always that way. There have been times when we were closer together but then women got the upper hand, matriarchy, and that lasted for millennia. Then men got the upper hand and that's lasted, oh, perhaps ten thousand years. It depends on how you're counting. The real revolution will be when neither sex has to dominate the other. It will happen."

"In my lifetime?"

"That's up to you." Venus poured the tea into exquisite red and gold cups. "Anyway, goddesses and gods cannot determine the future. We can try to sway it but we can't determine it."

The honey rolled down Frazier's throat. "You're a very good cook."

"Simple things. I leave the cuisine to Juno. She's so damned jealous about it that if one of us, even her adored Mars, cooks something better than she did or invents a new dish, she goes on a rampage."

"Bad."

"The worst. What's funny about her is that if you're in trouble—say you're having a difficult childbirth—she'll help if she hears you. She's good to her favorites."

"Like Jason and the Argonauts?"

"Oh, Frazier, that's so long ago. I was thinking of Craig Claiborne. She's just so jealous of her prerogatives. She can't share anything."

"Certainly not her husband."

"He was faithful for three hundred years. What else does she want? Anyway, all men will play around and if a woman doesn't know that, then she's a fool."

"Monogamy is impossible?"

"Nearly impossible."

"What about marriage vows?" Frazier was enjoying this.

"Whose marriage vows?"

"The Christian church's."

"Ha." Venus stirred her tea. "When those vows were first written the average life span was twenty-one years. Of course people could be faithful. Look how long you live now. Do you honestly believe that a couple who marry at twenty-five years of age and who live to eighty will be faithful? Impossible." She put down the teapot with a flourish of triumph. "You aren't made that way. You're just animals with a bit of intelligence. The more you violate your animal nature, the crazier you all get."

"Still"—Frazier wistfully stabbed at another delicious pancake—"I'd like to think my husband or wife could remain faithful."

"I keep forgetting that you're a Protestant." Venus raised an eyebrow. "Protestants take it all so seriously. Ask yourself this: Did we have a wonderful time?"

"Yes." Frazier beamed.

"Did I take anything from you?"

"No, of course not."

"Did I give you anything?"

"The best time I ever had in bed with anybody."

"A great gift. Sex is a great gift." Venus held her hand for a moment. "So, we shared our bodies. We gloried in the experience. I go my way and you go yours far richer than before we met. If I sleep with someone else, how can that take anything away from you?"

"But what if you fall in love with that person?"

"I am the goddess of love, remember?" Venus's warm smile washed over Frazier. "Not everyone you meet in this life is a long-term partner. But everyone you meet is an angel. They may be dark angels but angels nonetheless, bringing you messages from the gods. Sex is one kind of message. To deny the body, to deny the animal, is cruel because you're denying life. Life has its own imperatives and life is much older than reason. Stop trying to figure everything out and surrender to life."

"What about V.D.?"

"Frazier, you're an intelligent human being. You aren't going to be irresponsible. I didn't say you had to be promiscuous. I said don't deny your body. Don't deny life."

"My entire society rejects the body even as it uses it to sell products. A half-naked woman is wrapped around a liquor bottle; a handsome man smokes a cigarette. It's pretty schizophrenic, really. And then, speaking of being a Protestant, Christ tells me to die to my animal nature. To be reborn and transformed into some higher being."

Venus's voice vibrated with compassion. "I loved Jesus very much." She breathed in. "You must fulfill your animal nature. You are transformed into a higher being because you haven't denied life."

Frazier sat quietly for a moment. "I've denied life, haven't I?"

Venus leaned over and kissed her on the cheek. "Yes."

"I knew that when I thought I was dying. That's why I wrote those letters. I thought, 'Well, I've held back and withdrawn. Maybe I can blast some others out of their repressed cocoons.' And maybe I was having my last revenge—if you think about it. Oh, Venus, the trouble I'm in because of those letters."

"I know, but you told the truth. You can't be responsible for how people use it or deny it. It's like a talent. Up here we gaze down at you all and give you talents. What you do with that talent is up to you. You can't feel bad because your mother has become more rigid. You didn't make her like that. Your letter to Kenny Singer drew him closer to you."

"And cost him his lover." Frazier's eyes misted over.

"Billy Cicero would have dumped Kenny sooner or later. He's the kind of man who knows what he will do and then waits for some external event to justify his actions. You thought he was such a big part of your life, but the minute you needed him, poof, he was gone."

"You know, it's funny, this whole lesbian stuff. Do you feel like a lesbian?"

Venus smiled. "No, I feel like a woman."

"Exactly. Me too. And we love women because they're lovable, because there's something in that person worth loving, and although I've held myself back from it, I still believe it." She tapped her fork on the table. "But the common, run-of-the-mill prejudices about lesbians are all negative. For example, that I must be too ugly to get a man."

"We know that's false."

"Then I must be so beautiful I'm bored by men. See? You can't win. There's always some dumb reason why you're gay and they're not. I am hardly a genius, Venus, but I observe that Nature rarely makes mistakes, and as there has always been a percentage of the human population that is gay, she must have darn good reasons. I'd like to know those reasons but I do know there's no more wrong with me than with my heterosexual counterparts. I mean"—Frazier warmed up—"if a woman was abused by her father and she marries an abusive man, how can anyone say that's healthy? But she's better than I am because I'm a lesbian? I am so fucking bored with other people's stupidity I wonder how I lived my life before. How did I ignore it?"

"Because you valued things more than your soul."

Frazier thumped back hard on the chair. "I did, didn't I? I was really kidding myself."

"Your country has pushed Philistinism to new depths." Venus smiled ruefully. "Even Rome, and she went through some terribly vulgar times, didn't sink that low. All you Americans think about is money. Just awful."

Frazier wanted to leap up and defend her countrymen. She couldn't. The goddess was right. "We might find our way back to the heart, to valor, to beauty—abstract principles, but maybe that's why people worship profit. It's easy to understand."

"So is death. You're killing the spirit."

"I was part of that." Frazier tingled as Venus rubbed the back of her neck. "Look, Venus, everything you're saying about my country is true of me, and I don't know how to change America but I am trying to change myself, and maybe that's the beginning—one at a time. Maybe if someone sees that I am a happier person, a loving person, they'll think about themselves. Maybe they'll ask some questions."

"That's a good start, but you need to reach out. You need to struggle, to fight, laugh, grow. If you perfect yourself—as though that were possible—then you'd be a majority of one. You'd still be alone. People need one another. You can't go it alone."

"Hell, that's what I'm fighting for, but my so-called community is ass over tit because they know I'm a lesbian. They're like a bunch of school kids thrilled silly by a gorilla. Community! They're sitting in judgment of me. They're pushing me away."

"Frazier"—Venus's voice carried an imperial tone—"in Eastern Bloc countries gay people were considered mentally ill. Some were institutionalized. Others were imprisoned. Some committed suicide. It's not that bad in Virginia. Oh, there are pockets of violence but"—she lowered her voice—"isn't there violence every day against women? Rape. Child molesting. And what about violence against people who aren't white? No one is a special case. No one is exempt from trying to civilize humanity and replacing the love of power with the power of love. You have a duty to act and no right to expect approval. Anyone can find an excuse to keep from working for a better world. Being gay is a pretty good one, but you know, my little sex bomb, it won't work. Love is calling. Life is calling."

"I'm calling." Mercury appeared in the kitchen door. He was wearing sneakers with wings on them and gym shorts.

"Jesus Christ, you're wearing sneakers," Frazier blurted out.

"We don't use Jesus' name up here." Mercury glided over and sat at the table.

"We were having a heart-to-heart about the state of the world. I might have risen to Apollonian logic if you hadn't interrupted," Venus chided Mercury.

"Spare me." Mercury kissed Venus's hand. "You can use reason to justify anything. You know in your heart what's right and what's wrong, so I say shut up and get on with it."

"Are you both ganging up on me?" Frazier braced her hands against the table.

"What an excellent idea." Mercury smiled broadly and a crackle of electricity played across his lips.

"He's come to seduce you." Venus playfully pushed Mercury on the shoulder.

"And you have no such idea?" Mercury raised his eyebrows.

"She seduced me." Venus laughed with happiness.

Mercury appraised Frazier. "You are bold."

"She's irresistible."

"I know." Mercury, who had slept with Venus many times, agreed with Frazier. "We have a son, Hermaphroditus—well, she's a daughter too. I've always thought we should have more children but my beloved here has three children by Mars—she can't keep her hands off him and vice versa—and then she bore Eros but she's still being very tight-lipped about the father. She says he's fatherless."

"Well, Juno gave birth to my husband without any man's help, so I thought, why not? But we're getting off the subject. I know perfectly well you came here to try to win Frazier."

"We could all go to bed together." Mercury gleamed with golden light.

"You're bursting with lurid energy," Venus observed.

"I hope to holler." Mercury nodded in Frazier's direction, since he used a Southern phrase. "You know those letters you wrote to people?"

"Only too well." Frazier found him tremendously sexy.

"Well, think of the body as an envelope for the heart. I want a letter too." His eyes, almost amber, twinkled.

"Oh, brother." Venus shook her head.

Frazier blushed. "I think I'm going to blow a Fallopian tube."

CHAPTER
57

Venus kept a room for Mercury at Sans Souci. He couldn't exist without a large-screen television, which he could tune to every channel in the world as well as use to peer into people's lives. Mercury hated to miss a thing on earth, under the oceans, or in heaven. Vulcan fashioned a sleek silver telephone for him which cradled in the hand. Next to it on a slim, elegant rectangle were all of the various lines. Mercury had only to touch a glowing button—all even with the top of the surface, not a bulge anywhere—to get a line out. As human design goes, Mercury favored Bang and Olufsen, but Vulcan had created a thin metallic line in the wall so that when he pressed it, the compact disc, tape recorder, and radio silently emerged from the cream-colored wall.

Even the bed was spare yet sensuous. Mercury loved a clean line, whereas Venus preferred a baroque silhouette, but then no one could refuse Venus her excesses because she managed to make everything work. Her lust for gilded detail and vivid colors underscored her own personality. If she were an actress a director would say that Venus went over the top, but as she was a goddess, even that florid quality enchanted. Venus held nothing back.

As Frazier observed Mercury's room she wondered how these two managed an on-again off-again love affair over the centuries. It finally occurred to her that their very differences supplied the fascination.

Mercury's silken gym shorts, gold, clung to his tight buttocks. "Vi, why did we agree to get together for a family portrait?"

"Jupiter wanted one. He's feeling very nesty, I suppose," Venus answered. "I don't mind them as much as you do."

"I could live forever without seeing Dionysus again, or Mars." He held up his hand like a traffic cop: stop. "I know, I know, he oozes masculine appeal to you but he's got the brain of a squid and his damned wars are getting worse and worse."

"You can't blame him for war."

"Oh, yes I can. He eggs on human frailties." Mercury loathed his half-brothers.

"You'll never see any good in him. He's capable of incredible discipline and sacrifice and if we're going to talk about Mars, then you and I will get into a fight."

"Isn't Athena the goddess of war too?" asked Frazier, comfortable on the bed with its curved enameled headboard. She quite liked Athena, who possessed a grave beauty.

"Wisdom and war." Mercury picked music out of his vast supply, pressed a button on the remote for his CD, and luscious sounds filled the room, rock harp music with a strong rhythm.

"She never goes to bed with anyone, really and truly?" Frazier asked, remembering the stories she'd read about Athena.

"Oh, I flirted with her once to see if I could break her down. She got so nervous she went off and started a war." Venus giggled. "She didn't actually start one—that's unfair. Let's just say she assisted

Napoleon at Austerlitz. She was very fond of him and when the English poisoned him in captivity and he died she was morose for days."

"Look how you moped when Marlene Dietrich died." Mercury walked over to the bed.

"Yes, I loved her very much." A cloud of sorrow passed over the goddess's brow.

"You can't keep a human alive?"

"Not even Love can reason with Death." Venus shook her head.

"If one of you is in trouble and we're so inclined, we can help you save yourself, but Death does have the final power." Mercury sat next to Frazier on the bed. Venus sat on the other side of her.

"Can you die?" Frazier crossed her legs underneath her.

"*Gotterdämmerung.*" Mercury sighed. "Eventually, yes we can, but don't bring this up if you see Jupiter again. He gets very upset. He says, 'Who has the time to die?' He went to war against the Titans. He knows gods can die."

"I hope not anytime soon." Frazier wanted to touch his high cheekbones.

"Hardly."

"What about the Christian god, my God—can he die too?" Frazier blurted out. All those years of catechism tumbled in upon her.

"Sure he can. If he doesn't do a good job. He's so jealous. 'Thou shalt have no other gods before me.' You know, I faxed him the Ten Commandments a couple of years ago with comments in the margins. He was livid. No sense of humor, that one. Wants everyone to feel guilty and ashamed."

"Hates women." Venus lay back on a pillow, her arms behind her head.

"Hates sex," Mercury grumbled. "I don't know why so many of you down there pay attention to him. He's quite hateful and cruel."

Frazier, benumbed by this discussion of equals, and she a human, took a moment to get her voice back. "Yes, He is hateful and cruel, but when that's what you're taught from the time you can toddle, you believe it. Ideology need not correspond to reality to motivate people, and I suppose so many people feel so rotten about themselves they want a god to beat them, to confirm their worthlessness."

Mercury picked his feet up off the floor and whirled around to sit square on the bed facing Frazier. "You are a bright one, aren't you?"

"I told you she was—bright in some ways and just dumb as a hammer in others, mostly about herself." Venus stroked Frazier's back so she wouldn't feel too bad about honest criticism.

"I love Jesus, though. He brought mercy and forgiveness to the world."

"I am not big on forgiveness," Mercury admitted. "Except for Venus, none of us are. That may no doubt be a failing but my experience of Mount Olympus and the world is that if someone hits you, you'd better hit back. If the numbnut hits you again, take his fucking head off."

"Well," Frazier drawled, "that's effective."

"And solves nothing, but Mercury and I will never see eye to eye on that issue. Even Athena, who is so admirable and calm, gets revengeful. I think it keeps the ball rolling for generations, actually, and ultimately it gets dreary for everyone who isn't on the revenge cycle. I've got better things to do with my time." Venus leaned forward and hugged Frazier from behind.

Mercury, taking the hint, slipped off one sneaker. Frazier touched him. His skin shivered under her touch. "Wait."

"Why?" Mercury wanted to know.

"I want to see if you can make those wings on your sneakers flutter."

He put his sneaker back on, hopped off the bed and flapped the little wings. "On my helmet—you know the one you see in the ancient statues—I can make those wings wiggle too. We only wear those clothes for family portraits now. The rest of the time we wear whatever we feel like wearing, from any century. Some centuries really had great design. I've always liked the twelfth century. Very pure lines—the fabric draped beautifully. Of course, the dyes couldn't hold and they weren't terribly clean but if you concentrate only on lines, really good."

"I like today best, although it's gotten a bit too informal," Venus contributed to Mercury's idea. "But really the most incredible colors and fabrics. It's either that or the eighteenth century—a vast difference, I will agree, but female fashions from that period suit me."

"Everything suits you, but I like you best naked." Mercury kicked off his sneakers and leapt back into bed, his silken shorts showing the growing bulge underneath.

Venus pulled Frazier down on the bed and Mercury lay beside her. As Venus kissed Frazier between the shoulder blades, Mercury gently held her face in his hands and kissed her hairline and then her lips.

Frazier put her right hand on the side of his neck and then moved her hand down to his pecs. His muscles were hard and very well developed, but not massive like Jupiter's. Mercury's body suggested a human in his late teens or middle twenties, beautifully proportioned. Had he picked a sport he would have been a backstroker. He moved closer to her and she could feel his heartbeat in his cock, which rested against her thigh.

Venus reached around Frazier and embraced both of them.

Frazier lightly brushed her fingers over his shorts. Mercury exhaled in delight. She ran her fingernails over his thigh and returned to his shorts, where she slid her fingernails over the outline of his cock. Mercury shook. She reached in and touched him as Venus moved behind him and pulled off his shorts. A T-square of soft hair led to the instrument of pleasure.

"This is going to be great fun," Venus whispered in his ear and then moved down to his buttocks, where she kissed and bit him even as Frazier stroked his stupendous erection. Mercury was perfect in every respect and his penis was no exception. The head and the shaft were in balance, the balls not too saggy or small. Frazier rolled them in her hands just to feel the sweet skin. Mercury pressed against her and moved.

"Remember, she's human," Venus said as she reached between his legs and held Frazier's hand as they both stroked him.

Venus's long, slender fingers closed around Frazier's, gently squeezing her hand and Mercury's cock.

Frazier kissed Mercury on the lips. He knew how to kiss. There was nothing sloppy about his kissing. He took the tip of his tongue and traced Frazier's lips, then closed his lips and kissed her passionately. Venus kissed Frazier when Mercury was finished. After incinerating her, Venus then kissed Mercury. Although they had been kissing for centuries Frazier could feel the heat. Venus and Mercury genuinely liked each other, and in the long run maybe that was better than romantic love.

Frazier bit the skin between Mercury's rounded pecs and then she licked his nipples. Goose bumps covered him. She put her hands on his pecs, then tipped up on her fingernails and scratched him down to his groin. Then she nibbled her way down his rippling ab muscles and followed the line of his obliques to his cock. She started at the base, and using the tip of her tongue, barely touching him really, she moved along the underside to the head, which she circled with her tongue. The god arched his back in abandon.

Frazier raised her head as Venus hovered over her and she kissed a pendulous, magnificent breast before returning to Mercury's reddening cock.

She caressed his balls as she used her tongue harder and then harder until finally she put his cock in her mouth and sucked. She could feel his heartbeat in her mouth. He stood it as long as he could, then carefully pulled himself away.

Mercury embraced Frazier and pushed his cock inside her. She could feel his heartbeat deep inside.

As she looked over his shoulder she was amazed by the sight of Venus, now sporting a cock as lovely and erect as Mercury's, bearing down upon the god.

"Never let gender stand in the way of pleasure," Venus purred as she placed her hands on his rounded ass cheeks, separating them. "I've wanted to do this for centuries." His asshole opened, a rosebud of pleasure, and Venus, ever a worshipper of beauty, tenderly entered her friend.

Underneath, Frazier felt him shake. Venus mimicked his rhythm. If he used long slow strokes, so did she. If he moved shorter and harder, so did she. They moved, sleek as dolphins, the three of them together. It would be impossible to determine who suffered the most rapture. With a thunderous explosion they came simultaneously and Venus fell back on the bed laughing and hugging Mercury, even as she reached over to pet Frazier's hair.

Frazier pinched her arms with both hands to make certain she was alive. She counted her fingers. She counted her toes. "I have all my parts," she shouted jubilantly and launched herself on Venus and Mercury, laughing and kissing them.

"Why can't it be like this with humans?" Frazier wrapped her arms around them.

"You need to find the right human, or humans," Venus replied. She pulled the sash behind the bed and two nymphs appeared, bearing drinks filled with ice as well as cucumber sandwiches, scones, honey, and a variety of little cakes. The young ladies put the food on an arm that they pulled out from the bed, then left.

Mercury handed Frazier a glass of Louis Roederer Cristal, 1973. "There's Coca-Cola here too, for your chaser. Southern champagne, right?"

"Right."

Venus held up her glass, the light streaming through the pale golden liquid, bubbles soaring toward the surface. "To love, to laughter, to friends."

"Hear, hear," Mercury agreed as Frazier clinked glasses with both of them.

"This stuff is as good as nectar," Frazier opined.

"I think so too, but Juno, ever the traditionalist, insists there be nectar and ambrosia at all family gatherings. I much prefer this or a good hamburger. You Americans make the best."

"The French make the best pâté and champagne." Venus filled her mouth with champagne, then kissed Frazier, pouring the champagne into her mouth.

"Let me try that." Mercury repeated the procedure on Venus.

"Germans have the best asparagus, especially in May. Beer too." Frazier reached for another cucumber sandwich.

"Can we say anything about English cooking, or Indian or Japanese?" Mercury leaned back against the pillows.

"Best beef is in Kobe, Japan," Frazier said.

"Argentina," Venus disagreed.

"I'm off beef myself, but the best sushi I ever had was in a little inn in Tokyo and the best fried chicken I ever ate in my life was at a roadside café near Charleston, South Carolina."

"One of my favorite, favorite cities." Venus leaned against Mercury, using him for her pillow. "I have smiled upon that town."

"May I?" Frazier then leaned against Venus and the three of them ate and drank in contentment and peace.

"Know what I think?" Mercury wiped crumbs from Venus's lips.

"I can hardly wait," said his longtime friend.

"Blood makes you family; Fate makes you friends. I much prefer my friends."

"Me too." Frazier seconded the idea, then changed her mind: "Well, I don't know. I really love my brother and my father. I think Carter is going to grow up at last."

"Fantastic-looking man. I've thought of kidnapping him a few times. However, the last thing your brother needs in this life is another woman, even if she is a goddess."

"That's probably true, but I think this one he's got now, Sarah Saxe, I think she's good for him. Do you know our futures? Will my brother be able to help Armstrong Paving? He's not really cut out for business."

"No, we don't know the future, although Apollo has the gift of prophecy. But Carter—don't worry too much about him. If he stays out in the field doing the actual work he'll be happy. He doesn't need to run the business."

"That makes sense." Frazier smiled. "If I go to Apollo will he tell me the future?"

"Don't do that," Mercury counseled. "He'll tell you in a riddle or some lyric outburst and you'll drive yourself nuts trying to figure it out. Delphic Oracle kind of stuff. I can't tell the future, but I can see the present. Here, let me show you." He touched a sleek row of controls in the headboard. Noiselessly a tapestry rolled upward toward the ceiling, exposing a huge black screen.

"Don't tell me you all watch television." Frazier frowned.

"Not often." Mercury reached into the headboard and clicked a button. "Look."

The inside of the White House leapt into view. The bathroom to be exact. A figure sat on the throne, intently reading the newspaper, which hid his face.

"Don't be rude, Merc." Venus giggled.

"How was I to know?"

He beeped the remote again and the inside of La Scala appeared. A tenor and counter-tenor battled through an excruciating rehearsal.

"Can you show me anyone I know?"

"Sure."

Immediately Frank Armstrong was seen rummaging through the closet looking for his dress homburg. In doing so, he knocked down Libby's hat boxes. They clattered to the floor, tops flying off. Grumbling, he stepped off the little stool and began putting things back together. He noticed Frazier's letter inside an oval dark-blue box just as he was about to clap on the lid.

He removed the letter, studied the address and the date. He opened it and read standing up.

"Frank. . . ." Libby called up from the living room.

"What?"

"What was that racket I heard?"

"Knocked down your hat boxes. Don't worry, everything's all right," he answered in a loud voice even as he continued to read.

That fast, Libby appeared. The minute she saw what Frank was reading, and the open hat box, she broke into a swift trot, for her, and snatched the letter out of his hand.

"Don't upset yourself."

He grabbed it right back. "I'll be the judge of that. There's nothing in here I don't know. You had no right to keep this from me."

"You had a lot on your mind"—she was dying to read his letter—"and her letter to me was spiteful, cruel and well, awful, just awful. I didn't raise her to be like that. Anyway, I was afraid yours would be upsetting."

"It's not."

"Then let me read it."

"No, she wrote it to me, not you."

"I bet she tells you to leave me." Libby gritted her teeth.

"No."

"What does she say then? I mean, after all the years we've been married I ought to know. What does she say about me?"

"The letter is to me and about me. It's not about you."

Libby's voice registered disappointment. "Oh, well. Does she attack you?"

"She doesn't hold back any punches but she doesn't attack me."

"She was on drugs when she wrote those letters. Morphine. She couldn't have known what she was writing."

Frank reached down and placed the lid on the hat box. "I think she knew and I think she was on target, at least about me."

"You ought to let me see the letter." Libby's jaw tensed.

"No."

"Then there must be something in there about me, otherwise you wouldn't care."

"No, Libby, it's not all that bad, but it's a private communication from my daughter to me."

"You always loved her more than you loved me!" Libby shouted, a spontaneous explosion. "That's why she's a lesbian. I've heard about that. If boys are too close to their mothers they can't transfer their love to other women, and it's the same for a girl who's too close to her father."

"Give it up." Frank threw the hatbox up onto the closet shelf.

"I've got a sick child and you want me to ignore it?"

"She's not sick."

"She's certainly not normal." The cords stood out on Libby's neck.

"Who is? You? Me? Carter? The girls in the bridge club? My golfing buddies? Are they normal or are they just more committed to keeping up the phoney facade?"

"What phoney facade?" She took a step toward him, a threatening step.

"That everything is just"—he searched for the word—"peachy. That one is perfect, that one's mate is wonderful, and that one's children will all grow up to be successes and they, in turn, will marry the kind of people who care about appearances. The right job. The right religion. The right ancestors and the right color. The men wear double-breasted navy blazers with a silk rep tie for those luncheons at the club, and the girls wear floral print dresses with big hats. It's just a show."

"You're talking about our life! You're talking about our friends!"

"Maybe we don't have any friends, Libby. Maybe we just have other actors in this bourgeois play."

"Bourgeois?" Her eyebrows lifted, carrying with them the hard line of contempt. "I didn't even know you knew words like that."

Frank stood up ramrod straight. "I know a lot more than you give me credit for."

She crossed her arms across her still lovely bosom. "I'm all ears."

"I'm not a person to you. I'm a meal ticket. I'm an escort. I'm the genial host who mixes martinis in the summer, bloodys on Sunday after church, and scotch at night in the winter. I'm the guy who completes the picture but you don't know who I am. You never did.

You never wanted to. You just goddamn wanted me to play my part. I'm tired of acting in your play. I'm tired of paying for the privilege. I don't know how many years I have left, and I want to live them with some kind of "—he groped for a concept, for the words—"peace and maybe, maybe even love."

"Love?" She belted out the word. "Love? You never loved me. You loved your business. You loved your golf. You loved your precious Frazier. I worked for you! I hosted parties for those boring paving contractors, for clients. The food, the flowers, the compliments to their wives. And I gave you two children. I raised them. *I* raised them! You were working."

"I know, and I will regret that to my dying day."

"Why? I didn't do a good enough job? We've got a queer daughter?"

"Shut up, Libby." His voice was menacing and low. "I don't want to hear that word. She is what she is and it's her fate."

"Oh, is that like saying my child is a murderer but I love him anyway?"

"Not even close." Frank's eyes blazed. "Now why don't you get out of here and leave me alone?"

"Are you having an affair?"

He stopped for a moment. "No, I am not. I have never done anything like that, but lately I'm wishing that maybe I hadn't been so moral. I'm miserable with you. I've been miserable with you since early in our marriage, but I wasn't raised to desert my wife and children. I would like to know what it feels like to have a woman put her arms around my neck because she loves me, because she wants me, not because it's a way to keep me happy so she can get what she wants. And in time even that fades."

"We're too old for sex. It would be undignified." Libby, true to form, ignored the substance of what he said.

"I'd like to be undignified."

"That's all you men think about. Sex."

"That's not true." He finished putting the boxes back. "Anyway,

I'm not men. I'm me. One person. Male. No longer young but I'm not that old and I don't care what the calendar says. I've got a lot left in me and I've got a lot to give."

"Frazier's put you up to this. She wants everyone divorced because she's gay. Carter! Look what she's done to Carter and the sweet—"

He interrupted, "Libby, nobody puts anybody up to anything. People do what they want to in this world and if they blame other people for it then they're liars. Even if they believe the lies. Terrible things happen to human beings. Wars. Concentration camps. Political repression. Religious fanaticism. Illness. Rape. The list is endless and yet many of those people manage to find some joy in their lives, something positive. You don't. I'm leaving you and I know I'll be the bad guy. My every sin will be magnified. What you don't accuse me of other people will, because in this town there has to be a victim and a victor. Dumb, but a lot of people still believe that. So, I'm the bad guy because I'm leaving."

"I'll take you for every cent!"

"You already have."

"I earned everything in this house." She was ripshit.

"Wrong. You earned half of it and half is what you'll get. Nothing less and nothing more and if you want to squander your half on some divorce lawyer with fangs before you even get it, that's your choice. I'm sticking to my guns."

"We'll see about that." Libby put on a brave front as her world collapsed around her.

Frank walked into the bathroom for his travel shaving kit. Libby followed.

"This is a reaction to stress. The newspaper accusations. Frazier. Carter's separation. You'll be back." Frank kept on organizing things while Libby continued. "Men go through a phase like this. Oh, I know all about it. You'll go out there and date a few women, and you'll find out how good you've got it at home."

As he walked in and out of the bathroom, the closet, and back and forth to his chest of drawers, she followed him, talking all the while. She even followed him to the front door.

"Frank, Frank! You're having a mid-life crisis."

"I'm too old for a mid-life crisis." He opened the door, walked out, and shut it behind him.

Libby yanked the door open, standing there framed in the light from inside. Her mouth was open but nothing came out. Frank started the engine and drove down the driveway.

Mercury pushed the off button. "Guess we got more than we bargained for. I hope you're not upset."

Frazier replied, "No. I wish he'd left her years ago."

Venus said, "But he's done it now and that's what matters."

Venus held her champagne glass to the light. "Trust the people you love. That's the future."

"Huh?" Frazier was surprised.

"Trust them. Kenny wants to grow and learn. Your father is making changes the only way he knows how, and he's finally going to fight for his own happiness. Your father will be fine. Mandy has made a practice of counseling courage. Well, she can practice what she preaches. Everyone creates her own future. So don't worry about it," Venus said.

"Okay, okay, but I do worry about Carter's divorce."

"Divorce is absurd." Mercury downed his champagne.

"Divorce exists for the lawyers." Frazier reached for her Coca-Cola.

"Well, the lawyers belong to Apollo." Mercury smirked.

"No, they don't. You can't assign everything you don't like to Apollo."

"Well, they don't belong to Dionysus or Pluto, although they'll be as rich as Pluto eventually, because in America everyone sues everyone else if they live long enough." Mercury nestled a scone between Frazier's breasts. "Champagne and scones. Think we'll start a fad? Beats champagne and strawberries—I mean, everyone does that."

"Right now none of us here claims any lawyers. I will, however, claim any human being who seeks beauty"—she paused—"in any form. If a little lady in Bumfuck, Texas, crochets an afghan, I claim her. I even claimed the people who painted by numbers back in the fifties."

"You are a generous soul." Frazier laughed. "My mother went on a flower arranging kick so you'll have to claim her."

"It's difficult to claim Libby but I do give her credit. She has a good eye and she's passed it on to you. Poor Libby, I wonder if she'll ever get it."

"Get what?" Frazier twisted her head to see Venus more clearly.

"She's so busy trying to insulate herself from experience that she's becoming sterile inside. People have devolved into props for your mother. Do you know how horrible life would be if you could understand everything, control everything, predict everything? What a ho-hum. Better never to be born."

"I subscribe to logic more than my adored companion here." Mercury placed his hands on Frazier's shoulders and massaged them. "But she is right. There must be mysteries, rich and enticing mysteries."

"I think I stumbled on a big one." Frazier snuggled into his strong body. "Like why I am here."

"Mystery, myth, and magic." He kissed her ear.

"Perhaps the mystery is inside you. In which case you won't bore yourself." Venus considered another glass of champagne and then gave in to the urge. "Sex is certainly a mystery, and love an even greater one. Remember, Frazier, accept what you can't understand."

"Are you telling me to accept my mother? To accept those boneheads at home who are just dying to ask me why I'm a lesbian?"

"You're a lesbian?" Mercury mocked her.

"Actually, no. I'm myself." Sparks crackled in Frazier's green eyes. "I'll love whom I choose and work as I choose and as long as I treat people with respect and politeness I don't think what I do is anyone's goddam business."

"Well, why did you become a lesbian anyway?" Mercury merrily teased her. "After our megasex I think I have a right to know."

Frazier shifted herself so that she was now sitting inside his legs, face to face. "I became a lesbian out of devout Christian charity. All those women out there are praying for a man and I gave them my share."

Mercury whooped with delight as Venus laughed too. "At last, the religion makes sense to me. Oh, how saintly you are to deny yourself, my sweet." Mercury raised his glass in a toast.

Venus refilled Frazier's and they clinked glasses again. "But you will play with us, won't you?"

"Mercury, I would be thrilled to fuck you in any century, any continent, any, uh, transformation." Frazier lowered her champagne glass and put his penis in it.

"Ah," he sighed as the bubbles burst on his cock, "that's a deal."

"Venus, let's dip your breasts in champagne and lick it off." Frazier now put her champagne glass under Venus's left breast while Mercury did the same with her right.

"That tingles," Venus purred as they licked off the champagne.

"Here, roll over." Mercury tenderly pushed Frazier facedown on the bed. He poured some champagne in the small of her back, licked it up, then dribbled a little between her legs and licked that up too. "Better than ambrosia—oh, far better."

"God," Frazier moaned.

"Yes," they both answered.

She rolled over and beheld these two stunning specimens, perfection beyond perfection. Then she laughed, as did they. "If only I could find a human being who would play like we're playing."

"You might find one. I doubt you'll find two, at the same time anyway. When humans go to bed in threes they consider it kinky, not loving. At least these days they do." Mercury's mouth drooped a bit.

"You'll find someone. And the right person is always under your nose."

Frazier suddenly stiffened. "I have to get home to Curry and Basil."

"Don't worry. Your kitty and dog are being taken care of—really, we wouldn't do that to you," Venus reassured her.

"I'm so glad. All this talk of love made me think of them. Perfect love."

"Animals. Yes." Venus smiled.

"Not barracudas," Mercury said.

"Who do you know who keeps a barracuda for a pet?" Frazier lifted her right eyebrow.

"Neptune."

"That doesn't count," she told him. "He's the god of the oceans. I mean, he probably keeps fiddler crabs and moray eels too."

"Ever notice how every other fish restaurant in the world is named Neptune's Catch, Neptune's Glory, Neptune's World, and on and on. I'd hate to have restaurants named after me," Mercury noted.

"You've got Western Union," Frazier told him.

"Quite right too." He smiled. "You know all this hot sex and cold champagne have made me drowsy. Ladies, if you'll forgive me I think I'll go to sleep for a little bit." He rolled off Venus onto his side and was out in a second.

"They usually fall asleep after they come." Venus sighed. "It must be a greater effort for them, you know."

"We did gang up on him."

"Lucky devil." Venus reached for Frazier, pulling her toward her. "Comfortable?"

Frazier snuggled against Venus. "Uh-huh." She thought for a moment. "Do you believe people are straight or gay?"

"No. That's a silly concept, but then you people think in polarities these days. That's very destructive. You know—good or bad, white or black, happy or sad, man or woman, straight or gay, young or old. It's too simple, plus those ideas are not necessarily in opposition."

"Yes, but I think some few people are really gay and some few people are really straight."

"Poor darlings." Venus sighed. "But think of it this way. The human animal has a wide sexual range. The erotic possibilities are endless. Most of you are vaguely bisexual, although that knowledge is viciously suppressed. Right?"

Frazier thought a moment. "Yes, I think it's true that we're much more complicated than we realize."

"But there really are people who are absolutely straight and people who are absolutely gay." Venus brushed Frazier's cheek with her fingernails. "The purpose of the heterosexual person is easy to see: propagation of the species. The purpose of the homosexual person has been obliterated by you all down there on earth but it's plain as day to us."

"Well, what is it?"

"To serve the heterosexual. The totally gay person is designed to support the heterosexual. If everyone is involved in bearing and raising children, a delightful though exhausting process, nothing would get done apart from that. The community would fall apart."

"What about old people? They can help with the children," Frazier wondered out loud.

"Hey, when we started out, you all didn't live very long. Not in the numbers that you do now. Old people weren't a driving force in society and even with your longer life spans, elderly people can't keep up with children."

"That's true." Frazier nodded.

"Child-rearing must be done in the prime of life. Well, it's vital for the survival of the race that a small proportion of humankind in the prime of life not raise children. Those people, the stone homosexuals if you will, should perform the services needed by the others. It's essential for the species."

"You mean, like medical care or the arts, stuff like that?" Frazier's voice vibrated with fascination at this logical concept.

"Oh, that goes without saying. But cast your mind back ten thousand years, or three thousand if ten is too much for you. Better yet, go to the fifth century B.C. Athens. The war with Sparta. Already society had begun to shift, shall we say. But think of all-out war. The first line of defense should be the homosexual men. The second line of defense should be unmarried heterosexual men. The third line of defense should be lesbians. The fourth line of defense should be married men, and the last line of defense, obviously, should be the mothers. Humankind is developed to protect the children.

"And the reason lesbians are the third line of defense and not the second is sensible. The ovary will work regardless of whose body it's in. The egg is always more valuable than the sperm. So it's not wise to jeopardize any more eggs than you have to. I mean, one million men can die but if ten are left, let's say, and one hundred women are left, you will survive. Biology.

"It's blissfully simple, really, but then you all have just cocked up everything. Men and women were built to depend upon one another and to work as partners. Look what you've done to that."

"I didn't do it," Frazier protested.

"Didn't mean to sound accusatory," Venus apologized. "But, darling, what a mess on terra firma. You can't have a true partnership if one partner is more equal than the other, shall we say? How can people open their hearts to one another, be close, if one holds the whip hand or the checkbook over the head of the other one? It's absurd."

"Couldn't you come back to earth and help us out?" Frazier pleaded.

"And be turned into a movie star? Not on your life." Venus yawned.

"Tell me one more thing," Frazier begged.

"If I can."

"Do you think gay people, those people who are totally gay, do you think they are more creative?" Frazier felt drowsy herself.

"I think if Michelangelo were straight, the Sistine Chapel would have been painted basic white with a roller." Venus's laughter floated out the window to dissolve into the song of the nightingale.

CHAPTER
58

The delicate yellow of rosebuds attracted Frazier. She much preferred the understated roses to the bright reds that most people seemed to prefer. Venus created gardens of unsurpassed harmony on her country estate, and much as Frazier wanted to wander through the rooms of Sans Souci, she decided that she should wait for her hostess to give her the grand tour if she had the time. What Frazier wanted to see was Venus's art collection, since she assumed the goddess would possess the finest paintings from the centuries.

A lone gardener, his head turned away from her, expertly nipped at the rose stems. When she approached him he faced her and under the broad-brimmed straw hat was the imposing visage of mighty Jupiter.

He put his fingers to his lips. "Shhh."

"How did you know Venus was asleep?" Frazier wondered.

"I didn't. I don't want my wife to find us. She's a dutiful partner but she doesn't understand me."

Frazier smiled at the age-old line. "You like roses, I take it."

"Yes. I even like the humble geranium. Plants possess their own intelligence. They elected to stay in one place and let life come to them. Animals elected to move and go to life. Very simple really." He snipped another stem to promote growth. "Are you enjoying your stay with us?"

"Oh"—Frazier blushed—"I don't know when I've had so much, uh, so much of everything."

"There's more." He smiled with such light that Frazier had to shield her eyes.

"Sorry. You're so beautiful I forget that you're not one of us. I have a weakness for humans. Leda was fetching and Io and Europa. I loved Callisto, too, very much and Dionysus' mother, Semele, was a glorious woman."

"How can you remember all your amours?"

Jupiter laughed. "I had an affair with Mnemosyne—Memory, in English—and she gave birth to the Muses. I remember everything. Now don't get the idea that I'm fickle or a ladies' man. I'm not but I have been around for thousands of years and well . . ." He removed his hat, and his graying hair, close-cropped like a Prussian officer's, gave him even more of a virile appearance.

"What happened to your long hair?"

"A wig. For the portrait? This is so much easier." He ran his fingers through his hair.

"Are you interested in life on earth?" Frazier accepted the peach-colored rose he handed her.

"Sometimes. Things aren't the same down there. You people have calluses on your souls." Her puzzled expression caused him to explain. "You want answers for every question. You are overstimulated, yet emotionally malnourished. You are bombarded with non-stop information but the information is useless. You've lost your passion and soon you'll lose your sense of humor. People who need to feel safe every second of every day can't laugh. I used to feel sorry for humans. Then I became angry. Now, I'm bored—but not with you, my dear."

"May I ask you an unphilosophical question? A little fact. I'm not too good at philosophy anyway."

"Anything." He kissed the rose in her hand.

"Do you remember killing Rachel Redington on August 11, 1843? She was an ancestor of mine, only twenty-three, and she was sitting on the porch shelling peas. She had the metal colander in her lap and a storm came up suddenly and Rachel was struck by a bolt of lightning." Frazier's voice rose in anticipation.

Jupiter rubbed his close-cropped beard—the long curly beard was a wig too. "August 11, let's see. I do recall a pretty woman. Virginia summer." He brightened. "Wild pitch. I felt terrible, but then again she was spared living through that vile war you had in the 1860's. What in the world made you think of that?"

"My mother. We have this gigantic genealogy book and when I was little she'd turn to the page about Rachel Redington to prove to me that anything can happen to anyone at any time and I'd better damn well watch out. Scared the bejesus out of me. Oh, I didn't mean to use that name."

"Quite all right." He beamed benevolence. "You have nothing to fear in life, not you, not anyone, because every bad thing that you think can happen to you will—but not always in the form you imagine. Your valor is in overcoming these trials. I myself had to battle my own father and his Titans. I didn't know what would happen but I knew if I didn't fight, everything really would be lost. Never ask for an easy life. Ask for courage. I'll give it to you if you but ask." He draped his arm around her shoulders.

Although Jupiter was putting the moves on her, a game Frazier knew well, there was something paternal, kind, about him. "I'll remember that. Mnemosyne."

"From the sewer to the stars. Life goes on at all levels simulta-

neously. Once you understand that, you'll know there are no contra-
dictions. None. What appears to be contradictory is just two levels of
life colliding. See, the whole picture and every object, every person,
is in place." He strolled with her through the garden. "Don't seek to
understand this. That is for the gods. We've given you the gift of life.
Yours is to enjoy it. If you're sour, if you're lazy, you've betrayed
us—and yourself. Joy, Frazier, joy!" He lifted his arms upward and a
flock of Venus's white doves twittered out of the trees and flew
around them to return to their nests.

"Venus is telling me the same thing—in her way."

"Wonderful soul, my daughter." He reached down and held her
hand, swinging their hands as the tiny pebbles crunched underfoot.

It wasn't until Frazier glanced down that she realized they were
walking on diamonds, with a few rubies, emeralds, and sapphires
thrown in for color. She stooped over to pick one up. "Incredible."

"Here." Jupiter took the diamond from her hand, knelt down, and
picked up two more. He squeezed them in his hand, fashioning them
like clay, and handed her an exquisite emerald-cut diamond of seven
sensational carats. "To remember me by." He stood up.

Speechless, Frazier stared, transfixed by the pale fire in her palm.
"It's . . . overwhelming."

He roared, "I'll show you overwhelming." And laughing, he
enlarged himself to such a height she couldn't see his face. His penis,
quickly hardening, cast a shadow on the gardens. Jupiter reached
down and pulled out his member, as big as the Empire State Building. He rubbed himself a few times and sperm squirted across the
sky, except it wasn't white; the ejaculate filled the azure blue with a
rainbow of glittering colors. He instantly reduced himself, drawing
alongside Frazier as the colors, iridescent, melted into one another.
"Better than fireworks."

"I'll say." Frazier couldn't take her eyes off the sky. "I'm off
fireworks anyway."

"Oh, yes, you did make a mess—but you had help in doing so," he corrected himself. "Might I interest you in an afternoon delight? Even the king of the gods is a slave before you."

A mocking voice called from the house, "Daddy, that line's got gray hairs." Venus, dressed in jeans and a white cotton shirt open to her navel, barefooted, trotted out to her father.

Dejected, he said, "Oh, you've spoiled it. She'll never go to bed with me now."

"She can do as she pleases but don't you think Juno will see the sky? She can't be that far away—and when she observes your handiwork—she's going to be on you like a hawk on a mouse. Actually, she'll take it out on Frazier. She always does."

"Damn." Jupiter turned to Frazier. "I should have exercised some self-control." His voice lowered to a creamy baritone. "But that's the problem—around you I have no control."

"I wouldn't have missed that show for the world." Frazier grinned.

"Daddy, I think I've got to take her back home. You wouldn't want her changed into a bull like Europa, or think what she did to Aegina. Do you want a dragon to demolish Richmond? The Yankee armies were bad enough."

"Oh"—he rubbed his head—"that woman!"

"At least the women she destroyed or harmed had the benefit of sleeping with you. All Frazier did was watch your—"

"Truly impressive cock." Frazier smiled her biggest smile.

Jupiter emotionally turned to a puddle at this compliment. "If only we could have had even one night together. I promise you would not have been disappointed."

"Perhaps I will return."

He patted her hand. "You must go back home, much as we would love to keep you here."

A cloud on the horizon gave evidence of Juno's approach.

Venus grabbed Frazier's hand. "Come on, honey. Tits to the wind."

CHAPTER

59

"Ahh." Mercury moaned in his sleep, a pleasurable moan. Venus shook him again. He opened his eyes. "Huh?"

"Put your pants on. We need to get Frazier out of here."

Frazier, big-eyed, peered out the window as the cloud grew darker and larger. "She's picking up steam."

"That's not all she's picking up." Venus sighed.

"What's the matter?" Mercury wiped his eyes and swung his feet over the edge of the bed.

"Juno's about to pitch a hissy."

"Oh, no." He quickly tied on his winged sneakers. "Jupiter again?" Mercury remarked to Frazier: "Did you bang that old boy?"

"No, I did not," Frazier replied with dignity. "But he felt compelled to show me how big his cock was and he jerked off into the sky. The rainbow was really beautiful."

"He'll never learn." Mercury took Frazier's right hand while Venus took the left. "Hang onto us."

As they took off, Frazier heard Juno call, "Husband?"

Jupiter replied, "Yes, my sweetling. I'm here in the garden."

"And not alone, you lying son of a bitch!" Juno bellowed. She stormed, literally, into the garden.

As Jupiter contended with his bellicose partner, Venus and Mercury sped through the estate, escaping through the front door. Once out in the open they shot through the air and Frazier noticed that Mercury wore his ancient helmet.

Behind him the sky darkened, thunder and lightning engulfing Sans Souci.

Venus looked over her shoulder. "She's not buying it. And he's losing his temper too."

"As long as he occupies her for a bit. Once she puts her nose to the ground she'll be like a bloodhound."

"But I didn't do anything," Frazier protested.

"Oh, honey, since when does the truth have a thing to do with it? She wants to be a victim. She relishes the pain and she glories in inflicting it upon the object of his affections. If she had any guts she'd cut his balls off." Venus ducked a low branch on a cherry tree. "Actually, if she had a grain of sense she'd realize he is what he is and she'd better love him as he is. No one ever changes anyone else unless they want to be changed."

"We could go to your husband's forge." Mercury was thinking out loud.

"That Momma's boy?" Venus curled her lip. "He'd sell us out in a heartbeat."

"Not if you worked on him." Mercury, too, looked over his shoulder. The sky behind them, inky black, was shot through with golden and blue lightning. "Shit, those two are really having a Mr. and Mrs. I'm glad I never got married."

"So am I," Venus replied, tongue in cheek. She noticed that

Frazier had tears in her eyes, they were moving so fast. "Can you breathe?"

"Barely," Frazier gasped.

"You incline that way. Your bronchitis. Hang on a little longer until we're clear of immediate danger," Mercury advised.

"How about the chapel of Nicholas Fifth in the Vatican?" Frazier choked out. "Fra Angelico's. It's so pure and simple."

"What in the world made you think of that?" Mercury, worried, wished he had brought his tiny wristwatch TV so he could check locations before they wasted time getting there.

"I figured she wouldn't go near anything that was Christian," Frazier logically replied.

"Good idea," Venus praised her, "but you don't know the queen of the gods. She takes credit for anything beautiful, for any painting or statue in which a woman is the dominant figure. She even claims pantyhose. She swears it impedes rape. We'd look like three tourists and it wouldn't take her long to find us."

"Can't Jupiter help us out?"

"Do you want to be turned into a constellation?" Mercury said. "He can't control her."

"How come you two don't like her—I mean, apart from these rampages of hers?"

"She's not my mother," Venus answered.

"Nor mine, and she can be a vicious bitch to her stepchildren but, oh, how she dotes on Mars and Vulcan. She's cold to you until she needs you, and as you can imagine, she often needs me."

"She rarely needs me," Venus matter-of-factly added. "Juno only likes women who are obedient. And men. Kiss her ass and she's happy."

An explosion in the distance worried them. "Damn." Mercury grimaced.

"If even one mirror in my house is cracked I will tear out every hair of her moustache."

This made Frazier laugh and she nearly let go of Venus's hand. "Whoa."

"Hold tight." Venus grabbed her under the elbow. "Try that." The goddess pointed to a grotto below them. "We can hide until we come up with a better plan."

They dropped down and quickly entered the cool, moist cave filled with Cro-Magnon drawings. Odd bits of pillars bore testament to worship over the millennia.

"Maybe they'll blow themselves out," Mercury hoped.

"This is very old." Goose bumps appeared on Frazier's arms. "And very holy."

"The faith of centuries." Mercury traced a bison with his finger. "In the old days everyone got along, you know. The Norse gods were fine and we were fine and whatever gods the Incas and Aztecs believed in, everybody managed. Then the craze for one god took over and suddenly tolerance went out the window. Believe as I believe. Worship as I worship. Dress as I dress. Think as I think. It's deadly—and it makes it quite easy to kill."

"What do you mean?" Frazier couldn't take her eyes off the drawings.

"Well, if someone doesn't believe as you believe, then they are stupid or in league with the Devil. Off with their heads."

"Ah, yes, plenty of that in my century." Frazier was beginning to feel a prisoner of time—her time.

"See these stepping-stones to the altar?" Venus pointed to the ground.

"Smooth as the moon and worn down like half-moons." Frazier knelt to run her hands over the deep depressions in the stones.

"How many thousands of years did it take for them to shine like this, to be caressed by those myriad human feet? These stones are the residue of higher yearnings. Does it matter if the original supplicants in this grotto wore bearskins and worshipped the Ursa Major or, later, togas and worshipped Diana? Yes, this looks like one of her shrines. And still later they came, hiding and trembling to draw sustenance from one another and share the word of Jesus—the emotions were the same. The reaching for something finer, for something that offered tranquillity in the midst of chaos. It's all true. Pagan, Jewish, Muslim, Buddhist, Christian—the emotions are true. The doctrine is false."

"I pray I can remember all this when I get home."

"You will," Mercury assured her. He moved to the mouth of the cave. "Dammit to Hades. She's heading this way."

"Want to make a run for it?" Venus joined him to check the horizon.

"We have two things to our advantage," he said. "She's getting so nearsighted and she's too vain to wear glasses and she's not as fast as she used to be. She might pass us by. "

"Yes, but on the chance that she doesn't, let me see if there's a way out of here through the back."

"Let me go with you," Frazier offered.

"Stay with Mercury. If this is one of the ways down to Pluto, then you can't go there. If you cross the river Styx, that's it, Frazier. It really is the river of No Return."

"Charon, the ferryman, will take your money too," Mercury growled. "Actually, he's not so bad. He doesn't charge any more than the Staten Island ferry, but you have no idea how greedy Pluto is. Not only will you be stuck in Hades, you'll be flat broke. Hurry up, Venus. Her eyesight may be failing but she's not stupid."

Venus disappeared into the back. Bats flew up, she emitted a low, soft whistle, and they flew with her into the deep recesses of the cave.

Mercury left the mouth of the cave. He embraced Frazier. "Fasten your seat belt. We'll get through it." He kissed her on the neck.

Outside, the wind picked up and the rumble, rumble heralded the approach of the goddess, who was hitting the ground hard as she strode.

Venus, cobwebs in her beautiful hair turning to silver, motioned for them to follow. They hurried to her side. She led them to a tiny room off the main cave. "This will have to do. If she finds us, I'll have to hold her down while you two get out."

"She's big and strong and even though it was forever ago she was no coward during the war with the Titans. I'd better occupy her." Mercury's voice was hoarse.

"You're faster than I am. You need to get Frazier home." Venus stated the obvious.

The footfall was deafening and stopped at the grotto. The three froze, the plan unfinished.

Juno entered the cave. "I know you're in here. Give yourself up and I'll be lenient with you." She waited. "I know I have a reputation for vengeance but those stories are told by my detractors. After all, I'm a woman, too, and I know how seductive men can be, especially that man. He can talk a dog off a meat wagon. Now I will count to ten. If you don't voluntarily give yourself up I'll find you and it will be the worse for you, human. One, two, three . . ."

As she counted Venus crouched down, ready to spring if Juno tracked them down.

On seven a great huffing and puffing could be heard.

"Juno, you'll catch a cold in here." Jupiter had followed her to the cave.

"You don't care what happens to me."

"Of course I do, darling. You mustn't jump to conclusions."

"Ha! With your track record? I'd be a blistering idiot to believe one word from you. In fact I can always tell when you're lying—your mouth is moving!" She returned to her counting. "Eight."

"Honey, let's talk this over."

"I am going to find that human tart, that quivering piece of flesh and blood, and turn her into a python."

Cleverly Jupiter replied, "That's redundant."

"I have never changed anyone into a python."

"I know that, sugarplum"—his deep voice, sweet as honey, rolled over the words—"but Athena turned Medusa into a half-snake half-woman with that awful hair. You don't want to be accused of being a copycat."

This hit home and Juno paused a moment. "Athena would tell everyone that, too, and in her most judicious voice. I wish you didn't favor her so much. And that bullshit about her not having a mother—Metis was her mother and the whole world knows it."

"She feels motherless." He realized he'd get nowhere defending his daughter. "And I myself, much as I love her, have always thought she made quite a mistake in not allowing you to be a mother to her and teach her the womanly virtues."

"You never told me that."

"You never asked."

"You're trying to keep me from my task. Come out and show yourself, you little blond vixen! I won't turn you into a python. I promise. I'll cover you with cellulite. That's worse!"

"Lamby-pie, you're getting flushed in the face. Now remember your blood pressure. Let's get out of the damp."

"Did you go to bed with that girl?"

"I did not."

"Then why was the sky full of your sperm?"

"Iris was playing jokes on us. She's in charge of rainbows and I think she hasn't enough to do these days—with all the pollution in the cities, who can seek the rainbows? I'm sure she was playing a joke on us."

"Somebody shot the dots off Iris's dice. She's not smart enough to think of a joke like that."

"All right then. I'll tell the truth but you forced me to it." He held out the bait. She drew closer to him. "Venus's gardens appeal to me. I find solace and comfort there when business becomes too pressing. The rose fragrance curled into my nostrils and reminded me of you and suddenly I was overcome with desire—but, darling, you were nowhere in sight. So I jerked off and I called your name when I came."

Juno's eyes narrowed to slits. "Really."

"I can't stand humans anymore. They all go to therapists now. I can't sleep with them. Could you stand stories about their fear of the dark or their lack of self-esteem? Apart from that, I'm older now. I've learned something from the centuries."

How fine those words sounded to Juno. "What's happened to them? They used to worship me properly, and you, of course. Now they blame everything on their mothers. I'm bearing the brunt of this, metaphorically, and I swear I'll get even. Men are afraid to write about their mothers. They're afraid to admit they love their mothers. Sigmund Freud made cowards and liars out of them. These . . . these candy-asses caved in to a Viennese doctor without a fight. It's outrageous. Men caved in to an idea and it wasn't even an idea backed up by guns. Astonishing."

"I quite agree and I think we've got to do something about it." He put his mighty arm around her waist. "The Electra complex offends me as much as the Oedipus complex offends you, sweetheart. Drivel. Why, humans have no more backbone than a chocolate éclair." He bussed her cheek. "Say, how about a chocolate éclair and some coffee at your place? Then we could . . . play."

"I make the best chocolate éclairs," Juno bragged.

"And the best love." Jupiter, with a sigh of profound relief, guided his wife out of the cave.

Frazier, Venus, and Mercury waited a long time before venturing out.

"If we'd stayed in there long enough I would have had to use my Girl Scout skills." Frazier wiped the clammy sweat off her brow.

"Hey, bumping you off the local board of the Girl Scouts was a cheap shot." Mercury peeked out of the mouth of the cave. "They're gone."

"Just to be safe, let's wait a bit longer before going outside. It's entirely possible they could have another fight on the way to her kitchen." Venus sat on the altar. "Frazier, would you have made us eat bugs and start fires by rubbing sticks together?"

"I thought *we* could rub together," came the swift reply.

"My, my, we are feeling good." Mercury laughed.

"What I feel is gratitude. I thought I was going to spend the rest of my life looking like cottage cheese."

"You could invent a Girl Scout badge for surviving cellulite," Venus told her.

"Girl Scouts should have badges for adulthood and middle age." Frazier walked to the mouth of the cave. "Let's see. We could have a badge for surviving divorce. A badge for loss of job and loss of hair, badges for bankrupting yourself sending the kids through college, and certainly a badge for braving your first face-lift. However, knot-tying has to be done in bed."

"Ooo, I like that." Mercury experienced a twinge of lust. He would have liked to carry on but prudence dictated he get Frazier back to earth.

"Let's walk for a while and then we can pick up the pace." Venus, now outside, called them to join her.

As they walked along the ancient path laid with cobblestones, the sun popped out from behind the clouds and the raindrops on the leaves sparkled with tiny rainbows, reminding Frazier of Jupiter's multicolored emission.

"Do you two know about AIDS?" she asked. Why the thought occurred to her she didn't know. Perhaps it was because she couldn't imagine a god and goddess feeling pain.

"Oh, yes," Mercury said. "We can't contract it but we're aware of it."

"Do you feel pain?" Frazier wanted to know.

"Of course. Remember your *Iliad*? Mars and Athena mixed it up on the plains of Troy. I think she cut him on the thigh and he howled bloody murder. Healed right up, though."

"Mercury, was that Athena?" Venus asked.

"I'll ask her next time I see her. Maybe she put a human up to it. Anyway, yes we can feel pain but we heal very quickly."

"On earth, I think the Reagan and Bush administrations will be remembered one hundred years hence as the people who could have stopped the plague but chose not to because the right people were dying." Frazier's jaw set hard.

"The Republican Party has certainly sold out to the right-wing fanatics, the Christian fundamentalists, and the fat cats, haven't they? They're quite smug but they are right—AIDS *is* God's curse, but not on homosexuals and drug addicts." Mercury walked a little faster.

"It will be God's curse on them." Venus, saddened by any form of intolerance, finished Mercury's thought for him. "They will suffer for their lack of compassion and that Christian charity they bleat about, for as they turn their faces from the afflicted, so will we turn our faces from them, and the terrible revenge will be when their children die of AIDS years from now. They are so removed from real sexual behavior that they won't be able to figure out how it happened. I pity them as much as I loathe them."

"Hideous as they have been to gay people I don't wish it upon them." Frazier suddenly recognized that she, indeed, didn't wish AIDS on anyone.

"Forgiveness is very Christian or very Venus." Mercury reached out for her hand. "I don't believe in it myself. Sock me and I sock you. Or better yet, I wait a good long time and create a revenge of sublime elegance."

"Imagine if Frazier sought revenge against the people who have been unkind to her recently? It would take up so much time—and is Billy Cicero worth it? Or those silly Girl Scout ladies or even Libby, whose entire being is programmed to resist spontaneous pleasure?"

"Humans have short life spans. Maybe revenge does take too long but I like to see my enemies twist in the wind." The little wings on his sneakers flapped for a second. "What about you, Frazier?"

"I guess I don't mind seeing them in trouble, as long as my hands are clean. Not only do I not have the time to get even, I lose interest. I get distracted and sometimes by the oddest things. That wonderful Ben Marshall painting of Sir Teddy the horse. When I look at that I forget about what's going on around me. I love the painting that much. My flashes of hatefulness never last long."

"Maybe as you get older you won't have any at all." Venus smiled.

"As long as people act so silly about my being a lesbian or a bisexual or whatever I am, I think I'll have my little flashes."

"Most of those people are ignorant. They aren't malicious," Venus counseled.

"Who cares? The effect is the same. That was one of the reasons I was so circumspect about my life. Once people perceive you as gay, that's all they can see. I'm being robbed of my individuality. I may have been repressed before, I may have been emotionally dishonest, but I was seen as a full human being, not a category. I really hate this shit."

"I do too," Mercury agreed. "But worse things have happened to nicer people." He burst out laughing.

Frazier did too. "That's true."

"About all you can do in life is be who you are. Some people will love you for you. Most will love you for what you can do for them, and some won't like you at all. They won't like your voice or your accent or your sexuality or the color of your skin. You can't let them stop you."

"I don't—but it still hurts."

"At least you're not alone. Your Auntie Ru loves you and your Dad. Carter—he's working at it, and there's always Mandy." Venus smiled broadly, pinkish gold light surrounding her head.

"It's a paradox." Frazier noticed the smooth skin on Mercury's cheek, those sculpted cheekbones she had kissed. The sight of him made her shiver all over again. "No one will speak to your life but you."

"What do you mean?" He turned his head toward her, her amber eyes brilliant.

"I mean, black folks spend a lot of time trying to explain their reality to white folks, assuming the whites will even listen, women to men, gays to straights. You can plain wear yourself out trying to explain yourself to the so-called dominant group and then you haven't the time to discuss the environment or arms control or the economy or even the best restaurant in town. But if you don't do it, no one gets anywhere. I never realized how exhausting this would be, this coming out, if you can stand the phrase."

"Life." Venus smiled again.

"What?"

"Life is calling and she's not rational. Just think, no one has ever lived your life before. It's brand-new. I would worry far less about people understanding me than I would worry about not joining in Nature's grand dance."

"If only we had more time," Mercury murmured as they approached a door on the road—just a door, no house.

"Frazier, I love you very much." Venus kissed her. "You must go home now and I will give you my gifts if you're open to them. I want you to remember something."

Frazier, devastated that she would be leaving her friends, started to cry. Mercury put his arms around her. "Chin up, girl. Come on, we'll never really be too far away from you. I'm the god of communication, remember. The secret is: be clear and be simple. You humans make everything so complicated. Just noun, verb, direct object." He kissed her and she returned the kiss. "Life is calling." He repeated Venus's sentence, then handed Frazier to the goddess.

Venus wrapped her arms around Frazier. "Remember, there are no separate solutions. There are only community solutions. You fight for your place in the community. It doesn't matter that not everyone will accept you for yourself. What makes you think other people get accepted for who they are? Go back and work and reach out to the people who truly love you and reach out to new people. Hold your head up. You're as good as anybody. And you told the truth as best you know it. That in itself is a miracle. Hear me?"

"Yes." Frazier bawled.

"There, there." Venus hugged her tight. "Life is calling." She opened the door. "Go on."

Frazier hesitated, then boldly stepped through the open door.

CHAPTER
60

Frazier opened her eyes. She was flat on her back on the gallery floor. Her right hand was in her pocket. She felt the seven-carat diamond.

"My God, you had a terrible shock." Tears ran down Mandy's cheeks. "Frazier, Frazier, are you all right?"

Frazier looked into Mandy's tender eyes, into that kind and beautiful face. Venus had kept her word. "Mandy, life is calling."